Advance Reading Copy

Meltdown
GP James

ISBN: 9781948018074

400 Pages, 5 x 8

$13.95, Trade Paperback

Pub Date: MAY 16, 2018

DISTRIBUTED BY

INGRAM, FOLLETT, MBS, COUTTS, BERTRAMS, GARDNERS

FIC000000/Fiction/General

FIC030000/Fiction/Suspense

FIC031000/Fiction/Thrillers

CONTACT AUTHOR: GP James, writergpjames@gmail.com

CONTACT PUBLISHER: Nancy Cleary, nancy@wyattmackenzie.com

Published by Wyatt-MacKenzie Publishing, Inc.

Deadwood, Oregon

PLEASE NOTE:

This is an uncorrected pre-publication proof only.

MELTDOWN

GP JAMES

Wyatt-MacKenzie Publishing
DEADWOOD, OREGON

Meltdown
GP James

ISBN: 978-1-948018-07-4
Library of Congress Control Number: to come

Meltdown is a work of fiction. Names, characters, places, and incidents either are the product of the author's imagination or are used fictitiously. Any resemblance to actual persons, living or dead, events, or locales is entirely coincidental.

Editor: Richard Marek
Cover Design: Kerry Ellis

Wyatt-MacKenzie Publishing
DEADWOOD, OREGON

Published by Wyatt-MacKenzie Publishing
info@wyattmackenzie.com

www.gpjames.com

For Humanity

"Service to others is the rent you pay for your room on Earth."

-Muhammad Ali

CHAPTER 1

August the Sixth. Eight Twenty-Seven A.M.

His hazel eyes grazing the dials and gauges on the sage metal walls through the plate-glass window teleported him back to the seventies, making him feel older than thirty-eight, like he had been on the job for that amount of time and was cusping the turn of his sixth decade. Something in how the bottom of his gut rested on the ajar pencil drawer of his Formica-topped metal desk and how the cream metal shelf crammed with dusty manuals leaned with ivy plant tendrils dangling toward the orange fabric, wood-framed couch made him feel like he had never left, never gone home from the day he had started the job fifteen years earlier. He had grown into his desk chair like a potted plant, his waistline pressing into the arm rests and spilling over the sides. Repotting? He figured he might have to move the couch behind his desk. Trace Crane's office was sterile, stale, institutional—a house for insentience. It looked like a military command station from the Cold War. He didn't have nuclear missiles, but he had a nuclear *reactor*. He was always at the plant—4:00 a.m., 11:00 p.m., weekends, holidays. The nuclear reactor was a child that needed monitoring every second of every day. Trace was part of the foundation, a pillar in the wall. There were showers, cots, a kitchen. If he didn't have a wife and daughter he may never have bothered to go home.

Trace had been at his desk since 6:00 a.m., coffee in his left hand, paperwork under his right. As one of four control-room supervisors at Bear Mountain Nuclear Energy Center on the edge of the Hudson River in Buchanan, New York, Trace had reports to catch up on—maintenance, staffing, inspections, incidents. He was ready for his half-day. He and the other supervisors had agreed during the summer to rotate, relieving each other early on Fridays to allow them to spend extra time with their families. Hal Bernstein would swing in around noon and Trace would be on his way to his friend's beach house in Greenwich, Connecticut, with his wife, Avi, and his daughter, Brooklyn, for a relaxing weekend. No rigid schedule, no institutional office surroundings, no companywide-mandated internet restrictions, and, most importantly, no stress.

Trace rocked back in his ergonomic desk chair, his five-eleven, two-hundred-and-seventy-nine-pound body testing the hydraulics. He swept pieces of his hair from his forehead. His obsession with keeping it in line made him seem like a corporate, mid-century gentleman deploying a pocket comb upon his scalp every hour. His wan face was flushed, bloated from his poor diet and weight. He had a light speckling of freckles over his nose and cheeks, thin lips, eyebrows a medium density, his round face shaved clean. In the rare instance he let himself go his facial hair grew in light smatterings. Even at his age Trace's visage was cherubic. Despite his thinning hair he could easily pass for ten years younger. He had a boyish quality defined by the pudginess of his roseate cheeks, his freckles, and the jocular contortion of his lips. There was light in his eyes. Even when he was livid a touch of glee showed through; not much stripped him of joy. However, Trace had entered a dark period over the past couple years. His face was flat most of the time, eyes dim, lips bowing convexly. Stress, anger, and annoyance hung heavy in his jowls, ebullience springing free in unexpected smatterings of rising cheeks. Trace scratched at a patch of chronic psoriasis on his nose—a crust of pinkish-white flaky skin falling onto his paperwork. In times of severe stress scaly patches surfaced on the back of his neck, arms, stomach, and ankles between his fair, sparse body hair.

Trace looked up from his computer and scanned his office. At least once a day he thought how the space was desperately drab—cream block walls, gray berber, laminate-wood shelving, and metal-tube, vinyl guest chairs that said nothing but unaesthetic, dreary sixties and seventies. The only company-issued items in his office from the twenty-first century were his computer, his desk phone, and his desk chair. The lack of family photos and other personal belongings made some days at the plant bleak. Trace had to share the space with other supervisors when he was off duty and felt it odd to leave his personal effects across the surfaces. For communal comfort, he and the other supervisors agreed on pennants for the Yankees and Jets. He shuffled through a stack of vintage-car listings that laid atop an open book on rebuilding engines and restoring cars. He loved the 1970 slate-blue Mercedes cabriolet with maroon interior and top. There was one in rough condition for seven thousand, a steal. By the time he finished with it it'd be worth around seventy. Trace pictured himself in his garage spending hours lost in the innards of the luxury ride. Then he saw himself on Sundays cruising with Avi next to him and Brooklyn in the backseat.

He reached for a bag of potato chips, red stretch marks on the inside of his biceps protruding from his short-sleeve, company-issued button-up. He busted the bag open. *Chips before 9:00 a.m. The doctor says I shouldn't. High blood pressure.*

Hypertension. Onset of diabetes. I'm thirty-fucking-eight for Christ's sake. You try and do this job, doc, and see how high you get. He thrust his fingers into the bag and shoveled the fried slices into his mouth. Every time his teeth crunched potato he ascended closer to the next waist size. *Do I care? Sure. Can I get out of this toroidal loop of shit? Who knows...* Instead of towering walls of switches, monitors, and the backs of his control room staffs' misshapen heads, Trace pictured himself on a lounge chair at the edge of the sand where the tide fused granules to mud. Brooklyn chased the waves as they moved in and out, poking at bubbling sand-crab holes. Avi sat next to him, her fit legs draped over his large trunks, her arm around him, her head buried in his neck, her shoulder-blade-length locks of burnt umber whipping in her olive-skinned face, her emerald eyes looking sultrily at his hazels. They whispered to each other about how cute Brooklyn was. They kissed and hinted at the romantic evening the two of them would have later. It was perfect, but in reality they'd sit in separate chairs and watch Brooklyn play. There would be no whispering or romance. Trace would guzzle a beer and nod off while Avi looked at him in disgust. They'd arrive Friday in the late afternoon with enough time to chill by the pool or on the sand. Then they'd meet up with family and friends and have dinner.

Trace smiled, his yellowed teeth showing, crowns and fillings hidden in the rear, breath so acrid he swore there was a dead rat in the ceiling he couldn't pinpoint. He downed more coffee and rapped on his computer keyboard—technical reports, maintenance recommendations, staff evaluations, emails. As much as Trace was eager to be promoted in the future he was nervous about being away from the control room. All the paperwork annoyed and bored him. His true passion was the mechanics of the goliath machine. Trace stood and adjusted his pants, his stomach distended, his ass nonexistent to the point that it seemed it had been pushed forward and presented as his gut. His button-up draped his narrow shoulders. The weight didn't sit right on his frame, clearly a skinny man that had ballooned. Trace wiped his face with the back of his hand before plopping back down and starting back on his coffee. He pulled a pamphlet from under his keyboard for a charity retreat in Guyana he had been considering. He needed some solitary time and had considered going away for a couple weeks and joining a home-building group for the poverty stricken. It was that or a vacation with Avi to Bali, which she was dying to visit again. He wanted to turn things around with her but needed to clear his head first. The issue was he'd never get the time off for both trips.

Trace set his mug down. The love it warmed him with made his cold thoughts vaporize. Brooklyn had made it for him at day camp the previous summer. It was white with her handprint wrapped around it in purple paint. In yellow, red, and blue she had scribbled 'I luv yu dadee' across the opposite side. The men at the plant teased him about the mug. Trace didn't care. He'd drunk coffee from it every day since she had given it to him—pure, unabashed love from his daughter.

The mug rattled and danced across his desk. Trace scowled at the ceramic and reached for it. When he set it back it did the same jig. His desk swayed. He sat erect and eyed the length of his office wondering if he was hallucinating. His body vibrated. *Am I dying? Stroke? Doctor told you not to eat the damn chips!* He felt the vibrations coming up through his chair. The swaying of his desk intensified, a thunderous rumble like a timpani roll. Then the shaking hit like a mortar detonation, like Godzilla had grabbed the building and was trying to rattle all its contents out. The massive building rocked. Trace stood but was thrust back into his seat. He looked out on his control-room staff, spreading eyes gawked at him. *What the fuck is going on?* Trace tried to stand again but was adhered to his chair. Gravity had increased tenfold. The vibrations sent him skittering away from his desk. He clutched the armrests of his chair, feeling like he was on a mechanical bull. All he needed was a pitcher of beer and a good dare. His mug hopped toward the edge of his desk. He reached toward it. The mug leapt. Trace jumped for it. The mug smashed on the floor, coffee spewing, Trace landing on the carpeted cement next to it in a heap. His eyes rested on his broken mug. The side with the scrawled message had the handle still attached, the side with the handprint laid next to it, ceramic shards on the carpet. *I'll glue it.* He'd salvage it even if it couldn't hold liquid; he'd frame it in plexiglass.

Trace tried to press himself off the floor. The shaking intensified, pinning him to the carpet. He felt like he was in the bowels of a ship in the midst of a hurricane. His manuals and notebooks fell off the shelves, each thwacking the floor and splaying. Wood snapped, metal twisted, cement ground. Lights flashed and alarms blared inside his office; he heard the same cacophony from the control-room floor. *This can't be an earthquake. We're in fucking New York for Christ's sake. Maybe it's a terrorist attack?* Gauging from the force that shook the building, he swore one of the reactors had just exploded, but he knew that was virtually impossible. An object smacked into his side. He winced, grabbing his torso. He looked up, the ceiling tiles dancing like a five-line saloon crew. Then they came kicking one, two, three at a time. Trace rolled and the tiles pummeled the floor. One caught him on his head above his temple. Pain shot through his orbital socket and cheek bone. He winced, reaching for his face, his vision blurring. All quieted. Nerve-piercing pain radiated his skull. He felt like he was in the ocean, a vicious current tossing him. *I'm gonna fucking drown!* The pain stabbed down into his jaw and his nasal bone, then back up into his sinuses like he had just bitten into a subzero snow cone after a swig of hot tea. The cacophony returned to his ears. He put his hand to his mouth, choking on dust showering from the open ceiling. Trace swore someone had thrown flour into an oscillating fan. He couldn't comprehend what was happening. He was in it, whatever it was, in the moment, confused, his body and mind reacting but not calculating further to exactly what had occurred. He had been caught by surprise like a grazing rabbit being snatched up from a field by an eagle. He hadn't had one iota of presage in him while he clacked at the keys and dreamt about the beach. There was no rustle in the leaves or swooping squawk. A wicked force had engulfed him and his control room, sending them into phantasmagorical disarray.

Trace feared the building might collapse on him. *Is this it? Is this how it's gonna go down? In a windowless room, debris dumping on top of me?* He'd never know why. Workers would find his body with his control-room staff mangled, bloody, and buried under debris. He'd have no time to say goodbye to Avi and Brooklyn and the rest of his family and friends. This was his unexpected demise. Trace crawled across the floor. A fluorescent light bulb burst, shards of glass raining down. His hand pressed into bulb glass. "Ahh!" He recoiled and shook the glass off. He fell to his side and pulled the shards out. Blood leaked from his fingers and palm. Then the lights flickered and went out. *Dammit!* Glass burned in his hand, the floor still shaking, glass and metal rattling. *Station blackout?... Where's the fucking backup?...* He hacked, dust in his lungs. What seemed like five minutes of shaking had only been fifteen seconds. *When is it going to stop?* The building swayed, steel cried. Trace grabbed the handle of the mug Brooklyn had given him. 'I luv yu dadee.' *Daddy loves you, too, honey.* He braced himself for impact. Whatever it was he wouldn't see it coming in the dark. He wanted to be killed instantly. *Don't let me get mangled, stuck, and suffocate to death. Bring it!* The lights snapped back on with an electric pulse.

Trace flinched. The shaking subsided.

Trace looked around in disbelief. *I'm still here. Am I really here? Did it kill me? Maybe it killed me and I don't know it. No! If I were dead I wouldn't be in this fucking cave.* Sharp pain shot through his hand. "Ahh!" He pulled the last of the shards from his bloody palm. He felt he'd been tossed in a paint mixer. His office was in shambles, looking as though it had been unoccupied for decades, through several earthquakes, floods, looters, and a wrecking ball. Whatever the fuck that was was ungodly. It was supernatural. He was fascinated that the gargantuan control-room building could be effortlessly rattled. Trace pushed himself up from the floor. He stumbled, his equilibrium off as though he'd been at sea all day. Liquid dripped into his eye. He swiped at it with his arm. Blood smeared across his wrist. The ceiling tile. Trace touched the wound with his fingers. He winced. I guess they call 'em drop ceilings for a reason. The blaring alarms impeded his ability to think. The lights cascading through the room made him feel like he had taken MDMA and fallen onto the polished wood of the dance floor. He grabbed his desk phone from the floor and punched the keys. When he put it to his ear it was dead. He punched the switchhook rapidly and tried again. Nothing. He threw the receiver down and stood. Dust and debris fell from his button-up. He saw his blood on the phone, a bedroom murder where the victim was dragged away after calling 911. He grabbed a long-sleeve button-up from under debris on the floor, tore the dry-cleaning plastic from it, ripped a sleeve from the shirt and wrapped his hand. Through the glass Trace watched his men in the control room. CHAOS! PANIC! ALARMS!

Trace burst through his office door, spilling into the reactor-three control room. He skidded across the floor in his brown sporty bluchers, his facility badge whipping around his neck. "What the fuck is going on?" was all he could say. He scanned the reactor computer monitors and the sage-green, twelve-foot metal walls of monitoring gauges, switches, and indicators that looked like airplane cockpit controls wrapping the walls. Over six hundred alarm lights, many of them flashing in the nineteen-seventies institutional room, made it look like a spaceship had landed at the disco. Fluorescent bulbs that had shaken loose hung flashing from the drop ceiling toward the carpet.

"THIS IS NOT A DRILL," blurted repeatedly over the loudspeakers.

"Seismic event," control-room operator Jerry Zale barked. Sweat soaked his palms. He stroked his goatee, pulled at his ears, and pushed his glasses up on his hair. He was one of the most fit men in the control room, a navy vet who still did calisthenics every morning. He'd been at Bear Mountain for eight years since he was thirty-nine, and Trace had never seen him scared until two minutes ago.

Earthquake... Earthquake? Earthquake in Buchanan, New York? Trace scrambled to Jerry. "Reactor is scrammed. Rods are inserting," Jerry barked to Trace, the alarms drowning his words. Trace scurried behind a kidney-shaped desk and punched keys on a computer. He tugged at the shirt wrapped around his hand. "Pressure is dropping from twenty-three hundred psi," Jerry shouted from the reactor console.

"Coolant is falling," Valdern Aston shouted. "Main feedwater is down!" His voice sounded like James Earl Jones, and he had the towering build to support it. Bifocals perched on his flat, wide nose. His hair was a half-inch pile, thinning throughout, the sides gray. His demeanor was commanding—an early fifties navy vet. He presented himself like he was in his sixties and had been in the longest, greatest world war ever when really he'd just been floating on an inactive ship working with its nuclear reactor back in the seventies.

Every phone in the control room rang, LED lights pulsing.

"Hello," Trace answered. No one was there. He hit another flashing light. "Control room, Crane." Nothing. He hit another line. "Reactor-three control. Hello?"

Valdern and Jerry picked up the other phones. "Reactor three. Hello? Control three. Hello? Control three? Control room. Hello?" They shook their heads and looked at Trace.

"Phones are going crazy," Trace said. The clang of the iron door opening snapped his head up. Four crew members shuffled in, debris across their white company button-ups and khakis, panic exploding from their faces.

"Fire in the auxiliary building!" one of them yelled.

The alarms impeded Trace's thinking. His alabaster facial skin flushed. Good God. This is the big one.

The control room plunged into darkness.

CHAPTER 2

Trace's face was striped by washes of battery-driven emergency floodlights. He stared at the LEDs of the reactor-three control console glowing like a star system in the darkness. Blips of emergency lights revealed glimpses of ten additional crewmembers who had filed into the room. They checked gauges, yammered technical data to each other, and ran in and out of the control-room entrance. He felt like someone was going to flip the lights back on with a case of beer and cupcakes, busting up laughing. *We gotcha!*

"Declaring an unusual event," Trace bellowed to his team. He rapped at the keyboard behind the control room's teal, Formica-topped central command desk. The blood-soaked sleeve around his hand dangled across the keys. Then he spoke into the receiver of the direct line to New York Emergency Management. The computer and the line functioned on battery backup. "This is control-room supervisor Trace Crane from the Bear Mountain Nuclear Energy Center. I'm declaring an unusual event. We've got a station blackout as a result of what seems to be a seismic occurrence." *Seismic...* He couldn't believe it. *Earthquake in New York? What the fuck is the planet coming to?* The receiver pulled at his skin, sticking to the blood coagulating on the side of his face when he went to hang up. It had run down his white shirt collar and shoulder, making him look like he'd taken a gunshot to the temple. 8:49 burned back at him from his digital wristwatch. *Twenty-two minutes since the event had started.* Without electricity the only functioning gear in the control room was battery-driven gauges, alarms, and emergency lights. *In a few hours the battery-driven systems'll go dark if we don't get external power.* Typically the plant ran off its own generated power supply, but in a full shutdown emergency it relied on external power from the state grid. Trace thought the grid was probably compromised from the quake. Without external power the reactor typically drew electricity from three, large diesel generators that were kept on site for a station blackout emergency. The only problem was those generators weren't starting automatically as they had been designed to. *The pumps are all down, no coolant is circulating inside the reactor*—Trace's worst fear. Coolant also seemed to deplete at a rapid pace; Trace believed there might be a leak in the reactor vessel or piping caused by the quake. Without power the reactor was a truck blazing down a mountain in neutral without brakes. The core was going to continue to heat up and vaporize the stagnate coolant at an increasing pace until the fuel rods began to melt. *NO! Not on my watch.* Trace lanced his eyes at Jerry, who stood at the diesel-generator controls turning keys in the desk, attempting to manually start the generators.

"No manual start on diesel one," Jerry said.

Trace paced. "Keep trying."

"Trying manual start again on one." Jerry turned the key. "No start on one."

"Try two," Trace said.

"Manual start on two." Jerry shook his head. "Dead."

"Try three," Trace said.

"Manual start on three." Jerry turned the key several times. "Nothin'."

"Try them all again," Trace directed. He picked up his radio. "Hanson, are you guys down in the generator building yet?" Static swirled. "Hanson, it's Crane. Come in."

Inside the generator building Vic Hanson's radio squawked from his hip. He was fifties, medium build with a long, arching nose that sat under deep-set eyes. He reached for his radio. "Hanson here. Go 'head," he bellowed in a hard New Jersey accent. Gary Harrell was at his side—a black man in his forties, round face, honest eyes. Both men wore hard hats and swept their flashlights over the behemoth, cerulean-blue diesel generators that laid like three, dead whales in the massive hangar. Revealed in vignetting flashlight beams the room showed immaculately clean, paint fresh and shining, lined with steel piping of various widths. The concrete floor was painted a light, misty gray under the generators. A slate gray wrapped the edges with a yellow handrail running along parts of the access paths. "What's the status," Trace's voice chirped across their radios.

"Diesel two is sittin' quietly. Diesel one has a repair sign on it. They must've still been waitin' on parts for it from last month," Hanson said.

"Parts… What… What's three doing?" Trace said.

"Three? Three's comatose."

"Jesus." Trace wiped sweat from his forehead with his shirt-sleeve-bandaged hand. The temperature in the control room had quickly risen due to the lack of air conditioning and residual heat generated by the control consoles. The maintenance of the diesel generators didn't fall under Trace's watch. Had it, he would've had all three of them in top shape ready to fire. He blamed plant manager Ken Bramini for the flub. *Unbelievable!*

"Can you hear it turning over when... Jerry hit the manual on diesel two," Trace barked, "...when Jerry turns manual up here?"

"Is he hittin' it?" Hanson said.

"Jerry?" Trace called to him.

"Turnin' it." Jerry said.

"Yeah. Waddaya got?" Trace squawked into the radio.

"Dead as my grandmother," Hanson blurted.

"Try starting locally," Trace said.

"Starting locally." Hanson squawked off.

Trace, Jerry, and Valdern waited silently, alarm lights revealing their worried faces. There was no logical explanation for everything going wrong at the same time. *Phenomenon? Ghosts in the machine? Murphy's law?* Cascading issues had never happened during Trace's tenure. He nipped problems as they arrived, analyzed with instinct and intellect, and reacted. He was faced with something else now. A flurry of alarms snapped everyone's head toward the control console. "Coolant falling below two hundred forty inches," Valdern boomed. During normal functionality emergency feedwater kicked on and circulated coolant through the core once coolant dropped around one hundred sixty inches. Without power nothing would happen, and they had very little control, still the brakeless truck blazing down the mountain. The implications pushed acid into Trace's throat. He grabbed a roll of antacid from his pocket and bit off several tablets. His job's stress for heightened awareness and performance perfection coupled with the stress that had built up in his marriage made antacids part of his daily diet. Although, the tabs were futile against the eruption inside him. Ten boxes of baking soda couldn't alkalize his interior. Trace thought if the reactor became a runaway, melting locomotive he'd bolt out of there, find Avi and Brooklyn, and drive west. *Where are they anyway? Focus. Focus. Focus... They're fine. Focus...*

"Crane," Trace's radio blurted with Hanson's voice. "Diesel

two isn't starting. Repeat. Diesel two not turning over."

"Hit it again."

"Local start trying again. Stand by."

Trace waited, his stomach pulsating with the rapidity of his pulmonary system. *We need power. And we need it now!*

"Nothing. Local start not working," Hanson said.

"Keep hittin' it," Trace said.

"I'm turnin' it like a sixty-four Beetle."

"Take the panel off. Hot-wire that bitch if you have to."

"Removing panel. Stand by," Hanson said.

Gary Harrell pulled off the large wiring panel on the generator. Hanson held the flashlight for Gary and handed him a knife from his hip. "Panel off. Splicing wires," Hanson said into the radio. Gary reached into the panel and started splicing. Sparks popped. Vic and Gary recoiled. Gary grabbed the hot wire and saved it from touching the grounded sides of the box again.

"Get the red and the green," Trace heard Hanson say to Gary. "Maybe Santa'll show up."

"Here we go," Hanson chirped off. Gary touched the wires together. Beyond dismantling the generator, hot-wiring it was their only hope. If it didn't work Trace would phone for outside generators to be trucked in. *That's if trucks could even get to us.* According to the seismometer the quake was in the sixes. *How could a quake that big hit the East Coast?* Bridges crumbling, trees and power lines in the roads, buildings collapsing, and major traffic jams flipped through his mind. In perfect conditions they were looking at five to ten hours, maybe more, to get an external generator delivered. The generator would have to be ordered, paid for, and picked up. Even in crisis people wanted their money, especially when they were removed from the situation and knew little of the severity and consequences. Then there was setup time once it arrived. They'd be lucky if they had power by the wee hours of night. By then the core would be well into melting. Once power returned they'd be digging themselves out of quicksand with no certain idea of how the goliath machine would respond. Inside the windowless control room Trace felt detached from the outside world. Sure the building had shaken and the reactor was unstable, but what was going on outside?

A jolt of electricity shot through his body, snapping his eyes wide and his mind present. All the lights, fans, and machinery in the control room whined on. He looked around. *Good lord you gotta be fucking kidding.* Trace was just about to pen his eulogy, but it must not have been time yet. Trace puffed out a breath. "Yeah! Woooh!" He clapped his hands. "YEAH!" Jerry, Valdern, and the other crew in the control room cheered.

"She's alive!" Hanson's voice blurted from Trace's radio. Trace picked up his walkie. "Nice work." Power surged into Trace's arms and shoulders. He was a lion proud of his pride.

"Frankenstein's back, baby," Jerry yelled.

"Get diesel three up as well. We're gonna need the power," Trace said into his walkie. "Check those pumps," Trace barked to Jerry and Valdern, the smile quickly disappearing from his face. The news flashed on the LCD TV hanging above him. 6.4 IN PEEKSKILL emblazoned in cracked red letters animated onto the monitor. Aerial footage of Peekskill and the surrounding area looped on split screen next to the newscaster—smoke billowed from fires, water gushed, buildings and homes laid in rubble piles, cars stopped at the edge of collapsed highways. Trace grabbed the remote and toggled the volume.

The newscaster appeared, shirt so tight his bearded jowls spilled over his collar to his gold tie. "If this year wasn't already breaking records with the summer heat and natural disasters, here's another one. Less than thirty minutes ago a 6.4 earthquake was reported right here in New York, its epicenter in the town of Peekskill." The anchor lost his booming tone; his voice trembled. "We, too, felt the shaking some twenty minutes ago. Power is out in most of Manhattan, and the studio here is currently running on backup generators. Witnesses on the ground in Peekskill are telling us residents are absolutely shocked, panicking, power is out throughout the city and the surrounding areas. Buildings and homes shook for what seemed like fifteen seconds or more, and people were running terrified into the streets. Rescue crews have been deployed. There're reports of people trapped in crumbled buildings. Bridges and overpasses have been cut, sections collapsed, roads buckled." The audio garbled and the screen snowed with interference.

Avi, Brooklyn. Trace's chest tightened with fear. *I have to call them. I...* Trace picked up the desk phone and punched through various lines. He found a dial tone. Relief. He dialed Avi's cell phone. "The caller you are trying to reach is unavailable." Trace punched the switchhook and dialed again. "The caller you are trying to reach is unavailable. Please try your call again later." *Dammit!* The TV sucked him in. The broadcast blipped and squiggled, the newscaster's voice choppy.

"...ere's een considerable dam... age to Peekskill, and we can see from our eye in the sky many buildings have collapsed, smoke billowing, dust swirling, and several fire...s ...urning. To my wife, Shonda, and my daughter, Rachel—I tried to call and couldn't get through. If you can hear me get upstate and to shelter. I love you. My ife and aughter er in Westchester. Looking out the windows in Manhattan there oesn't eem to be any direct damage from the quake, ich occurred thir, thir, thirty-five miles to the, the, the north up the udson in Peekskill." The anchor put his hand to his ear. "What's that?... Okay... We have a... We have seismologist John Mattina from the USGS on the phone with us. Hello, John, can you hear us?"

John's voice sounded like it was coming out of a megaphone, his cell connection glitchy. "Hello, Al."

"John, can you explain to us what's happened here in the Northeast this morning?"

A graphic map of the Northeast U.S. appeared on the screen.

"As we know a 6.4 quake hit eekskill, New York, york, york at eight thirty-nin this morn nin, non, non, non," John said. Squiggly yellow lines spidered out on the map, indicating faults over the terrain. "This set off the Ramapo Fault System," the lines pulsated, "where it inter... tersects with the Stamford-Peekskill Fault Line, which origina... a... a... ates in Connecticut. Ramapo runs from there through New York, New Jersey, and into Pennsylvania. The fault shook for nearly twenty seconds, and in that time it set off faults all the way down the East Coast through North Carolina and all the way to the eastern edge of Illinois, triggering additional fault zo... o... o... ones. We thought our seismographs were malfunctioning, until we started getting calls from nearly twenty-six states. From the Peekskill epicenter alone shock waves have been reported as far down as North Carolina, as far north as New Hampshire and Maine, and as far west as Columbus. That fault... ault... ault—" There was static.

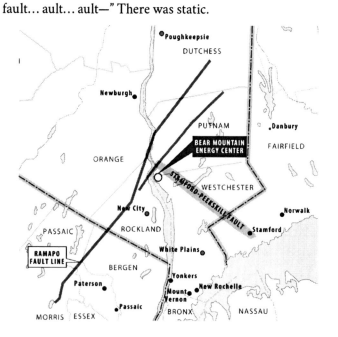

"Hello, John. John, you still there?" the newscaster said. He paused. "Looks like we lost him. That was John Mattina, seismologist at the United States Geological Survey." The newscaster put a finger to his earpiece. "And we have... Okay..." Aerial footage of the Bear Mountain Nuclear Energy Center showed on the split screen. The mammoth cooling tower just outside the control room spewed heavy amounts of steam. Trace thought it was like being at a game, the audience camera panning the rows about to turn on him. He'd hide under the bleachers if he had to. *They're way too close. The media would love to get through these walls.* Black and gray smoke swirled up from other parts of the facility grounds. *Fire?* "Gentleman." Trace pointed to the screen.

"That there folks is the Bear Mountain Nuclear Energy Center. Just one mile from the quake's epicenter in Peekskill," the anchorman continued. "Our chopper noticed the steam and smoke on their flyby." The split screen faded to reveal the newscaster with his female counterpart. Her champagne hair coiled down to her sapphire sleeveless shirt. Her nose pointed south like an arrow, her upper lip the bow, both registering as a contrived grin. "Haley Botnitz has just joined me in the newsroom."

"Boy, seeing the smoke from that power plant makes me nervous," she said.

"We hope everything is okay there. We are trying to get confirmation from sources on the ground," the male news-caster said.

Trace muted the TV. Jerry, Valdern, and several other crew stared at him. Reactor three had been constructed in the early nineteen seventies. What worried Trace was that the reactor was supposedly built to handle a 6.1-magnitude earthquake. A 6.4-magnitude earthquake delivering almost three times the impact had hit with the epicenter less than a mile from the plant. *There has to be structural damage.* Without seeing every wall and pipe he had no way of knowing. *Anything could be destroyed.* Also, Bear Mountain reactor three was rated number one in the country for the highest risk of core damage caused by a seismic event. No one ever imagined a quake of that magnitude striking the East Coast, except, clearly, the scientists. Seismologists knew something everyone else didn't—the Ramapo fault zone was a seething leviathan that could explode at any moment. Now it had. Trace experienced the chilling realization that their operating license shouldn't have been extended twenty years past the reactor's design life. Reactor one had been shut down permanently in the early seventies due to design flaws. Reactor two had reached its forty-year lifespan two years ago, and reactor three reached its design life two years after. Doubts and repressed fears of reactor safety and longevity flooded him.

"Jerry, we…" Trace grabbed his head. "I…" He touched the desk phone. "I need… I need a minute… I need a second… I need a second…" *Avi. Brooklyn.* He grabbed the desk phone and dialed Avi. The line was silent. He grabbed his cell from his pocket. He had no service inside the steel-and-cement-fortified control room. *Idiot. You already know that.* Instincts superseded his logic. Trace considered dashing outside to call, but he couldn't leave the control room. He was the leader. With pressure mounting he had to stay with his team. He dialed Avi's cell again. "The caller you are trying to reach is unavailable. Please try your call again later." He slammed the switchhook. "Shit!" The dial tone droned in his ear. He tried again. Same result. And then again. He knew Avi had been up since 3:00 a.m. Working in her home office. Although, he figured, she could be on the road because she had to take a break to drop Brooklyn off at summer school. They had enrolled her in the three-half-day-a-week program to get her ahead in the curriculum and take foreign-language classes with the hopes that she could test out of grades in the future. He wished he had told them to go out to the beach house early without him. They'd be there safe on the sand and he wouldn't be worrying.

Trace picked up the desk phone again and dialed his home line. A busy signal pulsed back at him. Trace scrolled through his smartphone for Brooklyn's summer-school number. *How could I not have the number?* "Christ!" He slapped the switchhook and dialed the operator in an attempt to get the number to Brooklyn's school. "All operators are busy now," said a robotic, female voice. "Please try your call again later." He smashed the receiver down and looked around the control room. Jerry, Valdern, and his other crew waited for him to act. "Shit. God-dammit!" *I should've taken the fucking day off like Avi had asked me to. I should be with my family. This can't be good. The house has probably collapsed. There's no way structures in Peekskill can withstand a quake like this.* Trace thought about going to search for Avi and Brooklyn. He looked at his smartphone screen wallpaper—a picture of his girls. He clutched his phone tight in his hand. He had to believe they were safe. "Please God let them be safe," he mumbled to himself. A flurry of alarms roused him.

"Coolant falling below two hundred inches!" Jerry yelped. Trace's eyes widened. His stomach seized.

CHAPTER 3

Avi Crane's umber hair was matted across her face with fresh blood. Metal shelving, bottled beverages, beer, water, juice, and bagged snacks had strewn across her. She slowly pushed her thirty-seven-year-old body from the debris. The front and top of her head felt like a battle-axe had been swung across it. She pushed her hair from her face and felt liquid on her fingers. *Blood?* She touched her head again, wincing. More blood. *What happened?* Lights flickered, blips of blurry color and packaging in her vision. She heard hissing, fizzing, static. A tone blared in her right ear, her hearing completely dropping out in her left in a bizarre auditory shift. She reached for her ear and then in an opposite shift her hearing returned. "Let's give 'em somethin' to …alk……bout… a little …ystery… fig… ure… out." Bonnie Raitt skipped over the ceiling speakers. Avi took stock of the aisle. Stark fluorescent ceiling lights glared in her emerald irises, blobs of blue and red mixing into purple in her vision. She winced and shielded her eyes. Every time light entered her vision a spear plunged into her skull. The end of the aisle looked surreal—everything fuzzy and slow. She felt faded from reality, removed, underwater. Between the shattered glass and pooling liquids other shoppers lay on the floor, debris on top of them. *Bodies. Are they dead? Kombucha? I was getting kombucha. No, beer. Trace wanted beer. My baby, I have to pick her up from the carnival, right? From the market, bank, zoo? What? School.* Pain lanced behind her eyes. *Trace. Where're you?* She envisioned him in the freezer section staring at pizzas. *No. He's at work.* She pulled her cell phone from her purse and dialed him. A teetering shelf adjacent to her cried and collapsed. Avi recoiled. Her phone beeped back at her. Call failed. She tried again. Call failed. *You're never available dammit! Answer the phone!* Avi hadn't realized the network was clogged and it wasn't Trace's fault. They had fought about him being unavailable at work in the past. Anytime anything happened at their home or with Brooklyn, Avi had to shoulder the burden because Trace was unreachable—in meetings or involved in a crucial refueling or repair process at the plant. Those arguments spun into fights about the dangers of nuclear energy, Avi's fears about living close to the plant, and Trace's job keeping him locked down from the rest of life. Each evening when Trace came home he was saddled with gargantuan stress that rendered him detached and emotionally unavailable. Romance in their marriage had become rarer than an albino panda and Avi was frustrated that Trace could never help with Brooklyn—rides to school, playdates, meals, baths, teeth brushing, and dressing.

"Let's give 'em somethin' to …alk… about… a little …ystery… to figure… out." *What is that singing?* At the front opening of the aisle blurry figures rushed past, climbing over stock that had spilled across the floors. A distorted man's voice giving repeated direction over the PA overloaded her aural senses, his words sounding like Charlie Brown's teacher speaking through a distorted megaphone. "Please wahwacuate the store wahwarefully. Watch your step. Please wahwacuate the store slowly and watch your step please…" *What?* "Wah waaah wa waaaaahh waaaaaahh…" *Ahh… that noise.* She grabbed her head. Static. "How about… love… uhhhvv… uhhhvvveee." POP! It sounded like the speaker jacks had been ripped out. Silence save for fizzing and distant commotion.

Avi moved to her knees, the backside of her black stretch pants wet. She touched her bottom. *Juice? Soda? I just got these pants.* She had been up since 3:00 a.m. in her home office working on an initiative for an advanced-energy technology startup, then skipped out to rush Brooklyn to summer school, and then to the store to pick up food for their trip to the beach. Avi had been consulting for the last three years with the energy startup to develop a zero-point energy-harvesting device. The technology was built using microtechnology to extract energy from quantum-level virtual particles oscillating omnipresently in the universe. Reminiscent of computer circuitry the device harvested the oscillations, amplified them, and converted them to alternating current that could be used by everyday electronics. Avi had planned to finish her work by midday, allowing her to join Trace and Brooklyn at the beach house for the weekend. Although, she was certain they were going to be late given all she had to complete, which included evaluating and reporting lab results from her team that was testing prototypes and picking Brooklyn up from school. Avi found it unfair Trace couldn't shuttle Brooklyn around because of his job demands. She despised it when he leaned on her like she was a stay-at-home mom when she was far from one.

Avi brushed dust and debris from her gray t-shirt. Her head ached down into her neck. She ran her hands around her face, across the thick, groomed eyebrows that sat above her darkened orbital sockets, across her cheeks, over her plump lips. She looked Italian or Middle Eastern—Mediterranean. She was Jewish, roots in Israel somewhere generations ago. She rubbed her neck. Her jaw ached. She slid her fingers across her chin, running them over a flat mole below her mouth. "Ahh!" she cried. When she moved pain lanced from her hip into her shoulder. She ran her hand down her side and her back, tenderness radiating. The aisle floor undulated. *Stop moving. Brook's at the farm, right? She's with grandpa? Is this just happening in the store?*

What IS happening? The last thing Avi recalled was her shopping list humming through her mind and reaching for sparkling water. *Earthquake?* She didn't know what one felt like. *This is New York, not California. Explosion?* She wobbled, her leg shaky. With her equilibrium imbalanced and all the debris on the floor she feared she would fall on the twisted metal and shards of glass. She tilted forward to her hands and crawled, her brown-leather purse swinging across her chest, plastic and cardboard packaging crunching under her limbs. The floor moving past her eyes nauseated her. Her pulse thrummed at the gash along her hairline, her entire cranium in agony. *Pressure. So much pressure.* She feared her brain had slapped into the side of her skull. Avi came upon a pair of blurry tan shoes protruding from a pile of snacks and bottled water. *Wicked witch? No.* An elderly woman was wedged between shelving, blood seeping from her head. *I'm at a funeral. No! My god. I'm hallucinating?* She crawled next to her. "Miss… Miss…" Avi shook the woman at her shoulder and recoiled realizing she was real and unconscious. "Help us. We need help over here," she called out to the end of the aisle, her vocal effort amplifying the agony in her head. Her voice was raspy, her accent somewhere between Philadelphia and Long Island. She had no idea who she was yelling to. Avi looked back at the woman, who reminded her of her mother—dry charcoal hair, large drop earrings, classy applications of makeup. The woman was someone else's mother and Avi would want someone to help hers if she were injured. "I'm gonna get you some help." The woman didn't respond. Avi feared she was dead.

Trace was fishing today, right. No. Golf? Football? No. He's at work, where he always is. Well, then, he's fine. Maybe. This's an earthquake. It might not be fine. She crawled forward. "Ahhh!" Pain pierced through her knee and shot down her leg. She leaned back on the shelf. A large shard of glass stuck out from her black pants. Her lucidity heightened exponentially as if she'd snorted up a mound of amphetamine. She inhaled quickly, wincing. Tears welled in her eyes. She reached for the shard, her hand shaking, grabbed it carefully between her thumb and index finger, and pulled it out. White-hot pain, bone deep, radiated down her leg. Avi angrily tossed the bloody shard into the open refrigerated shelving adjacent to her. The wound burned. She held it for a moment, writhing, her body trembling.

Avi continued crawling, reaching a man in his forties, his leg stuck under collapsed shelving. He struggled to pull himself out. "Can you help me?" he asked.

Avi crawled closer, squinting, the lights from above glaring in her eyes. She gripped the shelving and struggled to push it upwards. "Try now."

The man shimmied himself from under it. Avi saw his tibia was bowed. He grabbed his leg, agony twisting his face. "Do you see my son?" the man asked.

"The sun? No, we're inside. We gotta go."

"No. My son, my boy?"

"What? Shit." Avi looked around. "No. Where was he?"

"Right next to me." He grimaced.

"What's happening?" Avi beseeched breathlessly.

"Earthquake," he said.

Earthquake? Avi pushed bottled beverages, salsas, and bagged snacks aside looking for the boy. She thought she saw flaxen hair flopped over packaged goods and bottles underneath the shelving. She crawled closer and pushed aside debris to find the boy laying motionless under the shelf, his bloody countenance stark in her face. *Panic. Panic. Injured child. No. NO!* Adrenaline rippled through her stomach. Her breath staggered. She looked to the man, tears pushing over her lids. "He's here." The man crawled closer, grunting. He moved debris from the floor with Avi. The overhead lights cut out, leaving them in shadowy natural light. Pressure in her head lessened, the pangs rolling to a pulsating ache. *Oh my god. Oh my god. Where's Trace and Brooklyn? What's happened?* Her pulse doubled, heart knocking at her ribs. The man reached for his unconscious son. *Where are they? I have to know. The same thing could've happened to them.* "I… I have to go," she said frantically. "I have to go." Her chest tightened, suddenly she had trouble breathing.

"Thank you," the man said with a fleeting glance.

"I'll send someone." Avi crawled over collapsed signage, liquid, shattered glass, cardboard, and shelving to the end of the aisle. She staggered to her feet and stumbled into the main aisle, hyperventilating. "Please. I need help!" Her words fell into vacuity—useless, powerless, heard by no one. She couldn't muster a shout. She lurched forward. An alpaca came around the endcap of the aisle. *What the fuck?* Avi blinked. It was a lanky man with a bristly, gray mustache. He wore a red-and-black polo shirt tucked into khakis, a name tag reading "Harry" pinned on his chest.

"What's happening?" was all she could say.

"Earthquake," Harry said.

Avi winced, grabbing her head. "There's a woman in the aisle. She's pinned under a shelf. And a boy, too. They need… they need help." She was breathless.

"Okay. I'll take a look. You get outside."

Avi hobbled to the exit, stepping over produce, flowers, magazines, wine bottles, and candy bars. She grabbed her mobile phone from her purse. *What's the number?* She tapped at the icons, unsure of what she was doing. She hit the email icon; the camera took a picture of the floor. She scrolled through and stumbled upon the favorites icon. *Trace.* She selected his name from the list. Blood from her finger smeared across the screen. She pushed her bloody hair from her face and put the phone to her ear. No rings. A computerized voice squawked back at her. "The network is busy. Please try your call again later. Thank you." *What's goin' on? Why is...?*

She tried him again. "The network is busy. Please try your call—" She tried again and again and again, frantically stabbing at Trace's name.

Avi staggered outside, wincing from the sun's glare, migraine-level pain lancing through her skull. She tried her phone again. Same result. She made her way through the throng of people crowding the front of the store. "Uhhh…" She felt nauseated and tried to dial her daughter's school. "The network is—"

"Goddammit!" Avi grabbed onto a pillar and vomited. Embarrassed, she wiped her mouth with her shirt. She tore open a case of water from a stack that had collapsed and took a bottle. She cracked the cap off and rinsed her mouth out. Avi turned to the crowd of people. "Is anybody's phone working?" Everyone, phones in hands, shook their heads. Many were injured—cut, bruised, bleeding from hands, heads, and legs. Children wailed. Cars jammed the parking lot. Men and women wheeled out cartloads of food and water without bags. *Looting?* A security guard yelled after them, but quickly retreated to more pressing matters inside.

Avi needed to console Brooklyn if she was scared, tell her not to worry. *But where did I park? And where is she?* Her thoughts were a two thousand–piece puzzle dumped on the floor. She walked swiftly into the parking lot. A BMW came to a hard stop at her knees. *Jesus! Where the hell?*

The man driving the sedan honked. "Watch where you're

goin', idiot!"

Avi stared at him. *Asshole. Although, I should've seen him.* She pressed on. *Fuck it. Where is it? Dammit.* She stopped and pivoted. *Ah!* Her silver Toyota SUV glowed. She stumbled toward it. Every bounce on the asphalt pounded into her head and hip. She took her keys from her purse, hopped inside, and started the vehicle with the push of a button. A radio host's voice bellowed. "There've been confirmed reports out of Peekskill, New York, that a major earthquake has rocked the area. Officials are asking residents to stay indoors in safe, sturdy areas of their homes or move to clear, open, outdoor areas in the event of additional tremors. Reports of collapsed homes, fires, and—" Avi stabbed the radio power button. Silence. Focus. She clutched the shift and dropped it into drive. Her SUV lurched forward. She mashed the brake. *No, no, no...* She backed from her spot. The blare of a horn made her stamp on the brakes. Her SUV bucked. In her rearview a woman in a Mercedes sedan coasted behind her laying on her horn, glowering. *Bitch.* Avi realized she had a rearview camera on the dash LCD screen. *What an idiot I am. What's wrong with me?* She felt woozy and weak as if she had sat in the sun all day consuming vodka. A man in a black Acura stopped and waved her out. "Thank youuuu!"

Sun glare lanced Avi's skull when she backed from under the tree. Once she was in the line of cars waiting to exit, she fumbled with her sunglasses in the console and pushed them onto her face. *Relief.* Panic wrenched her stomach. She reached into her glove compartment and surfaced with a pack of sanitizing wipes, wiped sweat and blood from her forehead and threw the trash in a plastic tub on the passenger side floor. She inched forward in the line of cars, looked in the rearview and cringed at the bleeding gash above her scalp line. Stitches would be required, but Avi needed something to hold it for the meantime. She reached behind the passenger seat into her toddler bag—a change of clothes, snacks, towels, and toys for Brooklyn. Avi grabbed one of her baby's white t-shirts and tied it around her forehead. She looked in the mirror and fixed it. *Like G.I. Jane.* She looked out her passenger window. Beyond the parking spaces sat a berm of plants, the sidewalk, another berm, and finally the jammed street. *What am I gonna do? I need to get out. I NEED TO GET OUT NOW!*

Avi cut the wheel and gassed it. The SUV easily climbed the berms and sidewalk. She plopped down off the curb into the street, surprising herself. Her actions seemed to come from her subconscious. Angry motorists honked at her. The line to the intersection was gridlocked, her only hope a U-turn to circumvent the traffic. Instinctually, she threw her SUV in reverse and backed up over the curb. Horns blared. "Sorry!" She whipped her vehicle around, skidded down the curb, and squealed southeast on Main Street.

Nothing will keep me from my daughter.

CHAPTER 4

Trace stood behind the kidney-shaped central desk inside the reactor-three control room, a mug of coffee in one hand, his other resting on the laminate desktop. Every sip reminded him of the mug Brooklyn had given him lying in pieces on the floor inside his office. *I'll get to it. Focus...* The green metal walls of flashing lights, levers, and switches surrounding him looked like a space-aged stack of slot machines. The cacophony of alarms penetrating his brain impeded his ruminations. Omnipresent mumbled conversations droned in his ears, interrupted by snaps of switches. Trace's mind washed with worry about Avi and Brooklyn and how to respond to the reactor. Logical actions came in blips. It was mostly worry—bottomless anxiety and nothing more. He wondered if whoever had come up with the concept of putting six hundred alarms in the control room considered that twenty-five to fifty percent of them could go off at the same time during an emergency. Approximately twenty additional men were now in the control room watching the walls of gauges, blabbing into phones, scribbling on clipboards, and conferring with slanted jaws and scowls.

The notion of action surfaced. Trace picked up the desk phone and dialed Avi's cell. It didn't ring, only a computerized woman's voice crunched at him. "All lines are busy now. Please try your call again later. Message fifty." *Fuck!* He hung up and dialed the operator. A busy signal pulsed back at him. He dropped the receiver back into its cradle. *I'm helpless.* He saw Brooklyn crumpled and bleeding, trapped in a collapsed school building, Avi in a car accident, unconscious, paramedics nowhere in sight—her car teetering on the edge of an overpass. Dreadful media imagery from earthquakes around the world soared through his mind. He tussled with the thoughts. *Bring in the positivity!* He saw Brooklyn's school damaged then not, the bricks falling then intact, blood streaming from her face then not, tears in her eyes, her little pink, polka-dot backpack bouncing on her back as she ran terrified until Avi scooped her up. He envisioned Avi's SUV smashed, the windshield spidered, the airbags out, blood leaking from her head as she lay unconscious, slumped over the wheel.

Trace... A voice called to him. He fought to suppress the images, his brain in a vise. *Hey, Trace!* His house collapsed into a pile of rubble. *NO!* It stood strong and bright. He couldn't control his mind. Back and forth the images went, contorting and exploding from devastating to reassuring. *Crane...* He heard the voice again. *Hey, Crane!* Trace snapped his head up. "Coolant down to one hundred fifty inches," Jerry said. "You daydreamin' over there?"

"Uhhh… Thinking…" *Having nightmares... except it's day... daymares!* "Hit the high-pressure injection," Trace told Jerry.

"Injecting," Jerry said.

Trace felt the colossal machine moving in his viscera, a bellow of a beast caged in the depths behind several feet of steel and concrete.

"Coolant level increasing," Jerry said. "One sixty."

"Pressure's at seventeen hundred psi," Valdern said.

"One seventy… one eighty… one ninety…" Jerry said.

"Going up kinda fast isn't it?" Trace said.

Jerry nodded.

"Core temperature is seven hundred and rising despite the coolant increase," Valdern said.

"Two hundred… two twenty…" Jerry said.

"We're movin' too quick. How's that possible?" Trace moved to the control console and searched the vast array of gauges with Jerry and Valdern. So many switches, so many gauges. There was no fast way to troubleshoot. *Emergency feedwater. High-pressure injection. Get water in the reactor loop. Block valves?* Trace tucked his head and rubbed his hands together, alarms injecting him with anxiety made it hard to concentrate and move calmly. *Focus.*

"Pressurizer gauge is showing higher levels. Three hundred twenty at the pressurizer," Jerry said.

Trace snapped his head up. His chest shuddered with tension. *How could it be filling so fast? Stuck valve? Condenser?*

"Water level hitting three hundred sixty inches," Jerry bellowed.

Alarms wailed and seemed to pick up intensity like the warning in a cockpit while a plane nosedived to its demise. "Cut the injection pumps before we go solid," Trace demanded.

"Cut the pumps?" Valdern threw his arms up. "What you doin', Crane? Cut the *pumps*?"

Jerry hovered his hand over the switches. He looked back and forth between Trace and Valdern.

"We're about to go solid. Cut 'em, Jerry!"

Valdern moved toward Trace. "Hold up, Crane. You don't even know if these gauges are reading right. They're bouncing all over the place."

"You don't trust the gauges? You can't mistrust the instruments."

"The hell you can't," Valdern thundered.

The ten-man crew in the control room looked up from their instruments, phones, and computer screens.

"Water level three sixty-five," Jerry said.

"Cut 'em, Jerry!" Trace barked, his corpulent cheeks red, burning with heat.

Jerry toggled the switches. Trace and Valdern glared at each other.

Valdern stabbed his fingers in Trace's face. "You take responsibility for what you doin', Crane." His face twitched with tension, finger so close it blurred in Trace's vision.

"You better get your goddamn finger outta my face," Trace said through a clenched jaw.

"Or what?" Valdern retorted.

"Both of you relax. We're on the same team here." Gary trotted over from the back of the room and wedged himself between Trace and Valdern. Valdern's stare was cocky, his chin held high. Trace had a glower and a curled lip from the bad taste of impudence Valdern poured into him. From Trace's rosy, cherubic appearance one wouldn't think he was tough. But he was a lion in koala suit. Still, Valdern might make short work of him based on his military training.

"Water level three seventy. Still rising," Jerry said.

Trace turned to Jerry. "I told you to cut the fucking pumps!" Spit flew from his mouth.

"I did, I did, I did…" Jerry looked over the console and gauges, checking and rechecking.

Trace scurried next to Jerry. "Water goes past three ninety we're solid." If they let the vessel go solid they risked causing vibrational hammering that could fracture the vessel and piping causing a coolant leak. Trace thought they might already have a leak, but a solid vessel would certainly make the situation worse.

"Water level three eighty. Still rising," Jerry said.

"Dammit. What?..."

"Three-ninety. We're goin' solid."

"Shit!"

Choppy blond, late-twenties Skip Sinclair looked back at Trace. He had a forehead so long a jet could land on it. "Boilers're goin' dry."

"Dry?" Trace walked back toward Skip. "The boilers should be filling with the injection, not drying out."

"Pressure's at eleven hundred and falling," Valdern said. "Emergency pumps must've come on right after the injection."

"Cut 'em," Trace said.

"You cuttin' everything! We need somethin' runnin'!" Valdern barked.

"Cut 'em!" Trace demanded. "Now!"

Jerry cut the pumps one by one.

Trace watched the water level slow to a stop, pegging the gauge. He let out a heavy breath. Relief made him close his eyes. His shoulders were growing up to his ears with tension and he couldn't seem to rest them.

"Sumps are running heavy," Sinclair said.

Trace knew that meant coolant was leaking out of the reactor vessel or its piping somewhere onto the containment-building floor. He was now sure the piping must have been damaged directly from the shaking or possibly from the lurch of the coolant system during the station blackout. *Wonderful. Anything else?* The reactor was a trauma victim. *Is this bone broken? Is that organ punctured? Internal bleeding?* No matter how many monitors gave readings, some issues would be masked, and they didn't have the luxury of slicing the reactor open to hunt around. The reactor was housed inside a pill-shaped steel pressure vessel anchored in the center of a dome-shaped, steel-reinforced, concrete containment building, which was locked down during operation to contain radioactive gas or liquid that may escape the reactor unexpectedly. "Collection tank in auxiliary is filling quickly," Sinclair said.

"What's going on with the reactor tanks?" Trace asked. Sinclair raised his brows, triggering Trace to remember that the tank system was under maintenance. In the interim, wastewater had been diverted to the auxiliary building, which housed most of the reactor-support equipment and safety systems. "Christ." In the midst of everything Trace realized he was forgetting his notes about the reactor. Even though he was a reactor supervisor he wasn't in charge of facility maintenance. He didn't clean the decks. He was the captain of the ship. Once that tank filled they'd have to dump the potentially radioactive wastewater into the Hudson. Trace got on his radio. "Hanson, can we get a reading on the coolant going from the sumps into the auxiliary tank?"

"Copy. We're on it." They'd be several minutes before they had answers for him.

"Reactor pressure down to eight hundred pounds," Jerry said. "Pressure in containment increasing."

Low pressure in the reactor vessel and high pressure in containment didn't make sense. Also, core temperature was on the rise, which told Trace the core wasn't being cooled even though it was flooded. *A fire burning in the ocean? Impossible.* Trace was unsure of his next move. "Sinclair, roll that manual cart over here."

"Manuals. What the fuck do you need manuals for? You ain't qualified for this job if you need fucking manuals," Valdern said.

"C'mon, Val. You're gonna start again? Now's a good time for your attitude?"

"Watch yourself. I could damn near be your daddy. Earlier, you back there fumbling with the phone when we got split decisions to make. Now you wanna go through manuals?"

"If you're so confident, call the shots, then. What's the fucking move? Levels are all over the place. Everything's contradicting typical operation." Valdern had never liked Trace because Trace was younger than he, yet Trace was his supervisor. Additionally, it was a navy thing. Valdern had been a seaman and Trace hadn't. After Trace had received his diploma from Columbia University, a major in mechanical engineering with a minor in nuclear engineering, he fully immersed himself in nuclear energy. He started and ran the most popular nuclear blog on the internet, *Atomic Chronicles*, where he posted daily about industry happenings, advancements, and safety. He had spoken at the Nuclear Industry Summit in Washington on nuclear as the future of green energy, he was a regular speaker at the Nuclear Energy Institute, and a consultant to nuclear-technology companies producing reactor systems with enhanced safety features and operating efficiency. Trace was part of the Atomic Energy Council advisory group and was regularly consulted for his expertise by plant managers and supervisors at other Gener8-owned facilities. Amid his accolades, the general perception Trace gathered after starting at the plant was most of the navy guys looked down on the university guys. The navy vets called the university grads unis (U-knees), their own play on eunuch, referring to the crew as impotent or castrated. Resentment ran thick from Valdern, but Trace rarely engaged with him. When Trace had been offered the supervisor position, he had asked why Valdern wasn't getting it. Plant manager Ken Bramini had told him Valdern was an excellent operator, knew the ship top to bottom, but wasn't a leader, wasn't diplomatic, and had zero management skills. All that aside, he was still a major asset to the plant. Now, Valdern's dam that held his resentment was bursting. Trace took several deep breaths in an attempt to calm himself. He had to conserve his energy for rumination and judicious decisions.

Sinclair rolled the manual cart over and lugged the thousand-page behemoths to the central command desk. Dust blew from the covers as they thudded onto the laminated wood—1970s construction, single pages doubly thick with thinner modern inserts.

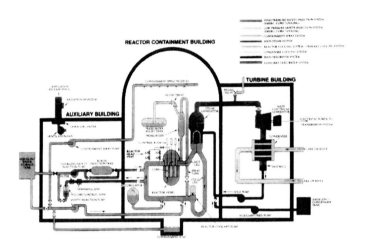

Trace began rattling off emergency procedures to his crew who verified the procedures back to him.

"We seem to be making the right moves," Jerry said. "Look at the vibration meters on the main pumps, though."

Trace saw the pumps' pressure gauges rising and falling and recognized they were probably sucking up steam and froth from the core. "We need to the cut the mains," he said.

Valdern spun around from the console. "Cut the mains? You've lost it!"

"We don't cut those pumps we won't have any in a few minutes. They'll blow out, and we could dislodge piping from the vibrations," Trace said.

"What we need is coolant circulating in that system," Valdern said.

"Exactly, and right now we're not gettin' shit." Trace went to the console and flipped the switches. The pump meters stopped lurching and the vibration-meter needles faded to a stop. Even though Trace couldn't hear what was going on in the containment building he felt it in his stomach. He sensed eerie stillness in the reactor. He had given the beast a sedative. All the pumps were cut, a seemingly awful idea, yet the only logical path the reactor had led Trace down. He had no idea when it'd wake up. Trace wondered if the reactor was the Mad Hatter pushing him down a garden trail to hell. He didn't know and he didn't know what other options he had, if any. To not respond directly to the reactor issues seemed ignorant to him. *If a baby cries put him on your shoulder, calm him. Then figure out why.* Trace was confident the system could subsist off natural circulation. Natural convection would keep the coolant moving as hot water rose and cold water fell.

"Jerry, what's our rad level in containment?"

"Nine hundred rem per hour and rising," Jerry said.

The rising radiation readings inside the reactor containment building indicated that there was a continuous release of radioactivity. That told Trace fuel was melting, which meant core damage stemming from a loss of coolant. He wasn't sure how it was possible since the reactor was supposedly flooded with coolant. *Or is it? Maybe Valdern's right and the gauges are wrong?* Trace thought a beer would be nice—a Vermont IPA and a slab of time to cogitate. He liked the froth in his mouth and the cooling trail the beer left from his throat to his stomach. Relaxation would ensue and his thoughts would flow. He wanted to evanesce and reappear in his garage workshop at his home. Repairing vintage amplifiers, speakers, receivers, arcade games, and cars led to lucidity. He had always found refuge in the garages of his childhood homes after his father had died. Working with his hands was a form of tai chi to him. Then answers would stream effortlessly. Trace needed that time now, but he wasn't going to get it. Making big decisions under pressure was a terrible idea, but it was the only choice he currently had.

CHAPTER 5

Avi sped down a local Peekskill road. *I have to call my parents...
My parents? My brother... Then... Where do I go? What about looters?
I should check the house. Fuck the house...* She envisioned people
running around with pistols robbing the innocent for food and
supplies. *Stop! One thing at a time. Get Brooklyn first then figure it
out.* Lush grass patches, weathered sidewalks, and flourishing
trees lined the streets of the quaint city. Colored, wood-sided
colonial homes, white-picket fences, dilapidated porches, and
Georgian-style, stacked-stone-and-brick buildings abounded.
If the modern vehicles and blacktop were taken away, the city
looked as it did in the early nineteen hundreds. Peekskill had
charm galore, but provisions to withstand high-magnitude
earthquakes were nonexistent. Avi navigated around a broken
water main that gushed into the street. Power lines sparked;
a utility pole had snapped and leaned on the cables. Vehicles
were pulled to the roadside, some containing drivers, others
abandoned. Car and home alarms pulsated in the distance. A
man staggered by, clutching his chest. The disarray of Peekskill
was hard for Avi to digest. Even though the sun blazed, the

city was overshadowed by ominousness. Avi felt she was in a war-torn third-world town waiting for insurgents to poke out with rifles or a land mine to explode under her car. Historic homes and buildings lay in rubble piles. Men and women hustled down the street, yelling. Others tried to pull loved ones and neighbors out from under smashed brick, twisted rebar, concrete, and wood. A little boy ran alone down the roadside, his face red, tears running in sheets down his scrunched face; he wailed. "No," Avi gasped, tears ran from her eyes. Brooklyn could be that boy, lost and alone, injured, no one to console her. Avi feared her school had collapsed, Brooklyn inside buried under the rubble, unconscious, unable to breathe. The early-1900s schoolhouse could've suffered a gas explosion given its antiquated piping and safety infrastructure.

"This is one hundred point seven WHUD out of Peekskill." A deejay's labored breaths distorted the mic. His voice trembled. "It's been confirmed through our news affiliate that a six point four on the Richter scale has hit the area. Our studio was shaking and we're currently on auxiliary power. I'm… we're… we're looking out the window and we can see water mains spewing down the streets. Power is out throughout the area and we're running on generators at the moment. People have called in saying gas mains are exploding. Everyone check your gas mains at your homes. If there are any signs of leaks shut them off and stay away. Matter of fact we're shaking again right now. It's an after shock." Avi's SUV rattled. She clutched the wheel. "Jesus."

"We're getting reports in that several overpasses, bridges, and highways have collapsed and've been compromised. The nine, six, eighty-seven, eighty-four. A section has fallen out of the Bear Mountain Bridge and at least two vehicles have been reported to have careened off into the Hudson. There are reports of people stuck in elevators, others trapped under rubble calling loved ones to come help them. We see people running and screaming in the streets—many bloody, those that can walk are carrying and helping others. Some emergency vehicles are beginning to show up outside. It's just awful. A woman is holding her child, both are bloody. The boy looks unresponsive. People are covered in dust and debris. Sirens are blaring everywhere. Also we've just heard from a source that an emergency has been declared at the Bear Mountain Nuclear Energy Center. We can see on the TV large columns of steam and smoke coming from the site."

Avi stabbed the radio off. The news made her panic more than she already was by verbally hammering everything she witnessed into her psyche. It was all shocking, images floating by in slow motion. The effects from the impact to her head made everything seem dreamlike, matte, vignetted. She felt like she was stoned, watching the ruination of her city unfold on thirty-five millimeter—her windshield the big screen. *Bear Mountain. Dammit, Trace!* The news of an emergency at the plant made her angry. *I told you, Trace. Dammit, I told you! Now we're in this mess when we could've been upstate living peacefully. Why don't you call? I hope you're trying.*

Mom's comin', Brooklyn. Avi grabbed her cell and tried Trace again. The phone beeped back at her. Call failed. She wondered if Trace was okay and if the nuclear plant was stable. Considering the damage around her she thought surely the plant would have suffered as well. She knew Trace would do everything he could. *Dammit Trace why didn't we move? Why didn't you listen to me?* She punched the gas. The wound on her knee burned against her pants. The blood was drying. *Stitches?* She didn't know. *Scar? For sure.* As long as it wasn't leaking she was content for the moment.

Avi reached an intersection. A small grocery store in a colonial block building had slid off its foundation. Across the street a gas main billowed like a flamethrower, sparking high-voltage lines. *Good god...* She hung a right and passed a jammed gas station, a line of over fifty vehicles wrapping around it. She crossed an intersection where a chasm had opened on the opposite side of the road, a car stuck in the fissure. Avi's pulse knocked, her jaw ached, her chest burned. She glanced in her rearview to check on Brooklyn, but she wasn't there. *Where?* Habit and instinct.

Avi's eyes focused back on the road. *Where am I?* She slowed. Her surroundings looked unfamiliar—heavily wooded with the occasional home crawling to the roadside. Mailboxes blurred. *Where?...* She arrived at another intersection and looked at the street signs, confused at how to get to her daughter's school. *Think. Orchard... No, Pemart...* She wiped her face with her hands. She was on Dogwood Road. *How did I?...* She must have been driving unconsciously. Road, signs, and cars washed in her vision, the trees breathing, dizziness swaying her head. She pulled her SUV to the shoulder and closed her eyes.

Brooklyn stood in the grass, smiling, holding a magnolia flower. Her silky brown hair coiled around her fair face, her hazel eyes looking directly into the camera lens Avi stared through. SNAP! The shutter clipped. A wailing emergency vehicle whizzing by blasted Avi's eyes open. She turned back onto the road and decided to go up Pump House and Gallows Hill and come back around on Sprout Brook. After several minutes she approached Albany Post Road. *Mama's comin', baby.* Avi accelerated onto the overpass. Ahead she saw rebar sticking skyward, the water below. She stamped on the brake and came to a hard stop near the edge. *Oh my god... Oh my god...* Her hands trembled. The overpass had collapsed. Amidst the concrete rubble below the trunk of a sedan stuck out of the creek, the rest of the vehicle submerged. *That could've been me.* She hoped no one was still in the vehicle. She wanted to help them, but there was no way she could. She dialed 911. Call failed beeped back at her on the screen. *Jesus.* She reversed from the edge of the overpass. She needed to get across to the city to find Brooklyn. *This is a nightmare. Why the hell did I go this way? What's wrong with me? There's no way I'm going to be able to pick up Brooklyn and get to the beach!* She shut her eyes.

Avi had graduated Columbia University with honors—a major in physics, minor in English literature. She had considered teaching and writing textbooks; however, she quickly found the idea boring and became enamored with renewable energy. Trace had inspired her to take professional risks, discover what resonated with her heart and soul. Avi entered an advanced studies program at Oxford and directly after took an internship at CERN Laboratories in Geneva. Back in Manhattan she entered the doctorate program at Columbia and landed a position with a startup called LBM Technologies, where she worked with a team developing renewable-energy building materials, including roof tiles, siding, and windows that gathered, stored, and delivered energy to the structure they resided on. Bettering modern societal infrastructure and helping the planet fulfilled her soul, mind, and heart.

After Brooklyn was born Avi started her own consulting business. She had decided the stress of traveling back and forth to the city and the cost of leaving Brooklyn with a nanny or daycare wasn't worth it. She wanted to continue pursuing her passion for advanced, renewable-energy technologies while raising her daughter and being present during her formative years. She couldn't let Brooklyn be influenced by strangers and Trace couldn't be around with his demanding work schedule. Even though Avi had decided to stay home with Brooklyn, she refused to be labeled a housewife. "I won't be one of *them*," she had said to Trace. "No way. Not happening." Avi was too independent. She had learned from her mother to be a woman, but when it came time for business her mother showed her how to pull on her pants and don a jacket.

Avi rounded the circle to the Jans Peek Branch overpass that crossed Annsville Creek. Cars heading toward the small bridge had turned around. Avi looked on perplexed. As she moved closer she saw two police cars blocking the road to the bridge. *No. No. No. No. No... It better not be collapsed.* She slowed her SUV and followed the other vehicles in a U-turn. She stopped at the patrol cars and opened her window. "What's going on? I need to get across to my daughter."

"Sorry, ma'am. Bridge is closed heading into the city. Your only bet is to take the nine and get north for a bit," the male officer said.

"But my daughter. I need to get to her," she beseeched.

"I'm sorry. Where's your daughter, ma'am?"

"At pre-school."

"Schools have emergency procedures. They'll notify you. Don't worry."

Avi removed her aviator glasses, her wet eyes pleading. Her nausea intensified. "Don't worry? Don't worry about my daughter? My young child? Don't worry about my four-year-old?"

"I'm sorry, miss. Look, I understand. You gotta keep it movin' now. Take the nine. Get north. Cut back around that way if you have to. But I'd advise you to stay off the roads. Most are closed going into the city."

The officer looked like a horned demon. *A woman going to find her young child—where's the compassion from this 'man?'* "Is this bridge damaged?" Avi asked.

"Is your head bleeding?"

"Shelf fell on me at the grocery store."

"You should get that looked at and wait for the school to contact you."

"Is the bridge damaged or not?" she asked with conviction.

"Not that we know of, but it needs to be inspected, ma'am.

We just gotta keep people outta the city. Too much damage there. Have to give room for emergency crews to get in." The officer waved her off.

Avi surveyed the bridge, pushed her aviators back on, and inched toward the roadblock. The officers stepped in front of her car. "Ma'am, I told you to turn it around now!"

Avi punched the gas; tires squealed. The two policemen scattered. She barreled toward the roadblock, t-shirt tied around her head, aviators on her nose, her cheeks and jaw taut, blood and sweat streaming. War! *I might regret this later.* "Aaahhh-hhhhhhhh!" She smashed her SUV through the roadblock.

CHAPTER 6

"I've declared a state of emergency in New York. Emergency crews have been deployed, and are working diligently to ensure the safety of residents in the area. It is my understanding crews are dealing with a number of issues—downed power lines and transformers resulting in power outages, pipe breaks resulting in a lack of water and sewage backups, people trapped in compromised buildings and homes, gas leaks, and more. Thus far we have forty-one confirmed dead and over two thousand injured. Both counts are expected to rise as emergency crews work through Peekskill and the surrounding areas," Governor Pagano's voice boomed from Avi's speakers. "An unusual event was declared at the Bear Mountain Nuclear Energy Center. The reactors were shut down. According to Bear Mountain parent company Gener8 there are mechanical issues they are dealing with, but there is no threat to public health and safety."

Avi barreled into the semicircle driveway that traced through the vibrant grass front of Brooklyn's school. Determination hardened in her eyes. *Mom's here. I gotchu, baby. I gotchu.* The Georgian-style, brick schoolhouse had slid off its foundation

and collapsed on one side, its steeple laying like a dead ana-
conda. The wood doors were pinned open and slanted, arched
windows shattered, exterior stairs buckled, and a flagpole
leaned, the American flag draping from it. Flashing lights from
emergency vehicles hypnotized her. "Oh my god! Oh my god!"
Avi gasped. *Brook...* It was exactly as she had feared. Brooklyn
bloody, pinned under rubble blipped in her mind. She tore into
the parking area, squealed to a stop, got out, and ran toward
the emergency workers. "My daughter!"

A brawny, ebony-haired firefighter put his hands out to
stop her from running past. "Hold on."

"My daughter." Avi pushed against him. "Please."

"Miss. We've got victims in there we're trying to extract.
The building is unstable. You can't go near it."

"Is my daughter in there?" Avi showed the firefighter Brooklyn's photo on the screen of her smartphone.

"Miss, I…"

"Please," Avi pleaded, tears surfacing. She looked past the
firefighter to the collapsed schoolhouse, smoke billowing from
one end, water being shot into the cloud. Stretchers moved in and
out full and empty, IV bags being held by paramedics. Rescue
workers in hard hats and jumpsuits hustled back and forth.
She didn't see Brooklyn. *Not on a stretcher. Not like this. Please.*

"Hey, Rodger. Come look at this real quick."

Another firefighter approached—lanky, auburn hair, pale,
freckles.

"Have you seen her?" Avi showed him the photo.

"Nope. We got a janitor, a lunch lady, a teacher, and three
kids. Not her though."

Pangs of fear stapled Avi's stomach. *What does that mean?
Is she dead? No! NO!* She saw her baby cold and blue. "Where's
everyone else?" Avi asked desperately.

"Evacuated. Took the busses outta here. Others went in

ambulances."

"Where?"

The redheaded firefighter shook his head. "The busses I don't know. Some of the ambulances went to Hudson Valley Hospital. Some went to Putnam. Some went to Northern Westchester. Helen Hayes. Depends on the injury and what kind of openings there were. Some might go to triage when that gets set up. Depends."

Triage. Avi saw her little girl alone on a stretcher. *Or maybe she's been taken by teachers or another kid's parents? I don't know where she is, dammit! Where's Trace? I should check the house.* Avi flashed the photo again. "Do you know if she was put in an ambulance?"

"Not sure, miss. There *were* young girls. Everyone was moving fast to get people out and away."

"God. What am I supposed to do?"

"The school representatives'll contact you, miss."

"So I'm just supposed to wait?" she said snidely.

The firefighter shrugged. "Unfortunately, yes."

Avi lunged toward him flailing. "No… No! I can't wait. I'm not waiting for anyone!"

"Miss… I…" The firefighter trailed off.

Avi thought firefighters were supposed to be courageous—resilient men and women who thrived on danger and aiding the sick, injured, distraught, and displaced. *He's compassionate. But that's it? What's the point? 'Oh sorry, your child is missing and might be dead or injured. That's too bad.' What the hell?* "Do you have a child? Would you just sit around when you know they're scared or could be injured?" Her pulse beat through her gums tightening on her teeth.

"Miss…"

"Please! Tell me something."

"Are you okay? Your head looks pretty bad. You look pale."

"I'm fine!" Avi snapped. "Can you help me or not?"

"All you can do now is call the hospitals. If no luck there then see if another emergency worker'll help you check evacuation shelters. But you're gonna have a hell of a time with either. I wish we could help, but I'm already short men and we've got an active scene here. People trapped inside. You have to understand."

"NO! You have to understand!" Avi grabbed the firefighter by his jacket. "You have to help me!" Tears spilled. "Please!" she pleaded. The firefighter looked at her unresponsively. Avi's arms trembled, her strength draining. The cacophony at the scene became acutely present in her ears: the spray of the fire hoses sizzling, truck engines rumbling, sirens whooping, air horn blasts, walkie chatter, shouted communication. *We've got a victim in the southeast corner, do you copy. Roger twenty-three forty-nine engine three. Copy. Over. Ten thirty-seven code one. Ten thirty-seven code two. Ten four code three. Copy. Over. Bring a bag and two stretchers! Three victims.* Avi felt light-headed. *Victims. Bag. Stretcher. NO!* She released the firefighter's jacket and staggered backward. The firefighter and school property rippled in her vision. Her eyes fluttered. She turned and vomited. Her legs wobbled, she felt like her soul was leaving her body, like all the blood and oxygen had drained out of her. Her chest, neck, and head tingled. Her legs buckled. She collapsed, her face planting into the grass.

CHAPTER 7

Inside the reactor-three control room Trace watched the end of Governor Pagano's press conference. His feet ached and sweated in his socks from standing for the past few hours. He drank a diet soda from a can in gulps. "With all one hundred and four nuclear reactors shut down throughout the country, the East Coast and areas of the Midwest and the South are feeling the effects the strongest. Over twenty-five million without power and it's not getting any cooler out there, folks. Crews are working right now to restore power and potable water services. Please, please, we ask the elderly, those who are sensitive to heat, and those with medical conditions to go to a relative's house who does have electricity or go to one of the many Red Cross shelters that have been set up in your area. That information is running at the bottom of your screen. We are New York. We're tough. We've been through a lot, and we stick together and we fight. So I ask everyone out there to be kind in this time, help your neighbors, band together, and support each other."

If people don't have power how can they see the bottom of the screen? Idiots. Many lights on the reactor-control console continued to flash, and a single alarm buzzed at a low volume. All the reactor pumps were still cut, and Trace was waiting to see how the reactor would respond. He didn't know what his next move should be; he figured he'd let the angry beast move first. He'd know soon if he was right and the vessel was nearly solid, filled with coolant, or if Valdern was right that the gauges showed false readings and coolant was actually low. He had his crew taking readings closer down the line to the reactor in an attempt to confirm if the gauges were off or not. Until then it was a stalemate.

The governor's speech was surreal to Trace. He swore it was part of a movie. Every time Pagano said 'New York' Trace was freshly shocked. He expected another city, another state, not his state, not his New York. Trace worried the media would sensationalize reports and panic the public more than they already were. If they did it could impede decisions being made at the plant and his team from stabilizing the reactor. He saw a speculative circus moving into town replete with harlequins, jugglers, trapeze artists, and tightrope walkers.

The newscaster returned. He had mocha skin and slate hair clipped neatly to his scalp. "That was Governor Anthony Pagano and his first briefing on this morning's quake. He touched briefly on the emergency at the Bear Mountain Nuclear Energy Center just one mile from the quake's epicenter. We here at News Ten are keeping a close watch on both events. Now we're going to go live on the ground with Larry Carpenter, who's been covering breaking developments at Bear Mountain. Larry."

The video cut to field reporter Carpenter, who stood on a grassy knoll, the steam stack of Bear Mountain in the distance behind him. "Thanks, Vincent. Earlier I was talking to residents about what they've been experiencing since this morning." The picture cut to previously recorded footage, Larry's mic under the chin of a fifties, mustachioed man at the end of his wooded driveway. "I heard a roar after the quake hit this morning."

"What time was that?" Larry asked.

"Between nine and nine-thirty I'd say. After the quake hit. My wife and I were on the deck having coffee when the shaking started. We looked at each other and wondered if maybe the coffee had too much kick to it and we were going crazy. Then we realized it had to be an earthquake. The whole house was rocking. We dashed inside and then the deck came down right after. We were lucky or we would've went down with it twenty feet to the ground. You see my house is leaning now, back deck is collapsed." The man pointed to the once stilted deck that twisted away from his home, half of it in a pile on the ground. "My wife gets on her iPad and there it is. Earthquake in Peekskill. So we wait for more information. We call some friends and family and then just stand outside in shock. Then I hear a roar. I look out through the trees over the Hudson and I see a column of steam launching up from the stack at Bear Mountain. We've seen steam from time to time, but this was different. It came out with such force. Like it had been built up and released because something's wrong."

The footage transitioned to a woman in her twenties with a stubby chin, jumbled teeth, and eyes like poached eggs. "I was still lying in bed. The quake had shaken me awake. I tried to get up but was paralyzed by the explosion. Books and anything on a surface came crashing down. A bookshelf fell onto our bed and fractured my ankle. Parts of our ceiling fell out, drywall broke apart all over us." The woman hobbled on a crutch showing her injury to the reporter. "My husband fought his way to our son's room and grabbed him out of a pile of ceiling drywall. Then we all just laid together on the living room floor and held each other. I could hear the sirens. We live right around the corner from the nuclear plant. I asked my husband what he thought it was and he said it was Bear Mountain. He said he had heard the alarms late night driving past the plant before. That really shocked us because we knew there'd been an earthquake and we know what happened in Japan."

Trace gawked at the TV. Residents' perspectives from the outside chilled him. He hated himself for being part of an event that spread fear through his community. He felt like a razor-toothed Santa Claus that baited children with candy canes before kidnapping them. A job that had been about supporting society with electricity was now feeling shameful. He didn't want anyone to be scared by the plant. He wished the public was more educated about nuclear energy; he thought it would abate their fear. Dealing with the system was daunting, but Trace believed in his team, their safety systems, and protocol. *It's my duty to restore serenity to my community.* Trace was confident they would mitigate the reactor issues. *It just takes time.*

The studio anchor came back to the screen. Then the picture split, the other side running footage corresponding with the anchor's dialogue. "Heart attacks and many cases of trauma are being reported out of local hospitals. Traffic is at a standstill on many highways because of overpass collapses. There've been reports of people driving on the wrong side of the highway in an attempt to get out of the Peekskill area. People are homeless, walking down the streets looking for loved ones. A mother lost her daughter when their home collapsed." Sound came up from the footage, the woman flailing hysterically in front of a pile of rubble that used to be her home, her husband holding her back from running into the pile. "West Point Academy suffered severe structural damage. Sections have dropped out of the nine, eighty-seven, the six, and the eighty-four. The Bear Mountain Bridge is severely compromised, part of it collapsed into the Hudson. Seismologists warn aftershocks can be expected for the next week or more. Residents throughout the New York metro area and along much of the Eastern seaboard are rattled. New York is in a state of emergency."

State of emergency... New York... The catastrophic footage astonished Trace. Any time he had seen destruction of that magnitude it had been somewhere else in the world—somewhere else he had never been that only existed to him through the tube—China, Haiti, Chile, California. The despair inside him over not knowing if Avi and Brooklyn were safe deemed his analytical mind inaccessible. Such a state eroded his confidence in stabilizing the reactor. *If I can't think I can't perform. If I know they're okay I can conquer anything.* He took several heavy breaths. Trace recalled the psychological exams he had to endure each year to discover how one would act in a crisis like he was in. The questions were superficial and speculative. *How would you respond to a loss of coolant? How would you respond to a fire? Why do you want to work in nuclear power?* No one had asked how he would respond if a devastating earthquake struck, sending the reactor into a tailspin, and he couldn't find his wife and daughter. *I have to go. Fuck this. I can't. I just can't. I have to get the fuck out of here. I'm useless, mentally incapacitated. I'm not an asset. I'm cancer. I'm gonna make bad decisions. I'm already making bad decisions. Right? Aren't I? Fuck. Where did my confidence go? You worked alongside the NRC as a consultant during Fukushima. You're recognized as one of the best reactor engineers in the country. You've won Supervisor of the Year five years in a row!* Trace trembled, his mouth dry, his stomach taut. Every cell in his being screamed FLEE! RUN! Trace headed for the door. "Crane, where you goin'?" Valdern yelled. Trace ignored him. He pushed the lever on the first door, and stepped through. He stared at the control room's wheel-locked, blast-resistant, gas-tight door. He turned the wheel. *I'm comin'.*

Trace pushed the door open and recoiled at the site of Bear Mountain Manager of Plant Operations Ken Bramini standing in front of him wearing a chalk-stripe suit. NRC Reactor Safety Director Harvey Asner and NRC Director of Investigations Bill Harris stood beside him. Trace's pulse beat rapidly in his neck. He idled in first gear with the gas to the floor. Ken's piercing eyes made Trace flinch. Harvey and Bill wore flat faces, all business.

"I was just about to ask to get buzzed in," Ken said. "Where you goin'?

Fuck. Dammit. What are you doin', Crane? Suck it up. Injudiciousness was upon him. *You'll find Avi and Brooklyn. They'll be fine... fine! This isn't some high-school fast-food gig. You've got lives at stake.* "K... K... Ken," Trace stuttered.

"Well. You gonna let us in or what?" Ken jibed.

Trace opened the interior control-room door and let Ken, Harvey, and Bill pass in a gust of rank aftershave, coffee, and cigarettes that expanded his nostrils like smelling salts.

"Thanks." Ken said. The men stepped in and Trace followed. *Now I'm stuck.*

"Alright. Everybody listen up. I wanna see this area cleared out. I want everyone who isn't working the system to get back. First, everybody huddle in for a second," Bramini said waving his arms. Jerry, Valdern, Sinclair and the other crew stopped talking into phones, typing at computers, and staring at walls of gauges. They circled in on Ken. He was five-and-a-half decades old, five foot seven. He was an ex-navy man, titanium through and through. He looked like he had cirrhosis, died twice, and somehow was still alive with the intensity of a thirty-year-old drill sergeant. He growled when he spoke, vocal cords wrought by cigarettes and gin. "Tell me what we got, Crane."

Trace took a deep breath. *Grow some balls and pull it together.* Trace shut his eyes and took another breath. "Main..." He paused.

"Crane." Ken demanded.

Trace popped his eyes open. "Main pumps are shut down.

We had low pressure in the reactor, temperature rising. Pressure building in containment with high rad levels in containment that are rising."

"All right. What's our move?"

"Pressure's on the rise in the reactor now. Temperature still rising, which is odd. I thought natural circulation might cut it for a while, but it clearly doesn't seem to be enough so we're gonna try to turn the main pumps back on and start circulating all that coolant we have inside the reactor." *If it's actually in there.* "That's as far as I know right now, sir. She's moment by moment."

"Alright. Sounds like you have some kind of direction. You're in charge. I'm gonna be in and out dealing with corporate and the NRC. You need me you let me know. But I'll be here for a while now at least."

Well... Here I am... I gotta steer this ship. Trace nodded at the orders. He was seventy-five percent relieved that Ken's presence had frightened him into not leaving the plant. The other quarter of him was focusing on Avi and Brooklyn. Trace was glad Ken had asked everyone to step back from the control consoles. The crew had ballooned past thirty, the congestion only adding to everyone's stress. Trace saw Bramini as a mouthpiece and a paper pusher. Men in his position were well studied and experienced, but once they sank into the bureaucracy of the industry they became rusty for the battlefield. The same would happen to Trace if he succeeded Ken's position. Now he wanted to rip into Ken about the diesel generator and wastewater tank situations, but it wasn't the time. He had to keep the team together and deal with Ken's managerial missteps later. *Perform your duties, stabilize the reactor, go find your girls, and go home. That's what you need to do.*

"Trace, come in, it's Hanson," blurted from Trace's radio.

"Go 'head," Trace said.

"Me and Gary are down in auxiliary. The containment tank is overflowing everywhere." Trace turned his radio volume down, nervous that Harvey and Bill from the NRC and Ken Bramini would hear it. Their ears pricked up anyway and none of them flinched.

Hanson stood inside the auxiliary building, fully suited, his booted legs in calf-high radioactive water. "Got twenty-five rads inside the room. Dirty water coming out of the floor drains. Gary, how those pumps lookin'?" Hanson looked over his shoulder. "Gary's lookin' at pump one and three of the mains," he said to Trace. "One's fractured. The other has some parts that burned up," Gary shouted. "Yeah, Crane, we got at least two pumps that're torn up. Water everywhere. Seems to be valve-control damage," Hanson said.

"Let's put a team on that pump repair." He looked back at Ken, Harvey, and Bill. Their presence would be less frightening if they weren't all in suits. Trace feared they'd write him NRC violations on the spot by handing him dozens of yellow carbon copies like speeding tickets. *We're not doing that bad. Are we?* "Remember, I need that core sample while you're down there." Trace said.

"Copy that."

"Jerry, where's our pressure?" Trace said.

"Seventeen hundred psi and increasing," Jerry replied.

"Temperature at six hundred and rising," Valdern called from the other side of the console. Trace filled his cheeks with air and danced his fingers along the laminate top. The core full of coolant and the increased pressure made sense, but the temperature rising didn't.

"Coolant is beginning to fall rapidly," Valdern boomed.

"We were almost solid. Where's it goin'?" Trace thought about the containment sumps running. The reactor made its move. *Now it's my turn.*

"I'm not sure we can trust the gauges. I told you we might not've been solid," Valdern said sternly.

Trace pursed his lips. *Yup. You did. You sure did.* However, the crew that Trace had sent to take readings from the reactor closer down the lines of piping and wiring had come back with the same readings as the gauges in the control room. The situation was maddening because the reactor's responses differed from the gauges. *Should I trust some gauges and not others?* The disparities were tearing him in half.

"Core temperature is at seven hundred degrees and climbing," Jerry said.

"Let's cut high-pressure pump two on," Trace said.

Jerry hit the switches. The team waited. "Nothing," Jerry said.

"Try 'em again." Trace whirled his hand.

Jerry shook his head. "Coolant's getting too low for the pumps to circulate."

"Alright, let's depressurize and get the emergency pumps to flood it again."

"Depressurizing," Jerry said.

Based on the radio report Trace had received from Vic Hanson and Gary Harrell several minutes earlier, he feared they'd have to start dumping into the Hudson if they couldn't contain the wastewater being produced by the reactor. The ramifications could be devastating to the Hudson Valley ecosystem given the increasing levels of radiation in the core coolant. Trace didn't like anything escaping into the river drains, even the slightest amount of waste, radioactive or not. If that happened he'd feel like his backyard was poisoned. It immediately made him think of Brooklyn playing in the dirt and getting some kind of contamination on her hands. *The core sample'll tell me more.*

"Vessel seems to being filling," Jerry said.

"Keep droppin' that pressure and we'll see if we can get the low-pressure heat removal to kick in."

"Dropping," Jerry said.

Trace rubbed his head. In it was a jumble of data, protocol, and perturbation. *Pumps burned up. Cut the high-pressure pumps back on... ECCS. No HPI then... Wait, no... depressurize to get ECCS if... but then if...* Trace let out a heavy breath. His moves had to be deft. He was a long-range sniper with one shot. In nuclear power there is zero tolerance for error. Not only was he worried about a possible oversight, he worried about the consequences and his job being in jeopardy. Harvey and Bill from the NRC and Ken Bramini perched over his shoulders like falcons—silent, analyzing, plotting. Their scrutinizing demeanors jangled Trace's nerves, thus putting more weight on the impingement of his analytical thinking.

"ECCS activated," Jerry said.

"Already?" Trace scowled.

"Annndddd... Now it's shut. Says core is covered. Doesn't make a damn shred of sense, but that's what it says."

"What?" Trace pondered why ECCS had shut so quickly and water-level gauges showed the core covered after such a short amount of time. No answers surfaced.

"I'm not buyin' it," Valdern said.

"Me either," Trace said. "Bring the pressure up again, Jerry."

"Pressurizing," Jerry said.

Trace wished he was in his backyard planting an apple tree with Brooklyn. He enjoyed showing her how to do everyday, simple life tasks. He wanted her to be a princess who wasn't afraid to get her hands dirty. "Okay, so first you dig the hole," Trace said, digging in the dirt next to Brooklyn. Brooklyn dug next to him with a trowel. "Then you fill the hole with water." Trace filled the hole from the hose that lay next to him. "Then plant food. Can you put the food in?"

Brooklyn grabbed a small package of fertilizer. "This?" she said.

"That's it." Trace smiled.

With a big smile Brooklyn dumped the fertilizer in the hole.

"Perfect." Trace offered his hand for a high-five. Brooklyn slapped it.

"Okay. Now we put the tree in." Trace grabbed the small tree. "What you do is you roll the plastic pot along the ground and push on it to loosen it up. Then, you hold the tree gently at its trunk and pull the pot off."

Brooklyn stared wide-eyed.

"Last, you massage the roots." Trace began massaging the root bulb. "Get your hands in here."

Brooklyn excitedly pushed her hands into the root bulb and squished the dirt. Trace leaned over and kissed her on the forehead.

"Crane," Jerry said.

Trace stared unresponsive at the control console.

"Crane?"

"Then you put the plant into the hole," Trace said. He and Brooklyn pushed the tree into place.

"Trace!"

"And pack it down tight."

"Daddy, you grew this tree from an apple seed?"

"That's right, I did. That seed's from the core of an apple you, me, and mommy ate together."

"It is?"

"Sure is. Probably grew because you licked the core."

"Really?"

"I don't know. Maybe… You see the core is important. Just like the apple you have a core, too."

"Trace!"

"I do?"

"Yeah." Trace ran his finger from Brooklyn's heart to her stomach. "Right there."

Brooklyn looked down at her torso, eyes spreading. "You have to find what's inside your core," Trace said.

"Like an apple?"

"Like an apple, angel. You can't get to the middle without chewing through the outside."

"But mama uses an apple corer when she makes pie."

Trace chuckled. "In baking it's okay, but not in life. You don't wanna remove your core. The core holds the seeds. Seeds that can grow another apple tree to give you all the apples you want."

"We have an apple tree," Brooklyn said excitedly.

"We do." Trace smiled. "We certainly do."

"Yo, Trace!" Jerry said.

"What?" Trace snapped to present, Jerry's eyes on him waiting for orders. "Hit it with a coolant injection and try the high-pressure pumps again."

Jerry toggled the switches. "Nothing."

"Christ!" Trace slammed his fist into the desk. He paced in a circle, then grabbed his radio. "Hanson, come in, it's Crane."

"It's Hanson, go 'head."

"High-pressure pumps are still a problem."

"No shit. We're lookin' at them now. Gonna be hours at best 'til we get them up."

Trace braced himself on the central desk. Sweat dripped into his eye and when he bowed his head he saw sweat stains under his armpits and across his chest accentuating his flab. *Ugh...* "Tell me about radiation levels inside containment."

"Fifteen thousand rem per hour at the peak of the containment housing," Jerry said.

Trace rubbed his neck. Fifteen thousand rem would kill a person in a matter of minutes. It was clear to him that fuel was melting inside the reactor. *The core is exposed.* Trace feared the possibility of radiation escaping containment and being disseminated over miles of surrounding counties, including his own, his family's, and friends'. *Where are Avi and Brooklyn? Please, God, let them be getting far away.* He was anxious to get the core sample, which would help him and the crew determine more accurately what was happening inside the reactor. The high-pitched blare of the control-room radiation alarm jolted his head up. Adrenaline shot through his chest like lightning. He looked at Ken, Jerry, and Valdern who gawked in disbelief at the flashing beacons along the walls and ceiling. Trace couldn't conceive how fallout had seeped into the sealed, double-filtered building.

"RADIATION IN THE CONTROL ROOM!" Valdern bellowed.

"EVERYBODY OUT!" Trace commanded. He and all the workers in the room darted for the exit. Paper blew in the air, phone receivers hung from their cables, chairs were left spinning, coffee left steaming. Everyone fled.

CHAPTER 8

*T*race. Where are you? I haven't been able to find Brooklyn yet. My head is cut. My hand is cut. My knee is cut. I wish I could hear from you. I hope you know that I've been trying. I haven't heard anything much about Bear Mountain. Has there been a radioactive release? Well... we'll definitely be moving now... I've been looking for Brooklyn. I wish you were here to help me. You'd've just felt it out and come up with a plan. Remember when we met sixteen years ago at Columbia? It was about nine degrees outside.

Avi was at one eleven and Broadway attempting to buy a coffee and berry Danish from a truck on the roadside. The morning rush-hour ensemble of squealing bus brakes, tires splashing through slush, horns, and engine rumble surrounded her. She'd've hit Jo's, Brewsters, or the Grind but was in a rush to get to class. Avi used to drink any kind of coffee, didn't matter if it was dishwater and twenty-four-hour-old grounds.

Avi sensed a strong presence behind her. She glanced. It was Trace. He was so slender that his jeans sagged off of his backside. He was bundled in a juniper-colored, quilted parka with a faux-fur-trimmed hood framing his face. He gawked at the overhead menu. When he looked down and found Avi, he smiled. His radiance cut the gray, snowy backdrop of the Upper West Side. She smiled back from inside a gray wool parka, a knitted ruby cashmere cap adorned with ear flaps and fuzzy dangling balls pulled over her head. *Cute boy.* "One fifty," the tough-faced cashier squawked in a thick Brooklyn accent. Avi dove into her jacket pocket for cash. Nothing. She checked a different pocket. Nothing. Then her tawny canvass messenger bag. "Shit."

"One fifty. Hurry up already, youngsta," the cashier yelped.

Avi felt a tap on her shoulder. Two crinkled one-dollar bills waved from a reddened hand in her scarf-wrapped face. She shifted her eyes to see the cute boy who had come up behind her a moment before. "Take it," Trace said.

"I…"

"It's all good, just two dollars," he said.

Avi reached for the cash, her smile stretching her frozen cheeks warm and exposing her lip ring from under her scarf. "Thank yooouu…"

"Coooome ooooonnnn. I gotta line formin' here," the cashier barked. Avi handed him the cash. The cashier immediately thrust two quarters into her other hand. She grabbed her coffee and Danish and stepped aside.

"Medium coffee. Tomato, bacon, cheese croissant," Trace ordered. Avi glanced at him. He glanced back at her. *Oh, he's looking!* She quickly turned away. Avi wasn't a shy girl, but she wasn't keen on giving acknowledgement to just any boy. They had to have light in their eyes, warm intentions in their heart. She noticed that light right away. Trace pushing the two dollars into her hand without looking for anything in return showed her the temperature of his heart. Avi checked her watch—7:23. She had a 7:30 English lit class. If she didn't leave thirty seconds ago she was going to be late. But something beyond her control kept her planted, steam warming her one ungloved hand. She kept looking at Trace.

The cashier snapped a waxed bag open and shoved Trace's croissant inside. Trace already had his cash set on the counter. The cashier set his coffee forward. Then Trace turned to Avi, catching her by surprise. She flinched and looked away into her coffee.

"Hey," Trace said.

Avi kept stirring, hoping that he'd go away even though she didn't want him to leave. She was nervous, caught by surprise, and worried about being late to class even though her Dr. Marten's combat boots hadn't moved.

"Hey."

Avi felt Trace closer to her. She looked up, her long eyelashes batting, her emerald irises beckoning. "Yes."

"Can I get one of those quarters from you?" Trace asked.

Her face began to reactively contract. "I… Uh… Yeah. Sure…" She had been expecting a different question. Avi came out with both quarters and dropped them into Trace's hand. He dropped one back into hers. "One is good," Trace said to her. Trace slapped the quarter down on the counter and took his coffee and bagged croissant. He moved next to Avi and grabbed napkins. Avi felt immune to the cold. She wanted to think it was another human's body heat near her, but it was Trace's aura. Trace pick up his coffee and looked to be taking off.

Her words, "You drink it black?" shocked her when they spilled out of her mouth.

Trace turned and chuckled. "Of course."

Avi recognized him. "You're at Columbia, right?" she said, still unsure how or why she was speaking to him. Her subconscious had bypassed her brain and was routed directly to her vocal cords.

"Indeed. Headed there now." He checked his digital watch.

"Matter of fact I'm going to be late. I got a seven-thirty."

"Me, too."

Trace started to walk. "You following me?" he said.

"Oh... No... I..."

Trace grinned. Avi laughed and stepped up next to him. They strode off quickly down Broadway, their boots sloshing through ice and snow.

"I'm Trace," he said.

"Avi," she said. "What class you headed to now?"

"Engineering lab."

"Is engineering your major?"

"Yep. Nuclear engineering."

"Hmm... What do you do with that?"

"There're various jobs, but I'm thinking nuclear energy."

"Scary."

"Why scary? It's lighting up these stores right now."

"Well... I don't know... You always hear things."

"Yeah... That's because people don't know what they're talking about. It's like saying sky diving is dangerous. Truth is... it is, but the chances of something bad happening are very slim, especially with two chutes available. You know... Life's dangerous. Gotta take a risk."

"That's an interesting way to look at it. True, I suppose."

"But whatever... You don't really need the degree to work at a power plant, but it helps if you wanna move up the ranks. How 'bout you?"

"Physics and English lit," Avi said.

"Physics, huh? How do the two of those work together?"

Avi giggled. "Who knows. Maybe I'll write textbooks."

Trace laughed. "Right."

"Trace is an interesting name. Never really heard of it. Sounds like something from the South."

"Yeah. My father was from Texas originally."

"Did you grow up there?" Avi asked.

"No. I was born in Jersey."

"Oh good."

"Why good?" Trace laughed.

"The South can get weird."

"True… and New York can't?"

Avi laughed. "Yeah, totally." She checked her watch. "It's seven twenty-eight." They were on 114th Street. "We're late."

"I have to go to one twenty. How 'bout you?" Trace said.

"One seventeen."

"Let's run." Trace broke into a jog. Avi loped beside him, coffee spurting from their lids. They dodged around other students and pedestrians, their heads bowed, fighting the wind. Avi smashed into a pile of slush; water and ice sprayed their jeans. They laughed. Trees, taxis, and cold faces of every color whipped by. They crossed 116th Street. Avi's foot hit the curb; she skidded on ice. Trace grabbed her under her left arm. Trace slipped. Their feet danced on the frozen sidewalk. They cackled. Trace steadied them out and straightened Avi upright. Their eyes sparkled at each other. They took off again.

Trace and Avi came up to 117th Street. Avi checked her watch—7:32. "Shit."

"Don't worry, it's only a few minutes," Trace said. "I'm headin' this way." He motioned to the northeast. "I'll catch ya later."

Avi watched Trace back-pedal away. *Don't leave. Aren't you going to ask me anything?* She smiled. She thought maybe he didn't 'like' her. She wondered if she was too nice, too friendly, too pure, not sassy enough. *Maybe he doesn't like my lip ring?* The doldrums rolled in. Avi hadn't met a physically attractive boy with honest eyes since she started living in Manhattan. "Thanks for the coffee and saving me from breaking my back."

Trace laughed. "Anytime. Gotta go." He waved and turned.

No… I wanted to ask you for your number or to have another cup of coffee or to go to Riverside Park and hang in the grass or... Avi watched Trace trot off. *Uhhh... Dammit...* Avi turned and started scampering toward the buildings. She thought maybe she'd see Trace again. She knew when his class was. Tuesday, 7:30 a.m., she'd be standing around Broadway and one twenty. Luckily the physics building was on the same block as engineering. *What happens if he takes a different route?* Considering he was a budding engineer, he probably traveled the same route at the same time. *Or would he? Maybe he doesn't have an engineer's OCD, maybe he's a mad scientist and disorganized?*

"Hey!" someone yelled. "HEY!" Avi looked over her shoulder as she trotted to class. "HEY!" The voice came closer. "HEY, AVI!" She slowed.

Trace came up beside her, out of breath, coffee spurting from the lid of his cup, his croissant bag swinging from his hand. "Hey..." He stepped closer. "You run fast," he said breathless.

Avi turned to him and smiled. *He better say the right thing.* She was tired of the social ineptitude of boys. Trace had started off swimmingly but then had drowned for some reason.

"Hey... There's a party tomorrow night on Claremont and La Salle. You going?"

"Haven't heard about it," Avi said.

"You should go. I think it's a tub of eggnog or something..."

"I'm lactose intolerant." *Shut up, Avi.*

"Well there's other stuff, too, of course. You wanna go? I'll pick you up and we can jog there."

Avi laughed. *Good, a sense of humor. He's back in.* She nodded. "Okay! Let's do it."

Mrs. Crane, can you hear me? Mrs. Crane. Avi. Mrs. Crane? Miss?

"Why are you calling me Mrs. Crane? We're not married." Avi noticed Trace's mouth wasn't moving, but she could hear voices. *Avi? Miss. Hello. Miss, can you hear me? Avi... Avi. Miss? Mrs. Crane, can you hear me? Mrs. Crane. Avi. Mrs. Crane? Miss?*

A hunky dark-haired man stood over Avi, looking directly into her eyes. *You're not Trace. Where am I? Is this a dream? Where's Trace? Am I at Columbia?* The pain came back. She winced, the sun peeking from behind his head, blinding her. The smell of vomit and rubbing alcohol sliced through her nose.

"Miss, can you hear me?" the man asked.

"Yes." Avi's throat ached. She coughed and tried to sit up.

"Miss, stay down." The man placed a hand on Avi's shoulder.

Her eyes adjusted. Smoke dirtied the bright sky. Her skin was wet, damp grass under her exposed skin. The cacophony of engine rumble, walkie chatter, command shouts, and water spray returned. Pangs hit the bend of her elbow. She reached for it, but the man grabbed her hand and gently guided it back to her side. "Avi." She heard a woman's voice.

"Where am I?" Avi asked.

"You're at your daughter's school," the man said.

"Avi?" Patti, another child's mother, with voluminous, center-parted auburn hair came into Avi's view. "Are you okay?"

"Huh?… Patti?" Lucidity was setting in. Avi's eyes focused. The ebony-haired firefighter she had shouted questions at towered above her. "What happened?" Avi asked.

"You passed out, miss," the firefighter said.

"What's that smell?"

"And you vomited. I suspect you have a mild concussion. We're gonna try and get you into one of these ambulances and have you transported."

"Transported?"

"To the hospital. You need to be looked at."

"Where is she?"

"Where is who?" the firefighter said.

"My daughter!" Avi feared her baby was dead. "I have to find my daughter." She tried to sit up. The firefighter placed his hand on her shoulder, but Avi pushed through and sat upright.

The crease of her elbow pinched again. An IV dangled from her arm. "What's that?"

"Some saline to hydrate you with meds to help wake you and help clear your head."

"Patti, did you find Brendan?" Avi asked.

"Yes. He's in the car with Eric."

"Oh thank god." Avi rolled to her side and attempted to push herself up to her feet.

The firefighter put his hand on her gently. "Stay down."

"Take this thing out of my arm. I need to go." Avi rolled away from him and got to her knees.

"Mrs. Crane, I'd suggest you go to the hospital for further evaluation."

"No time," Avi said. She lifted the tape around the IV insertion point, pulled the needle from her arm, and dropped it to the ground. Blood streamed down her forearm.

"Miss."

"I have to go. My daughter needs me." Avi staggered to her feet, picked up her purse and phone from the grass.

"Mrs. Crane, I can't let you drive this way." The firefighter reached for her.

"Avi," Patti pleaded.

"No." Avi took off into the parking lot toward her SUV. She was surprised at her defiance to firefighters and police. She had always been one to obey, but not knowing the whereabouts of Brooklyn had given her the rage and stouteartedness of a grizzly bear.

CHAPTER 9

The stark white of Trace's radiation suit and his rotundity made him look like the Michelin Man. His chubby face was squished into his mask, his steaming breath fogging the plastic shield, his nostrils flaring in disgust at his acrid breath. Staring ahead at the control console, Trace conceived the formidable walls of gauges and switches towering over his suited, masked men as a 1960s comic-book illustration for a story about astronauts traveling to another galaxy. Trace tapped a pencil on the desk in front of him. *Game on.* Radiation in the control room was an inauspicious indication that radiation could likely travel outside the plant grounds. Trace felt biologically connected to the reactor—pressure rising, temperature rising, coolant falling. His mouth was dry. *I could use another soda about now.*

Jerry and Valdern stood at the control console keeping an eye on the reactor. Trace was anxious to hear from Gary Harrell, who was trying to repair the high-pressure pumps, as well as Vic Hanson, who was in the valve room retrieving a core sample. He huddled around a central table with Bear Mountain manager Ken Bramini, NRC Reactor Safety Director Harvey

Asner, NRC Director of Investigations Bill Harris, and other crew—suited surgeons ready for an operation. Laminated maps overlaid with graphs, town names, distance markers, and traced circles sat before the men. Trace looked at a weather map on a computer LCD. "Dominant wind direction southeast," Trace said. Clyde Choe, a forty-seven-year-old Korean-Caucasian engineer with a long, sunken face and eyes set so close he was almost a Cyclops, scribbled calculations on paper and plugged numbers into a laptop.

Trace watched Clyde shade in areas on the map with a grease pencil, indicating where the release could travel if one had occurred. Trace had an inkling something had been released considering radiation had made it into the control room. But from where, he wasn't sure yet. He had a feeling it was from radioactive wastewater dumping on the floor in the auxiliary building. Every area on the map Clyde shaded glared at Trace—Cortlandt, Montrose, Buchanan. *Eric and Heidi live in Cortlandt, Dan and Geoffrey in Montrose, Kurt and Christie in Buchanan... Shit...* Trace wanted to call his friends and tell them of the potential danger. *If my damn phone worked I'd text them. Or if this damn computer system allowed for personal emails.*

Even though he believed a small release wasn't catastrophic, Trace worried about a continuous release or a large plume. He didn't want to poison his community; he wanted to continue to provide for it. Recently he'd been prodded by Avi to consider switching careers. Avi had fought a recent bout with breast cancer and previously battled Hashimoto's thyroiditis that left her with a chronic thyroid condition. When she began researching her ailments she came across articles about the Fukushima nuclear disaster. She made the connection between radioactivity and her diseases, convinced she was a victim having grown up near a nuclear reactor and now living in close proximity to another. She began to fear living near Bear

Mountain and Trace working there. After Fukushima and Avi's prodding, Trace had begun to question every aspect of nuclear energy and his career. Conflicted, he had considered working for New York ISO the state's energy-grid operator and moving his family out of Peekskill as Avi wanted. But he rejected the ideas every time they emerged. *Maybe I should've listened to her.*

Trace's eyes burned. Peekskill and the surrounding area was his home—his habitat for the past thirty-eight years. Trace was so familiar with the region he had named squirrels, birds, and deer he saw daily. *What are those guys gonna do? If heavy fallout leaks into the environment who's gonna tell them about it?* He hoped Avi and Brooklyn were fleeing town. *Just a message from them, that's all I need to get through. We're okay. I love you. Leave town. I'll find you when it's over.*

"It's Greco. Do you know where monitoring van three is?" Trace recoiled at the plant worker's voice squawking in his earbud walkie.

"Should be in its parking spot," Trace responded.

"Not there. Can't find it."

"What about one or two?"

"The testing equipment in one is malfunctioning and two has a flat tire, and the equipment is out for maintenance."

Heat flashed up the back of Trace's neck. He closed his eyes in an attempt to calm himself. Much of their equipment was either malfunctioning or left in disrepair. It was clear the plant was an old car never restored properly down to the frame—just bandages, tape over this, 'out of order' over that, equipment left unchecked, untested, and decaying. Again he was angry with Ken and other workers for the oversights. None of them had been Trace's responsibility. *These idiots.* He couldn't fathom how anyone could be so careless about a machine that had the potential to kill millions of humans and other biological organisms and poison the environment. It was like airplane mechanics ignoring engine and wing trouble on a commercial jet full of families. It didn't make one iota of sense. "Looks like you've got some work to do then. Try and get at least one of them up and running and get out in the field as soon as you can."

"Where should we head to?"

Trace looked at the shading on the map. "Head to Cortlandt." *Fuck, it's hot in here.* Sweat dripped down his face behind his respirator mask.

"Copy."

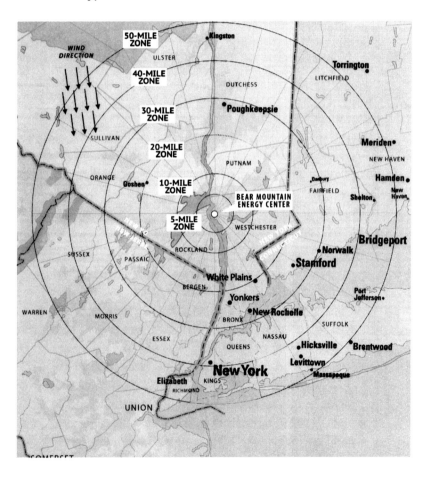

Clyde shaded other towns on the map in yellow and red indicating a path the release could travel if it wasn't stopped and increased in severity. Every town Trace saw sent a pang through his stomach—Ossining, Tarrytown, White Plains, Scarsdale, Dobbs Ferry, Yonkers, Bronx, Manhattan, Queens, and Brooklyn. *Brooklyn.* Yellow and red shading straight down the Hudson looked like bloodshed on a battle map. The river would carry fallout further out into the bay and onto the northern shores of New Jersey. *God. Not toward the city. Jesus.* Based on the wind direction, fallout traveling to Manhattan was a worst-case scenario. "We won't know how many millirem per hour we're dealing with until we get air samples." Trace had to report the release, but he had no idea what to say yet. He had to wait for the team to test the air. Then the release projection would be made based on the test results and the wind forecast. Trace sat behind the computer at the central desk and began to update his emergency cable. He felt like he was on an abandoned ship in the high seas writing letters to his loved ones. *If anyone finds this... We tried...* With radiation leaking into the control room and the possibility of a release into the surrounding environment, Trace upgraded the emergency from 'unusual event' to the highest-level 'general emergency.'

Power Reactor				Event Number: 512103		
Facility: Bear Mountain				Notification Date: 08/06		
Region: 1 State: NY				Notification Time: 8:49 [ET]		
Unit: [3] [ ] [ ]				Event Date: 08/06		
RX Type: [2] W-4-LP, [3] W-4-LP				Event Time: 8:39 [ET]		
NRC Notified By: TRACE CRANE				Last Update Date: 08/06		
HQ OPS Officer: ANTHONY CIRELLI						
Emergency Class: GENERAL EMERGENCY				Person (Organization):		
10 CFR Section:				HARRY FITZ (R1DO)		
50.72(b)(1)(i) — EMERGENCY DECLARED				ASHTON KERR (NRR)		
50.72(b)(2)(iv)(B) — RPS ACTUATION — CRITICAL				SAMUEL MURPHY (IRD)		
50.72(b)(3)(iv)(A) — VALID SPECIF SYS AC-				ERIC GREEN (R1RA)		
TUATION				CAMERON SALTS (DHS)		
50.72(b)(3)(v)(D) — ACCIDENT MITIGATION				BURT VORSKY (FEMA)		
				ANDY PINA (DOE)		
				SARAH BOYLE (USDA)		
				LESTER VU (HHS)		
Unit	SCRAM Code	RX CRIT	Initial PWR	Initial RX Mode	Cur-rent PWR	Current RX Mode
2	N/A	N	0	Refuel	0	Refuel
3	A/R	Y	100	Power Operation	0	Hot Shutdown

Event Text

UNUSUAL EVENT DECLARED DUE TO SEISMIC EVENT

"HU1.1 Seismic event identified by earthquake felt in plant and US Geological Survey (USGS).

"An earthquake was felt onsite at approximately 8:39 EST. The licensee characterized the earthquake as a 'severe' event. Tho licensee stated that, at the present time, unit three has been shut down due to a series of system malfunctions. The licensee is in the process of working with their emergency-response team and the NRC to stabilize the reactor.

"The USGS classified the magnitude of the earthquake as 6.4."

"Bear Mountain Unit two had been shut down for refueling and has not been affected during the event."

* * * **UPDATE AT 10:37 EST ON 8/06** * * *

"At 10:03 EST, coolant levels inside the reactor vessel have dropped. Pressure has fallen and temperature is rising."

* * * **UPDATE AT 11:41 EST ON 8/06** * * *

EVENT UPGRADED TO GENERAL EMERGENCY
"HG6.1 General Emergency declared.

"Radiation breached Unit 3 control room. Atmospheric release expected. Feedwater pumps down.

"The licensee notified state and local authorities and the NRC Resident Inspector, Bill Harris. Notified other federal agencies (FEMA, R1DO, R1RA, DHS, DHS NICC, Nuclear SSA, NRR, HHS, USDA, and DOE)."

Ken Bramini approached. "I need you in the chopper with me, Barnes, and the governor."

"What?" Trace scowled.

"Let's go. We'll have you back in under an hour."

"For what? We got a release happening. I need to be here."

"I know. The boys can handle the projection mapping while you're gone. Governor Pagano needs reassurance that we've got this thing under control. It'd be good for it to come from your mouth."

"Ken, you'll do just fine without me. It's ridiculous to pull me out of here right now."

"I'm not asking you," Ken growled.

Trace turned back to Ken. *Why don't we get a croissant and a coffee while we're at it? Screw it, let's lie at the pool and have mai tais. Maybe we'll bungee jump from the chopper?* He though it'd be great. He'd cut the cord, hit the ground, and search for Avi and Brooklyn.

CHAPTER 10

Trace followed Ken to the waiting Gener8 corporate helicopter on the helipad adjacent to the plant parking lot. Chris Barnes and Governor Anthony Pagano sat next to each other, separated by a small flat-screen TV and a burl-mahogany bar console. Trace's dirty khakis and white button-up coupled with his bloody head and hand were an odd juxtaposition against the custom suits Barnes and Pagano wore and the butter-leather seats and walls of the luxury chopper. Trace arrived at his seat, fearing he'd dirty the leather. He swiped his hand across the smooth texture before acquiescing and buckling himself in. The chopper lifted. Trace watched the plant shrink.

After Ken's introduction, Trace shook Barnes' hand with his left because of the bloody bandage around his right palm. Trace had met Barnes on a few occasions when Barnes had visited the plant. He remembered him sticking out like a pink hog between Black Angus, traipsing around in a seersucker suit, like he was fresh out of a French Quarter wedding procession. Oddly, he wore that same outfit now. His boater hat rested on his knee, gold, round, wire-rimmed glasses hanging from his shirt pocket. His complexion was a reddened tan somewhere between a live and a cooked crustacean. Barnes' bulbous nose sat between tawny irises set into bagged sockets below stiff, thinning, variegated silver hair pushed to the side. He was in his late sixties, built on a diet of fluorescent lighting, expensive Scotch, and lobster.

Trace knew Barnes as a bull. In his first year at the helm of Gener8 he'd taken the company from twenty-eight dollars a share to a peak of one hundred twenty-six dollars. He was a mainline of steroids and growth hormone. With almost fourteen thousand employees, Gener8 produced annual revenues of more than twelve billion and assets of over forty billion. Trace's and Barnes' interaction had only consisted of greetings, head nods, and small talk. Barnes made Trace nervous. He exuded a tenacious, commanding intensity that garnered him the code name 'the Barnacle' to company staffers and plant crew, but he was so formidable Trace and the guys couldn't bring themselves to chortle.

Trace shook Governor Pagano's hand. Pagano's large, muscular frame swallowed his seat, his knees higher than everyone else's, his head nearing the ceiling. Trace likened the former Wall Street whale, attorney, and NYU graduate to a Roman statue, clearly more imposing in person than he seemed on TV. Pagano wore a lilac-colored shirt and a flint-colored suit. He rested his deep-set lapis eyes on Trace and smiled. He wiped sweat from the smooth, creased, olive skin of his forehead up into his bristly slate hair. Trace noticed Barnes and Pagano studying the appearance of his clothing and his body weight. He felt like a slob and knew he looked like one, although he sensed the two juggernauts weren't passing judgment. There was respect in Barnes' eyes, concern in Pagano's. They were Washington generals looking at a Middle East infantry sergeant. Trace peered out the window. Bear Mountain looked like a mini war zone from above—an encapsulated Vietnam behind steel-reinforced concrete and barbed wire. The entire site was like a massive factory spread over acres. Two rectangular, red-brick, warehouse-sized buildings containing turbines paralleled the edge of the Hudson, which the control-room buildings intersected to form L shapes. Behind each stood a concrete-domed structure housing a reactor, the smaller auxiliary building for each attached to the containment domes. In the center of the property a significantly shorter dome housed remnants of reactor one, which had been decommissioned decades ago. Also in the center stood the white reactor steam-stack striped with red at the top. Behind, a massive administrative building and emergency-operations facility stretched between a sea of parking spaces. The wooded property was riddled with crumbled block buildings, fires, smoke, and workers scrambling in radiation suits and respirators.

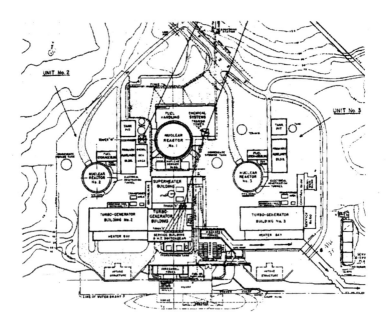

Trace resented Ken Bramini pulling him from the plant. Even if for only a minute it could be detrimental. Conditions with the reactor could take unpredictable turns at any time. *I should be down there.* Trace's right hand trembled. He gripped the armrest. Panic shuddered through him. *Anxiety attack?* He slowed his breathing. *In through your nose. Out through your mouth. What's wrong with me? Where's your confidence? My girls are fine. Think about the plant or you'll lose it.*

"So, you're telling me there's no radioactive fallout in that plume?" Governor Pagano said, referring to the steam billowing from the stack below.

"I'm not going to lie to you, there is," Barnes said. "But it's negligible. Less than you received at your last CT scan. Right now what—"

"Ho ho ho ho hold on a second," Governor Pagano scowled. "Rewind for me. Yes, there's radiation leaving the plant or not?"

"Yes," Barnes said. "But—"

"But nothing. Negligible, significant. It's all the same to me. There's radioactivity on the outside of those domes down there?"

"Yes, that's correct, but there's certainly a difference between negligible releases and significant," Ken said.

Pagano, lanced at Ken, eyes so sharp Trace could feel them piercing his own skin. *These two dumb-asses talking to the governor like that... stupid...*

"Lemme tell you something, gentlemen. This plant is a goddamn abscess. A fuckin' infected hangnail from the day I stepped into office. So I need you to be square with me. None of this dancin' around shit and comparing the radiation to CT scans. I see smoke, I see steam. I'm hearin' about radiation levels elevated outside the plant. I want it fuckin' square."

"The smoke we're seeing is from fires on the site related to the earthquake, some is oil burning on the turbine, both of which are unrelated to the actual reactors. The steam is my men venting to get the pressure inside the reactor under control," Ken Bramini said. "Isn't that right, Trace?"

Trace's stomach lurched. He stared at the smoke billowing up from the ground, wafting in the atmosphere like an expanding demonic cloud. Trace pretended he didn't hear Ken and stayed staring out the window waiting for the governor to launch back in. Nothing but the helicopter blades hummed in his ears. The side of his face warmed. He felt he was being watched. He turned slowly from the window to find six eyes beckoning. "Umm…" He was unsure how to elaborate. The situation below was still transpiring, they had all the pumps shut down, two of which needed repair, the plant was running on auxiliary power, radiation had escaped into the control room and was rising in the containment building, but he felt it was in his best interest to agree with anything Ken and Chris Barnes said. "Yes… right…" he said as if he was an automaton. *Just nod your head and get back on the ground.* He didn't want to be caught up in the bureaucracy.

"You know, Chris. This is why… This is why I wanted this plant shut down years ago. Goddammit, you stood in front of me and swore up and fuckin' down that this wouldn't happen."

Oh here we go… Bring me on the chopper so I can hear both of you get bitched out. Smart.

"Well… I…" Barnes stumbled.

"Do you know the bullshit I've had to deal with by still having those reactors operating? The letters, emails, phone calls from nuclear and environmental organizations, activists picketing at assemblies, long-winded conferences with you and the NRC. Bear Mountain's been an old dog with three legs and renal failure for years. You shoulda put her down already. Now we're in emergency surgery. Christ!"

Trace thought Pagano might punch a window out and choke Barnes to death. If he did Trace envisioned himself parachuting out of the chopper and landing in Peekskill to search for Avi and Brooklyn. Then he'd return to the plant.

Pagano turned back. "Do you know the kind of scrutiny I'm about to be under? I've had a clean, successful record for years as governor. You don't stabilize that reactor you're gonna tarnish my entire tenure."

"I've been working with these reactors since the day they went online," Barnes rebutted. "I have an engineering degree. I was stationed on the USS *Nautilus* nuclear submarine. I'm not just a figurehead. I understand the workings of all of our facilities nationwide. Before I took this position, I'd been on the ground for years. We're being straight with you."

Governor Pagano let out a breath. "That makes me feel better. All these times we've gotten together and you never mentioned that? Christ. What other secrets you got?"

Barnes shook his head.

"You know what worries me? The communication. We have to be side by side on this. I already have the president after me. I'm under serious watch. *We're* under serious watch. The world'll be looking at us. Just like Fukushima we're gonna have a spotlight on us big as the sun. I never heard of the town of Fukushima before that accident. This is New York, boys. We're responsible for a city that's the capital of Earth. A thriving ecosystem. Human lives, families down there on the ground." Pagano pointed. "This is fucking serious."

"We understand, Anthony. We walk this together," Barnes said.

"That's why we wanted you to meet Trace Crane," Ken said. "He's the control-room supervisor on duty and he's leading the charge down below. We have our finest on deck."

Finest on deck that isn't on deck... the helmsman of the ship is in the back havin' a beer and nap, but he's doin' a fine job steering? Get me outta this damn chopper. Trace connected with Governor

Pagano's piercing eyes. He could feel them boring holes into his skull. However, Trace respected him as a second-generation governor for donating his entire salary to the New York housing fund and standing up for his people.

"How do you feel about everything, Trace?" Governor Pagano asked.

Trace moved his tongue along the inside of his dry cheek. "Well…" Telling the governor everything would only anger him further. Pagano didn't need the details, but he needed the truth and he needed to be comforted before he threw Barnes and Ken out of the chopper at five thousand feet. "We're doing our best, sir. We're not gonna sleep 'til that reactor's stable. That's why we have emergency preparedness. Good thing is, you won't get a tsunami out of the Hudson. A Fukushima situation is out of the question. I want to make sure you understand *that*. The main reason they had issues out there was because the plant flooded. We're not going to have that problem. And this definitely isn't Three Mile Island or Chernobyl. We won't have operator mistakes. We know how to run our reactors," Trace said. Barnes' and Ken's bodies fell at ease to his statement. Trace's words were sincere. He had no other considerations for himself and his team besides stabilizing the reactor. There was no fluff to the situation, no cushion, no tolerances. Precision and stabilization success were the only options.

"You have to remember I care about New York as much as you do," Barnes said to Pagano. "We've got two plants in your state, three reactors, hundreds of employees. New York is one of Gener8's finest nuclear partners. These plants mean a lot to us. Not only that, it's my personal community as well. We have an office in Manhattan and my home is just on the other side of the Hudson in New Jersey. I swim in the water… I don't wanna see any of that damaged."

Pagano nodded. "Fine. But I wanna have another press conference and I want you and your team there. We give the public the proper information, we avoid some of the press speculation and sensationalism." The governor sighed. "Hard to believe we had a 6.4 this morning. Everybody's known about that fault line, but I swear it's never fazed me one bit. This's something the governor of California worries about. We're worried about snow, rain, flooding… I guess we *did* have a hurricane… Wasn't worried about those until Sandy touched down."

Trace peered out the window. The chopper swung over Peekskill. Being airborne removed him from the city, made him feel like he was staring at Legos or a video game. He saw crumbled highways, smashed and abandoned automobiles, smoke billowing from over a dozen fires, buildings collapsed, lines of cars moving like snakes in a labyrinth, and emergency vehicles swarming the streets. *Is Avi home with Brooklyn? Are they leaving town? Are they at a friend's or relative's?* Knowing others were down below injured, scared, homeless, and even dead edged off his confidence, made his hands clammy. *Be positive.* Trace had loved watching the lights of the city dazzle when he took off or landed on an evening flight at JFK. He took pride in Bear Mountain and the fact that he was instrumental in helping light up one of the most important cities in the world. He wondered if the people realized he and his team provided them with electricity so they could live modern lives without a concern for the basics.

"So we don't need to think about moving people?" Governor Pagano asked.

Trace sensed fear and uncertainty rise in the cabin.

"Trace?"

"Umm…" He looked to Barnes and Ken. "Nnnnoooo… Not currently, and I don't think we'll get to that point. We got this under control. Don't worry. I'm confident in my team," Trace said. *But am I confident in myself?*

Pagano leaned forward, cocking his head. "You're sure?"

"Certain," Trace spat out the word with wavering confidence. He envisioned the governor snapping his head off with his knobby mitts if his answer didn't hold up later.

"Because we could move some residents, a precautionary evacuation if you will?" Pagano opened his hands showing his palms.

"We wouldn't recommend that," Ken chimed in. "If it comes to that point you have a lot of factors to consider, even in a small evacuation. You gotta move hospitals, nursing homes, jails, it's a damn mess. You'd create a panic ripple where you don't need to."

Pagano's gonna have us all murdered if we don't stabilize. Trace was ready to be dropped back on the ground. The absurdity of Ken and Barnes wanting him in the helicopter had faded. He was now glad Ken had pulled him away. Sitting before Chris Barnes and Governor Pagano solidified his motivation to stabilize the reactor. That motivation stood partly on fear of Pagano strangling him to death. Responsibility stacked in heavier amounts on his shoulders. He had to make good on what he had promised to the governor. If he didn't he'd be unable to live with himself. *It won't come to that.*

CHAPTER 11

Trace pushed through the control-room door in his radiation whites, relieved to be back. Fueled on adrenaline his eyes were wide and alert analyzing the control room from behind his respirator mask. He was ready to conquer, ready to stabilize, ready to hear from his girls. Gener8 had the nations second-largest fleet of nuclear-power reactors, including twelve units producing ten-thousand megawatts. Thirty-five miles outside the center of Manhattan, Bear Mountain had become Gener8's flagship facility. Something about the proximity to New York City gave it prestige in the nuclear world. It was their Fifth Avenue shop, their Rodeo Drive outfit. Past incidents at Gener8 facilities skipped through Trace's mind: radiation leaks, commission violations, explosions, fires, radioactive water leaking into the Hudson, radioactive steam releases, oil spills. He had dealt with it all, but an earthquake at Bear Mountain was the biggest by far. *We got this.* "Jerry, what's our rad level inside containment now?"

"Just over twenty thousand rem and rising. Where the hell've you been?"

"In a chopper with Bramini, the Barnacle, and the Hammer."
Jerry shrugged. "Sounds like a set of yachts."

"Crane, it's Harrell. Come in," distorted Trace's earbud walkie with urgency.

"Go 'head."

"Hanson's in trouble inside the valve room. Pipe dislodged. Can't see. Steam everywhere. I think he's knocked out." Trace envisioned Gary Harrell watching radioactive steam spray from a giant dislodged pipe inside the valve room where Vic Hanson had gone to collect the core sample Trace had requested.

"Well, go in and get him!" Trace barked.

"Everyone down here is already overexposed. We had sixteen hundred rem measuring inside the room. Now it's twenty-four hundred when I put the extended telemeter in."

"Seriously, Gar? You need to save your man."

"I got a family I wanna go home to later. We need fresh crew down here to get 'em."

"Oh Christ… I'll do it myself. I'm comin' down. And I still need that goddamn core sample. Don't forget we got a reactor that's fucking overheating." Trace chirped off and started moving. "Jerry, I'm heading to auxiliary. Radio with anything imperative."

Jerry nodded. Trace paused at the door. *You have a family, too. Why would you risk overexposing yourself? Radiation isn't something you ever get rid of.* Trace dashed out the door. *Don't think like them. Don't let fear in.* He was confounded that Gary and his other men wouldn't go into the valve room to rescue Hanson but didn't have time to stew in the questions. People with good hearts still had their limitations. Trace clattered down a set of iron stairs. Altruism was in his DNA. He had learned from his father to help people, to dig his heels in when the earth under him faltered. From staying extra hours at the plant to covering shifts, Trace was always of service. When he was an adolescent he used to fight for a mentally disabled neighbor others ridiculed. Once he bought an Bear Mountain cafeteria worker a laptop so he could talk to his son who fought on the frontline in the Middle East. The man couldn't afford the technology on his salary, which was barely above minimum wage. Righteousness formed the fabric of Trace's heart. *I'm comin', Hanson.*

Trace rushed into the steam-laced valve room with an LED headlamp strapped to his head, the light refracting off the steam clouds, his visibility obscured. The room resembled the belly of a battleship—riveted steel and iron walls, pipes twisting overhead, along the walls and straight through the center of the room. Steam spraying and metal clanging resonated in Trace's ears, his breath heavy in his respirator. He walked with his hands out in front of him to avoid knocking into a pipe or beam. "Hansooonnn!" he yelled, his voice muffled behind his mask. His boots sloshed through water. "Hansooonnn!"

Trace saw Vic Hanson lying on the floor below a pipe spewing water and steam. He rolled him over. "Hanson?" He was unconscious, his eyes rolled back, his respirator mask shattered, blood across his scalp and face. His radiation suit was melted into his neck and lower jaw. *Jesus.* Trace's heart throbbed in his ears, his viscera desolated. Trace grabbed Hanson under his arms and dragged him toward the exit. His dosimeter beeped, indicating a rapid rise in his exposure rate. *Gettin' fuckin' microwaved in here.* He made it to the door. "Take him," Trace shouted to Gary and four other crew. "I'm going back in to get the core sample." Trace turned back.

"Trace," Gary grabbed Trace's shoulder, spinning him around. "It's not worth it."

"In your world. How could you leave him in there like that?" Trace barked.

"We're beyond our limits," Gary said.

"Fuck your limits. Goddammit! We got a man down, you save him. Fuck the regulations! Get him to decon and a fucking medic." Trace dashed back into the valve room. Trace felt the heat of the steam through his suit. He needed to stop the pipe from spewing so he could get a core sample. Trace crawled under the spewing steam to the safety valve and cranked the wheel shut. Silence ensued save for low grumbling and clanging traveling down the pipes from the reactor. *The beast is angry.*

Trace went to the main wall of wheel-valves that sat in front of a tangled maze of piping. He turned several old, iron valves, like inputting a combination to a massive vault. Hanson had turned many of them, he realized, and pressure in the system must've dislodged a pipe. If the wheels weren't turned in the proper order a pressure buildup and release could occur. Now Trace had to wait for the core coolant to reach the valve, which typically took several minutes, but he heard the pipes clanging, telling him the coolant was on its way. He grabbed the beaker Hanson had brought in from a steel table with the pair of forceps and held it under the sampling spigot. Trace released the valve. A foamy, yellowish liquid poured into the beaker. The forceps vibrated in his hand. He gripped them tighter. *Why is my hand shaking? Am I that weak?* Trace wrapped his other hand around the forceps and squeezed. He realized the vibration was from the radioactivity of the core coolant. *Jesus...* Trace cut the valve off. The pipes lurched. He looked up, questioning the sound. Everything seemed stable. The beast groaned.

Trace placed the beaker down on the steel table next to him. Holding it any longer would continue inflicting gamma rays upon his body right through his protective suit. His dosimeter blared; he was officially over his daily limit in less than five minutes inside the valve room. *Fuck it. I'll live.* Trace stabbed at his dosimeter, turning the alarm off. He took the testing instrument Hanson brought in from the table and dipped it into the coolant sample. Nineteen hundred and seventy-two rem showed on the digital readout. Trace confirmed his suspicions; he officially had a fuel melt on his hands. While it had always been his worst fear it was also his most distant. Trace, like most, worked in the industry because he believed in nuclear power. He was sure the systems were safe. Now he couldn't stop the flood of doubts he was experiencing. "Jerry, it's Crane, come in."

"Go 'head, Crane."

"We got almost two thousand rem from the core sample. We have a melt happening."

"Shit… Alright, copy. Noted."

"I'm on my way up." Trace chirped off. The pipes next to him clanged thunderously. "Jerry, what's the deal with the pressure in the pipes coming into auxiliary?" The explosion and shriek of sheering metal sounded like a ship being lacerated by an iceberg. A pipe burst and swung out, walloping Trace in the face, twisting his respirator off, and sending him to the floor. Steam and radioactive coolant spewed on top of him.

"Trace… Trace, come in, do you copy?" Jerry's voice blurted in Trace's earpiece walkie. "Trace?" Static. The other crew gawked at Trace's body through the glass insert in the valve-room door, unsure of what to do.

CHAPTER 12

Avi's SUV bounced over her newly buckled driveway. She felt moderately better; the saline and medication the firefighter had given her circulated in her blood. Her sleepy, lush, suburban neighborhood looked like a tornado had spun through it. The houses were a mix of sixties and seventies colonial repros. Appurtenances now resided on top of driveway-parked cars and the buckled street and sidewalks. Smoke twirled from a fire several houses down. On the corner water from a ruptured fire hydrant blasted into the air. In the center of the street water gushed through the blacktop, indicating a water main break. Neighbors picked up debris and loaded their vehicles.

Avi looked at her and Trace's Victorian revival. The three-storey house had partially slid off its foundation, the veranda pillars leaning, slices of wood siding hanging, the beveled-glass-inset, mahogany-framed front doors sloping. Devastation dried her mouth and twisted her stomach, acid sizzled in her throat. Her eyes burned; a tear slid down her face. Staring at the damaged masterpiece she and Trace had rehabbed, spent so many years in, gone through so many ups and downs in crippled her. *All that time. All that effort. And here it is... A pile of shit. A fucking pile of rubble!* She covered her mouth with one hand and shut her eyes. Her lips trembled; she gasped. Her and Trace's rocking chairs had been spun around by the shaking, causing them to face away from each other. She thought it a symbol. They had used to wind down together in the oil-rubbed rockers, enjoying the scents of the cedar-mulched beds of gardenia and jasmine tucked against the foundation and battered, brick-lined concrete pathways. Avi liked to marvel at the wisteria wrapping up the gray porch railing and cream spindles to the ornate detail under the roof. She reveled in birds making nests in the houses she and Trace had hammered together and hung in the cherry blossom tree in the property's front corner. Their late dog Norman ripped at the grass between the Japanese maples and the purple leaf plums while they shared a bottle of Sancerre, Avi holding newborn Brooklyn against her chest. It was all in the past; darkness had come and destroyed it all.

A telephone pole lay over one of her neighbor's SUVs. Avi was grateful it wasn't hers. She had decided to come home to use her home phone so she could call Trace and the various hospitals and shelters where Brooklyn might be. Now she wondered if the line would work. A crack of sparking electricity drew her attention to a telephone pole two houses down, the high-voltage transformer flashing wildly. She hoped it wouldn't set anything on fire. A basketball pole had smashed through another neighbor's minivan windshield, the ball out in the street. A heart-shaped leaf dropped onto Avi's windshield. The leaf reminded her of one of her favorite surprises. She'd sat in her car at the train station one night after work and flipped the wipers on as she always did to catch the advertisements from the windshield. She reached for the papers and took them into her car. "Laser surgery, lypo, gutter repair... *gut* repair..." *Interesting.* She unfolded a red slice of construction paper. She held a big heart between her fingertips. 'I love you honey. -Trace' was written in the middle. Avi realized if she had anything she had love—love for herself, for Brooklyn, and somewhere, some kind of love for Trace.

Avi exited her SUV and stepped onto the veranda. The wail of the security alarm made her wonder if someone had looted their home. It was unlikely in the neighborhood and she figured the glass-break sensors had triggered from the quake. Avi turned the front-door key and pushed the door, but it stuck due to the shifted foundation. She fidgeted with the latch before putting her shoulder into the wood and glass. The door popped open, sweeping through broken picture frames on the parquet. Photos of Brooklyn on a horse, on the beach, on a Ferris wheel, feeding ducks, sitting on Trace's shoulders stuck out of the broken glass. Beeswax candles and multicolored, patterned vases lay in pieces. She froze, mouth agape. Panic came in pangs to her abdomen, the security alarm battering her ears amplifying her anxiety. She stepped inside onto the slanted hardwood. *My home...* She turned to the security alarm panel and disarmed the system. She looked at the mess on the floor again. Her hands trembled uncontrollably. Anxiety burned though her chest to her neck and into her jaw. She cried, shoulders bouncing, shaking her head side to side. The waves of grief imbuing her felt the same as when she had heard of a close friend's sudden death. Intense nausea burned in her stomach, gastric acid rose in her throat. She closed her eyes, clenched her mouth, and swallowed repeatedly. It's just material items. *It's just material items. It's just material items. It's my home!*

Don't look at anything. Keep moving! Avi made her way through the foyer to the kitchen, glass crunching under her sneakers as she went for the nearest phone. Every dish and glass she and Trace owned had been flung out of cabinets and smashed onto the floor. *Just ignore it.* She grabbed the cordless from the granite countertop. Dead. She moved to the living room and tried the cradled cordless from the white side table with horse-leg base. It had battery power, but beeped back at her when she hit the talk button. "Shit." The base wasn't connected to the outside world because the electricity was out. *I should sweep this stuff up. Don't look at it!* Avi surveyed the living room she had so proudly designed. The doors to the TV cabinet were splayed open, the corner of the flat screen protruding, the Blu-ray player dangling by its cables, DVDs and CDs scattered into the herringbone hearth. Her literary-fiction collection had spilled out of the built-in bookshelves onto the aqua, gray, and black kilim. *Not the books... not the books...* Her massive oil on canvas of a valiant rhinoceros lay face down on the modern, gray pin-tuck sectional. The only items that hadn't moved were the iron Edison bulb chandelier and the kneeling Buddha next to the hearth she had picked up in Bali the year she had met Trace. She shook her head. *All that time putting this room together, dammit. Quit it. It's just stuff. You need a phone!*

Avi crossed through the foyer. The wall adjacent to her office had collapsed, partially blocking the entrance to the room. Lathe, plaster, and mesh had burst out of the wall, slices of sheetrock and studs hung from the ceiling, most of her black-and-white surrealist photography collection scattered on the parquet. Plaster dust and debris covered her desk and the floor. *My business. My computer. My files!* Every new discovery was like the glimpse of a corpse's blue feet when turning a corner. It was shock after shock delivered in stark blasts of smoking flash powder.

Avi crouched to her hands and knees and crawled underneath the wreckage along the parquet. She saw the phone cable hanging from her desk and followed the phone cable up to a pile of sheetrock. The phone was underneath, dusty, its face shattered. She picked up the receiver. Dead. *No!* Avi flipped the phone over; the cable was ripped out. She grabbed it from the floor, inserted it into the bottom, and picked up the receiver again. Dead. "Fuck!" She slammed the switchhook down. *What am I gonna do? Drive around aimlessly until I stumble upon something. Impossible. I need the phone!* Avi stood up with the phone and cable in her hands and realized it didn't snag at the wall. She crouched back to her knees and followed the phone cable along the floor through debris to the wall. She pushed sheetrock, papers, and books aside to reveal the jack. Avi plugged the phone cable back into the wall and picked up the receiver. She had never been so happy to hear the hum of a dial tone. She dialed Trace's mobile.

"You've reached Trace. Please leave a message and I'll get back to you as soon as I can."

"Trace, it's me. I wanna let you know I'm okay. I hope you are, too. I'm trying to find Brooklyn. Her school was evacuated and the kids were bussed to a shelter, but I haven't found where yet. Some were taken to the hospital. The school building mostly collapsed. Call me if you get this. My cell isn't working yet so I came home to use the phone. The house is a disaster so I probably won't stay here. And I'm gonna keep trying to find Brooklyn. Okay, honey. I—"

"If you're satisfied with your message, press one." A robotic woman's voice cut Avi off.

"I… lo—"

"If you want to re-record, press two."

"Fuck. Son of a…"

"If you want to delete and start over, press 3."

Avi pressed one, slammed the phone down, and dialed Trace again. His voicemail picked up. "I love you, honey. Call me." She hung up and dialed another number. An automated service picked up. "Thank you for calling the Bear Mountain Nuclear Energy Center. If this is an emergency hang up and dial 911. If you know your party's extension you may dial it at any time. Please listen to the following menu options. For security press one, for operations press two, for—" Avi punched in Trace's extension. A busy signal pulsed in her ear. "Dammit!" *Where are you, Trace?* Avi envisioned him unconscious under debris in the control room—alarms and lights flashing, smoke billowing from the controls. *Trace!*

Avi dialed the operator. The line was busy. "How the hell am I gonna get the hospital numbers? Dammit!" She opened her laptop on her desk, debris cascading from the lid. *C'mon, battery. Yes...* She had power. She opened her web browser and found a connection. She typed in *Hudson Valley Hospital.* The address and phone number came up. She punched the number into the desk phone. The line rang and rang and rang. She hung up and tried again. Visions of Brooklyn lying alone, cold, and unconscious on a gurney in a hospital hallway flickered in her mind.

Avi looked up the numbers for Putnam Hospital Center, Northern Westchester Hospital, and Helen Hayes Hospital. She dialed Putnam.

"Putnam Hospital," a woman answered in a gravelly voice.

Avi perked up. "Hello. Hi."

"Yes?"

"I'm looking for my daughter. She may have come in from Peekskill."

"What's her name?"

"Brooklyn Crane." Avi heard the woman typing on her computer. The pit in her stomach grew.

"Ummm... I'm sorry we don't have her. But there's quite a few patients that have just arrived and others that are still in transit."

"Okay."

"Give us a call later if you'd like."

"Okay... Okay... Are you sure? Can you check again?"

"I'm certain, miss. That's all the information I have at this time."

"Thanks." Avi hung up, dejected. She dialed Northern Westchester and Helen Hayes and received the same responses from both.

Avi considered who else to call. She tried the police department, but the phone rang almost thirty times before she gave up. She tried 911 and received a busy signal. She knew the city was in crisis, every man and woman for themselves. Emergency systems put in place only seemed to work on normal days. She picked up a picture of her, Trace, and Brooklyn in front of the lighthouse on Hatteras Island, North Carolina. She remembered watching the dune grass tip in unison when the breeze swirled, remembered strolls along sinuous sand paths lined with sloping driftwood fences. Avi took the photo to her chest and flopped onto the floor leaning against her desk. Tears of defeat cascaded. Her home, her business, and all her possessions were destroyed. She couldn't find Brooklyn and she couldn't get in touch with Trace. Alone and frightened, Avi's head pulsed with pain. She closed her eyes.

"You want to move to a new house in the heart of pricey Westchester *and* you want me to change jobs?" Trace's eyes pegged Avi inside their kitchen. He sipped coffee, set it to the granite counter, and tucked his white button-up into his khakis.

"Well... I..." Avi squeezed her mug of rooibos with both hands looking for comfort in its warmth.

"How insane is that? Seriously, who's going to pay for all of this?" Trace twirled his hands in the air. "I'm already taking care of my sister's kids... How can we afford all this?"

Avi was agape, stunned he had brought money into the mix. Starting her own company made their budget tighter, but it wasn't necessarily a hindrance to a move.

"Are we gonna live on your wages? We'll be in a two-bedroom apartment."

"C'mon, Trace. I've made plenty of money in this relationship. Made as much or more than you. What I'm asking is for you at the very least to consider moving us further from the plant."

"How far?" Trace asked.

"At least. I don't know. Twenty miles or more."

Trace rolled his eyes. "Twenty miles away? You get to work at home. I have a career at a company where I have to report in person. It's not that easy."

"Oh please. I used to commute to the city every day myself so I don't wanna hear it. We could get a good deal in Poughkeepsie."

"Nobody lives in Poughkeepsie. Poughkeepsie's for weekends. I'd be back living in Manhattan if I didn't work in Buchanan. What happened to your city spirit?" He sipped his coffee.

"We did that already, Trace. We had that phase."

"Oh phase." Trace snorted. "Whaddayou, ninety-seven years old? Jesus… My great-great-uncle, eighty-six, is still in the city. Out drinking martinis two and three times a week. Still dates, has a girlfriend. Gets hard-ons, no Viagra."

Avi cringed. "Well, maybe you can move back and he can be your wingman."

Trace shook his head. "You wanna move me upstate? Poughkeepsie's over forty miles from the plant. You want me to drive an hour each way after my ten- and twelve-hour shifts. Some days I can barely see to make it the two miles home."

"If there's an accident at the plant the fallout would most likely be taken by the dominant wind direction, which is east, out toward the sea. Living north makes sense." Avi was attached to their home. She had painted the walls, designed renovations for the kitchen and bathrooms, selected all the furniture and placed all the family-oriented, decorative accoutrements. Avi had created a warm, comfortable nest for them and was loath to leave it. However, it was best for her and especially Brooklyn that they move. She didn't trust the emissions from Bear Mountain or the safety systems in the event of an accident. She didn't want her little girl to have health issues like she had. Brooklyn had already suffered from spina bifida when she was born and for Avi that was more than enough motive.

"Whaddayou, Diane Sawyer? Are you even listening to me? Seriously, I'm not commuting that far. I'm just not gonna do it. It's not that easy. I'm stressed out as it is. Already losing my goddamn hair. You'll have me in a coffin at forty." Trace glared at her. "Maybe that's what you want?"

"I've had a thyroid condition *and* breast cancer."

"It's awful… absolutely awful. But none of that has anything to do with nuclear power and living near the plant."

"Oh my god!" Avi slapped the countertop. "The highest rates of thyroid cancer and thyroid disorders in the entire country are within a ninety-mile radius of eastern Pennsylvania, New Jersey, and southern New York. Sixteen nuclear reactors, thirteen still in operation, the densest cluster in the U.S."

"That hasn't been proven by the regulatory commission."

"You're in denial."

"I've been in nuclear energy for over fifteen years. I'm not in denial. I'm a goddamn expert!" Trace slammed his fist to the counter. "You're just stress and nerves twenty-four-seven. That's cancer."

"Oh bullshit. I have a fucking Ph.D. Where's yours?" Avi hated it when Trace downplayed her ailments. She felt grossly unsupported. She'd been pestering him for months about moving and he'd been blowing her off, but Avi had decided she wasn't going to be ignored any longer. She was aware Trace had NRC inspections and refueling going on at the plant and his stress level was soaring from extra hours and performance pressure. Still, Avi wanted Trace to consider the health of her and Brooklyn. Avi had considered moving upstate with Brooklyn and having Trace come up on the weekends, but it was too dismal to bring up. She was sure their relationship would disintegrate with that type of arrangement. They'd both feel like they were divorced—living in smaller homes, Trace only seeing Brooklyn on the weekends. It was no way for a family to live. Although, she might not have any other option if he didn't comply.

"I work at the plant. I don't have cancer. I'm not dyin'."

"You have a compromised thyroid though."

"I've had that since I was young."

"So did your mother and your sister. And you all grew up near Bear Mountain."

"My mother had Hashimoto's."

"And where do you think you get immune disorders like Hashimoto's?"

Trace threw out his hands. "Something with pregnancy."

"One way is radioactivity."

"Oh bullshit. For fuck sake." Trace downed his coffee. "I'm outta here." He shouldered his black-leather briefcase.

The cry of emergency sirens brought Avi back. *You should've listened to me!* Resentment poured thick onto her heart. She headed for the open front door, stepped onto the veranda, and listened to the omnipresent wail of fire and police sirens. Neighbors spilled out of their homes and gawked at the treetops, listening. A helicopter ripped by overhead.

Avi heard sirens from Bear Mountain in the distance. She wondered if an evacuation had been issued, but the sirens sounded like they were coming directly from the plant instead of the surrounding area. Trace had told her if she ever heard the sirens to grab the emergency bags he had put together, get Brooklyn and leave. In the same breath he had assured her nuclear was safe and even if an accident occurred and an evacuation issued she'd be okay, she'd have time to leave. Avi had believed him, but that was before Fukushima. *I'm not taking any chances.* She dashed back into her house, went for the laundry-room closet, and grabbed one of the black bugout backpacks Trace had prepped. A touch of love for Trace poked through her resentment when she opened the bag. *Enough to get me by if it gets really bad*—emergency radio, flashlight, pocketknife, freeze-dried meals, protein bars, emergency blanket, potassium iodide tablets, and a water-filter straw. She set the bugout sack by the front door and headed to the stairs with an empty brown duffle. Most of the family photos that had hung along the curving case were askew on the floor—frames split open, pictures protruding, glass spidered and shattered. Avi quickly grabbed each fallen frame and set them to the side of the staircase.

In Brooklyn's room pictures and toys crunched under Avi's feet. She tried to step around the mess, the disarray amplifying her anxiety. She set the duffle down and picked up Brooklyn's drawings, books, balls, stuffed animals, and sequined butterflies that had been suspended from the ceiling, returning them to their original locations. Avi scooped up pens, pencils, flipped up a little LCD TV, a mini table and chairs, and a basket of dirty clothes that had spilled out of the closet. She stood in the middle of the room, her chest heaving, sweat soaking Brooklyn's bloodstained t-shirt tied around her head. Feeling dizzy, she clutched the doorframe. She wanted to sweep up the broken bits and vacuum, worrying that Brooklyn would get glass in her feet. She wanted to put everything back in its original location and go out and buy replacements for anything broken. She rubbed her head. There was too much to do. She didn't have time. She snapped up clean clothes from the dresser, snatched a pair of sneakers from the adjacent sliding closet, put the shoes into the bag first, and then pushed Brooklyn's clothes in on top.

Avi turned toward Brooklyn's bed and smiled envisioning Brooklyn's ebullient face glowing just above the covers. Avi looked at the stenciling she had done above Brooklyn's bed—*Because I'm the princess, that's why.* It was fantasy to believe she'd have her little princess back in her bed by the day's end. *In the new house. In our new home. Where are you, baby?* She saw her on a bus with the other children being shepherded to a shelter. *I'm comin'. I'm gonna find you.* Avi gently glided her hand across the comforter. The room felt empty without her lustrous presence. *NO!* She put her hand over her mouth, a nauseating pang in her stomach. A helicopter thundering by at a low altitude rattling the house drew her attention to the ceiling. She dashed out the door.

Avi sacked her own walk-in closet for t-shirts, underwear, and socks. She took a set for Trace and snapped up her jeans and sweatpants that lay over her bed frame. The message she had stenciled on the wall above the bed beckoned—'I Love You. Yesterday, Today, Tomorrow. Always & Forever.' *What happened to that time?* She wanted to slap Trace repeatedly. His arrogance made her livid. Avi opened a drawer in her vanity and snapped up a small jewelry box containing a necklace and ring from her grandmother, two necklaces, a bracelet, two pairs of earrings, and four rings from Trace, including her original and an updated engagement ring. She considered wearing it. *No point.* She dropped the ring back into the box and put it in the duffle. Distant sirens and the helicopter circling reminded her to move.

Avi raced downstairs, spun around, and looked back. *Should I take more? No. They're just things. Will I ever see my house again?* She backed over the threshold and shut the door. Out of habit she pulled her keys from her pocket and reached for the deadbolt. She retracted her hand. The ajar door looked like a frown.

You've been good to us.

Avi tossed the bags onto the backseat of her SUV, hopped in, and started it up. Neighbors piled into their vehicles. She wanted to talk to them but didn't have time. She backed out onto the street and zoomed off.

CHAPTER 13

"What are you doing to me?" White-rubber-gloved hands latched onto to Trace. Eyes behind plastic shields quivered potently, frantic movements—twisting, grabbing at this body. His vision was blurry—muddled figures and orbs of light. He wrestled against three men that scrubbed and held him. He heard water spraying against a hard surface. Scrubbing, bristles scraping. His skin burned—itching, raw. The smell of industrial soap, alcohol, and acetone singed his nasal passages. "Let me up! Let... What." Washes of industrial tile, raw cement, and structural iron blurred in his vision. Water rained down on him. He saw steel bars at his side. Stark overhead industrial lighting glared in his eyes. *Wait. Where am I? Am I in prison?*

"Get... Get off me!" Trace gasped. "What... What's going on?" he panicked. "What are you doing?" His head and face ached with heavy, deep pain that felt like weights crushing his cheek bones and skull, the agony striking with every knock of his pulse. Every time it hit he felt his skull would split and he would pass out.

"Keep him still," someone in the distance called out. "Stay

still, Trace," someone else said in his ear.

"Trace, stay still, we're almost done. Can you see me?"

Trace wriggled. "I didn't do it... I didn't do it... I need..."

"You need a damn hospital is what you need," a voice above him said.

Trace found Gary Harrell's eyes like two planets behind a water-spotted, spacecraft windshield. Lucidity set in. "What's happened?"

"Pipe dislodged in the valve room."

"Valve room?"

"You were getting a core sample. First you went in to rescue Hanson."

"Hanson?"

"Yeah. A pipe burst on him and then the same happened to you. Knocked you down. Knocked your respirator off. Coolant and steam everywhere."

"Oh god... I've been contaminated?"

"Yeah your suit was compromised. They found you lying in contaminated wastewater."

Sharp ripples of adrenaline pulsed through Trace's abdomen. Reverberant yelling and coughing filled his ears.

"Hanson's in the other shower, but he's badly injured. You were lucky."

Trace didn't know the pipe was going to burst, but he had sent Hanson for the core sample. *It's my fault. He shouldn't have gone. I put my man in danger. But what else were we going to do?* Another crew member waved a Geiger counter across Trace's naked body. "Twelve-hundred rem."

Trace's eyes quivered. "I'm a fucking dead man."

"Is medical almost here?" Gary said into his radio.

"Arriving now," another worker replied.

"Don't worry, Trace, we're gonna get you to the hospital."

"Hospital... No!" Trace shouted in Gary's masked face.

"Trace…" Gary pleaded.

"No. No! NO. NO!"

"You need to go. What's wrong with you? They can start trying to detox you and see how much you've actually absorbed."

"Gary, lemme tell you something. There's only two ways I'm leavin' here. On my own two feet when the reactor is stabilized or in a fuckin' body bag."

"Don't be foolish."

"When the quake hit and I couldn't get in touch with Avi and Brooklyn I thought about leavin' and findin' them. But I knew I couldn't be selfish so I stayed. I knew I had a job to do—an obligation to the families out there. I'll be damned if I'm leaving now."

"Trace."

"You put me in a goddamn shielded suit and the only person my exposure threatens is me. I need to get back in the control room. I need to finish what I've started."

"But your Geiger readings," Gary pleaded.

"Shut up about them already. Take another reading and tell them you're mistaken."

"Trace."

"That's a goddamn order." Trace grabbed Gary by his suit and pulled his face to Gary's shield. "Do it."

Gary checked his surroundings. He grabbed the Geiger counter and pretended to scan Trace's body.

"Hey, Wiechert."

"Yeah?" Wiechert approached, face obscured behind his mask.

"That reading you took wasn't accurate. He's still within exposure limits."

"You sure?"

"Yeah, I'm sure. You wanna scan him yourself again? You think I don't know how to use a Geiger?"

"Nah. A toddler could operate one."

"Well, you better grow up then. Crane's getting suited up. Send the…" The medical team clattered into the decontamination room.

"Whadda we got?" A medical worker in a radiation suit approached Trace.

"Next one over." Gary motioned with his head. "He's good."

"Help me get my ass up and into a suit!" Trace barked.

CHAPTER 14

Trace's gloved fingers were numb when they struck the keys at his computer on his debris-covered desk. He was back from decontamination, dressed in his radiation whites, feeling woozy, his head and side of his face throbbing where the pipe in the valve room had struck him. Most of his body itched and burned from the decontamination scrubbing. A broken ceiling tile laid next to him. Dust and building-material particles were scattered over books, files, and papers on his desk. Half burned out and half askew the ceiling lights shined divergently, creating stripes and triangles on the walls. Trace was glad to be alive, and back in the control room updating his reports to Gener8 upper management, the NRC, and other federal agencies. His notes said the coolant sample contained evidence of a fuel melt. The high radiation levels in containment had already tipped him off, but the coolant sample had confirmed the melt. He never thought he'd put 'fuel melt' into a cable. It was a nightmare that every reactor operator had at least once in his career. He remembered having it a year ago after Avi started on him with her nuclear conspiracies.

While he continued updating his report he wondered how the dose of radiation he took in was progressing inside his body. *The symptoms will come. I should've left earlier. Now I'm being microwaved from the inside at level ten. Cancel! Cancel! Only problem is there's no button—no beeping confirmation.* Trace felt like the carousel in the bottom of the microwave oven. He was down in the catacombs—spinning, spinning, spinning, irradiated. *High power! Somebody pull the plug! Fuck! Fuck this place! Earthquake! Reactor issues! Now we've got fallout and a fuel melt! It's snowballing, goddammit! And I have to put a stop to it.* The albatross of public safety strangled him. *This's awful. Absolutely awful. I should've listened to Avi. We should've moved. How could I let my daughter be caught up in this?* He couldn't control nature, but he could control his family's location.

Trace's decisions in the control room had to be punctilious or he wouldn't receive the promotion to plant manager or the seventy-five percent pay increase. He foresaw himself reaching corporate, sailing his way up over the next twenty-five years, multiplying his income exponentially until he retired. He wanted himself and Avi to live a comfortable retirement where they could travel and leave all their perturbations behind. He wanted to send Brooklyn to the best university, have enough cash that she'd never have to stress, help her get a starter home or condo. Whatever she wanted. He and Avi had considered another child. He was going to need funds and Avi's current income wasn't going to be enough. Deeper still Trace had taken on the responsibility of financially supporting the two children of his sister. *This industry won't be left if we don't pull through this and even then there might not be one.* Trace envisioned himself driving a spear into the reactor control console. *Goddamn thing won't listen.* Trace stepped into the control room. "Jerry, gimme the stats?"

"Pressure's nineteen hundred psi. Temperature, eight hundred fifty. Radiation in containment at thirty-one thousand rem."

"That core ain't covered," Valdern said.

"You're right. You're right, it's not," Trace said. "We need to vent containment so we can release some pressure from the core and get the low-pressure injection pumps back on." Trace picked up the phone and dialed. "Ken. It's Crane. Listen, we need to vent containment, but we've got over thirty thousand rem inside. You might need to tell everyone to stay indoors."

"Give me a projection and I'll handle it," Ken said.

"Clyde'll work up a projection for ya." Trace hung up. "Clyde," he bellowed. "We're gonna vent containment. We're gonna need a projection sent to Bramini."

"Will do," Clyde said.

"Aight. Jerry, open them flappers, baby."

"Roger. Venting," Jerry toggled the switches to open the containment-building vents. "Okay, we're makin' room. Pressure on the descent."

"Good," Trace said.

"Crane, it's Gary. Are you available?" squawked into Trace's earbud.

"Go 'head," Trace said.

"The team just finished working on pump one. You wanna give it a go?"

"Copy that, Gar. Okay, forget the low-pressure pumps. Keep venting and then hit it with an injection and fire up pump one to try and circulate."

Jerry toggled the switches.

"Okay. Hit the injection," Trace said.

Val threw the levers. "Injection initiated."

"Coolant level rising," Jerry said.

"Crane, it's Greco. Come in," blurted in Trace's ear.

"It's Crane, go 'head."

"Ten millirem per hour in Peekskill and five millirem per

hour in Cortlandt," Greco said. Greco's field reading wasn't from the containment venting that had just occurred; Trace's team had confirmed it was from the ongoing wastewater leak inside the auxiliary building.

"Clyde," Trace barked. Clyde looked up from his maps, charts, and papers. "Bring that map into my office."

"Crane, do you copy?" Greco said.

"Copy." Trace squawked off and pushed into his office, Clyde following with the laminated maps.

"Throw it on that table." Trace pointed at the round wood veneer. Trace and Clyde looked at the maps.

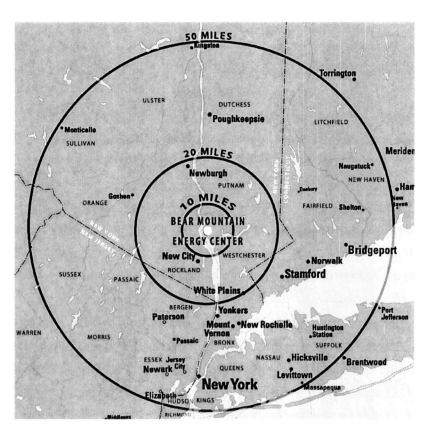

"Report is ten millirem per hour in Peekskill and five millirem per hour in Cortlandt." Clyde circled the areas on the map and wrote the measurement in his notes.

"Cortlandt's exactly how many miles?" Trace said.

"Four miles," Clyde said.

"Alright. Crunch some predictions based on Greco's field data in addition to the venting," Trace said.

"Got it." Clyde took the map and exited. Trace followed him back into the control room. "How we lookin', boys?"

"We got coolant circulatin'. Levels rising slowly," Valdern said.

"Alright!" Trace clapped his hands. "We're doin' this!" Even though the reactor still struggled and the core wasn't completely covered Trace was stoked coolant was circulating. Over several hours Trace planned to relieve more pressure in the system with the hope of mitigating many of their current symptoms and allowing more coolant into the core.

Trace walked back into his office and started tapping at the computer, updating his reports with release information from Greco's field data. A release of radiation outside the plant grounds was another piece of data in a report he thought he'd never write. The low-level release was more an ego dent than a threat to society and the environment. But worry twitched in his stomach. Trace was surprised by the concern. They were far from an evacuation as long as the release didn't multiply exponentially and the projections were accurate. At worst residents would be asked to stay inside. *Millirem is nothin'.* People panic based on ignorance. Fear grows, spreads, pervades. Rumors, speculation, and sensation heightening alarm. It would take much more radiation than they had released to bring noticeable harm to the people and the land. 'No safe dose of radiation' was a hyperbolic statement in Trace's opinion. Avi thought she knew what she was talking about, but she had no idea. Trace was more concerned about the quake damage and possibility of the reactor system continuing to malfunction. Now they just had to get more coolant inside to cover the core. Hanson's injury and the malfunctions they had faced with the reactor thus far gutted Trace, but he knew he and his team would prevail. They would persevere and they would reach cold shutdown. Trace figured at that very moment he had hundreds if not a thousand rem in his system and he felt fine. He knew residents and the environment could handle a few millirem. He didn't like that radiation touched the outside world on his watch, but it was the situation they were in. He suddenly was desperate to call Avi.

Trace spun around in his office looking for the desk phone, debris crunching under his boots. The phone rang. *Perfect.* He followed the sound of the ringer to the floor and dug under a pile of debris to find the blood-spattered receiver. The blood reminded him of his hand and head injury, both of which still twinged. He snapped up the receiver. "Control room. Crane." His voice muffled through his respirator mask.

"Hello?" Ken Bramini growled on the other end. Trace's excitement plummeted. He wished it was Avi. "Word in from the governor's office. He wants us to stop venting immediately," Bramini said.

"Stop venting? Ha… C'mon… seriously? We just started."

"Seriously. It's an order."

"Well order him to stop making decisions on how to operate this reactor unless he wants to suit up and come down here himself and sit in. And, you know damn well the governor has no legal jurisdiction over our operations." Trace coughed.

"I know… I know… Chris Barnes went back and forth with him. It's all fear based and media perception for Pagano. Barnes said we need to close 'em up. He's the damn CEO of this company."

"Not happening. By us relieving pressure in containment we can regulate coolant in the core. We're already looking positive."

"We're gonna have to figure it out with the vents closed for now," Bramini said.

"Fuck no. Ridiculous."

"Christ. C'mon, Crane. He's afraid we have excess radiation coming out with the steam."

"His suspicions are probably right, but we need to keep venting to try and rein the reactor in. I'm not closing them. The radiation is well below federal limits. Move people out if you're scared. Don't compromise the machine. You know damn well venting is not the main source of radioactivity leaving the plant anyway. Thirty, forty minutes ago you cleared us for venting. Now you're retracting?"

"Suddenly, I got every reporter calling and every resident staring at that steam. I hadn't considered it, but it's making us look bad," Bramini said.

"Look bad? We're trying to do our jobs here and wrangle the reactor. Who the hell cares about what people are seeing in the sky." Trace paused. "Listen… Venting isn't our problem. We got a core melt happening. Venting is part of the solution."

"What are you talking about?"

"I got a core sample. Coolant is highly radioactive. Additionally, reports are in from the field. Ten millirem per hour in Peekskill and four millirem per hour in Cortlandt."

"Dammit," Bramini said. "Why didn't you tell me before?"

"One thing at a time," Trace said. "I hadda open those vents."

"Well, now you gotta close 'em. Look, Barnes had a meeting in Washington as well. President Ramey is reared up. There's already been a nationwide order for all reactors, not just ours, to be taken offline immediately."

"You can't be serious? What's he going to do about the twenty percent of power missing from the grid nationwide?"

"No idea."

A phaseout. Decommissioning all reactors? The presidential considerations bewildered Trace. Fifteen years of his life were about to be over if he and his team couldn't stabilize reactor three. Utilities couldn't substitute the energy losses in the middle of a scorching summer. Trace always felt personally responsible during an outage. Families were going to be without power from coast to coast, people were going to suffer heatstroke, and the food in their refrigerators they used their hard-earned money to pay for was going to rot. "I'm telling you, it's not the venting. It's from auxiliary and the overflowing wastewater. The fallout from venting is a whole other thing."

"I'm telling *you*. Cut the venting," Ken said.

"You put me in charge. You gonna let me run this thing how it needs to be or you gonna dance all over my fucking toes?"

"This is coming from Chris Barnes and the governor. I understand what you're saying, but cut it the fuck off for now or I'm gonna pull you outta the control room again and make you sit in front of Barnes and Pagano and explain yourself. They'll have you lynched from the skids of the helicopter before you can say hello."

Tension ratcheted Trace's chest. *I don't do it, they'll get someone else to.* He detested the bureaucracy. "Fine. Fine... We'll close 'em up."

"The next thing I need you to do is take everyone but myself and Chris Barnes off of the control-room reports. We will be reviewing them first and disseminating from there."

"That's not protocol," Trace said.

"None of this is protocol. We've had a fucking earthquake in New York. Protocol's being rewritten. Everyone copied on the reports doesn't necessarily understand them and they're panicking at everything. It's detrimental to our operation. This is why we gotta shut the vents."

Trace saw logic in report control. "Fine."

"Also, cut the ventilation in the control room. My suspicion is radiation must be coming through there and we need to get that room clean."

"Shut the ventilation? Are you out of your mind? It's damn near a hundred degrees outside. It'll be like a goddamn oven in here."

"I need it shut. When the NRC comes through there that place needs to be in fucking order. Now do it!"

"Done." Trace smashed the receiver down. *I will iron this one out. I always do.* The journey had been too long and arduous to quit. He stood atop Kilimanjaro and would have to be thrown to the bottom to lose. Ken had just cut his rope. He and his team needed to free climb. He wondered how much force it would take to crush an entire industry? *An earthquake, a presidential decision, a failed reactor? My failure? I've come too far to have the collapse of Bear Mountain and Gener8 happen on my watch, too far to watch my industry crumble.* He repeatedly punched the cabinet behind his desk. *I. WILL. NOT. FAIL!* The cabinet door snapped in two and dangled from its hinges. Trace stepped into the control room, eyes blazing—one part anger, one part determination.

"Jerry, close the vents."

"Sinclair, cut the control-room ventilation."

Trace watched both of his men rest their eyes on him. He could feel their thoughts. *Aaaa... what? Aaaa... Are you delusional?* He figured they were wondering if a pink dinosaur was going to show up and do pirouettes across the control room floor. "I know… I know… Orders from the top… Just do it… Shut your eyes and do it…"

Trace didn't understand what the suits were doing. *How could Ken and Barnes keel to the governor? They know better than that.*

"Rad levels in control are rising," Sinclair said.

"Fuck Bramini. Cut the ventilation back on in here. That bastard's trying to microwave us." Trace said. He walked back into his office thinking of Avi and Brooklyn. He flopped down at his desk and sat, calmly focusing his awareness to his body. His pulmonary system shuddered from lack of food, injuries, stress, and caffeine he had assimilated via coffee and soda. *Maybe it's the radioactivity?* He pictured the isotopes humming through his cellular structure annihilating healthy cells. He chuckled. *I'm gettin' delirious in here.* Trace sat at his desk looking at the flashing lights and white-suited Martians in the control room. He shut his eyes.

When Avi had entered Trace's sight at the food truck on Broadway he had been immediately drawn to her positive aura and her infectious, vivacious smile. She had zest. She could see him, connect with him. An energetic gateway had opened between them. Now Trace was checked out. He had stopped caring, stopped being supportive, stopped compromising. He remembered she used to traipse around their apartment naked all the time—sit and read naked, cook naked. When she dropped utensils on the kitchen floor she would bend over showing her heart-shaped backside. She had been exuberant, amorous, flourishing. Now Avi kept the closet and bath doors closed while she changed her clothes. Over the past few years he could count their intimate moments on two hands. The staleness that had befallen their relationship astonished him. They were a patch of roses that no longer flowered—brown stems, only thorns left.

CHAPTER 15

Parked on the roadside, far from hungry, but knowing she needed to eat and hydrate, Avi forced a protein bar into her mouth. When she chewed it stuck like paste on her tongue. She choked it back with water. Her headache radiated into her neck and shoulders; she took pain relievers from her center console and swallowed back three capsules. Before calling hospitals again Avi had decided she would try to check shelters for Brooklyn and her schoolmates. Problem was Avi didn't know where the shelters were located. She was ready to ask police and other emergency personnel, but she feared she might get arrested for blowing through the Jans Peek roadblock earlier. She figured the cops had recorded her license plate number and she certainly wasn't hard to recognize with the bloody kids t-shirt tied around her head.

Avi turned around in her seat and reached for the black bugout bag, her arm trembling, her knee stinging. The fabric of her pants had dried into the wound and pulled against it. She opened the middle compartment of the bag and fished inside, retrieving a pamphlet. WESTCHESTER COUNTY

EMERGENCY PLANNING GUIDE. She opened the guide. RECEPTION CENTERS. She slid her finger down the page, breezing through the list. *Where is?...* She went through the list again, slower. *How?... Dammit!* Brooklyn's school wasn't listed. She was in a preschool summer program not a county-run public school. Avi thought the program might not even have an emergency plan for an earthquake or nuclear evacuation. She wondered if they would have gone to a reception center nearest to the school outside the evacuation zone? The pamphlet had a list of various public and private schools whose gymnasiums were considered reception centers. *Maybe they're all damaged?* Endless possibilities, but clearly the nuclear evacuation plan didn't include the consideration of a major earthquake. Avi perused the list of reception centers and narrowed down a group to search. *White Plains? Hastings? Bedford?* They were all at least twenty miles from Peekskill. Her theory of Brooklyn's school going to the nearest center collapsed. She sensed a journey ahead. Avi put the emergency pamphlet on her passenger seat, stuffed the remainder of her protein bar in the cup holder, and glanced at the smiling road sign. *Either way to happiness?* She sped off.

Avi pulled into the White Plains High School parking lot. Civilian and emergency vehicles were scattered, lights twirling. News vans with antennas sticking to the sky shielded the sun from reporters addressing cameras. "There've been reports that radiation *has* been detected off site," the newscaster's voice said over the radio. "Eye witnesses report a large column of steam spewing from the stacks at Bear Mountain. Gener8 states that the release is normal to the reactor's operation. They say the radioactivity in the steam is minuscule and well below federal limits. Governor Pagano has stated that no evacuation is necessary and Gener8 seems to be on track to stabilize the reactor. President Ramey is standing by in Washington ready to provide federal support if needed. Environmentalists state that no level of radioactivity from the plant is safe with some finding higher levels in the vicinity of the plant by using their own testing equipment." Avi cut the radio down. Emergency workers in reflective vests waved cars into the baseball and football fields to park. *Is this an internment camp?* Her body shuddered nervously, weakness in her hands. "Ugh…" She dropped her window when she reached one of the workers—a stout African-American woman. "Keep it movin' to the back. Parkin's out in the field." She twirled her arms.

"Excuse me," Avi said.

"Gotta keep it movin', girl. Straight to the back, park it in the grass."

"I'm looking for my daughter. Is there any way I can pull up front to see if she's there."

The worker put her hands on her hips, cocked her head, and flicked a glance at the front of the auditorium. "How you supposed to do that? Emergency vehicles up there blockin' it off. You park in the back; you free to leave when you want."

"I just need to check for my daughter. I'm not checking in. I'm not staying."

The woman tossed her hands. "Girl. I hear ya, but there ain't no room up there." She shrugged. "Nothin' I can do about that."

"Ooookkaaayyy… Thanks." *Helpful...* Her search wasn't going to be any sort of in-and-out service. Avi continued in line to the grass field until a worker waved her into a tight spot between an SUV and a minivan. Avi opened her door, hitting the minivan next to her. "Ah…" She slung her purse across her chest. When her feet touched the ground she wobbled, her knee aching. She placed a hand on her truck steadying herself. Her head throbbed, her pulse beat in her teeth, stomach acid in her throat. *Don't hurl.* She breathed deeply and swallowed. *C'mon. Calm.* Her nausea receded from the edge, enough for her to move.

Avi approached the auditorium entrance teeming with New York Emergency Management and Red Cross workers, the afternoon sun scorching down on her. A banner for each agency flapped in the breeze against moveable fencing. She shuffled into the serpentining line behind men, woman, children—octogenarians to infants—every race, shape, and size. *Are they gonna put shackles on me? Put me to work in the yard?* She envisioned stew slopping into steel bowls. *Quit it! You're not staying here.* Chatter was omnipresent; scared and confused faces abounded. A man in front of Avi had blood drying on the back of his head, dust across his clothes. A little boy with a bandaged head scampered past wailing. "Mommyyyy!" A woman with a bruised face and a blood-soaked leg bandage hobbled past. An elderly man stood doubled over, his breathing staggered, his wife rubbing his back. Anguish hunched everyone; no one stood tall. Families and friends reunited, hugging. Others stared at the sky mumbling prayers, their hands clasped at their hearts. Avi was in awe of the site, still in disbelief that it had become part of her current reality. She wished she had her family to hold close. She wanted Trace's support.

On the left of the entrance Avi saw triage tents; residents were being treated for injuries. At the front of the line emergency responders outfitted with vinyl gloves and particle masks screened everyone from head to toe with Geiger counters. On Avi's right stood quarantine and decontamination tents ready to receive anyone who might become exposed to potential fallout. The shelter atmosphere reminded Avi of a movie about a deadly epidemic. It seemed that the county was preparing for a public nuclear emergency. *Where are you, Trace?* No one had touched Avi yet and she already felt her privacy had been invaded. She wanted to get her child, take a shower in her own house, and curl up on the sectional with Brooklyn and maybe

Trace. "Uhhh…" Waiting in line frustrated her; every minute that ticked elevated her despondency.

"Excuse me. Excuse me…" Avi checked the woman's name tag. "Candi."

The woman, tall, soft, and saggy like melted marshmallow, with golden, choppy hair directed evacuees in a thick Staten Island accent. "Keep it movin' forward. Bags will be searched. No weapons of any kind allowed inside."

"Excuse me."

"Yes?" Candi said, stenciled brows raised, mouth agape, eyeing the bloody t-shirt wrapped around Avi's head.

"I'm not checking in. I'm just looking for my daughter." Avi showed the picture of Brooklyn on her smartphone screen.

Candi peered at the image. "I haven't personally seen 'er." She craned her neck. "Hey, Ralphy." Candi waved to a man in his sixties. "I gotta name for ya." She turned back to Avi. "What's 'er name, hon?"

"Brooklyn Crane."

"Crane," she yelled to Ralph. "Crane, Brooklyn."

Ralph scanned the check-in log on his laptop. He shook his head. "Nope, nothing."

He didn't say no. He didn't say no!

"How'd she come in?" Candi asked.

"With… with her school. She's in a preschool summer program." *Please. Please. Please.*

"Preschool summer program, okay. We've had several camps and summer-program classes come in." Candi looked to Ralph.

"No specific records on the youngest kids. We do have the school names," Ralph said.

"It's Blue Mountain Academy in Peekskill."

Ralph checked the list. "Okay, yes, they're here."

"I'm sorry?" Avi put a hand to her ear.

"They're here. They're on the list." Ralph smiled.

"Oh my god. Oh my god." Avi glowed. Relief made her feel faint as if stress had been her only fuel. She staggered and gripped the steel barricade to steady herself. "I need to go in and get her. What do I do? What do I do?" She envisioned Brooklyn inside with other children, teachers, and parents having a snack and juice. *She's fine. Fine and safe.*

"You'll still need to wait in line," Ralph said.

"Seriously?"

"If it was just the earthquake evacuation it wouldn't be an issue, but with the nuclear situation it's mandatory that everyone's screened before entering the reception center." Candi delivered the blow with the compassion of a barracuda.

"Oh my god. Can you go in and get her for me?" Avi pressed her hands together pleading.

"For one, I don't know what your daughter looks like."

Avi held up her smartphone with Brooklyn's picture.

Candi dismissed the photo with her hand. "And for two. We can't leave our posts out here."

"Please," Avi besought.

"I'm sorry. It won't be too long." Candi jiggled away.

Avi flopped her arms to her sides. *What the hell do you gotta do to get some compassion around here?* She tried to remain sanguine—twenty, maybe thirty minutes, she'd be inside with her arms wrapped around her little angel. The workers couldn't possibly understand Avi's fear for Brooklyn and the need to be with her. They had been trained to be dispassionate, but Avi wondered how they'd react if the roles were reversed. They'd be freaking out as she was. She wished she were in the lab—an early morning when no one else was around where computers, scopes, and research comforted her, where her cell phone didn't work and no one could reach her. The lab was her sanctuary. She'd have equations streaming through her mind, her fingers on scope knobs and equipment dials. She loved how the metal and plastic-dial ridges felt in her fingers, the smell of fresh tea and a freshly sharpened pencil, the rough texture of recycled notepaper under her hand.

Thirty-one minutes later an emergency worker wearing a particle mask and vinyl gloves circled a Geiger wand around Avi. Another worker checked the contents of her purse. *Where's the rectal exam? Ridiculous!*

"All clear," the man with the Geiger counter said. "Medical is over here to your left. You can get your head and leg looked at." The other worker handed Avi her purse.

You should get your head looked at. "Thanks." The first thing Avi was going to do was get Brooklyn. Then maybe she'd consider treatment for herself. She proceeded through the shelter entrance. Anxiety palpitated her heart; she smiled and furrowed simultaneously. Her hunt was almost over, easier than she had expected. The drone of a thousand evacuees inside the auditorium confused her, made her manic. *Brook. Brook. Brook. Brook. Brook. C'mon.* She approached a Red Cross worker, a man in his sixties with slicked-back silver hair, a crooked nose, and chapped lips. His skin was pale as a corpse, but his aqua eyes were radiant as a coastal sunrise.

"Excuse me. I'm looking for my daughter," Avi said frantically, showing the man the picture.

He titled his head, eyebrows arching. "Hmm… Lotta little girls in here. I haven't come face to face with her. Certainly doesn't mean she's not here."

"She came from the Blue Mountain Academy."

"Ummmhmmm… Yeah, nothing is assigned here. People and groups are scattered. Best for you if you start walkin' the rows 'til you find 'er. Cute little bugger, too."

Avi dauntingly scanned the vast rows of cots and evacuees. "Does anyone know anything around here?"

"It's gonna be alright." He squeezed Avi's shoulder. "Go on, kid, find yours. And getch're head looked at." He showed his straight, white teeth.

Avi nodded. *Don't be rude.* "Thanks." The man was an upgrade from the exterior receiving crew. *Take whatchu can get around here.*

Avi started down the first row of cots laid so close together there was just enough room for her two legs. She felt like she was invading the evacuees' privacy at every cot. "Excuse me. Pardon me… Sorry. Sorrrryyy… Excuse me." People gawked at the blood-stained t-shirt around her head, her sweaty face, her bloody pants, the anxious twist of her face. Others flinched at her desperate demeanor when she passed by. Avi scanned the rows from right to left looking for Brooklyn. Row after row she walked—up one, down the next, her stomach ratcheting with tension after each. *Where are you?*

A ball of light glowed ahead of her. Avi covered her mouth with her hands. There was no mistaking. Her little girl with toffee hair and butterscotch highlights sat with a group of other children, her back to Avi. *Oh thank god.* "Brooklyn." She called out, scampering closer. "Brooklyn." Strength and vibrancy poured into her aura in a warm rush, all tension in her muscles releasing. "Brook." She arrived at the group. "Brooklyn." Avi grabbed her. The girl yelped. "Hey!" the chaperone squawked. "What're you doin'?" Everyone turned toward Avi—eyes on her like she was a coyote approaching kittens. The little toffee-and-butterscotch-haired girl looked at Avi bemusedly.

No… "I'm…" Avi pulled back slowly.

"Don't touch her. You're bleeding," the chaperone clucked.

Avi stared, astonished. "I'm… Sorry… I'm sorry." She backed away embarrassed. The vibrancy of her aura plummeted, pangs arose in her rib cage. *Brooklyn… Where is she?* "I'm sorry, I'm looking for my daughter," Avi said.

"Well, that's not her," the chaperone barked, pulling the

girl toward her.

Avi took her smartphone out and showed the woman the picture. "Have you seen her? They look similar."

The woman shook her head. "You better get your head checked."

It was now clear to Avi that the girl's appearance was vastly different from Brooklyn's. She grabbed her head. *What's wrong with me?* The voice of a newscaster booming from the projected television broadcast at the head of the room became present to her. She turned to the screen. The newscaster stood in front of a collapsed, smoldering building, emergency vehicle lights glinting. "Over three hundred are reported dead, more than twenty-five hundred injured. Over seven thousand projected to be homeless. Peekskill and the Hudson Valley are trying to recover after a major earthquake, 6.4 on the Richter scale, rattled the area. Major highways collapsed, water supplies threatened, gas mains exploded, communities erupted in flames. The death toll has been rising all day long. But possibly the worst of it all is the catastrophe happening at the Bear Mountain Nuclear Energy Center in Buchanan one mile south of the quake's epicenter. Crews have been fighting to stabilize the reactor after systems suffered major damage and malfunctions. Almost half a million people live within the ten-mile emergency preparedness zone around Bear Mountain and almost twenty million live within a fifty-mile radius. Experts say if Bear Mountain melts and an evacuation is necessary it's possible that more than fifteen million people will need to be moved out of the area beyond the emergency preparedness zone. Executives from Bear Mountain owner/operator Gener8 Corporation say they have things under control while NRC officials are split, with some saying events at the plant are routine and others saying the situation is grim.

"Experts say the disaster at Bear Mountain has the potential to be more severe than Three Mile Island, making it the worst atomic calamity in U.S. history if things don't get better soon. The NRC has stated, while it is not likely, there is the potential for a massive release of radioactivity and there is potential for meltdown. Fires and damaged buildings have been reported throughout Bear Mountain property while experts work diligently inside the reactor control center attempting to stabilize the behemoth machine."

Avi continued through the rows of cots, tears streaming from her eyes. She reached the last rows in the auditorium without seeing her baby. Her pulse knocked in her neck. She put her hand to the artery. *I'm gonna have a fucking heart attack.* Her hands trembled. Her lungs surged with breath. Panic tightened her chest. She took her smartphone out. "Have you seen this girl?" She showed Brooklyn's photo to evacuees as she snaked back through the rows. "Have you seen my daughter?"

A black woman with two children shook her head. An Indian woman nursing her baby said, "No." A middle-aged Asian man shook his head and shrugged. She showed Brooklyn's photo to a legion of evacuees.

"No."

"No. Sorry."

"No."

"Aw, that's a shame."

"She's pretty."

"No, sorry."

"I haven't."

"Anyone? Have you seen this girl?" Avi shouted, her hysteria building, more eyes drawing to her. She trotted through the aisles flashing Brooklyn's picture. "I'm looking for my daughter. Has anyone seen this girl?" Every head inside the auditorium seemed to be shaking at her in unison. The multicolored faces blurred in her vision. She stopped at the end of a middle row;

desolation enveloped her. Tears cascaded down her face. *Where are you?* Fears of Brooklyn lying dead on a morgue table flickered. She was bloody, blue, injured, alone. *I'm back at square one. Dammit, no!* She grabbed her face and tried to choke the tears back, but she ended up crouching to the floor and howling like a toddler. "Brooklynnnnn!"

CHAPTER 16

Trace flipped the switch on the gas compressors inside the auxiliary building. They rumbled to a start. "We're taking on too much gas too fast in here," he said to the two crew next to him and the control room via his radio. Trace's boots sloshed in calf-deep water. He swept his flashlight around, following the water flow to an open storage-tank safety valve. "Ahh… Shit!" Clearly the tank had reached its pressure limit and was emptying to avoid fracture. Earlier, test results of the core sample by on-site chemists had told Trace the reactor coolant was loaded with radioactive gas. Trace had been gradually burping the system, but now he was pinned. He had to quickly release gases from the tank or risk losing all their reserve coolant. However, that meant they would have to vent the auxiliary building. He had to go against Ken just after he was told not to vent. *Although, Ken had only mentioned the containment building, right?* He spoke into his radio, "Keep the tank burping and open the auxiliary vents."

"Copy that," Jerry said over the radio.

Trace leaned back in a casting chair inside his control-room office. *Can't catch a break around here. Actually, we've got too many breaks!* Trace had just received communication from a team on the other side of the plant property. They were losing coolant out of the spent-fuel pool of reactor two, and it seemed at least three large cracks had opened in the walls. The team was keeping a continuous flow of water running into the pool to prevent exposure of fuel rods. However, containing the contaminated water leaking into the ground was a monumental task that would not get solved quickly and one Trace wouldn't be in charge of. *Why should I care about this reactor? Gener8 doesn't care about me. They just care about their facility. Why should I care when my wife and daughter are out there alone? My team and I are responsible for millions of lives and the environment on the other side of these walls. Who's looking out for mine while I look out for everyone else?* Trace detested the choice between the plant and his family. *You picked this job, idiot. You knew the responsibility. You didn't want it then you shoulda been a lab scientist.*

Trace looked at the door, tempted, but he couldn't leave. A leader was needed at the helm. Besides himself only Jerry and Valdern were competent. The crew were hounds waiting for barking orders. Trace and his team needed to work together to stabilize the reactor, but Valdern's resentment toward him had snowballed from thoroughly annoying to caustic, pressing acid directly into a gaping wound that had opened inside him. Additionally, Ken's demands to close containment vents and the lack of maintenance on the diesel generators and field-testing equipment made him feel Ken was working against him. *Why the fuck am I in charge?* Trace had always been confident with reactor operation, but now the reactor seemed to have a decision-making prefrontal cortex, prompting Trace to question everything he'd ever experienced, ever studied, ever trained for. *It's making me question my abilities. Are we making all the right moves?* To Trace it seemed he and his team were just responding to the reactor's various states and it was acting like a bipolar midlife crisis.

Trace navigated to a news website and streamed the live feed. A family was packing their van in their driveway. The sun-cooked reporter followed a perspiring, freckle-faced woman with a shoulder tattoo while she hauled luggage into the back of her vehicle. "There's been no damage to your home, tell us why you have chosen to leave town with your family?" The reporter thrust the microphone in the woman's face.

Her voice cut like a siren. "We don't have power. And we're afraid of being stuck without food and water." Her burly husband chimed in. "You've seen what happened at Fukushima and Three Mile Island. We're not waiting around for that. I'm not risking the health of my children."

The picture cut to a svelte woman with flabby arms and a weather-beaten face leaning out of the front door of her home. "I think we might leave town. I know not many people are, but I'm concerned about the nuclear plant. You know my father, rest his soul, used to work there." She shook her head. "I've heard stories. I'm skeptical."

"You think there's been a release of radiation?" the reporter asked.

"I've heard rumors that some people were detecting radiation with their own equipment and some relatives of plant workers are being told by the workers to leave town."

A montage of Peekskill resident snippets played. "We're not buying it!" a wasp-waisted woman in her forties holding a child said. "We've finally had that nuclear war and it's on ourselves," a bearded man said. "I'm scared for my family, my children," a horse-faced woman in her thirties cried. "What're we supposed to do? Sit around while radiation falls on us?" a tow-headed man said.

Trace dialed Avi's cell from his desk phone. The line rang twice. He heard a click and then static of an open line. "Hello? Avi. Hello?" A distant, garbled voice distorted the receiver. "Hello? Avi? Hello!" Distorted tones blared in his ear. The line disconnected. "Dammit!" Trace slammed the phone down. *Was it her? Her voicemail?* He dialed back again. "C'mon… c'mon… go through."

After no rings, a long pause, and a click Avi's voicemail picked up. "Hi, you've reached Avi. Leave a message and…" Brooklyn helped Avi finish the greeting. "Have a great day!" Her voice surprised Trace. It had been the first time he had heard it since he'd left their home that morning. The message tone blared. "Uh… I… A… Avi it's Trace. Listen… If… if you get this or… or can get this. I'm at the plant. We have a bit of a crisis over here." Trace coughed. "But I'm okay." *That's a fucking lie you've taken in over a thousand rem.* "We're gettin' through it. But get Brooklyn and get out of town. Just in case get far away north or south fifty to hundred miles if you can. Hell, two hundred if you can. Just go… just in case something happens. Call me if you can. My cell doesn't seem to be working. Call the control room directly or get emergency operations to put you through. And… and… I love you. Okay? I love you and Brooklyn." Trace hung up and dialed another number.

"Emergency operations, Flynn speaking."

"Hello, it's Trace Crane. Control-room supervisor at Bear Mountain."

"Yes, Trace," the emergency worker said.

"I need a favor. My wife and daughter. I haven't been able to make contact with them. I need to know they're okay. I need your help."

"Trace, you know we can't take personal requests."

"I need you to do this for me. I can't leave the plant. I'm stuck in here and the worry is killing me. I need your help."

"You know very well this is against protocol."

"C'mon, Flynn... Listen... Have you heard from your family? Do you know they're okay? I'm on the frontline here trying to save the reactor, protect the people. It's hard for me to think without knowing they're safe." Silence droned in Trace's ear.

"Okay... okay... But you can't tell anyone else about this. I'll only do it because you're a supervisor there. If others find out they'll all be asking. A lot of people been displaced. You're not the only one missing family."

"I won't mention it. You have my word."

"But where do I start? This isn't going to be easy."

"Take their information. Avi and Brooklyn Crane. Eighteen twelve Alpine Drive is our home address. Avi may've been there or on the road when the quake hit. My daughter, Brooklyn, was at the Blue Mountain Academy summer school. I don't know the address." *How could you not know it?*

"Okay. I'll see what I can find. And I'm sorry. I'm sure they're safe somewhere. Try to stay positive. We need you in there. The whole community needs you guys."

"Thank you." Trace hung up. He picked up the two pieces of Brooklyn's mug that lay on the floor and fit them together at their break. He rifled cabinets near his desk for super glue. He found a tube and ran a line of it around each side of the broken mug, pressing the two sides together and holding them tightly. Avi's voicemail and Brooklyn's mug would keep him going for now, but he needed to hear their voices live to take him all the way through. He walked into the control room. "How we looking now that the vents are closed?" Trace said.

"Coolant levels struggling to increase because of pressure," Valdern said.

"Goddammit. We just gotta keep circulatin' what we got for now 'til we can figure out how to get another injection into the system," Trace said. He was still astonished at Ken Bramini's direction to close the vents after they had started making headway with circulating coolant around the core. *It's fucking stupid.* The minimal amount of coolant around the core was better than nothing, but the core wasn't fully covered, which meant the top was surely melting.

"Crane," Gary squawked over Trace's earpiece. "We've got wastewater coming up through outside drains. Do you copy?"

Heat flashed over Trace's body. "I'm comin' out."

"Control, this is Thompson. Water's coming up through drains on the exterior."

"Control, it's Duval wastewater overflowing in auxiliary, copy?"

"Cortez to control wastewater…" Several more messages pinged across the radio. Valdern adjusted his walkie, shaking his head in disapproval. Trace pursed his lips and pushed through the wheel-locked exit.

Outside Trace stood next to Gary between the massive red brick and concrete buildings. It looked as though they were standing in Manhattan after a torrential rain. Steam wafted over them like subway exhaust. Trace watched wastewater spew from the drains set into the concrete. Water cascaded along his boots down toward the river, a dozen white-suited crew watching the flow. Radio chatter barked in Trace's ear. He turned his radio volume down and watched the radioactive lagoon, envisioning himself on a raft with a cold beer. *Take me to the river, drop me in the water.* It'd be a great getaway where he could be spat out into the Atlantic and never look back. He thought he'd land in the English Channel and Brian Eno would rescue him with ambient sound beds.

The cry of alarms howled through Trace's ears. He looked toward the Hudson River and sprinted back to the control room. He burst through the door. The flashing lights made his eyes flutter. If he was epileptic he'd convulse.

"River drains are open and we're dumping," Jerry said.

"Jesus Christ!" Trace clenched his right fist and raised it.

"Whaddaya wanna do?" Jerry said.

"Close 'em," Trace said.

"We do that we're gonna have wastewater all over the property, way more than we already have. It'll leach into the ground and into the river anyway," Valdern said.

"We need tanks brought in to take on the excess waste," Trace said.

"I ordered 'em, but they ain't gonna be here anytime soon. This shit ain't like McDonald's or buyin' a fuckin' t-shirt," Valdern said.

"Fuck!" Trace smashed his fist into the desk.

"You better let out at least a hundred thousand gallons to make it worthwhile," Valdern said.

"We need approval," Trace said.

"Forget approval. You know what the answer's gonna be," Valdern said.

Trace shook his head. "Shut the drains, Jerry." He looked at Valdern. "I don't wanna be on the hook for this shit. I'm next in command under Ken. I defy orders I put a mark on my head. Something goes wrong I'm done, not you."

"Water's already coming up through the floor drains. I'll tell you again, we're gonna have radioactive water all over the grounds. That gives the entire crew another obstacle to navigate. Regardless if the water goes into the Hudson through the drains or not radiation is going to be released into the environment. There's no damn difference! Good thing is the river flows down to the ocean. Most of it from here down is polluted anyway, especially close to Manhattan. I'd have more anxiety about it up north," Valdern said. "You need to make the right decision for the reactor."

Trace agreed with Valdern that the river was severely polluted anyway, but Trace didn't want to add to the problem. He didn't want to defy upper management, and he already had by turning the ventilation back on inside the control room. Ken Bramini, Chris Barnes, and Governor Pagano calling shots from the outside, putting political and media perception ahead of proper reactor responses that weren't publicly attractive, frustrated him. If Trace defied Ken's orders and something were to go wrong or contamination levels in the environment were raised too high, he could cause an unplanned evacuation or the poisoning of residents in the surrounding area. If the media and NRC found out everyone at Gener8 would point the finger at Trace to exonerate themselves and the company. Trace could potentially be hit with federal charges and prosecuted for the effects of his insubordination. His money would be siphoned off by legal fees and Avi and Brooklyn would have to live in undeserved stress because of his actions. He could go to jail. He could be sued and left destitute. Being a nuclear engineer was all he knew and had been trained for and no one would hire him in energy, science, or engineering after his name was tarnished. No one would want the responsibility. He'd be lucky if he could get a job swinging a hammer or repairing games at a local arcade. "Close 'em."

Jerry turned the levers. The alarms didn't stop. He turned back to Trace, shaking his head. "They won't close!"

Trace stared at the control console. Radiation leaching into the river, isotopes sloshing onto the banks of New York and New Jersey, seeping into the ecosystem around Trace's home, sickened him. He saw fish and birds being bathed in radioactive water, ignorant to the invisible, odorless, silent contamination. *Uranium geranium bubble bath—get you glowin' from the inside.*

CHAPTER 17

"CLOSE THE DRAINS!" Trace hustled up next to Jerry at the control console and frantically twisted the levers back and forth. "Son of a bitch! Come onnnn…." The alarms finally stopped. Trace's shoulders eased. The drains were closed.

"Now you know it's just gonna fill back up. You've got no choice but to dump," Valdern said from across the room.

Trace looked at his adversary and pressed his lips flat. What was best for the reactor system wasn't always the best for the environment, politics, and public perception. If he didn't treat the reactor properly the issues could grow, escalating the detriment to the outside world. During an accident mitigation there weren't always favorable options. He had to choose the best of the worst. Every door had a spring-loaded boxing glove behind it. Did he want to get socked in the jaw or the kidney? Either way he'd double over. *If this backfires I hope you understand, girls.* "Open 'em back up. Let 'er go for a hundred thousand gallons." The burning in Trace's stomach intensified. He walked into his office and plopped into his desk chair. He stared at a fallen wall clock resting on its face, jumping and pivoting from the sunken couch cushions with every stroke of its hands. It looked like a jumping-bean disc; there was life inside it. Trace understood, he was almost there—face down, his heart the only muscle in his body still pulsating. He'd fight to that edge and beyond to save the reactor and find Avi and Brooklyn. He hoped Flynn from emergency management would be in touch soon with a line on his girls. Trace was waiting on the reactor. *See how the reactor reacts?* It was a terrible conundrum. Coolant levels still struggled to increase because of the pressure buildup. They circulated as much coolant as they could, a small amount, until they could figure a venting workaround. Radiation was still rising in containment and leaking to the outside, but their testing showed they weren't above federal limits and thus no evacuation could be issued, only a shelter in place asking people to stay indoors. Trace feared failing all fourteen thousand Gener8 employees, their families, and tens of thousands of nuclear-energy workers nationwide. The fate of nuclear energy seemed to be his responsibility. If he didn't stabilize the reactor the collapse of the industry would be imminent. He envisioned himself being run down by armored men wielding javelins. Trace snatched up the ringing phone on his desk. "Yeah."

"I just received a report from you about a dump into the Hudson," Ken said.

He found one javelin. *Tuck and roll. Dodge!* "Umm… Hello?"

"What the fuck is that? I didn't authorize that."

"Hello?" Trace brushed his glove across the receiver creating static. "Hello? I think we have a bad connection. Who is this?"

"Crane!"

"Hello? I can't… I…" Trace hung up. *Luckily, I have a disaster to blame for bad phone lines.* He walked into the control room. Harvey and Bill from the NRC stood near the entrance in radiation suits. Harvey was the white pear shape, Bill the white pencil. Trace froze as if he'd seen a salivating jaguar. *Don't move and they won't see you. Do they know about the water dump? Shit.* The NRC inspectors approached. "Gentleman," Trace greeted them.

"We have reports of a water dump into the Hudson," Harvey said.

Trace nodded. "Unfortunately, yes. An uncontrolled release."

"Are you in control of your plant, Mr. Crane?"

Umm... Nnn... Yeee... "What the hell kind of question is that? Of course I am," Trace responded coarsely.

"You need to be holding everything in. We discussed that with Ken." Harvey thrust forward a short stack of papers into Trace's abdomen.

Trace looked at the papers, then back to Harvey and Bill. "What's this?"

"All your violations thus far. Dumping untreated into the Hudson. Radioactive gas releases into the atmosphere. Unmaintained diesel generators. Unmaintained field-testing equipment. I could go on," Bill said.

Trace scowled. "We're in the middle of an emergency here."

"We understand, Mr. Crane, but you need to get control of what you're letting out of this plant."

"We're bursting at the seams. Whether we dump or let it overflow on the property, it's going to make it into the environment."

"You need to start listening and stop playing like a maverick in here. Give that to Ken when he gets back."

"You're citing us in the middle of a crisis? The hell is wrong with you people?" Trace grabbed the papers and stared astonishingly at Harvey and Bill. "You think we want this? Want to release into the environment? This's ridiculous."

"We'll be back around, Mr. Crane," Bill said. The men turned and exited.

Trace looked down at the violations. *Ken's really going to kill me now. I thought the commission was on our team?*

The desk phone rang. Trace looked at it and the flashing red light seemed to beat like the bloody heart of a steer. "Mmm…" *Could be Avi… could be… anyone… It's definitely Ken.* "Hello."

"Off-site radiation's on the rise. What's going on in there?" Ken barked.

"It's the water dump and I hadda burp gases." Trace shoved the NRC violations under a reactor manual, tucking them away as if Ken could see through the phone.

"When I said no venting I meant no releasing anything into the environment! You're workin' against me. I've gotta do damage control on the outside with the state, press, *and* Chris Barnes. Stock is already down five points. Barnes is going ballistic!"

"I don't give a damn about the stock. I'm trying to save a reactor here!"

"You'll give a damn when your investments turn to dust by Monday. This affects all of us! The second the accident was announced and the market opened this morning our stock dropped five points. When news gets out about the decommissioning and phaseout talks in Washington we'll probably drop another five. That's about thirteen billion in losses in less than twenty-four hours. We're a whale with a really big harpoon in us."

Ken was right, but Trace had to focus on what was best for the reactor. He believed if he did then the money would be fine because the accident would be mitigated. His father had told him, 'Don't focus on the money. Do the right things, take the right steps, and money will be okay.' That's what Trace was sticking with. "Close the Hudson if you have to. The release isn't good, but it's sure better than letting it spill all over the plant grounds. Move people. What's the reluctance with that?"

"There's over four hundred thousand people in the ten-mile

radius around the plant. Hospitals, nursing homes, prisons, orphanages, thousands without cars, elderly, handicapped… It's the last thing we wanna do. It'll cost us millions, and it'll cost us lives. Cost us our jobs, too, if we jump the gun. That's the last resort. We're not nearly at that level right now. We're not above federal limits."

"Exactly. Now that you've heard yourself say what I've been tellin' you, get off my ass. You're lucky I didn't open the containment vents. We're here trying to stabilize the reactor. We can't worry about politics and public image. We need to do what's right." Trace slammed the phone down.

The governor was ignorantly swaying Ken's orders. Trace had always had an issue with governors who didn't have a clue about nuclear-reactor functionality. Most of them believed they had legal authority over venting decisions when they didn't. Even when Trace, Bear Mountain, and the NRC advised state officials they stuck with what *they* wanted most of the time. Trace knew he had to be careful making unauthorized decisions that could upset the governor because Gener8 still needed the governor as an ally. They had to stick together through the disaster and into cold shutdown. Trace understood Ken's and Barnes' attempts to protect the reputation of Bear Mountain and Gener8. He understood the consequences of the stock prices plummeting. However, the threat to the people and the ecosystem surrounding the plant was paramount. The only way to mitigate all threats was to stabilize the reactor. Trace and Ken were Siamese twins wielding knives at each other. Trace was cutting himself loose. During his career Trace had learned that sometimes a little contamination had to be risked to make an overall save. *Sometimes you have to risk one man's life to save two hundred. Sometimes you have to let out water and gases containing several thousand curies of radioactive isotopes to avoid letting out millions.* "Jerry, how's our coolant?"

"Coolant's surprisingly on the rise," Jerry said. "Very slow, but rising incrementally."

"Interesting. So we could potentially get full coverage in several hours?" Trace said.

"If it stays like this, yes," Jerry said.

"Nothin' to do but wait." He flopped back in a chair and closed his eyes. He and his team may've surprisingly brought some sort of stability to the reactor, given the limitations placed on them. He was amazed water was getting into the pressure vessel without them continuing to vent. They still had to get the core fully covered with coolant and get the temperature to drop. Then he'd have to stay at the plant until the reactor reached cold shutdown, but that could be in the next twenty-four hours if everything stayed positive. Trace thought their training and safety protocol may have been working after all. Had they mitigated the main issue by burping gasses and dumping wastewater, or did the reactor just decide to be friendly? Trace wasn't sure. Daily operation of the reactor was simple, crisis was what they had trained for, but crisis never unfolded like training drills. Crisis was a metastatic, mutating cancer. Trainings would be held after the occurrence to prepare for possibility of the same event in the future. The problem was events rarely repeated themselves. It was simply like running with your head behind your heels. It was symptom response—move first, think after. *They bomb a plane, they train on planes. Next time, they bomb a subway. Go figure. Big scare... No—astronomical scare. But we may've nipped it before it got uncontrollable.* The next time Bear Mountain upper management and the NRC returned Trace hoped he and his team would be ready for champagne and back pats. *Nice job. We're good.* They'd check the boxes off, sign the reports. *Good job, boys.* If all went right there'd be a few days of no sleep, the reactor would be shut for investigation, and everyone would get on their way. *Still, we'd be under major scrutiny. Sure my job would be at stake, everyone's would.*

Trace worried about the entire community—the destruction the quake caused, the injuries, the displaced families and businesses. He wanted to tell Avi he was sorry. She had been right in asking for them to move away from the plant. The risk becoming palpable made him understand living close wasn't worth putting his wife and daughter in jeopardy in case they couldn't control the reactor. At the same time Trace hoped they would reach cold shutdown just so he could prove Avi wrong and show her their safety systems and protocol worked. He'd take her for a nice dinner and let her pick out a good bottle of Syrah or whatever her palate fancied. Then he'd have the nuclear talk. She wouldn't agree, but the proof would lie on cold shutdown, no evacuation, and no contamination of the surrounding area.

Trace hadn't been sweet to Avi in years. He wanted to again. When it was all over he was going to try to be a good husband again. He wasn't going to roll over and say nuclear was bad, but he would agree to move his girls away. Then he'd seriously consider if he was going to work in the industry any longer. Fear about his health from the radiation he had absorbed in the valve room suddenly crept up on him. Pangs at his sternum were the assailant's knife. His joy was being stolen, poison pervading his mind. *How could I treat my love like I had? How could I stop doting on her? You're fine. Quit it! Be in the now. Be present! No... No... Fuck...* Anxiety came in burning tension in the left of his chest. He sipped in a big inhale.

CHAPTER 18

Avi rapped on the redwood door of the unlit farmhouse. "Lea!" she called out. Brooklyn's blood-soaked t-shirt around her head made her feel like a refugee standing outside a quartering house in the middle of a war zone. Her shadow projected by her SUV's parking lights spilled tall onto the battered stone facade. Avi had spent the past several hours calling hospitals again and checking more than a handful of shelters. There was no sign of Brooklyn anywhere. Was she still under the rubble of the schoolhouse in the dark, alone, injured, unconscious, and cold? *Is she dead?* Staying sanguine was difficult even though Avi was a perpetually positive soul. Unrestrained grim scenarios formed in her psyche and played on loop. Poison was taking over her mind. She needed a glass of wine, several glasses, and a rock in her hammock.

Drops of water ticking off tree leaves, cement, and metal gutters offered tranquility she couldn't surrender to. Avi felt drops on her shoulders and looked up into the plum sky, the rain illuminated by the moon. Humid air warmed her neck and nostrils. Avi pounded on the door again. "Lea!" She pushed the unilluminated doorbell button and heard nothing. *They don't have power.* "Leaaaa!" She called out again. *What am I doing?* Avi was delirious without sleep, her stomach bricked out with tension, her mouth arid. *She's probably not even here. I'm such an idiot. I should've stayed at the shelter.* "Leaaaa!" She turned back to her SUV. Rain came down in sheets. Her clothes and hair began to soak. Heat flashed across her neck and chest. She reached for it, wetness. *Panic attack? Nerves? Stroke? Heart attack?* Her skin burned.

Avi reached her SUV and pulled at the door handle. Locked. She reached inside her purse for the key, rain and darkness obscuring her vision. She tilted her bag open in front of the parking lights. Her keys were missing. She scampered back to the driver-side door and put her face to the window. Her keys lay on the center console. "Shit!" Avi pulled at the door handle again. "Damn!" She pounded on the window. "Why!… Why!… WHY!" She wailed. *What the hell am I going to do now?* She couldn't bear to go back to her house. It wasn't safe, the structure could collapse without warning. She abhorred the idea of staying at a shelter. She would be curled in a ball on a rigid cot, mind racing, eyes plastered open. *Brooklyn!* Avi was stuck, her phone didn't work, and she was miles from town out in farmland. Walking anywhere of distance would be brutal. She considered running to a neighbor's house or into town. *Someone might be around, maybe?* No one was in town when she had passed, power was out, it was 3:00 a.m., and visibility was obscured from the rain. Avi crouched, her back to her car; she squatted on the stone driveway and bawled. *My life is falling apart. Why? Why is this happening? Dammit, Trace, do you know how angry I am at you right now? Your stupid job and nuclear energy has cost us so much.* Avi felt she had been living for Trace's career over the past several years. *No more! I'm done. You're on your own after this.* Even when Trace was physically present he was still absent—just a body, a grumpy, negative, apathetic mass. *Now our home has been destroyed and Brooklyn is missing. I'm sitting in the fucking rain! Where are you?*

The latch of a heavy deadbolt sounded like the cock of a bolt-action rifle. Avi looked toward the house. An orb of light moved across the window, torrential rain hampering her vision. *Is... is that someone or am I hallucinating?* She squished her eyelids together and opened them. The orb was still present, teetering. Avi stood and waved her arms. "Lea!" she cried. The door creaked opened. Avi scurried toward it, a towering shadow stepping through.

"HEY!" A man bellowed, his appearance still obscured, but becoming clearer to Avi. He extended his arms, something metal and gleaming clutched in his hands. "WHO IS IT?"

"Tim. Tim! It's me, Avi," she pleaded from the ground.

"Avi?" Tim lowered his arms. He stood tall on the porch, his gray-plaid pajamas hanging on his lanky frame. He was seventy-five with brittle, charcoal hair and a right-side lean. His cheeks were smooth like a forty-year-old's, his mouth drooped on the right, his eyes biting with such intensity they could make an army back off. Tim held a pistol in his wrinkled hands.

Lea stuck her head out the door, her short sable hair matted and spiked to one side. She was forty-three with a deep mocha tan, a chiseled face, and a loose body. She looked like someone's mother, a nurturer with a warm smile. "Avi… Oh my god. Lea swatted at Tim. "Dad, put that away."

"What?" he said.

"Go!" Lea yelped.

Tim retreated.

"Avi," Lea said. "Sweetie… What?" Lea embraced her tightly. "Are you okay?"

Avi shivered in Lea's arms and shook her head. "Brooklyn?"

"Where's Brooklyn?"

Avi shook her head. "I don't know." She choked up.

"Jesus. Come inside." Lea helped Avi over the threshold and walked her across the rustic wood floors into the kitchen at the rear of the house. Lea's hands on Avi's shoulders sent comforting vibrations through her body. She and Lea had become like sisters, like family, ever since meeting at Columbia University nearly twenty years before. They had traveled the world together, attended each other's family celebrations and tragedies, and become confidants. They were each other's maid of honor, they shopped for their weddings together, saw the birth of each other's children, coached each other through job interviews and job loss. Avi had helped Lea through her mother's death and her divorce. Lea had helped Avi through her battle with cancer, personally keeping tabs on her hospital treatment while Trace was locked away at work. They shared great literature, spoke on the phone for hours about their existential aspirations and the state of modern society. Their running joke was they were wives and if Avi left Trace, she and Lea would move in together and have a happy, platonic family.

Tim had just finished lighting a number of large candles on the central wormwood island. He pulled a chair for Avi. "Thank you," Avi said.

"Dad, you wanna get some towels?" Lea said.

"Sure," Tim left the room, the beam of his flashlight cutting him a pathway in the darkness.

Lea filled her teakettle, put it on the stove, and lit the gas burner with a match. She turned to Avi. "What's going on? What's happened to your head?" Lea scanned Avi. "And your leg?"

"Brooklyn," Avi shook her head. "I can't find her anywhere."

"Av, start from the beginning. Where were you hurt at? Is that from the quake?"

"I was at the grocery store when the quake hit. A shelf fell on me, hit me in the head. Then I crawled onto some glass. My head is killing me right now. I might have a mild concussion. I'm seeing colors and spots. The pressure in my head is unbearable."

Lea opened a few of the distressed walnut cabinets and searched. She surfaced with a bottle. "Extra-strength migraine." Lea shook two pills out of the bottle, grabbed a glass from a cabinet, and filled it with water from the purifying tap at the sink before setting the pain-quelling duo in front of Avi. "Take those," Lea directed.

"I should put something in my stomach." Avi grabbed the pills and tossed them back with the water.

"What would you like? I have a few things in the fridge that are slowly warming. And I have a loaf of fresh bread my dad picked up yesterday morning."

"The bread'll work," Avi said.

Lea put the baguette in front of Avi along with a dish and a napkin. The bread stuck to Avi's tongue and mouth. She still had no appetite but needed to put something in her to soak up the acid and stop the painkillers from irritating her stomach. Tim returned with towels and draped one around Avi's shoulders and handed another to her so she could dry her arms and hair. "Thanks," Avi said. Tim laid another on the floor under her feet.

"Okay. Continue," Lea said.

"Trace is at the plant. I can't get ahold of him. Brooklyn was at preschool. The school collapsed and I can't find her."

"The building what? Was she in there?"

"I don't know. I don't think so… Not at the time I arrived, anyway. So they said. The other kids were taken to hospitals or evacuated. I've checked a few shelters and I've been calling hospitals with no luck." *I should still be out there looking.*

The teakettle blew. Lea cut the gas. She grabbed a mug from the cabinet and dropped a tea bag in it from a ceramic jar on the counter. "Chamomile. Let it steep for a few minutes." Lea set the mug in front of Avi.

The steam sent warm, comforting vibrations through Avi's face and shoulders. She nibbled at the baguette.

"Was there damage to your house?" Tim said from his perch on a counter stool.

Avi nodded. "Terrible."

"Oh god."

"It's leaning and everything inside is broken. I can't go there."

"What do you think might be going on at Bear Mountain?" Tim said.

Avi pursed her lips. "I don't know."

"You think there's a meltdown happening?"

"Dad." Lea gasped.

"What?" Tim held out his hands. "We can see the steam stack across the Hudson. It'd be nice to know."

"Don't stress her out." Lea scolded him.

"All I know is what I've heard on the news," Avi said. "Trace always swore it was safe, but I stopped trusting. I told him I wanted to move away from the plant."

"Oh geez." Lea looked over at her father then back to Avi. "Honey."

"Now something's happened." Avi's hand trembled when she sipped her tea. "I have to find Brooklyn."

Lea nodded. "We'll help you. What can we do?"

Avi shook her head. "I don't know. We need to call hospitals again. Visit shelters. Call the police maybe. Call other students' parents whose numbers I don't really have." Her voice cracked. "I don't know." A tear dripped into her mug. "I locked my damn keys in the car, too!"

"Okay. I think you need rest first." Lea rifled through a drawer at a built-in desk next to the refrigerator and surfaced with a penlight. She held Avi's lids open and shined the light into her eyes. "You're slightly dilated. I think you're right about that concussion. Mild at the least."

"You're lucky you're not active at the hospital right now or you'd be on duty," Tim said.

"True."

"I say we get you cleaned up, Av. You shower. I take care of your wounds and you lay down. You need at least three or four hours' rest. You leave me whatever info you have and we start making calls in the morning. Then when you get up we can venture out to shelters or wherever you need to go."

"We should do something now. I should be out there."

"What are we gonna do now? It's three in the morning. It's more a disservice to yourself. You need to have your wits about you for this kind of search."

Avi knew Lea was right, but guilt burned in her stomach. She couldn't power through the night looking for Brooklyn and had exhausted many search avenues already. *It's not your fault. You're doing the best you can. It's not good enough. This is not a 'best you can' situation. It's win or lose.*

Lea's two young boys appeared in the kitchen. "Mom, what's going on?" one of them said.

"Hey, sweeties. Sorry we woke you." Lea walked over to her boys. "Our friend Avi is here." The brothers gawked at Avi and rubbed their eyes. Lea kissed them both on their foreheads. "Dad, will you?" Lea tilted her head toward her sons.

"C'mon, guys. Let's get you back to bed," Tim said moving toward them.

"And can you fish Avi's keys out of her car, too?" Lea asked her father.

"In the mornin' when it stops rainin'. I got a slim jim in the garage." Tim spun his grandkids around and put a hand on each of their backs, pushing them forward out of the room.

Avi wished she had Brooklyn to usher up to bed and tuck in. She wanted to hold her tight and bury her face in her neck, and tell her everything was okay. She wanted to have Brooklyn's head on her lap, stroking her hair, reading a story to her as she drifted off. *Maybe* A Light in the Attic *or* James and the Giant Peach. She sipped her tea. "I wanna see your view of Bear Mountain."

"It's out on the deck, honey. You sure you wanna do that?" Lea said.

"Yes." Avi clutched Lea's arm. Lea helped her from the chair and guided her toward the French doors.

Outside the rain sounded like a finger-snapping orchestra on the awning over the deck. In the distance beyond trees and the Hudson, Bear Mountain stood out like a space station in the dark expanse. Faint alarms echoed in the distance. Washed-out red, blue, green, and yellow lights flashed under wafting steam. Floods of white light spotted various areas of the plant like lunar landing pads. The small amount of steam being released concerned Avi. It seemed to her that plant operations wasn't venting, thus holding everything in due to pressure regulation or a major release of radiation inside the containment building. Black smoke curled from another area of the plant. *Fire?* Avi wondered where Trace was in the mess. *Is he okay? Is he inside the control room? What's he doing at his very moment? How's he feeling? Is he sleeping? Is he thinking of me and Brooklyn? He has to be... but he has a job to do.* Avi thought she should call her brother and parents but couldn't muster the energy. They lived in Florida so she wasn't worried. She wished they could join her to help look for Brooklyn. She yearned for their love and support, but she didn't want to bring them into the disaster zone.

The humid night air reminded Avi of weekend nights with Trace at their home. Before Brooklyn was born they'd lounge on the flagstone patio in front of the firepit, Avi would stir up bourbon-based craft cocktails and feed Trace desserts she had picked up in the city. She relished breathing in the fragrance of viburnum and orange blossom while watching the sky twinkle.

It had been ages since they had had that time. Avi loved putting treats into Trace's stomach. She believed food and drink were one constant in every human life. People made love amidst food and beverages, fought over them, married, celebrated birth, death, closed business deals.

Avi's love of sharing food was part of why she embarked on a career in renewable energy. In her research she had learned over three billion people, almost fifty percent of Earth's human inhabitants, relied on unventilated and inefficient wood burning, charcoal, biomass, or dung cooking stoves. These cooking methods caused their operators, mostly women, to inhale toxic smoke on a daily basis, greatly increasing their chances for respiratory and heart disease. Thousands died each day from having archaic cooking environments they used to feed their families. Avi believed the renewable, off-the-grid technologies she helped create were an avenue into mitigating third-world issues. Due to a lack of funds in many third-world countries, traditional energy systems costing billions of dollars cannot be afforded and the import of fuels cannot be reasonably considered. Therefore, more than ninety percent of the population in developing countries went without.

Avi had found it astounding to learn more than one-quarter of Earth's people were without electrical energy. She hoped her technologies and charitable-outreach programs she affiliated with would allow developing countries access to refrigeration for food and medicine, proper cooking stoves and ventilation, hot water, sanitation systems, and communication. With those tools developing communities would see increased literacy and life expectancy. In Avi's heart she wanted everyone to live the best life they could no matter their social or financial status. She wanted to abolish social classes and classifications of first and third worlds.

Avi didn't want to admit it to Trace, but she missed the city.

She didn't want to live there again nor did she want to live near Bear Mountain. It was about missing good times with her husband—her confidant, her best friend, her lover. Avi hoped they would be reunited soon and could work on restoring their relationship. She wanted to be in sync with Trace again, back on the same team, not adversaries. She wanted Trace to be sweet to her again. Avi wanted his support and knew he needed hers. Lea's hand rubbing Avi's back brought her present. Coupled with the warmth of the tea mug in her hands Avi found a tinge of comfort. "Thanks," Avi whispered.

CHAPTER 19

Trace lumbered across the plastic-lined, cement flooring that met plastic sheeting hanging from the block walls inside the decontamination area of the emergency operations center. The windowless space was institutional, reminiscent of an old emergency-room corridor with very few doors, the kind of space found in the bowels of a gymnasium that could be scrubbed and hosed out. Trace reached an intersection with a short corridor that led to a large room set up for crew check-in and decontamination. The room was top to bottom tile with stainless-steel accoutrements, yellow plastic tents, gurneys, showers, testing instruments, and medical supplies. Two suited crew members waved Geiger counters over other crew that entered. Trace waved to them. "Gentlemen." They acknowledged Trace. He hoped they wouldn't stop him and try to scan his body because they would find he had been exposed to hefty amounts of radiation earlier. If word spread, Trace would be forced into quarantine at a hospital, which would keep him from the plant and from Avi and Brooklyn.

"Hey, Crane," one of the decontamination crew called out.

Trace cringed. *Just what I didn't want.* "Yeah."

"You get checked in already?"

He detested lying, but he had to do what was right for himself. Nobody was going to look out for him. "Yep, all good here." Trace could feel the crewman wondering. Trace waved, glad he had his respirator on to conceal his nervous face.

"C'mere for a second?" The crewman waved him over.

Trace froze. His heart doubled its speed. The crewman continued to wave. If Trace didn't go he'd inflate their suspicions. He lumbered toward the decontamination area and arrived before the two crewmen.

The crewman approached. "Listen. We heard what happened to you in the valve room."

This guy tries to grab me I'm runnin'. I'll slug him right across the head. "Yeah," Trace shrugged, "no big deal." Trace sat his shoulders back, let his chest rise, and stared into the crewman's dark dots. The other worker watched them from a few feet back. It seemed like an intervention to Trace.

"You're lucky you only came out with minimal exposure."

Trace's shoulders released. The tense air in his chest fogged his respirator mask. "Yeah, man. Sure is."

"Thanks for holdin' it down in there."

Fuck is wrong with this guy. Small talk... Small talk could've given me a stroke. "That's what we do. We're lookin' good in there."

"Alright. Have a good night, then." The crewman patted Trace on the arm.

Trace's lips curled in a grin. *I should punch you in the face.* He arrived at a locker room where a group of crew undressed. Tired faces covered in dirt and sweat came and went, blood on their hands. Trace nodded to Gary Harrell, Clyde, and Sinclair when he walked in. He placed his respirator in a bin with others. "Gentleman."

"Crane," they said in unison. Trace started to shed his protective suit. "How you guys holdin'?"

Gary shook his head. "Shiiiittt… Like tape on water." A smile stretched his round face, big teeth shining. Trace, Clyde, and Sinclair laughed. Trace saw Gary as the counterbalance to Valdern. One unflappable and jubilant, the other acrimonious. Trace wished he could carry the same infectiously positive attitude Gary had. *I used to be like that. What's happened to me?* Trace wanted to give Gary shit about him not trying to save Vic Hanson earlier but refrained. He was sure it wasn't malice on Gary's part; he was just scared. Plus, Gary had lied about Trace's radiation exposure so Trace could stay at the plant. Trace continued to undress. He sat on a wood bench between the lockers and started unlacing his boots. "You talk to the wife and kids?"

"Yeah, I heard from 'em," Gary said.

"How?"

"Happen to get through on the house phone."

"Really?"

"Yeah. But you know I live north like forty miles, so… They're not having too many issues up there."

"Ahh…" Trace nodded and removed one of his shoes. *Just where Avi wanted to live.* "Lucky you."

"Yeah. God's kept them all good for me. Where's your fam at?"

Trace removed another boot. "I live three miles away right here in Peekskill."

"Shit." Gary's face dropped. "Damn. You haven't heard anything?"

"Nothin'." Trace shook his head.

"Sorry 'bout that man. That's hard."

Trace exhaled fear and dejection. "Yep." He pulled at his socks. "Clyde, how 'bout you?"

"I ended up gettin' through to my in-laws. Kerry was in a car accident with the kids. Kids are a little bumped. Kerry's got a broken tibia and a fractured wrist. Cuts on her face, etcetera…"

"Geez, man." Trace feared Avi and Brooklyn could be in the same situation or worse. *I have to talk to them.*

"Yeah." Clyde pursed his lips.

"That's gotta be hard," Trace said.

"Yeah. Killin' me. But at least I know they're all gonna be okay despite the injuries. My in-laws are there and Kerry's sister, so that's keepin' me calm."

"Don't go askin' Sinclair now," Gary said.

Sinclair grinned.

"That's the single man right there. Where your family live? Florida or somethin'?" Gary jibed.

Sinclair nodded. "There're some perks to being twenty-eight."

Trace chortled. "But from Florida? I don't know about that. Panhandle?"

Gary and Clyde chuckled.

"Central, thank you. I didn't grow up in the swamp," Sinclair laughed.

"Gary, you'd've already known if it was the handle. He wouldn't be able to sit in the same room as you." Trace removed his suit. Gary and the others busted up.

Trace placed his equipment in the applicable bins. The room looked well used, towels strewn across the floor, lockers left open, boots on the tile. Gary stood fully dressed. "I'll catch ya later, Crane."

"Yep, me too," Clyde said.

"Me three," Sinclair said, wedging his foot into a shoe.

Trace waved them off. Then he tidied the place, picking up items off the floor and putting them in the dirty bins. He unbuttoned the top buttons of his shirt and paused. Guilt of being away from the control room deluged him. His left chest burned again. He put his hand over his heart. His mind blipped with technical analyses. Tension built in his jaw as if it had been wound with a key unbeknownst to him until now. He pulled his socks back on, then his suit and boots, then fished his respirator out of the bin, squished his face into it, and trudged out the way he had come.

The control-room gauges, computer monitors, and LED alarms blurred in Trace's vision, his radiation suit and mask suffocating him. His eyes closed. Bliss came in warm tingles, melatonin drenching his body. His eyes reopened. Light glared in his eyes, washes of sage, white Martians, strange silence, click, click, clack, switches being thrown, pens against clipboarded paper scraping in his ears, everything aurally magnified and agitating. *Where am I?* It was 3:00 a.m. Trace sat at the central desk watching blurs of night crew checking dials, data, and reports to get up to speed. At that point they were essentially baby-sitting the reactor. Coolant levels had finally crept to a level that seemed to be keeping the core from heating further. The colossal machine was the happiest it had been since before the quake. Trace and his team had to wait until the next morning to see if the temperature would start dropping, and then he'd have to convince Ken and Barnes to allow him to vent. His feet and legs were aching from standing for nearly eighteen hours. The side of his head and face felt tender. He was lucky the pipe had caught him mostly on his respirator mask. He realized if it hadn't he'd have a fractured jaw, cheek, and nose, which would've kept him on the sidelines indefinitely. *Pumps are up. Coolant circulating. Core covered. Is it really covered?* He questioned the machine again. Trace and his team had followed protocol. They had conferred with the reactor manufacturer, NRC, and other experts. They had responded to all the reactor's ailments and it seemed to be resting now. Either it was on the mend or its veins were temporarily laden with morphine.

"Hey, Traubman." Trace picked his head up and looked at the suited night-shift operator. "I told you about ECCS and the pressure… and… you know… the…"

"Yes, sir. Got it," Traubman said.

"Okay. And the temperature… temperature we gotta watch, plus the release inside containment. If that keeps rising come wake me, because…"

"Don't worry. We got it. Don't worry."

"Alright… alright… uhhh… and the sumps… you gotta watch the sumps… and…"

"Trace! We got it. Go… get sleep." Traubman shooed him away.

"Fuck sleep, Traubman. I've been here since minute one. I'll leave when I damn please!"

"Oh godddd… I know… We got it. We need you sharp. Just go lay it down for a few."

Trace realized Traubman was right. His hand trembled when he pushed his respirator up and sipped cold coffee in a futile attempt to keep himself coherent. It wasn't happening. Trace was certain no amount of caffeine could restore him. *I'd fall asleep on cocaine right now.* He had hit a wall and crashed. Done. Through. Burnt. Fried. Toasted. Charred. Cooked. Didn't matter if the room caught fire and burning babies needed rescuing. He was dust in the wind, delirious, adrenals drained, and vitamin deficient. Trace was hungry, but being saturated with caffeine and stress left his stomach vacuumed with tension and so intensely knotted he felt like he had tight abs, which wasn't the case. Between the stress and bad diet his insides were a conflagrant entanglement. His mouth was parched; he needed water, too. The state of the reactor meant more to Trace than it did to others because he was there when the quake hit and the behemoth machine started functioning off its own directive. It was his job to be in the control room and see through the containment of the beast. Yet, Trace realized he'd reached a state of uselessness and incoherence. He had to step out.

Inside the locker room Trace removed his khakis, button-up, and undergarments. He shivered, his body temperature low from lack of sleep and food. He looked down at his gut, disgusted and glad he was alone, embarrassed about his flabby physique. He took a towel, washcloth, and sandals from a locker that bore his name, slipped the sandals on, walked to the showers, and fired one up. The warm water sent vibrations through his body. He shut his eyes. Trace wanted to curl up on the floor and pretend he was under a tropical waterfall thousands of miles from Bear Mountain. He opened his eyes—institutional tile, no palm trees, no boulders. He pumped liquid soap onto a washcloth and began to scrub, the harsh chemicals drying his skin. His distance from the control room worried him. He wanted to grab his radio and ask what was going on even though it had only been fifteen minutes since he had left. He pumped shampoo into his hand, shut his eyes, and scrubbed his scalp. He was back under the waterfall. He smiled. The shower made him feel like he would after a normal work day where'd he go home, eat, wash, and flop in front of the TV for a film. *But I'm not home!*

Trace turned his fingertips around his ring finger. The absence of his wedding band saddened him. He had gained too much weight and one day he couldn't squeeze it on. He had thought it was an omen and Avi had been devastated by it. Yet he had felt relieved without the ring pinching his skin. He realized it had given his ego freedom from his marriage, which had become insipid and constricted. *No women were lookin' at me anyway.*

Now Trace wished he had his white-gold band around his finger. He saw Avi and Brooklyn home snuggling together in his bed, Brooklyn asleep, Avi wide-eyed, cell and house phones next to her, waiting to hear from him. He envisioned the house damaged. If it was he hoped they were at a friend's or had left town and gone to a hotel, at worst a shelter. What if they're injured or dead? *What if they're both fucking dead? I'll go mad. Absolutely, fuckin' mad.* Considering the dose of radiation he had absorbed he might not live anyway. *So be it. If they're dead then I'll die and be with them.* Trace shook the grim thoughts from his mind as he rinsed. He stepped out of the shower, toweled, and changed into new undergarments, khakis, and a short-sleeve button-up.

Trace trudged down a carpeted hall in the operations center, exhausted, his body aching. He arrived at the kitchen and looked in the vending machine. It had been run through. A few lonely hangers left—a sandwich in cellophane, cheese puffs, a granola bar, chocolate candies. Everything but the granola bar looked like a stomachache. He dug in his pocket for his wallet. He patted around his others. "Shit…" He realized he had left it in his desk along with his house keys. *Dammit! Dammit! Dammit!* Trace smashed his fist into the vending-machine glass. The cheese puffs dangled from their coil. *Hmm…* Trace grabbed the vending machine and rocked it until the glass and metal beast slammed into the wall. He dropped the machine and let it wobble. The cheese puffs dropped. *There's one advantage to having body weight.* Trace reached in and grabbed his take. He tore the bag open and shoveled the puffs into his mouth. He opened the fridge. The inside had been ransacked—only a dozen sodas, juices, and waters remained. He took a water. Next, Trace went to the cabinets, opening them two at a time while still dumping cheese puffs into his mouth. Dishes, containers, glasses, tea, coffee, almonds. *Almonds.* He finished the bag of puffs and set it on top of an overflowing trash can, soda dripped from a crushed can that teetered on top of the recycling heap. *Damn stampede of animals came through here.*

Trace devoured the almonds by the handful. *God, I'm hungry!* He cracked open the water and guzzled back half the bottle. "Ahh…" More almonds. He went to the filtered-water station, stuck his bottle under the spigot, and pushed the blue plastic tab down. Brownish water ran from the machine. Trace quickly let go of the tab. "Damn." He dumped some of the water out into the tray. Most of the brown was gone but a bit had mixed with the bottled water. He looked at it and shrugged. He drank. The taste hadn't changed, but it was clear to him that the water pipes may've been compromised from the quake and were taking in contamination, most likely soil, hopefully not sewage. *I thought this water was filtered.* He opened the sink spigot. Murky water spewed and didn't stop. *Is this all we have?* Trace wondered if anyone was on top of the provisions for the crew. They wouldn't last long without food and clean water. He didn't know who to talk to about it. He had to contact office services, but none of them were there. *I need to lie down.*

Trace waltzed into the hall. Open doors revealed crew-members sleeping on cots in the offices. One man was curled up in the hallway against the baseboard. Trace stepped around him. *Like a homeless shelter.* He arrived at the operations nerve center and looked through the entrance glass. The graveyard shift sipped coffee, watching computer monitors and televisions displaying facility surveillance and news. Laptops sat open along tables, the crew hunched over them, phones to their ears. A large, grainy image of the floodlit reactor-three containment building sat on the big screens. It looked like a spaceship in the middle of the desert.

Trace couldn't bear to poke his head in. *Rest…* His eyes were heavy, his brain tangled. A surge of adrenaline gushed through him, but he felt mentally listless, inert and alert at the same time. He trudged down the hall and found a large room lined with cots, a few available. He slipped inside quietly. Snoring abounded. He found a cot by a wall next to Jerry.

Trace sat on the nylon and moved the blanket to the end, the pillow to the head. He lay back. The room was hot and he assumed building management was trying to conserve power while they ran off auxiliary systems. He slipped his khakis and button-up off, leaving himself in a pair of white boxers and a white undershirt. His body ached like he had summited Everest and been dragged over icy boulders back down to the bottom. He was the most exhausted he'd ever felt in his life. His mind was a spate of thoughts—a caffeine-laden gerbil sprinting through a labyrinth. *The pressure's too high, temperature's too high, coolant's too low. Pumps... pumps one and two... blocks eight and nine... generator, diesel, station blackout... Avi, my love... Brooklyn...* His thoughts rambled, his logic, concentration, and coordination nil. His head ached on one side, his legs sore, acid burned in his throat, and his facial skin felt like it was drooping onto his neck. He needed to get at least a few hours of REM sleep. *Ha... REM... the irony... Maybe a little bit of REM sleep is MILLIREM sleep...I'm fucking delirious.* "Hey, Jerry," Trace whispered. "Hey, Jerry. You awake?"

"What?" Jerry grumbled.

"What do you call it when you get a little bit of REM sleep?"

"Not enough," Jerry muttered.

"Millirem." Trace chuckled quietly.

"Go to sleep."

Sleep. Right. Like that's gonna happen. Trace felt responsible for the disaster. Just his involvement in the industry made him feel culpable. The research Avi had hammered him with surged out of his recesses. "What about the tests that Dr. Arnold Rapp did in Massachusetts, where he found increased leukemia rates around a plant there? And what about Dr. Jack Johns who documented high child-cancer rates around that plant near San Diego? What about Three Mile Island? They had soaring cancer rates after that reactor melted down. Counties are only prepared to evacuate ten miles around a plant in the event of a radioactive release, but we both know particles can travel for hundreds and even thousands of miles. How are you prepared for animals being exposed? They won't be able to reproduce, or be used for a source of meat, milk, or eggs. Even worse, the land could possibly be declared uninhabitable for decades. The Nuclear Regulatory Commission receives ninety percent of its funding from companies like yours. The energy companies pay for the commission."

It's not all true. It's not all true! Now Bear Mountain was doing everything Avi thought it would. *How did you know? Did you have a premonition? I'm a piece of shit. I should've listened to her.* Dejection made his mouth dry. *How could I endanger my family? Idiot... Quit it. We got this under control.* When it was all over Trace would agree to any house Avi wanted, wherever she wanted. Even if they stabilized the reactor he wouldn't want his girls living in fear. Indignation surfaced. He and Avi had been at odds for years, a slow downturn after she had gotten sick and besieged him about the perils of nuclear energy. He felt invaded, resentment pervading him. He was disappointed that Avi had become so motherly, a nester that only drank herbal tea and didn't want to leave Peekskill unless it had to do with moving upstate to somewhere more remote.

Avi? Are you there? He hoped he'd wake up, Avi pushing his arm because he was breathing strangely. He had developed sleep apnea from his ballooning weight and stress. Many nights he would catapult up in bed, gasping, with Avi asking him if he was okay. *She hasn't awakened me yet. I'm still knocked out cold, the clutches of a demon pulling me further into the depths of this nightmare. Where are you, my love? I pray that you and Brooklyn are okay.*

Trace took out his smartphone and found a voicemail from Avi from the day before that had been downloaded. He listened to it. "Hi, honey, it's me," Avi said.

"And me!" Brooklyn blurted.

"We're on our way home to make dinner. Your favorite, crab cakes. And we have baklava. Yum… Don't come too late. Love you." "Love youoooo, daddddyyy," Brooklyn belted. Trace's chest flooded with euphoria that quickly plunged to despair. In front of Brooklyn Avi always put on her best face and tried to show Trace love as an example. Avi didn't want their daughter to experience their animosity. *How could I take it for granted?* The joy of having two people that Trace loved so dearly, that were so kind, overwhelmed him when he didn't know if they were safe. *You can't control it. Sleep.* Trace shut his eyes and tried to usher in more relaxing thoughts. Visions of him with Avi and Brooklyn on the beach playing with a frisbee floated through, Avi's brother's ashen mutt, Toby, chasing the disk and biting at their legs. He envisioned weekends on lounge chairs in the backyard. Before Brooklyn arrived winter nights were spent on the sectional catching a movie, balsam fir crackling on the hearth.

Trace and Avi were stretched out on the sofa. A bottle of Merlot sat empty on the coffee table. Sometime later their clothes were on the hardwood, Trace running his hand over Avi's peaks and valleys. He loved her soft, fit curves, fitting perfectly in his hand. Her hair hid her face, one emerald iris glowing through the strands looking seductively at him. Trace swept her hair back and tucked it behind her ears. He liked to see her cheeks, lightly scarred from teenage acne. She was embarrassed by it, but it was faint and Trace found it sexy. It made her real to him, not some wispy, artificial daisy. *Where did that connection between us go?* They had become the odd couple—the fat guy with the cute woman. 'How'd he get her?' people thought when they were together in public. *I'm the dumpy dude with the beautiful girl. I don't deserve her anymore.*

CHAPTER 20

The warmth of mid-afternoon sand cradled Trace's feet. The sea air opened his nose; he could taste the brine, a sultry breeze feathering his face. He wore a beige linen suit and stood at a driftwood trellis wrapped in white linen. Avi's favorite flowers, lavender magnolias and delphiniums, adorned the edges. Avi's uncle in a powder-gray suit stood in the center of the trellis waiting to officiate the ceremony. Trace looked down the flower-lined passageway between the branch chairs. Avi appeared from behind a seagrass berm, her father on one arm, her bouquet and the train of her strapless chiffon-and-lace dress in her other hand. A pitch-perfect a cappella quintet striking up Phil Collins *Groovy Kind of Love* in such harmony Trace thought a choir of angels was singing at him from the heavens. Avi's eyes shimmered when she hit the aisle. A string quartet fading in on the chorus resonated in his ears as if God stroked the chords of the universe. Avi burned bright when she walked toward Trace, blurring all scenery and people around her. Her smile was broad. "Avi?" Trace called. "Avi!" He lurched from the altar, but he couldn't move. His feet felt like they'd been cemented to the ground. He looked down and saw they had fused with the sand and turned to glass. He tried to move again, flailing his arms toward her. "Avi!" He watched flames engulf her, her body fading into the grassy bluff behind. "Nooooo!"

Trace's eyes shot open. His chest heaved, his pulse thrumming in his ears. He looked to his side for Avi. Drop-ceiling tiles, carpet, cots, and cream drywall were hazy in his vision. It took him a moment to realize where he was. *Fuck. It's all really happening, isn't it? Or is it? I was on the beach getting married. Why was she burning?* He noticed some cots had emptied, but most were still full. Jerry and Valdern were still asleep. He checked his watch and squinted. Five twenty-eight a.m. blurred in Indiglo. *Two hours of sleep. No fucking way I'm getting up.* His body was cold and stiff, acid burning in his esophagus. *More sleep.* He shut his eyes, but he felt strangely awake, his mind humming, yet skipping like a scratched record—coherent and incoherent thoughts intertwining. *The pressurizer. Close the vents? Earthquake! Is the core covered? What about ECCS? Hanson! Feedwater is down!* He opened his eyes, knowing another wink would be impossible, and just lay there dreading sitting up. He was anxious to get back to the control room to see if the reactor had filled with more coolant and if core temperature had dropped. Trace hadn't spent a single night apart from his wife, not a single night where he didn't know where Brooklyn was. He took his phone out of his shoe, fumbled with the touch screen, and dialed Avi. The line didn't ring. Her voicemail picked up immediately. Trace hung up and dialed again and again, always with the same result. He composed a text message to her. *I love u honey tell Brooklyn I luv her call me at plant if can I'm stuck here dealing with reactor let me know ur ok.* Trace dropped his phone back into his shoe with disgust. *Goddamn technology never works when you need it. Why was Avi burning? Was it an omen? Can't be... Can't be... Why would she be hurt? Why?* He felt vast emptiness under his ribs. *Suck it up.*

Trace pressed himself from the cot. His body tingled and ached down to his bones, his hands and forearms numb and weak. The gash on his head and the cuts on his hand burned. His eyelids felt like they had weights on them. Trace pulled his pants on, pushed his arms through his button-up, and collected his belongings. *Coffee.*

He lumbered into the emergency operations center kitchen. He grumbled at the appearance of the room—institutional nineties laminate flooring and countertops, wood-veneer cabinetry, white plastic chairs and tables, crumbs on all surfaces, an acridity of cheap coffee and rotten cream wafting. It was a discomforting experience he never wanted to wake up to. He found a paper cup and squeezed out a hot brew, considering someone might have heated the contaminated water from the sink and disguised it as coffee. *You're crazy.* He rifled the cabinets. Pretzels and Grandma's cookies. *Breakfast.* He started with the cookies. Trace was surprised at the energy he had. His adrenal glands were working overtime and he figured it wouldn't be long-standing. *I'm gonna crash later.* Trace sensed a presence behind him. He turned. Ken Bramini stood scowling in a charcoal suit holding a steel-blue suit covered in plastic. Trace found it odd. Ken only wore suits for meetings. *Another governor encounter? What's he want me to do, his dry cleaning?* Trace knew they had plenty of steam for that. Hang that suit over the venting tower. *Oh right, we're not venting.*

"You caffeinated!?" Ken's voice banged like gunshots.

Trace recoiled and looked at the cup in his hand. *It'd be easier to press that suit with this coffee.* He bit into another cookie and stared at his boss.

Ken pushed the plastic-covered suit into Trace's chest. "Put this on."

Trace glanced at it apathetically and pushed the remainder of the cookie into his mouth.

"We're goin' on the *Today Show*. Chopper waiting outside."

Trace took a pull from his coffee. Then another and another. It burned his mouth and throat. "What?"

"The *Today Show*. The morning show. You, me, and Barnes. He wants you there." Ken put the suit into Trace's open hand.

"What? Why? I've barely slept. I gotta get back to the control room. What the hell's going on?"

"You'll be back. Like I said, Barnes wants you there. The public needs to hear from a man that's been on the inside the entire time. It'll help assuage their fears. It's important. People're freaked out. We've got lawyers callin' us, environmental agencies, activists. People are leaving town, stress is causing anxiety attacks, miscarriages, heart attacks, heat stroke. Our shareholders are in an uproar."

Ken's voice felt thirty decibels louder to Trace than it actually was. *Stop screaming!* He couldn't understand why Ken enjoyed thriving on disaster. He seemed to love it like Trace loved food. "Well, gee. A nuclear reactor is halfway to meltdown, I wonder why people are freaked out? I don't do press. That's your job."

"You a team player or not? This is how it goes." Ken jabbed his finger into Trace's chest. "You can get dressed or get lost. And why the hell are you being so damn insubordinate anyway? We never had this kinda interaction. I know this's hard, but that's what we train for. You gotta toughen your ass up, man. C'mon!" Ken slapped Trace on the shoulder.

Toughen my ass up... What is this, the navy? I'd like to drop your ass inside the reactor core. Why they wanted him on the news befuddled Trace. *What am I a corral pony?* He was too tired to fight. His body tingled with numbness. He felt the plastic over the plush suit fabric sticky in his hand. Ken walked off. *How could the man have so much energy so early?* Trace figured he must've gotten at least four or six hours. *How could anyone sleep? Maybe he didn't. Maybe it was adrenaline or copious amounts of coffee?* It was the military training. Trace figured Ken was up doing push-ups, but Ken hadn't taken in a blast of radiation like Trace had. *Why did I agree to this? Actually, I don't think I said yes.* Ken's eyes were convincing. The magical blue was mesmerizing, drew you in. You wanted to swim in it, pet the turtles. He had to play along, he had to follow Ken's orders. Or did he?

CHAPTER 21

"Brooklyn?" Avi shuffled on a cracked linoleum floor in a dank, exposed-brick corridor, pipes serpentining above. "Brooklyn." The droplights flickered, sparks sprayed from exposed wires in the ceiling. She couldn't pinpoint the acrid scent singeing her nostrils, but it seemed like a combination of sulfur, burnt rubber, and death. Brick, concrete, and wood rubble was scattered before her like remnants of a detonation. Children moaned and cried out.

"Help!"

"Help me!"

"Mommyyy!"

"Brooklyn?" Avi called out, staggering through the corridor. "Brooklyn!" Avi came up on a massive pile of debris—bricks, desks, plaster, chairs, books—everything thrashed and mixed together as if a tornado had dropped it all there.

"Mama," Brooklyn cried from the pile. "Mama!" Avi dropped to her knees and crawled into the wreckage. Her little girl lay bloody, pinned under concrete, wood beams, and brick. Avi recoiled.

"Brooklyn! NO!" She covered her mouth.

"Mama. Help me!" Avi heard Brooklyn's voice, but it didn't come from her unresponsive body. "Mama?"

Avi snapped her head around. "Brook? NO! NO! Please, God!"

"Avi," Trace said.

"Trace?" From a bird's-eye view Trace stood in front of the containment building housing the troubled reactor in his radiation whites with the hood off. The containment building vibrated. Then the concrete-and-steel structure started to melt. "Trace!" Avi screamed, her voice thin and raw. The building exploded.

Avi's eyelids spilt open. She gasped. Her heart palpitated. *Fucking... what kind of nightmare?...* Blurry washes of morning sunlight squeezed through the shutter slats wrapping the room in horizontal illumination. Her tired eyes fell back closed. Her edge rounded when she realized she was at their friend's beach house. Trace was in the kitchen cooking up a feast, Brooklyn playing and eating bits of food he fed her from the stove. When they were at the beach house they tended to reverse roles. Trace couldn't stay in bed so he'd get up and project his anxious energy onto a task. Avi, on the other hand, enjoyed a couple extra hours under the covers. She smiled. A great day at the beach was ahead. Even though their marriage was rocky Avi would enjoy herself. Two days of bliss. She and Trace would be mostly disconnected from each other, but the tension would run low.

Avi turned to her side. Her body and head ached. She grimaced. *Why?...* "Ahh..." She opened her eyes, shielding them from the morning light. She looked at the bedside clock. *8:47. That's not... What clock is that?* She realized it wasn't from the beach house. *Where?* She sat up. Her knee screamed in pain. She saw a bandage around it and noticed her clothes—clean, billowing terry shorts and a t-shirt. *Whose clothes are these?* Thoughts of the earthquake, driving around the city, and visits to shelters looking for Brooklyn inundated her. *Are they dreams? Nightmares? I'm at the beach, right? No. No?* As strange as her memories were she knew they weren't dreams. They were her current unimaginable reality—a fracture of her universe. Avi tore the covers off and swung her feet over the side of the bed. Heat pervaded her upper chest, neck, and lower face. It was warm to her touch. *It's hot in here.* She wobbled, her equilibrium off. She opened the bedside shutters—lush trees, grass, small farmland, rows of crops. *Lea's house?*

Avi slid off the bed. Her feet hit the hardwood. When she sprang up she lost her balance and knocked into the bifold closet. She clutched the wall. She shuffled to the door.

Avi stumbled into the kitchen to find Lea, Tim, and Lea's two boys in their pajamas. Tim worked the stove as Lea set her boys up to eat. Warmth pervaded Avi's body. She found comfort in the breakfast scents and Lea, her father, and Lea's sons functioning as a family. Avi enjoyed Lea's boys' cherubic faces, their smiles. Their obliviousness to the disaster unfolding outside their home made Avi jealous. She found beauty in the purity of a child's mind and heart. Brooklyn wasn't receiving the same isolation. *If she's still alive. Of course she's still alive!* Avi figured she was either alone or with strangers. *Either way she's probably terrified. I should be there for her. I should be protecting her.* The disaster was going to scar her soul, going to alter how the rest of her life progressed. *She could end up with PTSD.* It could tear down all her securities, she could be clinging to Avi's leg until adulthood. *It's not fair!*

"Hey," Lea said. "C'mon. Sit."

"Did you find Brooklyn?"

Lea shook her head. "Dad and I spent an hour calling hospitals, shelters, and emergency numbers after you went to sleep. We didn't come up with anything and the lines are out again now."

"We have to find my baby, Lea."

Lea went to Avi and hugged her. "Take a breath, sweetie. That's what we're going to do today. Right away, okay. Try not to panic. We're gonna eat, get dressed, and start lookin'. Start goin' to shelters and start calling more numbers. Don't you worry."

Avi coiled her arms around her friend. "Thank you."

"Of course. How're you feelin'?"

"Confused. Achy. My head is splitting. I feel like I drank a fifth of vodka." Avi put her hand to her face. "When I woke up I thought I was at our friend's beach house. I thought everything was a nightmare until I moved and felt my body."

"Oh honey." Lea guided Avi to a chair at the reclaimed oak slab. "Sit."

"No. Let me stand a minute. I want to see if I can keep my legs under me. I'm a bit off balance."

"What's going on with your chest and neck and your face? Let me look at that."

"I don't know. Whaddayou mean?"

Lea pulled Avi in front of a mirror in the hallway attached to the kitchen. Her head was bandaged, her knee bandaged, her hair bedraggled, her eyes puffy, her complexion wan. She looked like a apparition from a horror film. "God…" she gasped. "Look at me." Avi cringed. She felt detached from her countenance.

"Don't worry, you're still cute. You've been through a lot. Look at that rash, though." Lea's words sounded underwater. Avi stayed staring at the mirror. *Rash?* Her mind and body ached like she'd been trampled by elephants.

Lea put her hand on Avi's chest. "Feels warm."

"Yeah. Looks like a burn," Avi said.

"Did you get sunburn yesterday or the day before? I didn't notice it last night when I was bandaging you." Lea said.

Avi shook her head. "Wish I had. That'd meant I was at the beach. I don't know what it is. Wasn't there yesterday."

"Maybe something you ate? It's probably stress. Heavy, heavy, shocking stress can do this."

"Yeah, you're right. I remember feeling a hot flash last night before you came to the door when I was freaking out in the rain."

Lea nodded. "I'll give you something topical for it to try and calm it down."

"Thanks."

"Come. Sit. I wanna hydrate you with saline. I have some that I keep around just in case somebody drinks too much wine on a weekday." Lea cupped her hands and whispered. "Me."

Avi chuckled. Then she winced, her head pounding, pain radiating into her teeth.

"I'll give you painkillers for your head and the rest of the aches as well. Then you need to try and get some food in you." Lea sat Avi at the kitchen table. "I'll be right back."

Tim placed a tall glass of vanilla liquid in front of Avi. "Have that first. It's a protein drink. Will be easy for you to get down. Your car key is there on the counter, too."

"Thanks." Surprisingly, she was a bit hungry. Not necessarily a great appetite, but she needed to put something inside her stomach. Avi knocked back half of the shake. Her stomach lurched. She burped and Lea's boys laughed. "Excuse me." She rubbed her stomach, her nausea returning. She would've preferred poached eggs, toast, and fruit. But she knew she needed to keep the shake down so her body could absorb some nutrients.

Lea returned with a bag of saline and a syringe. She saw the shake in front of Avi. "Good idea, Dad." Lea took Avi's arm and wiped it with an alcohol swab at the crease of her elbow. "You had an IV recently?" Lea asked, referring to the syringe mark on Avi's arm.

"Yeah, when I passed out at Brooklyn's school. Paramedics hooked me up."

"Geez… Okay. I'm gonna put this next to it."

"Mama's a nurse!" one of Lea's boys said.

"That's right, guys."

Avi barely felt the syringe pierce her arm. Lea hooked up the saline and Avi felt it swirl into her veins. She was immediately back on the grass at Brooklyn's school. Then she was in the hospital lying in bed with breast cancer—IVs and monitoring cables dangling from her, medication in the hanging bags. Avi detested everything medical after her bouts with Hashimoto's and breast cancer. Just the IV made her feel sick again as if she were on the brink of death, alone in the abyss, her mortal clock speeding. She closed her eyes.

Avi brushed Brooklyn's hair while she sat on the vanity in her bathroom. Avi whispered in her ear, "I love you."

"I love you, too, mama," Brooklyn said. Avi watched Brooklyn's jazz dance class. Then they sat on the grass in the park reading together.

Lea's kitchen came into focus—the wormwood island, the distressed cabinetry, the stainless refrigerator. Oxygen flowed easier into Avi's nose. The IV fluids took affect, clarity returning to her mind. Lea placed three ibuprofen in front of her. "Take these after you get a little more food in you." Lea handed her a tube of cream. "This is for the rash. I'll let you rub it on after breakfast."

"Thanks. Then we get in the car and start looking for Brooklyn," Avi said.

Tim came into the room with a battery-operated, handheld TV, antennae splayed in the air. "Look."

Anchor Lance Grable's voice distorted the tiny TV's built-in speaker. "This is a special edition of *Today*. This morning I have with me Chris Barnes, president and CEO of Gener8 Corporation, the owner and operator of the Bear Mountain Nuclear Energy Center. Along with him is Bear Mountain General Manager Ken Bramini and…"

CHAPTER 22

The glaring stage lights made Trace feel like he'd been pulled over at 2:00 a.m. after a night at the bar, spotlights so bright they exposed his innermost secrets, blemishes inside and out-side his body and soul he hadn't known existed—fear, anxiety, freckles on his hands. He sat next to Ken and Chris Barnes in stone-blue club chairs watching Lance deliver his opening across from them. Three cameras off the stage pointing at the trio felt like sniper rifles. Trace felt exposed, raw, naked—left out in the tundra with a hungry polar bear as the only pos-sible source of warmth. He had cleaned himself up the best he could, combing his hair to the side, rinsing blood off his face and hands, before donning the steel-blue suit Ken had given him. The large wound at his temple and cuts and bruises along his jaw showed through the layers of makeup he'd been coated with before taking the stage.

Beads of sweat tickled the hair follicles on his thighs, armpits, and chest, the radiation whites he wore under his suit creating a convection oven. He had worn the protective suit unbeknownst to anyone to minimize radiation exposure he could potentially spread to others by being outside the plant. Luckily, Trace was overweight and his suit was roomy, thus allowing radiation whites to fit underneath. He shifted nervously in his chair, the radiation suit crinkling. He hoped no one could hear it as loud as he could. He looked rumpled and loathsome sitting next to Barnes, who wore a cerulean-blue suit with a white sky-blue-striped shirt. Trace felt cheap, out of his league.

Last time Trace was on a news program he had been interviewed about the positive aspects of nuclear energy and the low carbon footprint compared to coal-powered plants. Now he slouched in front of cameras, engulfed by his worst fears. The prized, flagship plant was catching all the malfunctions activists had been yammering about for years. Trace, Barnes, and Ken were public targets ready to be sprayed by questions. Flying over Manhattan earlier had been difficult. As the sun rose he saw his beloved city below mostly dark—power outages because of the quake and shutdown of Bear Mountain. Trace felt responsible. The black holes in New York City were a depiction of holes in his heart over what was happening to residents around the plant. *Be confident. You've got coolant around the core, dammit. You're doin' good. It could be much, much worse. Stay optimistic. The reactor's on the mend.*

"Welcome, gentlemen," Lance said.

"Thank you," Barnes and Bramini said.

Trace said nothing; his voice wasn't working yet. He felt oddly alert from the copious coffee and pastries he had consumed in the greenroom. His hands and feet tingled, but his mind held nothing, not a word. It was as if he had reached the apex of meditation. Everything was still, he was present, just there, sort of daydreaming in stasis live on one of the most watched morning shows in the nation.

Lance stacked note cards in his lap. "We asked you all here this morning because people are concerned. There's—"

"NO NUKES! NO NUKES!"

Everyone in the studio except Trace turned startled to the street window behind them. Trace turned slowly. He was so tired he had no adrenaline left to react. A young man pounded on the glass. "YOU LIE!" Police and security tackled him while he continued screaming. Protestors behind him pressed against the crowd-barricade. Sticked signs with X's drawn through reactor steam stacks and anti-nuclear statements pumped into the air. The crowd cheered for their fallen man. Trace looked on; his mouth arid. *Crazy. But they're not a hundred percent wrong.* The crowd broke into chant. "Shut 'em down! SHUT 'EM DOWN! Shut 'em down! DECOMMISSION! Every dose is an overdose! Every dose is an overdose! DECOMMISSION!" Trace wished the public had a better understanding of how nuclear reactors functioned, but he understood their fear. In the past Trace and others from Gener8 had tried to educate the masses as best they could. *Does it really matter? It's my job to deal with the reactor, not theirs.*

Trace, Ken, and Barnes turned back. "Okay. Some folks out there are a little unhappy," Lance continued. "So… There's an ongoing nuclear accident happening at Bear Mountain, which for viewers that don't know is in Buchanan, New York, approximately thirty-five miles outside of where we're sitting right now in midtown Manhattan."

"Right, Lance. If I could interject for a moment. This is not a nuclear accident. I want to make sure that's clear, and I've said it in our press conferences. This is a system response to the earthquake that occurred yesterday morning," Chris Barnes said.

"Oooo—kay. As I understand it there is a system malfunction happening currently that is putting the reactor in jeopardy."

"A system malfunction, yes. The reactor in jeopardy, no," Bramini said.

"You see, Lance," Barnes said. "This is why we're here. We want to clear everything up with the residents of New York so they can understand exactly what is happening and exactly what is not happening at Bear Mountain."

"Okay, Chris. Tell us," Lance said.

"In short. The earthquake yesterday caused the system to shut down as it normally should. During that shutdown our crews encountered some unforeseen system issues. They are still dealing with buttoning up some of the issues now. However, as of late yesterday the reactor has been under control and we have coolant around the core. Our teams are now monitoring the reactor to ensure that cold shutdown occurs with continued stability."

Trace looked at Barnes. *Wow, he's really puttin' butter on that one.* Barnes downplayed too much for Trace's taste, but he understood. Barnes had to make people feel safe. If not, panic would continue. Trace understood why they had brought him along. *Security. Placation.* No one was lying, but they were omitting and he was sure the comfort of his presence convinced viewers. Trace felt like a wounded child at a firearms regulation assembly. *See, it's not that bad; the boy took two to the chest and he's still alive.* Even though the reactor's prognosis had grown more positive, Trace and his team were still in a holding pattern due to the inability to vent containment based on Governor Pagano's demands and Barnes' decision.

Avi, Lea, and Tim watched the portable TV Tim had propped up on the kitchen table. A tear slid down Avi's face. She looked at Lea. "He's there. Why is he there?" Avi was glad he was okay. Makeup covered injuries on his face, head, and hands, his dark, sunken eyes reveling his unrest. She never thought she'd see him on TV and now she felt Trace only existed inside the tube, beamed over a satellite from a different realm. He looked okay for the moment, but what about after the telecast concluded? She wouldn't see him, know if he was still safe, know what awaited him, or the physical and emotional pain he was going through. She couldn't imagine being inside the control room several yards from a malfunctioning nuclear reactor. She may've been angry with Trace, but she empathized with his position. *But it's what you wanted!* There's no way he fully considered the level of disaster, decisions, pain, and stress that imbued him. Saving the reactor from meltdown was Trace's responsibility. He had billions of eyes on his performance, millions of lives and vast swaths of land relying on him. *Did you think about that, Trace? Did you consider it?* She wondered if he had been the teen out of high school who had leapt to the frontline in the Middle East without first considering the worst scenarios that could afflict him. Death wasn't even number one on the list. Having to live a life as a pile of flesh with missing limbs, third-degree burns, and a colostomy bag was the top. *Did you think about that, Trace? Have you learned your lesson? You need to put your family first and nothing else!* Avi picked up the cordless phone from the counter. She pressed 'talk.' There was no dial tone.

"Av... The phones don't work," Lea said.

"I... I should call the station. I should... Dammit!" She slapped the phone down. "I should... I should go to the city and get him." Avi stood.

Lea clasped her arm. "By the time you get there he'll be back to the plant. These newscasts last, what, five, ten, fifteen minutes at most. Don't waste your time. You need to focus on Brooklyn. Let him do his job."

"His job is to help his family!"

"Yes. But it's also to stabilize the nuclear reactor."

"I need him. Dammit, Trace. I'm so mad at him. I told him I wanted to move! I told him!" Avi smacked the table, rattling the breakfast dishes.

Lea tugged Avi by her arm. "Sit."

Avi reluctantly plopped back onto the chair.

Lance Grable continued, "Now we've seen reports about radioactive steam—venting—that was occurring, which I understand is part of the reactor's operation. However, apparently there has been radiation detected outside of Bear Mountain property in Buchanan, Cortlandt, and Peekskill. What can you tell us about that?"

"I can tell you that only minuscule amounts of radiation have been released into the environment. Levels are well below federal regulations and there is no threat to public health and safety," Ken Bramini said.

"We've heard reports from environmental agencies that they've found increased levels of radioactive isotopes in the Hudson as of early this morning," Lance said.

"We do our own testing of the surrounding environment, waterways, and air. If there were anything to be concerned about we would absolutely let the New York Emergency Management Office know so the appropriate action could be taken."

Avi's biggest fear blurted out of the little TV—radiation released into the environment. She was livid with Trace. His words swirled in her mind. 'Nuclear's safe. Nothing can happen. Don't worry. I know what I'm doing.' *What ARE you doing?* Avi immediately wanted to leave town, but she wasn't leaving without her daughter. From her research and experience Avi knew airborne radioactivity was capable of infecting every living organism and inanimate object in its path.

When isotopes infected a living organism, they hid in its tissue, organs, and bones for the rest of that organism's life and even as the organism existed as dead matter. Over eight thousand square miles had been contaminated by fallout in and around Fukushima. Sixty-three thousand square miles had been contaminated in and around Chernobyl. *Was it happening here?* Avi covered her mouth with her hands.

"What people have to understand," Barnes said, "is that the radiation detected off site is not harmful. It's less than the background radiation everyone receives from space, less than your last dental X-ray. And… With public health and safety in mind, in agreement with the governor's office, we have ceased all venting activity. The dump of water into the Hudson is part of normal plant operation once we can't take on anymore water in our tanks. That water was being used to cool the reactor. We want everyone to understand that we have the situation at the plant under control. So much so that we brought our control-room supervisor who is leading the team, Trace Crane, here with us to ensure everyone that we are taking all necessary steps to stabilize the reactor and protect the public. Isn't that right, Trace?"

Trace looked at Barnes and then to the news anchor. He was cornered, a noose around his neck, hundreds of millions of eyes staring at him. He was afraid to divulge details on national television that might trigger Barnes and Bramini to come down on him. *Just confirm the truth.* He nodded. "Right. The reactor is surrounded by circulating coolant and we are attempting to decrease the pressure and temperature of the core now that we have adequate coolant to work with. That's our focus right now. I'm confident by the end of today we should be taking major strides in decreasing the temperature of the reactor's core. Then, like Mr. Barnes said, we'll be on our way to a cold shutdown." *Wish it was as easy as it sounds. That's what we're here for, to make it sound good while we kill ourselves to repair the reactor and make it look easy to the public.* He likened it to a concert—technicians behind the scenes losing their hair by the minute tweaking sound and lighting to make the talent look good on stage. *We better not get any feedback.*

"Will Bear Mountain survive this event and ever come back

online?" Lance asked.

Oh god, not that question.

"Absolutely," Barnes said.

This guy's got balls to come swingin' with that kind of bravado.

Barnes continued, "Reactor two was down for refueling when the quake hit and it's in good shape. We won't be firing it up until things settle at the plant. Reactor three will need repairs, but we'll have her back up as well. This's New York City's power. We won't leave the city dark."

Trace wasn't sure he believed Barnes' or even his own words. If the reactor stayed stable and temperature decreased there were still a multitude of obstacles to navigate. He wasn't sure he believed Bear Mountain would survive. It all hinged on what unfolded next at the plant. He needed to get back to the control room. More importantly he needed to know Avi and Brooklyn were safe. He was outside the plant, a prisoner on home leave. He wondered if he should return to the pen or grab his girls and split town. But they were close to stabilizing the reactor, and it was his duty to be there. He caught a glimpse of himself on the director's monitor. His forehead was covered in sweat, his face flushed. He looked like he had the flu or a gun to his back. Pressure to perform pulverized his fortitude.

The taping with Lance Grable concluded with Lance delivering a close-up monologue about natural disasters, nuclear energy, and humanity. Trace was relieved it was over. He never wanted step onto a news set again. He didn't have the stomach for it. Oddly, one would think Trace's stomach could handle just about anything, but it was a voluminous hot-air balloon floating tremulously in the breeze. POP! Deflated. Trace shook hands with Lance and wondered if the guy ever stopped showing his whitened teeth. *Guy's got more dopamine in his head than a meth addict.* Trace strolled off to the greenroom. He stuffed half a glazed donut into his mouth.

"We're gettin' the chopper back in five," Ken said, stirring cream into a coffee.

Trace nodded. "Imma hit the head first," he mumbled with a full mouth. He strode down the corridor, passed the bathroom, continued to a door at the end of the hall, and pushed through it. He heard street noise. He stepped outside and held the door. He looked back down the corridor through the sliver of glass in the interior door. Ken stepped out of the green room. Trace swiftly moved outside and let the exit door shut. He hustled down 49th Street, his hand high in the air. Cabs, town cars, and trucks passing and then a yellow Prius came to a stop. He hopped in the back. The Somalian driver's tawny eyes inquired in the rearview. "Peekskill," Trace said. The driver's eyes stayed on Trace.

"Sir, Peekskill no good. All roads shut from earthquake." He waved his hands.

"I need to go. The highways still work. I was just in a helicopter looking at them."

The cabbie shook his head. "Sir, I'm sorry. Too much mess. Take too much time."

Trace rolled his eyes. "Fine. Take me to that ATM up there." Trace pointed to the banking logo on the right a thousand feet ahead in Rockefeller Plaza. The cabbie pulled ahead and over. "Wait here, I need to get cash."

"Sir, I'm not going to Peekskill."

"Don't worry. We're gonna go to Harlem."

"Okay, sir." The cabbie sat back.

Trace split through throngs of tourists gawking and pointing, maps in hands, camera phones snapping, between New Yorker's striding to their weekend jobs, briefcases and purses swinging. He arrived at the ATM, dipped his card in, and punched in his passcode. He withdrew a thousand dollars—ten hundreds. The machine opened and pushed his card out, followed by the cash.

Trace pocketed both, trotted back to the taxi, and hopped in. "Alright, let's go." The cabbie took off into traffic.

Trace peeled off three, one-hundred dollar bills from the fold and held them through the plastic window. "Here."

The cabbie turned back. "What's this? You pay at end."

"We're goin' to Peekskill."

"Sir…" The cabbie hit the brakes making Trace lurch forward. "Take it. That's three hundred. We gotta make two stops. When we get to the first stop I'll give you another two hundred."

The cabbie took the money and sighed. "Okay."

"And you better drive fast."

CHAPTER 23

"It's right here. The green and beige with the veranda." Trace braced himself as the taxi came to a hard stop in front of his leaning Victorian revival. He froze. The morning sun was a spotlit smile on his house. He wondered if the rays would cause the materials to come alive and self-repair. Trace felt disconnected from his home, some sort of energy break that made it seem like it wasn't his. He owned it, he had been there the morning of the day before, but now there was some kind of distance, some kind of objectivity to the sight of it. *Wow.* The destroyed roads, buildings, and vehicles he had seen on the way to his neighborhood fascinated him. He was in the middle of the remnants of a significant natural disaster. The view from inside the plant and up in the helicopter didn't fully express the extent of the detriment. In New York City it was business as usual as if this disaster was taking place eight thousand miles away. He wondered if people realized that the catastrophe was only thirty-five miles north, next door, down the street, a jaunt. Trace was fully immersed. He'd been in the plant and now on the outside. He felt the fear of being a civilian surrounded by sensationalized press, alarms, sirens, smoke, steam, and destruction, but mostly the fear of not knowing exactly what was happening at Bear Mountain. Trace's buckled driveway was empty. He thought maybe Avi and Brooklyn were inside and Avi's car was stuck somewhere. Trace pulled the door release and turned to the cabbie. "I won't be long. And I'll give you that other two hundred when I get back in."

"Don't worry, sir. I wait for you."

"Thank you." Trace exited and scurried along the concrete path winding through the grass between the trees to the crimson veranda. He was grateful his home hadn't completely collapsed. Unsure of his home's stability, he stepped gingerly onto the veranda steps and used the cream railing to ascend. He reached the front doors and noticed the right one wasn't closed all the way. *Was it ajar from the quake or had Avi been home? Did someone break in?* He put his shoulder into it and the door popped open. Trace stepped inside. Glass and ceramic crunched under his shoes. *Wow.*

To his left he saw Avi's partially collapsed office, plaster dust spread across the parquet as if it had been shot from an air gun. Trace looked in. "Avi!" She wasn't there. He went to the living room and saw their books spilled on the floor, the Blu-ray player dangling, DVDs and CDs scattered. Nothing that couldn't be cleaned up, nothing compared to her office. "Avi!" Trace walked back through the house into the kitchen. The cabinet doors were open, dishes and glass spilled across the hardwood. Antique chalices his mother-in-law had passed down from Avi's great-grandmother lay in fragments on the granite. His face flushed with heat. *Quake went for all the good stuff.* "Avi!" He couldn't deal with analyzing the destruction. The backyard was the only area that seemed the same as the morning before, untouched by the destruction. He wanted to lie in the hammock and hide.

Trace headed back to the front of his house and ascended the stairs. "Avi!" He reached the upstairs hall and tore into Brooklyn's room. Nothing. He rushed into his bedroom. "Avi." He checked the master bath. "Fuck!" He wondered if they had been there but hadn't seen any signs that Avi had been in the house when the quake happened or that she had returned after. She could've been in her office severely injured, but he hadn't seen blood. *Maybe it was covered with debris? Maybe she called 911 and an ambulance had come? No, she was dropping Brook off. Or was she?* He took his cell phone from his pocket, turned it on, and dialed her. "The caller you're trying to reach is unavailable. Please try your—" Trace hung up. "Fucking technology." *Home phone. Home phone!* He realized that he should've turned his mobile on in Manhattan where service was available. *You idiot!* All he had been thinking about was getting a cab and getting to Peekskill. *You're making too many mistakes.* He went to the cordless next to their bed and picked it up. *No dial tone. No dial tone? No... No power... No fucking power! NO POWER! That's my department. Christ!* He smashed the phone back into its cradle, took off out of the room, lumbered down the stairs, and jogged out to the front yard. "Fuck, fuck, fuck!" He recognized his neighbor Vijay's gunmetal Audi sedan coasting down the street. Trace trotted into the road, waving his arms. Vijay stopped and dropped his window.

"Trace?"

"Hey." Trace put his panic-ridden face through the window frame.

"What's going on? Shouldn't you be at the plant? Are you okay?"

Trace was certain he looked like a clown that had just come out of the psych ward with his bruising, dried bloody cuts, and television makeup he had never washed off. "Have you seen Avi and Brooklyn?"

Vijay pursed his lips. "No." He shook his head. "I just went to check on my warehouse. I was home all day yesterday, all night. Hadn't seen anyone come to your house."

"Shit. I… I'm trying to find them." Trace puffed out a breath. "I… Will you call me if you see them?"

"Of course. Certainly. Everything's closed out here. Nobody's at work. Some local stores are open. Food and such. But the shelves are bare. People are scared and just staying home with their families if their house didn't fall down. We took in some friends whose house collapsed. Sirens going all hours, fires burning. People are really worried about the nuclear plant. News says, 'stay inside with the windows and doors shut.' Lot of people skeptical about what's going on."

"I understand. We're doin' alright in there." *Are we? You've been exposed to a high level of radioactivity and you're wearin' protective whites under your suit.* "You have a pen and paper?"

Vijay reached into his center console and surfaced with both. Trace wrote down a phone number and handed it back to Vijay. "That'll get you to the control room."

"Okay. What's going on with the reactor? Is it okay or? I heard it's covered with coolant, but… And people say radiation has been released and…?"

"We got coolant circulating. The temperature should be on the decline." *Should be? I should be there. I should know! I need to get back.* "The situation is still concerning. We've got work to do, but we got it under control. And, yeah, radiation was released, not significant amounts, but some, a good amount. But…"

"Trace, you must tell me. Is my family safe here?"

Trace looked over his shoulder to the taxi. Then turned back and licked his dry lips and pressed them together. "Right now, yes. Anything changes for the worse, you'll see it on the news. Don't worry." Trace still wasn't sure he trusted his optimism. *Are you being honest with yourself?*

"Thank you. Thank you for what you do." Vijay grabbed Trace's left hand to avoid his bandaged right. "Take care of yourself. We wish you luck and we're behind you."

Trace watched Vijay drive off. He was unsure of where to go now. He figured Avi would go to a friend or relative's house or leave town and find a hotel. *That's if she's not dead or severely injured. Oh stop it! Michelle's, Paula's, Lea's, Dave's, Josh's?* Trace didn't know any of their numbers and only knew where a couple of them lived. *I could be driving around all day. What kind of husband am I?* He couldn't remember where Brooklyn's school was, but it was crazy to think she'd still be there. *Possible?* He didn't know where the paperwork was or what the phone number was. *Idiot! I should know this shit.* He felt like an awful father. Even though he had been physically absent, he had been emotionally available and supportive to Brooklyn, but he relied on Avi to have all the vital information. *I'm not THAT bad. I hope they're not separated. I hope my baby isn't alone. Avi must hate me right now—detest me.* He figured she'd divorce him when it all ended. *I don't blame her.* The disaster was the finale. *Drop the curtains.* He turned back to the taxi, entered, and thrust two hundred dollar bills forward to the driver. "Let's go."

CHAPTER 24

"Avi!" She heard Lea call after her as she ran to her SUV. "I'll be back... I'll be back," Avi yelled. She entered the vehicle, locked the doors, and started the engine. Lea tugged at the driver's side door handle. "Avi!" She pounded on the window. "You shouldn't be driving right now!"

"I'll be back." Avi threw her SUV in reverse and zoomed down the stone drive. Twenty-nine minutes later she crossed the Tappan Zee Bridge and turned north toward Peekskill. Twenty more minutes and she neared Buchanan. She was sad the Bear Mountain Bridge had collapsed because the route she had just taken to circumvent it made as much sense as driving from Connecticut to New York by way of Ohio.

Avi sped down a road near Bear Mountain, the plant a couple miles ahead. A few minutes later she saw roadblocks and police. She stepped on the brakes. It was a familiar scene and she wondered if any cops were present from the roadblock she blew through the day before or if there was an APB on her license plate number and the police in front of her would notice. *Fuck it.* She slowly approached the roadblock and dropped her window. "I'm trying to get through to Bear Mountain," she said to one of the officers.

"Roads to Bear Mountain are closed off. Big crisis going on in there." The officer stepped to Avi's window, arms across her burly chest. She was built like a square-jawed jiujitsu master. Avi was sure she could snap a tree with her attitude or use her musculature as a riot wall.

"My husband, he's one of the control-room supervisors. He's in there now and I haven't been able to get ahold of him. Is there any way to reach the inside of the plant?"

The cop shook her head. "Unfortunately, we don't have any direct communication with the plant."

"Is there another way for me to get through?"

"There isn't. Like I said, all access to the vicinity of the plant is closed off to the public."

"But my husband's in there. I told you that. Our daughter is missing. I need to see him. I can't get through on the phones."

"I'm sorry. Look…" The officer rested her hand on Avi's window sill. "There's nothin' I can do. Strict orders. I really wish I could."

"Can't you radio a supervisor or something?"

The officer raised her brows before putting her radio to her face. "Five twenty-one. We have a woman whose husband is a worker at Bear Mountain. She's here at block one looking to contact him. Please advise."

Static from the radio hissed. Avi stared at the black box waiting for fangs and a tongue to appear. SNAP! *Give me something!*

"Five twenty-one. Captain Willowby here. That area beyond the roadblock is restricted. Access only by personnel in radiological protective gear. No civilians can enter. Further, we have no direct communication with the interior. Unfortunately, I'd suggest she just wait it out. Understand he's in there workin', doin' what he has to do to help the reactor." The captain chirped off.

"Copy." The officer looked at Avi and pursed her lips. "Sorry, hon."

Avi sank dejectedly into her seat and rubbed her face with both her hands. Again the lack of empathy from an emergency worker befuddled her. She realized no one could understand the pain that pervaded her unless they were going through it or had gone through it themselves. Avi saw humanity as one and in a time of crisis she believed everyone needed to help each other instead of adhering to cold-hearted protocol. Lions stick with lions, zebra with zebra. *I'm an idiot for coming here! Why don't you try to find me, Trace? You should just leave that damn plant, focus on your family, and get us out of here!* She envisioned herself beating a punching bag with Trace's face on it. Did Trace love Bear Mountain more than her and Brooklyn? *Quit it!* Trace had a job to do. She knew his responsibility to the community. In the living room Trace twisted wire into a heart in front of Avi. "Each strand is a part of us winding together," he said, grinning. So much joy enveloped Avi's face that her cheeks met her eyes. The sunlight flooding the room brightened, Avi's jubilance amplifying the rays.

"It's beautiful." She kissed Trace's neck. Later, she put the heart on her nightstand so she could go to sleep and wake up with it there every day. After their relationship had spiraled into the abyss she buried the heart in a drawer under makeup. Now she envisioned the wire heart unwinding.

"Miss!" *Miss? Miss what? What did I miss? I miss our love.* Knock! Knock! Knock! "Miss!" She continued to hear the sound of heavy, blunt metal hitting glass and a muffled voice. "Miss!" Avi opened her eyes. "Miss, you gotta move it!" The police officer rapped her flashlight against the window. Avi realized she must've unconsciously pulled to the roadside and spaced out. *What's wrong with me?*

CHAPTER 25

*D*ecommission! DECOMMISSION! Decommission! DECOM-
MISSION! Down with nuclear! DOWN WITH Gener8! Down with
nuclear! DOWN WITH Gener8! The thundering call and response
from between the trees on the forest-lined road sounded like
a spear-wielding aboriginal war group approaching. Trace
listened to the chant through the cracked window. *Is it in my
head?* He looked at the sun-drenched canopy, cloudy white
beams in the fog rolling through the forest. A patrolled roadblock several thousand feet from the Bear Mountain Nuclear
Energy Center main entrance came into his view. The cabbie
slowed the Prius. Dozens of vans from every news outlet lined
the street, their satellite antennas sticking up above the trees
like a pack of giraffes. It was familiar to Trace. Activists had
been campaigning on and off for years regarding the relicens-
ing of reactors at Bear Mountain. He felt like a politician in an
armored car rolling up to the press, protestors, and barricade.
What an awful way to live.

Trace wondered if people realized the time and effort he
and his team put into providing electricity so they could live

modern lives without concern for the basics and luxuries: electric stoves to cook meals for their families; ovens to bake a holiday pie; curling irons and blow dryers to get ready for work or an evening; washing machines and dishwashers to keep their essentials clean; stereos to help assuage their emotions, get pumped, or drive a party; computers to communicate and make a living; mobile phones and tablets; the internet; video games; air conditioning and heating. All of it was possible because of Bear Mountain. The cell phones they used to record and up-load the protest had been charged on Bear Mountain's power.

A police officer came to the rear driver's side window of the cab. Trace lowered it and showed his Bear Mountain badge. The officer nodded, tapped on the car, and waved to his counterparts to open the barricade and let Trace through.

The cabbie tipped his eyes at Trace in the rearview mirror. "This safe up here?" he asked. Trace locked eyes with him.

"Absolutely." The cabbie would only be there for a moment, thus exposing him to a minuscule amount of radiation that wouldn't cause any health concerns or even be noticed. The taxi pushed forward. A silver SUV similar to Avi's passed by. *Now you're really dreamin'.* "Wait. Stop!" Trace yelped. The cab-bie stamped on the brakes. Trace lurched forward and braced himself against the plexiglass wall. He tore his door open and ran after the SUV. He reached the accelerating vehicle and pounded on the rear window. "Avi! Stop! Avi!" The SUV bucked to a hard skid. Trace smacked into the back corner and spun around before scurrying to the driver's window. He saw Avi inside. Her brows lifted so high they would've left the atmo-sphere if they weren't attached to her face. Trace tugged at the door handle. "Open the door!" She flailed her hands across the door trying to figure out how to open it. Finally, she unlocked it and Trace ripped it open. They dove into each other's arms. "Oh my god, Trace," she squealed.

"I love you, honey." Trace kissed her neck and face. "I'm so glad to see you. Oh my god. I've been worried."

She choked out words. "I saw you on the news and... and..."

"Where's Brooklyn?"

Avi put a hand to her mouth. "I don't know. I've been looking for her."

"She's missing?"

Avi nodded.

"Jesus," he gasped. "You went to the school? And..."

"Yes. Yesterday. The school was damaged, everyone evacuated. I've checked hospitals and shelters. I went home."

Trace ran his hands through his hair. *My girl. Where is she? The school staff must have her somewhere. Unless she's hurt?* He pulled back from Avi so their chests were no longer touching. He was afraid his suit might not be enough to protect her from his radiation exposure. Nothing was enough when it came to protecting his wife. He wanted to tell her about his exposure, wanted to tell *somebody* because he had told no one, but he didn't want to upset her any further nor rouse alarm that something might be wrong with him.

"The house is destroyed," Avi said.

"I know. I was just there looking for both of you."

Avi locked eyes with Trace. "You were?"

"Yes. Of course. Where do you think Brooklyn is?"

"I don't know. Shelter, hospital, with other children's parents, morgue, buried in the rubble."

Trace let out a breath.

"Miss, I told you. You gotta clear this roadway!" The female officer approached, pulling Trace and Avi from their reunion. *The hell is this woman...* Trace held his Bear Mountain badge up, stopping her. "She's my wife. We'll be outta your way in a minute," he boomed.

The officer acquiesced. "Alright."

"What's going on inside?" Avi asked.

"Was chaos yesterday. This morning things are looking pretty good. We may be stabilizing."

"We need to find our baby, Trace."

Trace nodded. "What happened to your head and your chest and neck?"

"A shelf fell on me at the grocery store. That redness, I don't know. I spent the night at Lea's house."

Trace brushed Avi's cheek.

"Get in the car. We need to find Brook," Avi said.

Trace looked back toward the plant. He saw the cabbie staring, at him wondering if he should stay or go. Trace turned back to Avi. *Find Brook or stay here? Find Brook or stay here? Find Brook or stay here? You have a job to do. So what? Your family's more important.* Anxiety rose inside him, his heart thrummed against his ribs. "You have to know they'll probably arrest me later and certainly fire me if I go."

"She's worth it," Avi said.

"Slide over. I'll drive," Trace said. Avi scooted to the passenger seat. Trace plopped down in the driver's seat and shut the door. He touched the gas. A moment later he heard pounding on the rear driver's side glass. "Trace!" He hit the brakes and saw an Bear Mountain security guard in full radiation whites at his window. *Dammit.* Trace dropped the glass.

"Control room's looking for ya," the guard said. "They said something about a bubble. They got an issue in there they need you on. I've been looking for you and Bramini for an hour. Caught wind on the radio you were out here requestin' entry in a taxi."

"Bubble?"

"Yeah, that's all they said and it didn't sound good."

Trace stared at the guard. *Hydrogen bubble. Can't be. Could it?* "Give me a minute."

The guard nodded and retreated. Trace turned to Avi. She

shook her head repeatedly.

Trace grabbed her hand. "I have to…"

Avi pulled her hand back. Trace reached for her.

"Don't. Don't!" she snapped, waving her finger at him.

"I'm responsible here. You understand, don't you?"

"It's always the plant before us. Always! Brook's missing. What the hell else do you need to happen!"

"Babe. Listen. Please. This is hard for me, too. Very hard for me to sit in there while you and Brook are out here… But this's serious and you know it. I have a community to worry about here. This ain't some finance job. This is the frontline of war. This's tearin' me apart inside, but I don't have a choice."

She shuddered. "I know. I know. I know you're right. But where do you draw the line. Where do you give in and take your family and run?"

Trace shook his head. "I don't know. I really don't know. I signed on to serve the community. When you do that you give up a part of yourself and your family."

Avi swallowed back her resentment. Talk about a quandary. This was a conundrum of mammoth proportions. Trace was stuck between public safety and his wife and daughter. *Do I wanna get eaten by the alligator or the crocodile?* "Stay in touch through the control-room direct line." He scribbled it down on a pad from the center console. "Either that or emergency management. Let me know when you find her." He coughed. Avi was okay. Knowing that, he could move forward, but Brooklyn missing eviscerated him. He had confidence that Avi would find her. She was tenacious, smart, resourceful. He was sure his wife could handle it, but what worried him was that Brooklyn was injured or dead. Trace pulled Avi in, hugged and kissed her. "I love you. You find our girl and I'm gonna stabilize this reactor and be with you both soon, okay?"

Avi nodded into his shoulder dejectedly. "Okay."

CHAPTER 26

When Trace stepped into the control room the hydrogen-detection alarm felt like a hammer drill playing staccato thirty-second notes on his skull. He saw Jerry and Valdern watching the monitors from behind their full-face respirator masks and radiation whites. The plant was more crowded than ever with more than a hundred personnel from the NRC, EPA, and DOE having arrived on site. All twenty-plus crew inside the control room wore the same suits, white-vinyl figures moving in slow motion performing futuristic surgery on an entity from another galaxy. Between the seventies decor, the radiation suits, and his delirium Trace felt like he was watching a skewed rendition of *2001: A Space Odyssey*. Presage crept up Trace's neck and his skull in a warm tingle. His pulse beat in his fingers. Faster… faster… He tromped to the console. "What's happened?"

"We have a hydrogen buildup detected inside the reactor," Jerry said.

"Where?"

"Top of the pressurizer," Jerry said.

Trace closed his eyes. His face flushed with heat. He was immediately furious for acquiescing to Ken for the *Today Show* and leaving the control room. *You imbecile! You should've been here to watch this.* There was no guarantee that he would've known about the hydrogen earlier or have been able to do anything about it. *You shouldn't've even tried to go to sleep. You should've been here with coffee in your hand and your eyes glued to the gauges!* Trace was again livid Ken had ordered the closing of the reactor containment vents. Before Trace had gone to sleep he had believed the core was covering with coolant. He had told the public just a few hours ago they were nearing a path to cold shutdown. *How could I be so brazen? How could I lie? You didn't know...* Trace had thought he was going to return to smiling faces, his men kicking back in their chairs, hands behind their heads, watching the reactor's temperature dropping. Sure there would be other obstacles to navigate with the continued need to vent to bring the reactor stable, but Trace never expected a hydrogen bubble. The gap between the state he thought the reactor was in and cold shutdown had seemed like a jaunt from L.A. to Vegas. Now he had a mission from Earth to Venus. A pressure cooker of reactive gas brimmed. "How could this happen? I thought the core was covered."

"Superheated steam," Valdern said, staring at Trace. If he had fangs he would've sucked Trace dry. "You were here late, Crane. The telltale would've been that the temperature wasn't dropping at all. You shoulda picked up on that."

"I did... I did... It... Ffffuck... I figured it needed time to decrease. I figured now by morning we'd see the change."

"I told you this yesterday. You didn't wanna listen goddammit!"

"Oh bullshit. You weren't a hundred percent on it!"

"Well at least I thought of it. And where the fuck you been anyway? Gary said he saw your ass on the mornin' news. What the fuck is that?"

"Bramini pulled me aside before you all got up. Not my idea."

Valdern's lips crinkled in disgust behind his mask.

How could I not think about the steam? Valdern was right. The reactor was so hot water inside had become superheated steam, thus keeping actual water out of the core and pushing the water gauge up, giving them a false coolant reading. Dealing with a malfunctioning reactor was like flying a plane remotely from the ground on instruments during a storm with no visibility of the aircraft in the sky. Trace began to question his adequacy for his position. *Valdern should've had it.* Guilt washed over him. *My head is a fucking dust cloud. Get it together!* "Jerry, let's try and decrease pressure again." Trace pushed his respirator up and guzzled his coffee.

"Trace!" Jerry said, referring to Trace removing his respirator and drinking inside the contaminated room. "Don't worry about it, Jerry. I'm fine." Trace coughed. No one but Gary Harrell knew Trace had been severely contaminated with radiation. A few more millirem didn't matter the least bit, and the coffee was well worth it. "Decrease that pressure, Jerry."

"Decreasing," Jerry confirmed.

Trace couldn't believe how overly optimistic he had been. He had trusted the machine and the reactor had fooled him like a sweet-talking panhandler. The behemoth had become his adversary. *How could you after I've treated you so well?* He closed his eyes and breathed deeply, trying to calm himself. Brooklyn blew bubbles from a wand while she sat in the bathtub. Her giggles reflecting off the tile walls of the room enraptured him. *Shame she can't blow this one away.* His eyes rolled open to the monitors in front of him. "Damn, damn, damn. Bubble is expanding. Go back up."

"Increasing," Jerry said.

"Crane!" Valdern boomed. "You know what the fuck you're doin'?"

Trace found Valdern's face scrunched, his eyes flaring.

"Seriously, Crane. You're fucking with hydrogen. Whaddayou think you're tryin' to do going up and down in the pressurizer?"

"I'm trying to get water in the fucking pressure vessel. It's barely ten in the fucking morning and you're startin' already? Jesus Christ, man."

"You're playin' with fire," Valdern said.

"Actually, he's playing with hydrogen," Jerry said.

Valdern glared at Jerry.

"We gotta try somethin'. You have other suggestions, lemme know," Trace said to Valdern. He dialed Ken Bramini from the desk phone.

"Yeah?" Ken answered.

"We have a hydrogen bubble at the top of the pressure vessel," Trace said.

"Crane?"

"Yep."

"Where the fuck have you been? We're still in Manhattan waitin' for you. Where the fuck did you go? We got the cops here and everything. Jesus fucking Christ!"

Trace pulled the receiver back from his ear. He could feel Ken's rage through the line. "I came back to the plant. I couldn't find you guys."

"You went to the fucking bathroom and never came back!"

"I don't know. All I know is I took a taxi and I'm here and we got a hydrogen bubble."

"Christ. I thought the core was…"

"Covered… Yeah, me too. Turns out we have superheated steam giving us false readings on the coolant gauges."

"Unbelievable!"

"Yeah. Hydrogen detectors were going off when I returned. We currently have about three percent at the top of the vessel."

"From what?"

"By-product of the zirconium fuel rods melting," Trace said. "I told you we hadda melt!"

"You need to get coolant through the vessel now!"

"No shit. Coolant's too low to get high-pressure pumps to circulate. When we inject coolant it flashes to steam because we're superheated."

"Drop pressure, then. What about the emergency pumps?"

"We have. It causes the bubble to expand. Hydrogen is already at three percent. We hit between four and six and we risk explosion."

"Is there oxygen around the core?"

"Some, yes."

"How?"

"I'm assuming we have cracks in the pressure vessel or piping."

"You should've never cut the high-pressure pumps in the first place," Valdern interjected.

Trace's eyes flared. "Really. We were going solid. Systems are fucked up. Shouldn't've cut the pumps. Pffff... C'mon. Who's fucking team are you on?" He put the phone back to his mouth. "What we shouldn't've stopped was venting."

"The governor is on our backs. What... Look. Do what you gotta do, but keep it quiet."

"Are you asking me to lie?"

"Lie? No. I'm askin' you and everyone else to keep their mouths shut about what we're doing there because people on the outside don't get it. They see steam and think it's a radioactive plume. Then they overreact."

"Fine. But you do realize if we open the vents at some point everyone *will* see the steam in the sky? Doesn't make any sense.

You should've never pulled me out to Manhattan this morning. I coulda been in here and possibly avoided this shit. Now we've been on national TV telling everyone everything's okay, don't worry, no big deal, there's coolant around the core. Look at it now!"

"That's on you, Trace. You told us there was coolant around the core."

Trace's facial muscles hardened with such tension they trembled. Rage flashed in waves of heat from his shoulders to his neck to his face. He felt murderous. If Ken was in front of him he'd strangle and beat him until his hands broke. Then he'd string himself up. *My fault... My fault!*

"I'm on my way in," Ken said.

Trace put the phone down and stared at Valdern. "When you've got constructive solutions and not criticism, lemme know. Until then have some goddamn respect. Jerry, what're our readings outside containment at ground level?"

Jerry checked the digital readout. "Seven hundred rem."

"Seven hundred?"

"Seven hundred," Jerry confirmed.

Radiation was passing straight through four-foot-thick concrete and half-inch steel. Trace realized the core had been melting since yesterday and had never stopped. Saving them from a full melt was the minuscule amount of coolant circulating in the core, not nearly enough to come close to cooling the reactor. It was a trout fishing line holding a shark; one twist and it'd snap.

Trace saw Skip Sinclair ripping his respirator mask off, his shoulders bouncing, tears dripping from his wan face. "The hell you doin'?" Trace said. Skip shook his head and choked on his words.

"We're all gonna fuckin' die in here."

Trace moved to Skip and grabbed him at his arms. "We're

gonna be fine." Trace rattled him. Skip looked down, his body trembling. "Look at me," Trace said. "Look at me."

Skip turned his reddened, wet eyes up.

"We gotchu man, don't worry. We need you in here, stable. Alright?"

Trace cracked open a soda from a nearby desk. "Here. Guzzle that. Your sugar's probably low. Makin' your head crazy."

Skip took the soda and downed most of it. Trace took the can from him and set it back to the desk. "Put that mask back on or you're really gonna be in trouble." Skip nodded, continuing to choke back tears. Trace massaged his shoulders and biceps from the front. "You're good, alright? Look at me again."

Skip locked eyes with Trace.

"I'm not gonna let anything happen to you or anyone else in this plant. Believe that. Go take a seat for a minute." Trace pointed to a desk chair. Skip complied.

Trace turned back to the front control-console wall and wondered if his job was worth it. He had given all his days, his energy, his entire adult existence to nuclear. Every time he had questioned his career something had burned inside him that said it mattered. He was performing public service by sending electricity into his community. No matter their gender or age, anytime someone had asked Trace what he did for a living and he had told them he was a nuclear engineer their eyes danced. People immediately thought he was a genius, a rare organism that they had the honor of getting a glimpse of. He was an annual night-blooming flower, an albino tiger. 'Oh, look you're one of them. Wow. What do you do?' Sometimes he'd encounter skeptics or adversaries and they'd interrogate him about Fukushima, Three Mile Island, and what-ifs about Bear Mountain. All those people made the job worthwhile and kept him going. The job was about people. It was about community. *It has nothing to do with me anymore. Of course it's worth it. What you're doing matters. You can get through this. You've made it this far. Put your head down and plow.* Trace would rather die trying than let the tristate area be destroyed.

CHAPTER 27

*Y*ou know what I need? I need a burger. Something greasy with *Gruyère, bacon, and pickles. That'd fix my stomach right about now.* Trace drained sixteen ounces of coffee into his cup from an urn sitting on the oak-veneer conference table inside the emergency-operations building nerve center. One urn read 'decaf.' *Who the fuck brews decaf for a nuclear disaster?* Trace had shed his radiation suit for the clean environment of the building, which he was surprised existed considering the release. At least one ventilation system was working as it should. His button-up was partly tucked in the back of his pants, shirt-tails hanging over the front, revealing the bottom of his gut. His facility badge attached to its lanyard hung over his back. His hair was matted. He scratched at the light stubble on his cheeks and the burning psoriasis on his nose, attempting to avoid the tender, bruised patches near his jawline. When Trace had stepped into the control room earlier, the news about the hydrogen bubble was like hearing about a complication during a surgery Avi had had. *There's an issue. We're not sure what may*

transpire. She's touch and go. We're hoping for the best. But when I
had gone to bed she was okay... I should've been in the control room.

Trace took a seat at the conference table and stared at the wall. The news in the background seeped into his subconscious. "Many hydrants are ruptured throughout the city. Many firefighters don't have adequate water to battle fires. Law enforcement has reported two murders—a carjacking where a man was stabbed and a road-rage incident where a man was shot. They've also arrested and detained another nine for various incidents. Local hospitals are reporting three children born yesterday. One was delivered in a car stuck on the highway on the way to the hospital.

"This just in. Reports of half a dozen people being admitted to local hospitals with radiation burns." Trace turned to the large flat-screen TVs at the head of the room. All the emergency-operations staff stopped what they were doing, increased the volume, and watched from their partitioned desks. The newscaster continued, "The victims are believed to be residents of Peekskill." *Avi? No. You just saw her.* "Sources are claiming radiation has been released from the ailing nuclear reactor and isotopes are floating over the Hudson Valley. Gener8, the governor's office, and the NRC have stated that the release of radioactivity from Bear Mountain is not a threat to public health and is well below federal limits. Outside sources say we should be deeply concerned. We have Cal Zumsteg with the Union of Concerned Scientists here in the studio. Cal, tell us. Do you think these residents received the radioactive burns from fallout that came from Bear Mountain?"

"Hi, Patrick. Yes, it is very possible. If you recall last night we had rain. That rain could potentially bring an abundance of those floating isotopes straight down to the ground surface and have the potential to burn your skin with the right alignment of factors."

"Turn it down," Ken barked when he burst in with Valdern, Jerry, Harvey Asner from the NRC, and other crew. "Turn that shit off and pull up the conference images."

Trace didn't see how radiological burns were possible unless the release concentrated in one area undetected before the rain. *Potential cracks in containment? Wastewater in the Hudson? Gases escaping out of auxiliary? Everything together? Things are really spiraling now. A bubble. Public radiation exposure. It's all over for us. I'm responsible...* Good god I'm responsible... Devastation came in a draining sensation to his stomach. He hoped the burns were a false alarm and doctors would figure out that the civilian health issues were from stress and anxiety. Trace needed to communicate with his ground crew again. But they only had one testing van operational and had to rely on the EPA, NRC, and other agencies for their assistance in monitoring the environment. Even still, it was nearly impossible without hundreds of people and testing vehicles to analyze every acre of the surrounding area. Finding radiation pockets was like ghost hunting—wisps of invisible matter tucking into corners.

Everyone filed around the conference table—lethargic bodies hunched over steaming mugs and Styrofoam cups. Ken Bramini was the only one upright and rigid. Several scientists from consultant firms, national nuclear labs, research institutes, universities, and the reactor manufacturer appeared on the videoconference screens at the head of the room. Others said hello on the speakerphone at the center of the table. Everyone had his glasses on, pens at the ready. Trace danced his fingers on the wood veneer. *Now we're in the thick of it. The brains are here. Everybody's gonna piss in the bucket, see who's got the best range.*

"Let's talk about the bubble," Ken Bramini said.

"Bubb-ulls," Jerry said.

"And not like the chimp," Trace said.

"What is this, a fucking joke?" Ken said.

"We haven't slept much, Ken, relax." Trace went to the dry-erase board at the rear of the room and drew a large, vertical capsule that represented the reactor. "That's the pressure vessel," Trace said. Inside the top of the capsule he drew a large bubble. "That's the hydrogen buildup."

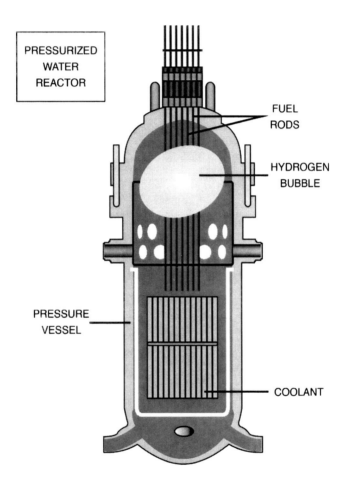

PRESSURIZED
WATER
REACTOR

FUEL
RODS

HYDROGEN
BUBBLE

PRESSURE
VESSEL

COOLANT

"How the hell did we get a bubble to begin with?" Ken said.

"Well—" Trace started.

"It's 'cause Crane had us shut all the pumps down," Valdern interjected.

Trace glared at Valdern. "That's ridiculous."

"You're no navy man, Crane. I worked on those ships for years."

"That's bullshit!" Trace snapped back.

"Is it? Only reason you're in charge is 'cause you went to that fancy-ass school."

"If you're up for the task, Val, step up," Trace said.

"Gentleman," Ken barked. "We have a bubble in the core. Y'all can take it out in the yard later."

Trace pointed to his reactor sketch. "When we try to lower pressure to get ECCS to kick on the bubble expands." He drew a larger blob at the top of the vessel. "We're at three percent hydrogen right now. We hit between four and six percent with the amount of oxygen we have present and our chances of combustion are extremely high, a pin sittin' against a balloon. Since coolant has been leaking from the vessel, it's possible we have a breach and oxygen may be slipping into the vessel."

"Can't you vent the hydrogen from the core into containment and hold it there?" a physicist on the TV conference screen said.

Trace shot a sidelong glance to the bespectacled man on the TV at the head of the room. *Did he seriously just ask that?* "There's oxygen in the containment atmosphere." Trace turned his hands up. "We do that we risk explosion."

"Hold on. Containment is so large that the amount of hydrogen released to it would be trivial," Harvey Asner from the NRC said. "Also, combustion is unlikely because the hydrogen has no ignition source."

Trace returned to his chair. "The oxygen *is* the ignition source. Considering the temperature inside the reactor right now it's very possible."

"Why don't we do a controlled burn?" Ken said.

"Even if the hydrogen just burned the pressure pulse created could compromise the reactor vessel. It's essentially an explosion," Trace said. "If the vessel is fractured then a breach of containment *is* likely."

"You could blow down the system and push the bubble out," one of the scientists on speakerphone said.

"Ridiculous." Trace leaned back in his chair. "We blow all the coolant out of the core and then the fuel starts to heat at three to six degrees a second. We'd have twenty minutes max to fill 'er back up or we'd have a full melt. You might as well evacuate to Colorado."

Ken rubbed his freckled head. "What do you suggest, then?"

"We use a valve in auxiliary that is part of the safety injection system, which will let the hydrogen pass from the top of the pressure vessel directly into a sealed tank in auxiliary where we can filter and burp it out."

Ken's brow furrowed into a deprecating abyss. "What, are you insane? No one can go inside auxiliary to turn that valve; they'd be overexposed in less than a minute. We've got radioactive water all over the place."

"It wouldn't be anything instantly deadly," Trace said.

"Well. There you go. Who the hell's going to *slowly* kill themselves for this?"

"I'll do it." Trace said quietly. He certainly wasn't going to tell them yet that he had already taken in over a thousand rem. Everyone in the room fixed their gazes on Trace.

"That's ridiculous. Like I said, you'll be overexposed almost immediately," Ken said.

"But it won't kill me," Trace said.

"Yeah… not right away…"

"Whaddaya think, Val? Good way to get rid of me, right?"

"Ain't nobody wanna see you die, even me. It's a noble move, but stupid," Valdern said.

"Noble move to vent noble gas," Jerry said.

Trace chuckled. "Christ you're on a roll. Too bad hydrogen isn't a noble gas."

"Yep… Sorry, guys." Jerry sat back.

Ken looked at Trace. "I'm not authorizing you to do that. Hell no. Completely against all policies. Absolutely no way it's happening."

"We don't have any other options," Trace pleaded. "We've tried natural convection, forced circulation. We've steamed and liquided out the pressurizer… We've tried to push the bubble through the makeup and letdown system, but the valves failed. Nothing's worked."

"I say we blow the system down and push the bubble out. It's the most expeditious option," Ken said.

"Then you better start evacuating now. It's going to blow up in your face," Trace said. "We gotta make the right decision here. You were on national TV telling people we're on the path to cold shutdown, sittin' there smilin' like everything's good."

"You were there, too, Crane. I wasn't moving your mouth."

Trace pictured himself slicing a knife into the crevasses on Ken's face, tying him to his chair, and leaving him to drain. "I was following you and Barnes' optimism when I shoulda been in the control room watching the reactor!"

Everyone in the room and the scientists on the TVs sat uncomfortably in silence.

"I heard it before. Cut the bullshit. The blowdown is all that makes sense right now, and that's what we're gonna do."

"Again, ridiculous." Trace stood. The meeting was superfluous to him. He didn't need to hear everyone else's reckless ideas. He had figured it out, but for some reason everyone needed to speak to justify their existence. No one could ever just say, 'Yeah. That's it. Let's do it.' "I've given you a solution. Again, Ken, don't put me in charge and then pretend I'm not. You guys are fucking reckless. RECKLESS!" Trace kicked his chair, sending it crashing into the wall. "Do whatever you want. I'm done with this shit!" He stormed out of the room.

CHAPTER 28

Avi and Lea strode toward a shelter entrance at a school auditorium. The humidity in the air made Avi feel like she was walking through goo. It slowed her down, added to her lethargy. Adrenaline and caffeine in her system cut through in stabs of heightened awareness. She had slipped into a pair of black yoga pants and a lavender t-shirt Lea had given her. Lea had donned jeans and a white t-shirt, her hair freshly spiked. Avi's head bandage showed under her burnt umber locks. Her anger at Trace for not coming with her made her facial muscles so taut she thought she was creating permanent wrinkles in her skin. Since Brooklyn was missing she had trouble being rational and understanding Trace's position. In her mind nothing should be more important than their daughter and their family.

Red Cross and FEMA banners flapped against a moveable steel barricade that wrapped the perimeter, emergency crew with Geiger counters stood ready, paramedics tended to the injured, food and beverage rolled in, trash rolled out. The familiar setting petrified Avi—homeless families of all classes, elderly, handicapped, and injured, waiting in line to be checked in. Questions jutted from everyone's dismal, perplexed faces—why, how, what's next, when will it all be over? Hearing the news of a radioactive release from the plant was still clattering in Avi's head. Even though Gener8 and the governor had reported the release would not exceed federal limits, she didn't feel secure. She believed no amount of radiation was safe beyond what organisms received naturally from their existence on Earth. She was sure nuclear and environmental agencies couldn't test every square foot of land space or every stream of air. A high level of isotopes could be lurking just down the road from a negligible level. The juxtaposition between her work in advanced renewable energy technologies and the disaster fascinated and infuriated her. *Maybe people will listen to me now!* Avi desperately hoped Brooklyn was inside.

"I can do the talking," Lea said.

"Thanks," Avi said. They approached a fifty-something male crewmember. "Hello." Avi saw Mel on his name tag, which reminded her of her grandfather. "Checking in?" Mel asked.

"No, just looking for her daughter. She would've come in with the Blue Mountain Academy from Peekskill," Lea said.

"Okay."

"Have you seen her?" Avi showed the man Brooklyn's picture on her smartphone.

Mel shook his head. "Can't say that I have."

"Do you know if her school has come here?" Lea asked.

"Not sure. There's definitely a bunch of kids in there," Mel said with the compassion of someone giving directions to a liquor store.

"Do you have a list of check-ins?" Avi asked.

"The perrrrrson with the logs from yesterday is taking a break. Honestly. Honestly. Honestly, I'd say best thing to do is go in and take a look. We just have to have you—"

Avi interjected snidely, "—scanned by the radiation detector. Then you go through security and that's it!" She ended with a grin.

"Yes," Mel said. "Very good."

"Right." Avi rolled her eyes. *Damn this process!* She was tired of uncaring responses, body scans, and bag searchers. *Am I a criminal for trying to find my daughter?* Meanwhile, she was certain somebody had snuck into a shelter with drugs, a gun, and a knife. *Anyone giving jaywalking tickets this weekend? Ridiculous.*

"Roger." Mel waved to an early-thirties Korean-English man in black shorts and a blue paramedics t-shirt. Roger approached. "Wand 'em up," Mel said.

Roger waved his Geiger over Lea from head to toe. "Good." He started on Avi at the top of her head. When he reached the lower portion of her face the Geiger counter blipped. Roger stopped and held the wand steady.

"What's that?" Avi said.

"Well… It's… hmm…" Roger checked the Geiger box. He moved the wand over Avi's lower face, neck, and upper chest. The Geiger blipped rapidly.

"What's happening?" Avi asked.

"What's this rash?" Roger asked.

"Stress."

"Hmmm…" Roger checked the Geiger box again. "Have you been exposed to any radioactive material?"

"What? No. What kind of question is that? I didn't shoot JFK either."

"It's a stress rash," Lea said. "Her daughter's been missing since yesterday and her husband works at Bear Mountain."

"Have you been in contact with your husband?" Roger asked.

"No. He works at the plant. How am I gonna be in contact with him? I haven't seen him since yesterday morning before the quake." *I'm not telling this guy anything. I had the rash before I saw Trace earlier today anyway. But could he have transferred radiation to me?*

"It's a stress rash," Lea said. "I'm an RN. I know."

"The Geiger is picking up on it. When did you notice the rash?"

"This morning," Avi said with dead eyes.

"Okay. Step over this way for me. Follow me," Roger said.

Avi strapped her arms across her chest and stood still.

"C'mon." Roger waved. "This'll only take a minute."

Avi's lip curled, her face dismal. *Everything's a minute around here. My four-year-old is scared and alone. 'No problem. Can we see some ID first?' Let me make you wait and ask you a bunch of superfluous questions.* Avi and Lea reluctantly followed Roger to a tented area containing additional crew, testing devices, and medical equipment. "What are we doing?" Avi asked.

"I wanna try this other Geiger on you." Roger took it from a stainless table.

"What is this research and development?" Avi jibed.

"Just stay with me here. It'll only take a second to make sure you're all good." Roger turned the machine on. The snap of the dial and the electronic whine of the device sent a pang though Avi's gut.

"Okay." Roger ran the wand over Avi's rash. The Geiger blipped rapidly. "Yup. As I thought. You've been exposed to something, miss. Have a seat here." He pointed to the sheeted gurney.

Avi stayed standing. "How could I be exposed? This is ridiculous. I've gone nowhere near Bear Mountain." *That can't be it. Everyone there would've been in radiation suits if it was a problem. Trace wouldn't've hugged me.*

"Can't be," Lea said.

Roger waved over one of his paramedic counterparts. "Hey, Jordie. Can you take a look at this please?"

Jordie was a smooth-faced, early-forties Dominican that

looked like he moonlighted as an underwear model. *If it's the rash then it's definitely not from Trace. But what if I had the rash and then radiation was transferred to that area from him or from being near the plant. Too coincidental. Doesn't make sense.*

"I'm getting a gamma reading from her rash," Roger said to Jordie.

"Let's see."

Roger waved the Geiger wand over Avi again. The machine blipped.

"Yep," Jordie said. "Do you have any idea how you may've been exposed to radioactive material?"

"No," Avi said. "I haven't been. This doesn't make sense. I… I had radiation therapy for breast cancer a few years ago, but that was on my left side."

"I understand. Yeah… that's definitely not it. We're gonna need to transport you to the hospital for further evaluation. We need to make sure the contamination isn't systemic and the hospital can treat your infected area."

"I'm not going anywhere. I'm here to find my daughter. I don't have time for this."

"Miss, we understand, but you clearly've had exposure to radioactive material and need to be further evaluated. We can't let you inside the shelter. This is for your own good."

My own good? Jordie turned around with plastic, gauze, and tape in his hands. "Have a seat so I can cover the area and then we can get you on your way."

Avi recoiled and marched out of the medic tent. "C'mon, Lea."

"Miss, you can't…" Jordie pursued her. His gloved hand latched onto Avi's wrist.

"Get off me!" She wrestled against him.

"Miss. We need to take you in."

"No!"

"Security to triage. Security to triage," Jordie squawked

into his radio.

"Get—Off—Of—Me!" Avi screamed.

He followed her. "Miss. This is for your own health and safety."

"Avi, wait." Lea held her hands up.

Avi turned back. "C'mon."

A policewoman arrived, her ponytail of ebony braids pulled so tight to her crown her penciled eyebrows arched. "We may need to restrain her," Jordie said.

"Brooklyn, Lea. I need to go inside." She turned to the medics. "I need to go inside," she said sternly, glaring. The policewoman gripped Avi's arms.

"Miss, we need you to take a seat and follow the medic's instructions."

"My daughter," Avi wailed. "Dammit! Get the hell off of me!"

"Avi. Go with them. I'll go inside. Just go with them," Lea said.

"Lea…" Avi cried. "Lea! What the fuck is this? Let go of me!" Avi wrestled against the policewoman. "How dare you!"

"Miss. Don't make me have to arrest you. We understand what you're saying, but you need to follow the medic's instructions first."

"Bullshit!" Avi screamed.

Roger spoke into his radio. "Kisco Medical Center this is triage at Kisco Elementary shelter. We're coming in with a radiation burn. Copy?"

"That's a copy. Team will be ready to receive. Over."

"Go," Lea said. "Just go, Avi. I'll look for Brooklyn. Then I'll come find you at the hospital. Tears traced tributaries on Avi's face. Lea turned around. "Go! Don't be stupid. I'll be right there to find you."

The policewoman and the medics pushed Avi's body back onto the gurney, her tearful gaze still on Lea walking toward the shelter entrance. *Why is this happening to me? Why? Why!*

This better not be from you, Trace! Avi wriggled against the hands latching onto her. "Miss, relax and calm down. Relax!" Thoughts of going to the hospital petrified her. With everyone surrounding her she felt like a mental patient being taken unwillingly. "Relax. Lie down. Lie down!" Again she wondered where the compassion of the emergency workers had gone—wondered if it had ever existed. She was a mother who hadn't seen her young daughter in over twenty-four hours during one of the worst disasters in U.S. history. *How could they not understand?* Avi hoped Brooklyn was inside and Lea would find her and bring her to the hospital where she was headed. Then they'd all leave town.

"Get off me!" They thrust Avi into the ambulance, the doors slamming at her feet.

CHAPTER 29

Trace sat against a wall inside a hallway of the control-room building enclosed by blast-resistant, gas-tight doors. His head throbbed, his hand burned, his radiation suit and respirator making him feel acutely claustrophobic. He closed his eyes and listened to the clanging pipes overhead, wondering if there was an encoded message in the noise. He was trying to deduce logic from the bubble meeting he'd had inside the operations center earlier. He couldn't accept the decisions that were being made by a team of 'experts.' Trace was over it. Fed up. Done. He felt he should've gone with Avi. *Why should I stay? I'm dying from the inside anyway. What's it gonna matter? There're other guys here that can do what I'm doing. Fucking up... That's what I'm doing. Dammit you took this job on. You knew the responsibility.* A soldier wouldn't stop fighting because he couldn't get his family on the phone. The soldier had taken an oath to serve as had Trace. *You have a responsibility to this community.* Trace suddenly felt Brooklyn was in trouble. *She's hurt.* He sensed her soul crying out. *It's all in your head. I think I can feel her. No! She's fine.*

ABC, CBS, FOX, CNN all wanted to talk. The *New York*

Times, the *Wall Street Journal*, the *Daily News, USA Today*. Anything new? Any updates? How can we help? There was a celebrity offering a machine that supposedly could filter the air of towns around the plant in case of a heavy radioactive release. If the reactor suffered a hydrogen explosion the ramifications would be devastating. People would need to be evacuated. *That bubble pops, we're done. I'm done.* Everything Trace cared about sat under a guillotine—fate holding the rope. He and his team had to be precise and confident with the bubble mitigation. Before the bubble meeting Trace heard Hanson had died due to head trauma and radioactive coolant entering his mouth, poisoning his body. *I should've never asked him to take that core sample.* His children were now without a father, his wife without her husband. A tear dripped from Trace's eye. *This is too much.*

The squeal of the iron wheel-lock door opening raised Trace's head. *Can't get a damn minute alone!* Clyde poked his head into the corridor. "Hey, a nuclear physicist from Yale is on the line for you and an engineer from Germany called earlier—" Trace raised his hand to stop Clyde from talking. Over the past twenty-four hours the longest the control-room phone didn't ring was four minutes. Trace had heard from almost every agency, political and environmental office in the country—NRC, DOE, EPA, USDA, FEMA, DHS, Red Cross, NRDC, Union of Concerned Scientists, Riverkeeper, academic scientists, activists, Governor Pagano, and the White House. Even international associates called. Everyone wanted answers, everyone had suggestions, but no one was fixing his problems. "Take a message from everyone. I don't wanna talk to anyone else or hear anyone's suggestions."

Clyde nodded. "And… local channel six is looking for info… and a radio station has called… daily news and…"

"How the fuck?… Tell them to call fucking publicity at headquarters. How in the hell are they getting through to the control room!" The media was looking for any little strand they could latch onto. A disaster acting as a major revenue generator for the media sickened him. More papers sold, more traffic visited their websites, more people watched their telecasts and listened to their radio broadcasts. Later all the data would be quantified and used to sell advertising. He thought journalists should be more compassionate, put their microphones down, suit up, and help emergency teams. Clyde exited. The latch of the iron door returned solace to Trace in the form of solitude.

Trace realized he hadn't considered the bubble because he had followed Ken's plans and not his own. *This is why I never played by the rules. Rules box you in, strap you down. Rules give you a hydrogen bubble.* Most weeks Trace put in fifty to sixty hours and some weeks, especially during maintenance and refueling, he put in seventy-two hours or more. His life was the power plant. He was a fuel rod inside the reactor. He had given his soul to Bear Mountain—ripped it right out of his protective suit and handed it over. With all that he had given to the plant he would be damned if he went along with Ken's reckless solution for the hydrogen bubble.

Trace recalled when he and other plant personnel had been asked to stand on the line against protestors outside the Bear Mountain grounds and in Manhattan. During one intense protest, while the Fukushima disaster unfolded, Gener8 had bussed employees into Manhattan to fight back against protestors. Trace and his colleagues had been asked to pass out pamphlets to demonstrators and spectators on the safety of nuclear power. Trace remembered being screamed at and having the material thrown back in his face. "Stop drinkin' the Kool-Aid!" people yelled. Trace remembered willingly fighting against protestors; he believed wholeheartedly in nuclear energy and their jobs. Now he felt ashamed for having been on the street. *Maybe the people were right.*

Hello, beautiful. I miss you deeply. Trace wanted Avi to know that the depth of his love for her had never changed. *I know what we have and I know what we've had. I know the spirit you are.* He adored her for her altruism and empathy—unadulterated kindness. *I know you can see all of me. It's hard to find the purity of our hearts in this world and we need to cherish our bond.* She'd fight for him in life; she'd be at his side no matter. *You've supported me in all that I've strived to be and all that I am.* The past thirty hours had been sobering—smelling salts under his nose, a cane across his face. *I've awakened. I've become clear. Let's get back to our life. We're still young, not even forty. Let's get back to that life. Let's enjoy each other again.* Trace stood up, determination in his eyes. He leapt to the wheel-lock door, disengaged it, and took off quickly down the hall.

CHAPTER 30

"Get off me! Get the fuck off of me!" Avi wrestled against four nurses strapping her to a hospital bed, the fluorescent ceiling lights glaring in her eyes. She was in the section closest to the door, two other patients by her side, the curtains pulled between them. Her pulse knocked in her forearms, veins engorged, hands hot. The strength coursing through her muscles felt superhuman, she could overturn cars, had enough rage to kill with no remorse. She flailed her legs and arms, slamming down repeatedly like a psychiatric patient. "GET THE FUCK OFF!"

"Calm down, Mrs. Crane, please. We can't let you leave because of your radiation exposure. Not until we hear from the doctor."

"THIS'S BULLSHIT! I need to find my daughter. And what the fuck do you people care!" Spit flew from her lip. "Strapping me down like a fucking prisoner. How dare you! You should all go to hell. All of you!" The straps gripped her wrists and ankles.

"Calm down, Mrs. Crane, or we'll need to administer a sedative to you."

"Don't you fucking dare. I do not consent to any of this!" The nurses exited.

"Get back here. Goddammit!" Avi wriggled against the restraints. All she had set out to do was search for her daughter. Her chest heaved. *This's ridiculous!* She shut her eyes in an attempt to calm down. After her adrenaline dwindled, she felt desperately alone as she did when she had been admitted years ago for breast cancer, a lone lady ringing the bell at death's door, unsure if anyone would answer. Avi was at least glad the nurses didn't try to force her to change into a gown this time.

Why is this happening? She should've never let paramedics drag her off to the hospital. *What a terrible mistake. What did I do to deserve this? I'm trying to find my daughter and they put me in a fucking hospital!* Despair set into Avi's heart. She wondered if she'd ever drive Brooklyn to school again, pick out her clothes and dress her, cook for her, play with her outside in the yard, go on rides with her in the park, spin around sillily in ballet skirts until she dizzied and fell laughing, take her to swim lessons, build sand castles and pick shells at the beach, attend dance class, brush and braid her hair, read to her, deliver money as the tooth fairy, deliver gifts as Santa, hide candy as the Easter Bunny, celebrate birthdays, celebrate Mother's Day, dress up for Halloween, go trick or treat, attend play dates, and drink wine with other moms. She looked to the door. "Lea!" Ebullience spread over her face.

"What the hell have they done to you?" Lea went to Avi's side and released the restraints.

"I was trying to leave."

"Jesus. Av..."

"I don't give a damn. And neither do they. They wanna keep me here while I'm trying to find Brooklyn... Not gonna happen." She lowered her voice. "You didn't find her did you?"

Lea shook her head.

Avi melted into the bed. There was no more disappointment to be had. She had been disinfected of expectation, stripped clean with ammonia and copper wool. "What're we gonna do? You have to get me outta here."

"I'll work on it. Have the doctors been in to discuss anything yet?" Lea asked.

"I've been waiting for test results and them to return," Avi said. A stack of newspapers was left at the doorframe by an orderly. Lea scooped them up. "You want something to read?" she asked Avi. They shuffled through the papers together. The headlines glared with fear and sensation. *BLACK RAIN! PEEKASHIMA. HOUSTON WE HAVE A MELTDOWN!—High levels of isotopes measured throughout the Hudson Valley. HATE TO BURST YOUR BUBBLE. Bear Mountain IS READY TO POP!—A potentially explosive hydrogen bubble has been discovered inside the reactor.*

"Breaking news out of Bear Mountain." The line drew Avi and Lea's attention to the TV. "We have confirmed reports that a hydrogen bubble has been discovered inside the troubled reactor. Bear Mountain crew and officials from the NRC are currently convening over the situation to determine whether the bubble is at risk of exploding. We have former NRC inspector Hans Grovin to talk with us now." The split screen showed the news anchor and Hans. "Hans, tell us about this bubble and what it could potentially mean."

Hans spoke with a German accent. "Hydrogen is a by-product of melting zirconium fuel rods inside the reactor. The presence of hydrogen tells us that there is certainly some sort of superheating and melting happening inside the vessel."

"And what are the implications of the bubble's presence?"

"A hydrogen buildup can be dissipated via a multitude of methods; however, that really depends on the state of the reactor. Part of the issue with hydrogen in the system is that when it comes in contact with oxygen it becomes combustible."

"And that's what happened with the reactors in Fukushima, correct?"

"That's correct."

"And if this bubble were to burst?"

"Burst! No." Avi yapped at the TV.

"We could certainly be looking at a breach of containment and wide dispersion of radioactive isotopes into the environment."

"Would you say that's one of the worst possible situations they could encounter at the plant?" the newscaster asked.

"Absolutely. From there you'd have no protection around the core to the outside environment. It'll mean widespread evacuation for sure and a desperate cleanup."

"How would millions of people be moved without pandemonium ensuing?"

"They wouldn't. The state is only prepared to move between four and five hundred thousand within a ten-mile radius of the plant. Given the levels of radioactivity, a further radius would need to be evacuated if containment were breached. Possibly up to fifty miles where there are approximately twenty million people."

A map of the New York metro area appeared on the screen with a reactor steam-stack indicating where the Bear Mountain Nuclear Energy Center resided. "Take us through the fallout on the map," the anchor said.

"With winds coming from the northwest, if containment is breached fallout'll blow through Manhattan," Hans said. An ellipse of red stretched from Bear Mountain down through Manhattan and Long Island and out into the Atlantic Ocean.

"Is it possible to evacuate New York City?"

"Evacuate New York!" Avi turned to Lea, then back to the TV. "They gotta show maps! And pretend. Draw it out on the screen like it's a football replay analysis. Morbid."

"Possible? Sure. In a civilized manner? Absolutely not," Hans said.

"What does an evacuation of that magnitude look like?" the newscaster asked.

"Madness. Absolute madness and gridlock like no one has ever seen. People would need to literally walk off the island. It would be the largest civilian evacuation in the history of modern society."

"What level would you say this event measures on the International Nuclear Event Scale, the INES?"

"Right now they're rating it a five. If that hydrogen bubble goes it's a seven for sure. That's the highest level and would be on par with Chernobyl and Fukushima."

"Thank you, Hans." The screen cut to a close-up of the newscaster. "That was former NRC inspector Hans Grovin. Experts are warning if the hydrogen bubble blows it'd be like a volcanic eruption. The top of the containment building would blow off, spewing billions of radioactive isotopes into the environment. Many are saying a wide-scale evacuation would be impossible to execute safely and efficiently. And then there's the aftermath. Cleanup and restoration efforts are estimated to cost in the hundreds of billions. The atomic side of the cleanup would take at least ten years."

Evacuate New York? What are you doing, Trace! You better stop that bubble. You turned your back on me and Brooklyn for it so you better make good! Avi turned to Lea, her face contorted in astonishment, the nightmare of meltdown palpable. Avi resented Trace every time news of the reactor situation intensified and the chance of meltdown and evacuation increased. She knew he was doing the right thing, but even so she'd divorce him when it was all over. *If any of us make it out of here. If Brooklyn is dead I will not go on, and I swear to god Trace, I'll take you out with me.*

A short spindly man, black hair glossy like a show dog, and a nurse with short magenta hair and double-wide hips walked in. "Mrs. Crane. Dr. Cheng."

Avi cut the volume down on the TV. "It's Dr. Crane," she said curtly.

"Pardon me. *Dr. Crane*. Medicine?" the doctor replied.

"Physics."

The doctor nodded respectfully. "Well, we've got some tests back." The doctor referenced Avi's file and pushed at his space-aged, rimless glasses. "Good news is the radiation exposure isn't systemic. You somehow've taken a local dose to your skin. It is, however, fairly radioactive. We found the isotopes iodine and cesium in the rash before we washed it. Gamma energy from the area is decently strong. None of this is life threatening. However, it is a hit to your system. I'd recommend that we keep you a few days to keep treating the area topically and administering meds intravenously that can help combat the radiation and attempt to rid the exposure as quickly as possible."

"I can't stay a few days. My daughter is missing and I need to find her. I need to leave now."

"I understand, but I can't discharge you without the proper care. Have you contacted the authorities about your daughter? Is your husband or any other families members available to help find her?" the doctor asked.

"My husband works at Bear Mountain. I have no one else around here. So please discharge me."

"I'm afraid I can't do that considering your condition. Radiological exposure can be a threat to others and, therefore, we must keep you for monitoring and administering of medication to ensure there is nothing more to your ailment."

Avi swung her feet over the side of the bed. If her eyes were flamethrowers they'd singe off the doctor's hair. "You can't keep me here!" She jabbed her finger into the file resting in the doctor's hands.

"I'm sorry," Dr. Cheng said.

"Dr. Cheng," Lea interjected. "I'm Avi's friend, Lea Rosanato. I'm an RN and I used to work at Putnam. I could administer the intravenous meds and the topical treatment to Avi if you release her. I'm licensed for home care."

"I don't know if that's a good idea. Mrs. Crane should stay. The authorities should help look for her daughter."

"The authorities are seriously preoccupied right now. They can't focus on it. Further, Avi's case is something she could seek outside treatment for and the hospital can transfer care. She has every right to it. You can pull me up in the system. I'm in there."

Go, Lea! Avi cherished her friend.

Dr. Cheng rested his eyes on Lea. "Okay. Fine. Fair enough." Dr. Cheng turned to exit. "Oh." He turned back. "There's one more thing, Mrs. Crane."

Avi's eyes beckoned.

"You're pregnant." He looked at Avi's file. "Approximately two months I'd say."

Avi stared at him, her mouth partially ajar. *Pregnant? Pregnant... How did?...* She remembered the night she and Trace knocked back a bottle of wine at the beach house. *Wow... Wow... Why now?* "Av... Oh my god," Lea said.

"Don't worry, Mrs. Crane. Your radiation exposure won't affect the fetus." Dr. Cheng and the nurse exited.

Lea embraced Avi. *Pregnant.* The news shocked Avi so heavily she couldn't form another thought. There was just the word pregnant in lightbulbs suspended in a stark white room, Avi behind glass peering at the display. To have another child she needed Trace around. She didn't want to be a single mother, let alone a single mother with two children. She considered abortion. Avi wasn't certain she and Trace would stay together when the disaster ended. There were too many factors to consider and it all teetered on their reactions when or if they reunited. Vindictiveness pooled in her psyche. She feared she would lash out at him and he would be belligerent. A powder keg would detonate and their union, which had tipped its apex long ago, would plummet to its demise.

Avi hoped for the sake of their children, their relationship, and the East Coast Trace could mitigate the hydrogen bubble. *You owe me that.* If anyone could accomplish the task it was Trace. She knew he'd fight, but what really worried her was if the reactor was still under his control.

CHAPTER 31

Trace strode quickly along a concrete service road between buildings inside the Bear Mountain grounds. He wore his radiation whites but had left his respirator mask behind. The afternoon sun warming his face comforted him like he had just awoken inside the cool interior of his friend's beach house and stepped outside onto the terrace. The sun fed him, bathed him, surrounded him like a warm towel. Trace was exhausted, his legs weak. But his disagreements with everyone about how to mitigate the hydrogen bubble had been an injection of adrenaline to his nervous system that kept his eyes open in determination and kept his feet tromping. Trace passed towering concrete storage casks, some cracked and leaning from the quake. He stepped over serpentining hoses, sloshed through inches of ground water left from rain and the containment of fires. Distant alarms droned in his ears while crewmembers in radiation suits whipped past him in white flashes. Trace reached the barbed-wire fence separating the interior facility grounds from the parking lot. Two armed guards in radiation whites and respirators with assault rifles stood at the ready, side arms strapped to their hips, backs facing Trace on both sides of the large sliding gate. Another guard sat in the booth paralleling the fence. Trace approached.

"Crane," the guard bellowed, glowering from behind his respirator.

Trace nodded and faced the fence.

"How's it going in there?" the guard asked.

Trace pointed to the gate. *Shut up with the small talk and open it!*

"Where the hell's your respirator? Are we cleared to be without?"

A corner of his charcoal SUV beckoned from the parking lot.

"Crane?" The guard stepped in front of Trace. "You alright?"

Calm yourself, Trace. Talk to this man and calm down. It's not his fault. He doesn't know. Trace looked up, eyes bloodshot and sharp to the point that they seemed conical, tension so tight in his jaw it would take both his hands to move his mouth. "I'm... I'm good," he said flatly through his teeth.

"Where's your respirator?" the guard grumbled.

"Inside."

"We're under mandatory issue."

"I know. I had to just run to my car for a second. Grab something."

"Crane."

"Gotta get something from the car. Figured I'd be quick. I've had that damn thing on since yesterday. A few minutes' break won't overexpose me, and it's damn well worth it to get some fresh air."

The guard nodded. "I hear ya. What's the situation in there?"

"We're battling. There's a hydrogen bubble."

"What's that mean?"

"That means if you haven't already called your wife and kids, do it. We got a fucking mess in there," he said bitterly.

"You're saying it could explode?"

"Maybe."

"Christ."

"Yep. Pray to him, too, we're gonna need it."

"You know we're on lockdown. No one in, no one out. Strict orders. Not even to the parking lot."

Trace cocked his head. "You talk to your wife and kids since yesterday?"

"Yeah… well, cell service is on the fritz, but somehow an email snuck through to my phone and they let me know they're a-okay."

"Good. I haven't talked to mine or heard anything from them at all. I have a picture in my car of them that I want. I need something in the control room to help get me through."

The guard nodded. "I hear ya. Quick to your car and back. Fast before anyone strolls out here. Use the pedestrian gate."

"I appreciate it."

The guard nodded and returned to the booth.

Trace pushed through into the parking lot and strode to his SUV, unlocking the doors with the remote as he approached. He shed his protective suit, stomping it off his thick legs onto the ground. He entered his vehicle and closed the door. Then he quickly closed all the air vents. Trace looked back toward the guarded gate. No one watched. He started his truck with a button push, slapped it into reverse, punched out of his spot, and zoomed through the parking lot. He looked back toward the guard gate. The guards looked at each other. The guard he had been talking to exited the booth and stared.

Trace hit the main access road that led to the property perimeter. He split through emergency vehicles and trailers that spotted the shoulders of the road.

"Gustav, it's Feresten, come in," squawked from Trace's radio. Trace reached to turn the volume off.

"Trace Crane has taken his vehicle from the lot."

Trace recoiled from the radio.

"Could be headed your way. Charcoal SUV."

"Copy."

Panic ratcheted Trace's stomach. He pushed the SUV to over forty-five on the twenty-mile-an-hour access road, rounded a curve, and then the main gates came into view—towering latticed steel with barbed wire and cement barriers funneling the road to both sides of a guard station. The gates were closed and two more guards armed with assault rifles stood facing Trace. *Ha! Like a prison. What a fucking joke. Got us locked down like lab chimps.* Two more guards stepped out from the booth and signaled Trace to stop. He punched the gas. The two armed guards raised their rifles. Trace gave it more. "Shoot me! Do it!" Sweat ran from his scalp. The guards screamed and waved their arms. A security SUV darted in front of Trace. He impacted the vehicle, tires skidding. The steering-wheel air bag socked him in the face, burning his skin. Glass sprayed from the windshield. His SUV fishtailed. Trace fought the wheel, the air bag thrashing over his face and chest. Blood streamed from his nose. He couldn't see anything but air bag, glass shards, trees, and buildings whipping violently in patterned blurs. The SUV spun, bucked, hit a curb, and flopped onto the passenger side. Trace's head whipped against the doorframe with a crack. The SUV slid across the dirt and smacked into a tree, finally coming to rest. Trace hung from his seatbelt, his face bloody and powdered from the airbag.

CHAPTER 32

The tree groves she passed permitted dappled sunlight to flicker on the windshield, causing Avi to think she saw emergency lights. She sat in the passenger seat while Lea drove them in her minivan down a tree-lined county highway. She looked out the door window and saw Brooklyn running along the roadside grass dodging between trees. Avi blinked. Trace's face appeared in the window. Blood streamed from his forehead. Feared cinched Avi's stomach. Trace's face morphed into Brooklyn's bloody face twisted with terror. Avi shut her eyes again and turned forward. *You're hallucinating.* She was glad to be out of the hospital and back on the hunt for Brooklyn. She didn't like how angry she felt, but the times where authority had attempted to stand between her and her daughter incited rage she couldn't quell. She didn't know any other way to be heard by insentient emergency workers. When she had roared, they seemed deaf.

Avi saw a farmhouse in a distant field that had slid off its foundation, the owners walking around it assessing if the structure could be saved. She and Lea crossed a buckled intersection, the asphalt fractured as far as Avi could see. She saw a porch that had been twisted off a colonial home, the steps lying on their side. *Sad.* "The hydrogen bubble! Could Bear Mountain burst!" The radio reporter's voice cut from the door speakers. Avi's shoulder muscles hardened, tension radiating up the side of her neck into her head and jaw. Her knee twinged. She wondered if Bear Mountain really could explode. She turned to Lea. "What's with all the cars on the road?"

"I don't know," Lea replied.

A helicopter buzzing overhead drew Avi's and Lea's attention. Avi dropped her window and poked her head out for a better view. The women caught up to a fire truck that drove slowly ahead of them. A man's voice blurted from a bullhorn. "Turn around and go back to your homes. No evacuation has been issued. Please stay in your homes. No evacuation has been issued."

The two emergency vehicles zipped by using the opposing traffic lanes, sirens blaring, lights flashing. Avi gripped the armrest. "Seriously, what the hell is going on?" Lea said.

Avi tossed her hands. "There wasn't an evacuation called. We'd've heard about it on the radio. And they're telling people to turn back to their homes. I don't get it."

They turned into Lea's neighborhood, a nondescript street off the main road. Avi and Lea noticed an influx of neighbors packing their vehicles and heading out. Lea slowed her van. "Drop your window," Lea said. Avi complied.

"Hey! Hey, Alice!" Lea waved. Alice Rosen, forties, marigold-colored hair, waved back and approached. "What's going on? Where's everyone going?" Lea asked.

"We're leaving town. You heard about that bubble? They said the nuclear plant could explode." Alice fussed with a duffle bag in her hands.

"Yeah, we heard, but…" Lea looked to Avi.

"Some said it wasn't a big deal and others are saying it is… they seem unsure," Avi said.

"We're not taking any chances," Alice said. "We're leaving."

"Was there an evacuation issued?" Avi asked.

"Mom!" Alice's boys yelled in unison from behind her.

"No. No evacuation—"

"Mom!"

Alice turned back to her boys, "One second, guys," then back to Avi and Lea. "It seems irresponsible of them. I mean, I don't know what they're waiting for? A lot of people are leaving, but really it's only a fraction of the population."

Avi looked at Lea, her lips ironed flat with concern.

"We're looking for her daughter," Lea said. "She was at school when it all happened."

Alice's face fell solemn. "Oh my."

"We checked all the shelters we could find around here and we've checked all the hospitals," Avi said.

"I heard hospitals were so full around here they were taking people into Columbia Presbyterian in Manhattan," Alice said.

"Really?" Avi asked.

Alice nodded. "Yep."

"Thanks, Alice. We better get goin'. I'll talk to you soon." Lea put Avi's window up and touched the gas. "I need to call that hospital," Avi said.

"Maybe the house phones are working, but do you think we should be evacuating?" Lea asked.

Avi took a deep breath. "I don't know. I don't know… I wish I could talk to Trace again. But either way there's no way in hell I'm leaving without finding Brooklyn."

"Of course," Lea said. "Of course."

Avi and Lea walked through the foyer of Lea's home toward the kitchen. Avi was jealous yet happy for Lea that her home wasn't compromised by the earthquake beyond a few wall cracks. The floors reminded Avi of her own sanctuary. She wanted to walk through the doors of her Victorian home, feel the coziness of the nest she and Trace had created, the warmth of family photos and possessions surrounding her. She wanted to be with Trace, Brooklyn, her parents, and her brother at her reclaimed picnic table in the dining room. "Let's check the phones," Avi said.

Lea picked up the cordless. "Power's still out so…"

"Don't you have a corded line?"

"No… I… I wonder if the phone in the basement… It's an old one… We can try it… I hadn't even been thinking about it… Wasn't sure who I was gonna call anyway," Lea said. "C'mon."

Avi followed Lea to the basement. "Dad likes to watch football down here," Lea said, referring to the dated, rear-projection, big-screen TV.

"Or you mean you send him down here to watch it?" Avi retorted.

Lea laughed. "You know how it is." She picked up the phone. The dial tone hummed.

Avi's hand trembled when she reached for the keypad. She dialed the operator. "Columbia Presbyterian Hospital, please."

"Medical Center… Please hold, I'll put ya through," the operator said.

The line rang. "New York-Presbyterian Columbia University Medical Center," a nurse answered hastily. Voices, foot falls, doors, and stretchers clattered in Avi's ear.

"Hello?"

"Medical Center," the nurse said curtly.

"I'm… I'm looking for my daughter, Brooklyn Crane."

"Okay. When did she come in?"

Avi heard typing. "I… Um… I don't know if she did, but she's missing from the earthquake. Do you have people from

Peekskill there?"

"Ah… Yes. Lots of 'em. Okay, Crane you said, right?" The nurse typed.

"Yeah." A moment passed and the receiver fell silent. "Hello?" Click. "Hello?" *If you'd like to make a call please hang up and try again. If you need help hang up and dial*—Avi hung up. "Shit! Got disconnected." She dialed the operator back. A busy signal barked at her. "Damn!" She finally got an operator and asked for the hospital again. The line rang dozens of times and no one answered. "Shit!" She slammed the phone back into its cradle. "Goddammit!"

Lea rubbed Avi's shoulder. Avi scooped up the phone again. "Who're you gonna call now?" Lea asked.

"My voicemail. Maybe Trace's tried to call me or… I don't know… Some other kid's parents or something about Brook…" Avi dialed. After one ring her voicemail picked up. *Hi, you've reached Avi. Leave a message.* Avi stretched her finger for the asterisk. *Have a great day!* Brooklyn's voice mixed with hers. The message tone beeped. Avi hit the switch hook and dialed again.

"What happened?" Lea said.

Hi, you've reached Avi. "I forgot Brooklyn's voice is on my voicemail. I want to hear it again." *Leave a message. Have a great day!* Avi hit the switchhook, redialed, and listened. She recalled back in December when Trace had given her a new smartphone for Christmas. Avi and Brooklyn recorded the greeting together sitting by their Christmas tree surrounded by wrapping paper. Brooklyn twirled in her cartoon-print, footed pajamas, Avi sitting on the floor leaning against the sofa smiling, Trace snapping photos. They ate cookies and cooked cinnamon pancakes with bacon for breakfast.

Avi hit the switchhook and dialed again. She pressed the asterisk and entered her passcode. *You have four new messages. To hear your messages press one.* Avi tapped the digit. *First mes-*

sage. Click. *To listen to your message again press*—Avi pressed three. *Message erased. Next message. Avi, it's your brother. Calling to make sure you and everybody are okay. Call me. Mom and Dad wanna know, too. Next message. Uh... I... A... Avi, it's Trace. Listen... If... if you get this or... or can get this. I'm at the plant. We have a bit of a crisis over here.* Trace coughed. *But I'm okay.* He paused, machines rumbling in the background. *We're gettin' through it. But get Brooklyn and get out of town. Just in case get far away north or south fifty to hundred miles if you can. Hell two hundred if you can. Just go... just in case something happens. Call me if you can. My cell doesn't seem to be working. Call the control room directly or get emergency operations to put you through. And... and... I love you. Okay? I love you and Brooklyn.* Tears welled in Avi's eyes. She realized the message must've been before she and Trace had run into each other. She needed new information. Although, 'get out of town' might still apply. *To save this mess*— Avi stabbed two. Next message. Avi, it's your brother again. Can't seem to catch *you. Tried the house, no answer. I've texted and emailed. Hope you guys are all right. I've been watching the news. I'm sure Trace is at the plant. It's crazy what's going on. Get in touch if you get this.* Avi pressed two to save. *No more messages. To go to the main menu press...* Avi dialed.

"Who you calling?" Lea asked.

"Control room. Trace. See if we can find out more about what's going on." After several rings the line disconnected. Avi tried again. Nothing. She looked at Lea, her eyes wet with despair. "Can't get through. Of course," she said bitterly. She dropped the receiver into its cradle.

"What should we do?" Lea said.

"Let's go to the hospital. What else are we gonna do?"

CHAPTER 33

Large hands grabbed Trace's shoulders. The guard from the perimeter booth stared into his face. Trace's mind was both dazed and acutely present. No thoughts fired, only sensory observations.

"You okay?" the guard asked.

Trace tried to brush the guard's hands off. Blood gurgled in his mouth.

"Help me get 'em out," the guard said over his shoulder. Another guard climbed onto the side of Trace's SUV. The first guard reached over and unbuckled Trace's seatbelt. Trace fell from the seat into the hands of both guards. They dragged him out of the SUV onto the grass.

"You alright?" the guard asked again, kneeling next to Trace.

Trace moaned, his eyelids opening and closing, his chest heaving with breath. Blood gurgled from his mouth.

"Crane? Can you hear me?" The guard turned back to his men. "Is medical coming? Might need that ambulance after all. He might have a head injury." He turned back to Trace and clapped his hands in front of his face. "Crane, can you hear me?"

Trace winced and tried to push himself up.

"Stay down." The guard guided him back to the ground.

"I'm fine…" Trace mumbled, his eyes barely open. "I'm fine… I gotta… I gotta go… I gotta get outta here. The flowers. The flowers are attacking." He looked like he was drunk.

"What? Where's your suit and respirator?" the guard asked.

Boots clomped toward Trace. "The flowers," Trace said.

"You stupid motherfucker. What the fuck is wrong with you? Whaddayou crazy?" one of the armed guards screamed. "You almost fucking ran us over." The guards helping Trace pushed the angry guard back. "Pipe down. Pipe it down."

Trace pushed his heavy frame up onto his elbows.

"Stay down," the guard said.

"I'm fine… I'm fine…" Trace rolled to his knees. He looked to the site perimeter. Trees and pavement blurred in his vision, his face burning, head throbbing. He dashed toward the exit, off the block like an Olympic sprinter.

The guard chased after him. "Get back here!"

"Hold it!" another yelled.

The vehicular arm gate and stone-wall entrance blurred ahead. How he would get from the outside to Avi and Brooklyn he had no idea. *I'll need a taxi. How the hell am I gonna get a taxi? I'll hitch a ride… Shit, I'm slow…* Something hit him in the back. His legs crumpled. One of the guards was on top of him, a knee in his spine. "Get off me!" Trace yelled.

"Stay down," the guard said.

Trace's arms twisted behind his back. Handcuffs ratcheted, the steel pinching his wrists. "What are you doing! I'm a goddamn supervisor here."

"What the fuck is going on?" Ken Bramini appeared. The guards flipped Trace over. "Crane. What the hell is this?" Ken stood over him in his radiation whites.

"I'm outta here. I'm done… Tell them to let me go." Blood

leaked from his mouth.

"Whaddayou mean you're done? You're outta here? We're in the middle of a fucking crisis. We have work to do. You're supposed to be implementing the hydrogen bubble initiative."

"I don't want any part of it. I'm gettin' the fuck outta here and I'm gettin' my wife and kid and I'm gone."

Bramini stepped closer. "You're not going anywhere. We're on lockdown. Where the hell is your suit and respirator?"

Trace said nothing.

"He took it off," one of the guards said.

"You took it off? Crane. Seriously, what is this?"

"I don't agree with the hydrogen initiative. And I don't know that I can do anything more. I'm not moving forward. My daughter's missing. My wife's out there injured, lookin' for her. That's more important. So let me go." Trace wriggled against the handcuffs.

"You're under contract. Under contract to operate this facility, under contract to be here in a disaster. We're on lockdown. No one in, no one out. You go out onto that road you endanger anyone you meet with potential radioactivity you've picked up on site. I'll have you arrested on both counts. Take the cuffs off him."

The guards eyed Bramini dubiously. "Do it," Bramini said. One of the guards unlocked the cuffs and removed them. Trace rubbed his wrists.

"You want that on your conscience, then walk out that fucking exit."

"It's your fault this's happened, Ken. You shoulda never made us close those fucking vents. You've created a pressure cooker, goddammit!"

"Barnes' and the governor's orders, not mine! I told you that."

"Bullshit. You put me in charge, you let me do what I do."

"You follow my orders. I can take you in and out of charge

as I see fit. I make the final decisions here, not you. And I've decided how we're gonna handle the bubble. We've already started."

"You're an idiot." Trace spat blood.

"What's it gonna be? Which way you walkin'?" Ken said.

Trace looked to the perimeter. He rolled to his knees and stood. His body ached and trembled. He looked at Ken and the facility behind him—ominous hell—then back to the exit—illuminated liberation. Trace thought about the implications of leaving. Old, stout, bald, freckle-headed Ken Bramini wasn't messing around. Ken would have him arrested if he left. If the media got ahold of the story he'd be in a dredging net across the bottom of the Hudson with every rusty, mangled scrap latching onto him, every poison suffocating his pores. If Bear Mountain completely melted down the guilt that would imbue him would be far worse than the guilt he'd feel for not going to find Avi and Brooklyn. *I have to know they're okay.* He grabbed his head. *They're fine... they're fine... It's gonna be okay... Avi's out there alone searching for our baby.* Trace turned toward the exit gates and walked. The guards jumped after him.

"Hold it," Ken said, calling off the guards.

It's over for me anyway. If I don't go now I might never go. I might never see them.

"Crane," Ken called out.

Trace kept walking.

"Crane," Ken barked.

Trace kept walking forward. *Fuck that motherfucker and fuck this job!*

"Crane!" Ken yelled.

Trace stopped and turned around, an inferno in his stare. "What!"

"Fine. Your way," Ken said.

He cocked his head. "What?"

"You come back we do it your way, dammit," Ken said.

Trace glared at Ken. Ken's concession came purely out of necessity, without moral base. *I can smell his turpitude.*

"Let's talk about it. Your way. We need you in there."

Trace walked back toward Ken and the facility, determination in his eyes. He knocked Ken's shoulder when he passed him. *Sorry, girls. I gotta save the reactor first. I hope you understand.*

CHAPTER 34

Avi and Lea moved briskly through the doors of Columbia University Medical Center. The waiting area was crammed like a hip Soho lounge—all the chairs occupied, people sitting on the floor. Wheelchairs and stretchers rolled past and distorted codes pinged off the intercom. They arrived at the front desk behind a line of people. Avi cut to the front.

"Av," Lea called after her.

"C'mon." Avi waved.

"We're looking for Brooklyn Crane," Avi blurted to a reception nurse. "My daughter," she added.

"Miss, there's a line of people. You'll need to wait your turn," the nurse said gently.

"My daughter. She's been missing for two days. I can't wait any longer." Avi turned toward the line. "Is anyone in this line looking for a missing child?"

"Av," Lea attempted to quiet her. "Av."

"Anybody?" Avi said. "My daughter's been missing for two days. Do you all mind if I cut in front?"

Everyone in the line nodded, others gestured acceptingly.

"It's okay," a woman leaning on a stroller said.

"Go 'head."

"Please." A man in a thawb and a fez motioned to the front. "Go."

"Thank you." Avi turned back to the nurse. "Alright. We got approval. Please."

The nurse shook her head in disbelief at Avi's tactic. "Brooklyn Crane. Okay. Child?"

Avi glared. "Yes, child."

The nurse rapped on the computer keyboard. "Our records have been going crazy with the patient influx. Still giving me problems. IT's trying to fix everything. Fifth floor is children's care. Sign in here real quick and take the elevator. They'll have records up there."

Lea scribbled her and Avi's names on the log.

They waited at the elevators. "Fifth floor," Avi gasped. *C'mon. C'mon. C'mon.* Avi jabbed the up arrow. *What happens if she's not here? Then what? Morgue?* The elevator arrived. Avi pushed in; Lea followed. Avi watched the numbers flip on the digital screen. Two, three, four, five. She scurried out onto the linoleum, Lea in tow.

"To the nurses station," Lea said.

Avi banked right and shuffled to a stop at the counter. "I'm looking for Brooklyn Crane. She's my daughter." Her body hummed with anxiety.

"Okay. Crane. Let's see." The nurse moved with the urgency of a sloth. She had one lazy eye that looked intermittently at the ceiling. "All right. Can I see your ID or driver's license?"

"ID or driver's license? Seriously? She's my daughter. Is she here?" Avi smacked her palms on the counter.

"Av… Just give it to her," Lea said. Avi rifled through her purse and slapped her driver's license on the counter. The nurse poked at the keyboard.

"Okay. We got 'er. Yep. She's down the hall."

Avi looked at Lea in disbelief. She didn't know if she should faint or run. Her hands trembled. *Minor injuries? Intensive care? Is she conscious? Brain damage?* "Which room? Which room!"

"Fifty-one o nine. Just give me a second to sign you in and—"

Avi sprinted off, leaving Lea and her license at the counter. She rounded the corner, anxiety stinging in her veins. *Coma? Paralyzed? Can she talk? I'm comin'!* 5109 blurred in her peripheral vision. Avi squealed to a stop. She looked inside the room and saw three beds, a multitude of tubes and wires running to all of them. "Brooklyn?" She scurried to the first. "Brooklyn?" to the middle, "Brook?" to the bed next to the window, "Brooklyn?" Avi saw her butterscotch hair protruding from a bandage, oxygen under her nose. "Baby?" Avi froze. Sharp ripples in her abdomen radiated into the middle of her back. She covered her mouth. "Brook," she gasped. Tears pressed to her lids. Avi touched her arm. "Baby, can you hear me?" Lea hustled in and stood bedside. "Angel." Avi stroked Brooklyn's cheek. "Baby, can you hear me? It's mommy." Brooklyn didn't respond. Avi scanned her little girl—IVs, tubes, bandages from scalp to toe, cables running from under her hospital gown, a cast on her wrist. The bandage around Brooklyn's head matched Avi's—rose and ochre blotted in the gauze fibers. Avi sensed Brooklyn's pain as a searing-cold draining in her bones. She felt like her flesh had been flayed open, gelid air hitting her raw nerves jangling her soul. She wanted to take Brooklyn home, un-bandage her, wash her, put clean clothes on her, feed her a home-cooked meal, tuck her in bed, rub her back, and whisper her a story.

"Brook, honey." Avi clutched her arm. Brooklyn slowly opened her eyes.

Brooklyn stared unresponsively at Avi.

"Baby?"

"Mama?" Brooklyn said groggily.

"Oh, sweetie." Tears cascaded down Avi's face. She kissed Brooklyn all over and hugged her. "Oh thank god." Avi wondered if nurses had sedated her in the hospital and she was hallucinating. She had thought she'd be burying her little girl when it was all over. Or worse she'd never find her at all. Brooklyn's warm, little body pressed against Avi's. *She's really here!* She buried her face in Brooklyn's neck and smelled her sweet, smooth skin, her soft hair like silk on her nose. Brooklyn's heart beat against Avi's chest. Never in Avi's life had she felt relief of such magnitude. She had never lost anything so great and had it return. Avi pelted Brooklyn's neck and chest with kisses.

"Ow!"

"Sorry, sweetie." Avi pulled back. "What happened? What hurts?"

"My tummy and my arms and my legs."

Avi never loved a soul as much as she loved her daughter. *Trace, you're so lucky I found our little girl.* Looking at the coils of wires and tubes attached to Brooklyn made Avi's nausea return. She felt faint, blood leaving her head, static in her ears. The room blurred. She clutched the bed to steady herself. Then the feeling faded, lucidity returned. "I love you so much, honey—so, so much."

"I love you, too, mama. Where've you been?" Brooklyn said.

"We've been looking for you since yesterday. What happened at school, honey?"

"I... don't know. I woked up here."

"What's the last thing you remember?"

"I was at school... and... and then shaking... and then big loud sounds... and then that's it."

"Oh, sweetie." Avi kissed her again.

"Where's daddy?" Brooklyn asked.

"Daddy's at work, honey."

"I want daddy, too. Can he come?"

"I wish he could, baby, but he can't leave. There's been an accident at the power plant where daddy works, and he's there trying to save it."

Lea wrapped her arms around Avi and rubbed her back.

"How do we know what's wrong with her?" Avi whispered.

Lea wiped her eyes, stepped back from Avi, and reached for the chart at the end of Brooklyn's bed. She flipped through the pages. "Trauma to the head. Contusions to the abdomen. Fractured ribs. Internal bleeding. Fractured tibia. Fractured wrist."

Avi ran her hand through her hair. She held her hand against her face and took a big breath. She didn't want to hear any more. The words describing what had happened to Brooklyn gashed her insides. Avi caressed Brooklyn's arm. She kissed her on the cheek. "I love you, honey."

"I love you, too, mama." Brooklyn smiled.

Avi pulled back the covers on the bed. "Can you wiggle your toes?"

Brooklyn moved her toes, wincing. "It hurts."

"Okay, honey. Okay." Avi returned the covers, relieved that Brooklyn wasn't paralyzed.

"Are you hurt, too?" Brooklyn asked.

"Mama hurt her head and her knee." She smiled. *My girl has such compassion.*

"What's on your neck?" Brooklyn asked.

"Oh." Avi touched her bandaged neck and chest. "Mama was burned."

"Can I have some juice?" Brooklyn said.

"I'll go find some," Lea said.

"Thanks," Avi said. *We're gonna be fine.*

CHAPTER 35

Bloody dirt crumbled from Trace's face onto his chest. He rubbed off remnants from the car wreck while he slouched at the oak-veneer conference table inside the emergency operations center. He looked like he had been dragged behind a pickup truck and dumped into a ditch. He hadn't even considered cleaning himself up after the crash. His mind was focused on three things—Avi, Brooklyn, and the hydrogen bubble. His emotions had hardened, his trepidations had receded, and his despair had turned to a calm cantankerousness. He had been taken to the escarpment of his psyche, gelid winds so raw on his bones he felt he was burning. He had broken through to the other side, been reborn. It was something like the phenomenon of drinking oneself sober. He was clear and he simply didn't give a fuck any longer. He was going to save the reactor and see his girls soon. He was acutely focused, serenely focused like a Shaolin monk. Had Ken not conceded Trace would've kept walking. Now he had to believe Avi and Brooklyn would understand his decision to turn around.

At the head of the room flat-panel TVs blipped with every

major news outlet and on-site reactor data. Emergency operations staff had their faces in laptops, gabbing into telephone headsets. When Trace leaned back in his chair his head, neck, and shoulders ached. He unmuted the TV next to the conference table and flipped through news channels.

"I don't know why we have to tell you everything we're doing," Chris Barnes said.

"Conflicting statements from the governor's office, NRC, and Gener8," the news anchor said.

"The hydrogen bubble is unstable. Explosion is possible." A scientist dug his pen into a page.

"It's not a nuclear accident. It was a failure of machinery outside the core," Barnes said.

"Experts say residents could need to worry about increased cancer rates for more than thirty years in the area."

"The core is most likely melting. They've had a loss of coolant," a scientist said.

"While meltdown is considered a possibility, officials say there's no imminent danger," the anchor said.

"What would happen is the radiation would spew out of containment into the atmosphere. Rain would send it down to the earth and push isotopes right into the soil, the crops, everything coated in radioactivity," a scientist drawled.

"A large amount of radiation escapes into the environment, we're talking teratogenic mutations. That's the exposure of fetuses to radiation. If pregnant women are in the area and absorb fallout then the fetus is exposed. It's ugly—malformations of the brain, skull, and eyes. Mental retardation, stillbirths, cleft palates and lips, clubbed feet, fused fingers and toes, additional limbs. Then you have genetic mutations. This's stuff that gets passed down generation to generation. Radiation exposure alters DNA. That's what people gotta understand. It's not a house fire. Put it out, a few people died, it's over. Radiation lives on and on and on…"

"Safety systems functioned as designed. There was no catastrophic accident. The plant is in a stable condition and operating normally," Ken Bramini said.

"High winds are spreading radioactivity," a wheelchair-bound scientist said.

"Brief puffs of radiation. Not a threat," Chris Barnes said.

"If it's serious they're not gonna tell you because they'll start a panic. I think they tell you what they wantchu to know," a fifty-something woman with spiked platinum hair and bug eyes said.

Trace muted the TV. He saw why the public was panicking—facts were intertwined with fiction and misinterpreted statements that would confuse anyone. He had heard of the panic evacuation and hoped Avi and Brooklyn had hightailed it out of town if they hadn't previously.

The latch of the emergency operations center door brought Trace present. Valdern and Ken entered and sat at the conference table. Trace glared at Ken momentarily before deciding he needed to be emotionless. Valdern unrolled a piping schematic for the auxiliary building. "Alright… Here's your pathway," Valdern said. "You see this here." He dragged his finger across the paper and pointed to a small vertical pipe with a black bow tie indicating a valve. "That's valve eighteen forty-seven. That's what you want. It's not the easiest to access. It's probably forty, forty-five feet off the ground. It's small ladders into catwalks and such. So you gotta go underneath here and up."

Trace hoped his adversary was giving him a solid plan.

"You lookin' at me like I'm sending you to your grave. Now you know I wouldn't do that. We got business to tend to here and I know this facility."

"I trust ya." *Do I?*

"Good. I'm approximating the reading inside auxiliary is two thousand rem. That wheel valve needs to be turned probably close to a hundred revolutions. You're gonna need some tools because it probably hasn't been turned in... actually, it's probably never been turned. So I don't know what kinda corrosion you dealing with there. You need to go in with a team and each of you has about thirty seconds before you're overexposed. You take turns spinnin' that wheel 'til it stops."

"No team. I go alone," Trace said.

"Jesus Christ, you're frustrating." Valdern exhaled deeply.

"You go in with a team," Ken said. "There's no compromise here."

"It's gonna be chaos trying to move guys through that maze safely in the short amount of time we have." Trace said. "Those ladders and catwalks are one-way streets. Guys gotta wait to go in and to go out, which cuts our time to turn the wheel to practically nothing for each person."

Ken stabbed his knobby finger into the table. "I'm not debating with you."

"I'm already overexposed. I go in alone. I'm as good as dead anyway."

"Huh?" Valdern looked at Ken

"Whadayou talkin' about?" Ken said.

"When that pipe burst that knocked me out when I went in to get Hanson," Trace said.

"What pipe burst?" Ken said.

"Yeah. You weren't here I guess. I was exposed when I was knocked out. Coolant and gasses got into my suit. I've probably taken in close to a thousand rem."

"What!" Ken's face crinkled. "You went to the... you were at the morning show. You sat next to me and Barnes. When? Yesterday? You traveled to Manhattan and... My god! You—" Ken turned crimson. "What the hell's wrong with you!"

"Don't worry. I was wearing a protective suit under that

polyester thing you gave me."

"Jeeesus…" Ken snapped his head to the front of the room as if he was trying to shake off what Trace had told him.

Trace coughed into his hand. "Now… I'm not gonna debate with *you*, Ken. You wanna save this reactor I go in there alone and handle it. If not I walk out that door and really leave this time. Then you figure it out. You send a team in there you're gonna overexpose all of 'em. Your ass'll be fried by the company and the commission." Trace lowered his voice and leaned in to Ken. "I'm helpin' you out here."

"You got some fuckin' balls." Valdern's face spread. Trace felt his first shred of respect from him. "Damn. Stupid, though. Why the fuck haven't you gone to the hospital?"

"What the hell are you doing? You're a walking fuel rod," Ken said with fascination. He pushed himself away from the table and crossed his arms over his chest.

"Don't worry. I don't plan on huggin' ya. It's fine. I've been washed and in a suit a majority of the time. This whole plant's contaminated. Don't go thinking it isn't. Those isotopes are on everything. Even you."

CHAPTER 36

Avi had moved to a chair next to Brooklyn's hospital bed. Lea had gone to the cafeteria, leaving them alone with the other two children in the room. No other adults was the important aspect—just mother and daughter. Nothing against Lea, but there was a connection Avi could only tap into when alone with her baby. Now that Avi had Brooklyn her outrage toward Trace had ebbed, she was becoming more concerned about him. She thought with all the safety and communication systems at the plant he would've figured out a way to get in touch with her. *Is he too busy? Is he hurt? Dead? Unconscious? Dammit, Trace, I'm sick that I haven't heard from you.* Even though they had been stuck in a dreadful period of their relationship, Avi still loved Trace and cared for him deeply. She wanted him to be at the hospital with her. She needed his support and so did Brooklyn. Avi took out her mobile phone and dialed Trace's. It went straight to voicemail.

"Where's daddy?" Brooklyn asked.

"He's at work, honey. I've been trying to call him."

"Well, he should answer."

"I know, baby." Avi grinned. "He's busy."

Avi turned to Brooklyn's neighbor on her left side. "What's your name?"

"Sarah." She had freckled fair skin, a gap in her front teeth, and curly, voluminous, auburn hair. The girl wore a neck brace and had injuries similar to Brooklyn's.

"I'm Brooklyn's mom. Where's your mom?"

"I don't know," Sarah said.

"You haven't seen her at all?"

Sarah shook her head.

"Aww…" Avi rubbed Sarah's shoulder. Avi looked over at the third bed and saw Brooklyn's other roommate, the girl's blue eyes looking back through her feathery lashes.

"That's Simone. She sleeps a lot," Sarah said.

"She's awake now." Avi smiled. "Hi, Simone." She waved. Simone waved back. "Where's your mom, Simone?"

Simone began to cry. She choked out words between gasps. "I. Don't. Know."

Simone's grief sliced Avi's heart. She put her hand over her chest. "It's okay, honey. Do you girls wanna hear a story?"

Simone nodded. Sarah said, "Yeah!"

"Yes!" Brooklyn squeaked.

Avi recited *Oh, the Places You'll Go!* from memory. After ten minutes serenity befell the room. When she stood her knee ached. Faintness engulfed her. She gripped the chair until blood returned to her brain. Simone was asleep. Sarah had also drifted off peacefully. Avi lay down and snuggled into her daughter, her mind and body finally relaxing after two days of fear and anxiety. She sank into the bed, the coolness of the sheets comforting her. Her lack of adrenaline revealed how tired she was.

Avi wondered where Trace was at that very moment. *You've been on my mind. All day, every hour, every few minutes I oscillate between thinking about Brooklyn and you. Are you injured? Are you eating? Have you slept? I remember our times. I know your sweet heart—your kind, honest eyes. That's what swept me. I knew inside you were beautiful, pure.* Avi reminisced how Trace had pushed the two dollars into her hand at the food truck and wasn't looking for anything in return. *We need to cherish each other like we had in the past.*

CHAPTER 37

The beam of Trace's xenon helmet light refracted in the thick smoke and steam inside the auxiliary building. He stood in a foot of radioactive water fiddling with the light switches on the wall, but the power was out and he didn't have time to troubleshoot. His flashlight beam gleamed along the maze of iron and steel pipes and catwalk that twisted several stories up into the building. He moved forward, his waterproof boots sloshing through the water. He felt like he was in the Manhattan sewer system; the dead rat in the corner made the notion palpable. Intense heat along with a vibrating sensation Trace swore was ionizing radiation penetrated his protective suit. He approached a ladder and looked up. Pointing his headlamp through the catwalk above revealed decades of dirt and corrosion thick on the pipes. *I'm gettin' cooked now. Where is that valve?* He ascended the ladder. Since everyone was exhausted Ken had suggested they wait until morning to make their move on the valve, but Trace wasn't having it. He had a witch's work to do—contain a witch's brew. The sooner the better, and he wouldn't sleep anyway with the hydrogen bubble still looming inside a cauldron of radioactivity. The sound of rumbling and steam escaping echoed nearby. Trace wondered if the rumbling was the reactor, which didn't make sense to him. *Might be the pumps.* There was a caged beast behind the walls. *Don't awaken it... Keep going!* The iron catwalk clanged as he clomped along.

Trace reached the vertical middle of the building and climbed another ladder, squeezing his rotund frame through the small opening in the grated platform above. The catwalk wobbled when he put his weight down. Ahead, the platform and rail twisted down to the right where he needed to continue his ascent. A pipe adjacent to him had dislodged at some point earlier, taking out the catwalk next to it. He figured it may've happened the day before when he and Hanson were there attempting to collect a sample. He breathed into the fear knotting his gut as he thought about getting smacked unconscious by another pipe. Hanson's death hung in his consciousness again. Trace envisioned his own face melting. *Quit it!* He stepped forward gingerly, holding the rails, and saw a ladder less than ten feet away. He took another step. The catwalk whined. He stopped and surveyed the grating and rail, hoping it would hold. He continued forward several more steps. The catwalk twisted downward. "Shiiiit!" Trace grabbed a pipe above him and felt the platform peel away from his boots, his weight transferring to his arms. He moved his feet to a pipe next to him and listened to the catwalk cry, twisting away, dislodging the platform and ladder structure above that he needed to climb to access the valve. The iron clanged thunderously off pipes and infrastructure before splashing into the water below. "Perfect," he grumbled. His hands gripping the pipe above his head made him look like a nervous jungle tourist on a two-line rope bridge. He spoke into his suit radio, the compression of his shoulders pushing into his neck constricting his voice as if he was fighting a multiday stretch of constipation. "Val, it's

Crane. Catwalk's been compromised. I'm hangin' here like a tightrope walker."

"What happened?"

"Pipe burst from earlier dislodged the supports. Imma have to scale the pipes from midway to the top."

"We told you to go in with a team... You need assistance?"

Trace looked up into the maze of iron and steel, dreading the ascent. *I sure do.* "Nah. I'm good." *No one else is comin' in here.*

"Copy that. Careful on the climb. You don't look like the pull-up type."

Trace chuckled. "Kiss my ass," he said breathlessly. He looked down through the tangle of pipes, his light shimmering on the water twenty-two feet below. *Yeah, that wouldn't feel good.* Trace monkey-walked his way thirteen feet along the pipes to a vertical run. He slowly climbed upwards, feet and hands on metal strapping, supports, pipes, whatever he could use. *God, I'm out of shape.* He hacked, the cough deep in his chest. "Where's the valve? I don't see it."

"Don'tchu listen? I told you it's on the left side of the walk," Valdern said.

"Yeah, well, I'm not on the fucking walk anymore. I'm climbing pipes like Koko the gorilla in here. You know, after this, I hope you go home and get laid for fuck sake you're so goddamn ornery." Trace surveyed the pipes above. The painted labels, stickers, and metal tags nearly impossible to read from his angle. "Well, this is a fantastic fucking nightmare. I'm lost in here gettin' cooked sous vide."

"I don't know what you sayin', Crane. Gimme a landmark in there so I can direct ya."

Trace scanned the pipes. Nothing. Smudged, corroded numbers and letters. He faced where he had come from and then up into the room, looking for the valve. "I see valve eighteen fifty-two above me. Am I close?"

"Yup. Next row above that to your left, right of the boron-injection tank."

Beyond eighteen fifty-two Trace saw pipes and dislodged catwalk in his path. "Great." *I'm gonna be walkin' upside down, diagonal into a different realm.* He continued forward, struggling to pull himself upward. He saw the boron-injection tank above to his left. "I think I see it." He focused on a collection of valves at the end of the tank.

"Good. Can you get to it?" Valdern asked.

"Imma do my best. Over." Trace continued to climb. Determination and adrenaline propelled him. Every pull of his weight made Trace hate himself, made him want to run nine miles a day and lift weights. He pulled himself up another foot, his biceps burning, his wet boots slipping squeakily on the iron. Trace reached higher and tried to pull himself up one last time. His arm muscles locked. He stopped and held himself steady, his respirator mask suffocating like a wet towel over his face. He lifted it and gulped in a breath. *Bad idea. Radiation.* He pulled his respirator back down. The seams were now loose. *Oh fuck it.* He looked at the wheel valve above several feet to his left. *It's right there, c'mon!* Trace reached, gripped the pipe strapping and pulled himself up twice more with two bellowing grunts. He was on all fours on a horizontal pipe that led to the valve. He shimmied along the iron and arrived at the wheel valve, which was attached to a vertical offshoot of pipe. He stood, wrapped his arm around the offshoot and stabilized himself.

Trace took a straight steel bar strapped to his side and stuck it through the handwheel. He leaned on the bar, struggling to get the wheel to budge. The valve had been there for over forty years and may have never been turned. "C'mon…" He put more weight onto the bar. "Dammit!" He went at it again with all his mass. The wheel turned with a splitting cry. Trace lost his footing. He reactively snatched onto the horizontal pipe his feet had stood on, gripping it in the fold of his elbow of his right arm, his weight yanking with such force he felt his arm would tear off his torso. His feet dangled. The steel bar plummeted forty-three feet to the murky water. Trace's shoulder and arm muscles burned, joints and ligaments tearing from his body. His arm started unfolding at his elbow.

You fall, you ain't gettin' back up. Trace swung his left hand to the pipe. His fingers grazed the bottom. He swung his arm again, his fingers slipping off the side of the pipe. Again he went at it, that time yanking himself up with his right arm. His left hand caught the iron. The strain in his right shoulder lessened. He swung his feet to a vertical pipe in front of him. The tips of his boots teetered on the edge of a pipe coupling, his body leaning away from his feet, putting him on a diagonal. *This is to save the reactor. To save the East Coast.* "Ahhhh!!!" He climbed his hands one in front of the other along the pipe until he was vertical. His chest heaved and his calves trembled. *Damn, that was close. I need a moment. Fuck. You imbecile. C'mon!*

Trace climbed back up to the valve, gripped the handwheel, and tried to turn it. It wouldn't budge. "I need that bar." He tried the wheel again, sweat streaming down his red face. Either the wheel was going to budge or his head was going to pop. "C'mon! Motherfucker." He let out a deep roar. The wheel moved half a revolution. "C'mon!" He turned it again. Every revolution took all his energy, every vibration in his being, all his soul. Adrenaline made him feel superhuman. He had strength like a junkie on PCP and bath salts. He'd eat someone's face if he had to. "C'mon!" Cuts on his hand burning under his gloves felt good. The turning became easier, full revolutions ensuing. The piping shook. Trace recoiled, eying the pipe. He didn't want to get smacked by a burst pipe again. *Keep goin'.* The wave of shaking subsided. Trace went back to turning. Turning. Turning. Turning. Trace's arms burned and trembled. "For Christ's sake, c'mon already!" The wheel finally tightened to a stop. "Val, it's Crane, come in. Valve is open. Repeat. Valve is open." Hearing the flow of gas and coolant in the pipes allayed Trace's trepidations. He felt victorious.

"Copy. Now get outta there," Val said.

Trace dreaded the descent but felt exultant, standing high in the building, king of the pipe jungle. He'd pound his chest if he didn't have to hold on. He had completed one-third of his mission. All he needed was cold shutdown and his girls. He was ninety-five percent sure the bubble would be dissipated without complication. He couldn't envisage an undesirable outcome, nor could he handle one.

The water falling from the decontamination shower on Trace's neck and shoulders sent soothing waves through his muscles. *At least this time I can scrub myself.* He coughed, a nasty hack that bellowed under his ribs. *I'm getting worse.* The interior of his body vibrated; he wasn't sure if it was exhaustion and caffeine or radiation he had absorbed. If Trace ever walked out of Bear Mountain he hoped by some miracle he would live. *Maybe I've taken in less than I've thought. Maybe I'll be that bizarre case that lives.* Doctors arched over him, gawking, charting notes, astonishment twisting their faces. "You're an anomaly," one of them said. Trace hoped that would be the case; his life hadn't been fulfilled yet. He had to make things right with Avi and he had to stay alive for Brooklyn.

Trace scrubbed his pale skin with soap and Radiacwash, moving the brush across his stomach and arms. Injuries on his face, head, and hand burned. He loathed his appearance and couldn't understand how Avi continued to look at him after his weight had ballooned. *Wonder if they can do lypo on my corpse? I should have time to make my funeral requests before the radiation takes me. I think cremation'll do. Let the wake be a bow tie around an urn.* Even though Trace loathed himself, he felt accomplished for having opened the valve in auxiliary. He was anxious to get back to the control room to see how the reactor was responding, though he knew it would take hours for the hydrogen to expel and results to show. Trace's stomach bubbled. He hustled out of the shower to a toilet stall. His stomach retched and whatever was inside him blew out his bottom. *Radiation sickness or stress?* He rubbed his face. A wave of exhaustion cast over him. He checked his watch—4:00 a.m. He figured he'd get two to four hours on the cot if he was lucky.

CHAPTER 38

Avi sat next to Brooklyn, watching her chest rise and fall. The doctor had stopped by forty-seven minutes before and told her Brooklyn would need a few more days at the medical center before she could be released for home care. Lea slouched in a chair by the bathroom door, leaning on her hand, asleep. The glow of the rising sun refracted through the window, casting shadowy rays on the foot of Brooklyn's bed. Avi smiled. She watched dust dance in the beams. She saw the particles as a higher power entering from the divine realm to help heal Brooklyn. She approached the window, looked to her right between buildings toward Central Park and watched the morning sky glow ochre and violet across the clouds. *Magnificent.* Her first sense of calmness in forty-eight hours radiated through her. She had slept soundly next to Brooklyn all night and finally felt somewhat rested. The colors of the sky reminded her of when she and Trace used to sit in front of a shipping dock on the Hudson watching the sunset. The dock was one of her favorite structures in the city. It encompassed character, fortitude, and maturity—attributes she believed to be important to the soul. She wanted to be that dock when she grew old.

"SHUT 'EM DOWN! SHUT 'EM DOWN! SHUT 'EM DOWN!" A crowd chanting roused her. She looked to the street. Protestors marched down Broadway, pumping staked signs skyward emblazoned with reactor steam-stacks and Gener8 and Bear Mountain logos with X's through them. "Down with NUCLEAR! Down with Gener8! Down with NUCLEAR! Down with Gener8! Down with NUCLEAR! Down with Gener8!" blasted out of bullhorns. Avi turned back to Lea and pushed her on the arm.

"Lea. Look." She pointed out the window.

"Huh?" Lea awoke, wiped her eyes, and hobbled next to Avi. The ladies said nothing to each other. If Avi didn't have to stay with Brooklyn she'd gladly join them. *I'd lead them!* She dragged her fingertips over the satin skin of Brooklyn's arm. Hunger set in. A chocolate, blueberry, banana smoothie would be nice, but she wasn't going to find it at the hospital.

"You hungry? Why don't I go down the street and get us something?" Lea said.

Avi nodded. "Really? That'd be amazing."

"Of course." Lea headed for the door. "I'll be back." She exited.

Avi was concerned about research she was supposed to have turned in two days before. Even though she was sure her client, Particle Power, would understand the delay, she felt anxious she wouldn't be able to fulfill her commitment. The nuclear disaster showed just how important her work was. Now that she had Brooklyn she was ready to go to the lab and push forward. If safe, clean, renewable energy production had already been adopted New York wouldn't have been dealing with a nuclear catastrophe. According to Avi's research, zero-point energy had an estimated generation efficiency of ninety-nine percent. It was an inconceivable figure considering traditional fossil fuel and nuclear systems carried efficiencies between thirty and forty-five percent. Single nuclear reactors produce anywhere from a few hundred megawatts to just over a thousand, with the largest facilities registering a total capacity peaking in the three thousand range. Avi had calculated that a zero-point energy system could produce more energy in a hundred-thousand-square-foot warehouse than the total nuclear capacity of some entire states. The research was astounding and she was eager to share it with her client.

Avi kissed Brooklyn on her head. Now she needed to hear from Trace. She reached into her handbag and surfaced with the jewelry box she had taken from her home the day before. She opened it and slipped her original engagement ring onto her finger above her baguette-diamond wedding band. Even though she had an updated platinum, two-carat, cushion-cut diamond ring she had chosen to wear the original white gold with diamond spec Trace had given her fifteen years ago. She wanted that bond between them to return, a bond that was rich in love, care, and emotion that superseded material possessions. The scales had tipped the wrong way. The bigger, clearer her diamonds had become and the more precious the metal the more their bond had diminished. She'd wear a plastic ring pop if it would repair their union.

Avi turned to the wall-mounted LCD TV. Governor Anthony Pagano filled the screen. "It has come to my attention that many residents in the area have been leaving their homes, panicking after hearing news regarding Bear Mountain. No evacuation has been ordered. I'm asking everyone to please not leave your homes. By many fleeing the area in an uncontrolled manner dangerous situations are being created on the roads, paths for emergency vehicles are being blocked, and additional chaos is being created. There is nothing to run from. I can assure you my office is on the pulse of the happenings at Bear Mountain and I will personally notify you if an evacuation is necessary."

The picture cut to news anchor Hanna Herrera. "This just in. Reports out of Morristown, New Jersey, witnesses say they saw the wife and daughter of Gener8 CEO Chris Barnes arriving at the Morristown Airport. Witnesses question whether the nuclear magnate is ushering his loved ones out of town because of the looming hydrogen bubble inside the troubled reactor. However, moments ago Governor Pagano said he and his team are on the pulse of the situation and an evacuation has not been ordered. Zac Hamm spoke to residents earlier today." The picture cut to an all-American field reporter who stuffed his microphone in different faces of worried residents from around Bear Mountain.

A lanky, bearded man, sixties, veins like caterpillars under the skin of his muscular arms packing bags in the back of his minivan said, "What's going to happen in ten, fifteen, twenty-five years if radiation is leaking? We won't know 'til we all get sick. Then it's too late."

"It's not what they're telling us. Lies, lies, lies…" A woman, seventies with curly gray hair. "They oughta shut all these nuclear plants down for good."

"I'm nervous, yes, but it's my job," a man in a hard hat and a button-up said. "I work at Bear Mountain and I've reached my daily radiation dose, but I'll go back in if they call me."

"We're worried we might never be able to go back to our home," a woman in her fifties said, "but we've left anyhow. We didn't wanna risk it. And now were here at my sister's house in view of another nuclear power plant. I'm feeling like there's very few places in the country, if any, where you can go far, far away from nuclear power."

"I had to leave my business," an Indian man with bulbous cheeks said. "I have a café. It's a small business. If we don't have customers we don't make money. No one is coming in and business has been slow due to the economy. We're already barely hanging on."

"My husband and I live paycheck to paycheck," said a woman in a white tank top with frail arms. "I'm a waitress. He works construction. We don't work, we don't get paid, and I have four kids to look after. We're going to have to rely on credit cards. Just a few days, a week or two will compound the debt we already have."

The program cut to a commercial break. Cheerful music played as appealing, ethnically diverse families danced across the screen. A bubbly woman's voice-over began to coincide with the footage, "What are the things you care about most? Do you care about your family? — Your environment? — Your health? — Your future? — Well, so do we. As the nation's leading alternative energy provider, we here at Gener8 care about you and everything around you." Chris Barnes appeared on the screen, walking in a green field near a river. "I'm Chris Barnes, CEO of Gener8. We proudly produce for our great nation clean energy, which helps you create, grow, and thrive all without the carbon footprint. So these guys," Barnes stepped up next to a massive redwood tree and placed his hand gently on it, "can continue to grow and thrive, too." The screen cut to a blue sea with the woman's voice-over following the matching onscreen text. "Grow. Thrive. Generate. Gener8."

Avi shut the TV off. People's stories were too heartbreaking for her. The sensation of the newscast was a verbal machine-gun assault. The fatal grenade in the trench—an image-recovery campaign for Gener8 and Bear Mountain. *The fear people are in—it's awful.* She faded back into her chair, leaned into the side of Brooklyn's bed, and caressed her baby's arm. No matter what transpired Avi believed she'd be okay. She had Brooklyn and that was paramount.

CHAPTER 39

After a dreamless three hours and nineteen minutes of sleep Trace had awoken with a surge of energy. He downed a coffee and ate nothing, his appetite nil. He should have been waking up at the beach for a relaxing day. He should've been dreading a Monday or have been anxious to get back to work, but instead he was behind fortified walls trying to stop a civil war. Trace stepped inside the control room in a fresh radiation suit. "How's she lookin'?"

"Wooohhhhh!!" the twenty-plus crew in the control room cheered and applauded. Workers came up and slapped him high-fives and gave him fist pounds.

"Nice job, Crane."

"Yeah, Crane! Fuckin' hero, man!"

"Wooooohh!" Everyone clapped. Valdern came up and extended his hand. Trace hesitated, realizing Valdern had reverence for him. He chortled thinking it took a death sentence to show Valdern that he had the guts to be in charge. Trace took his hand. Valdern drew Trace into his chest and patted him on the back. "You got balls, Crane."

Jerry stared at the sage-metal wall of switches, levers, and gauges. "Bubble's dissipating."

"Good," Trace said. Coolant was already rising and they were certain it was no longer superheated steam; the reactor temperature was dropping. The core had been melting, but Trace was glad containment held strong, keeping the New York metro area safe from catastrophic doses of radiation. His beloved reactor was being stabilized. At the very least Bear Mountain, Gener8, and he wouldn't be saddled with the stigma of a nuclear meltdown and evacuation. He hoped some of the media weight would shift back to the earthquake and focus on the effective efforts his team employed in stabilizing the reactor. Trace wanted to share the moment with Avi and Brooklyn. He wanted to be grateful again and return to the wonderful life they used to live.

Trace envisioned himself sitting in the plant cafeteria. He reached into his lunch bag and pulled out a glass container housing a gourmet meal Avi had whipped up for him. A slip of paper fell from the top. He turned it over. In Avi's cursive it read, 'Ingredients: Chicken, sweet potato, Love, and Joy.' Trace smiled. Warmth pervaded his veins. He loved being loved by Avi and he loved loving her.

On several occasions when Avi worked late at LBM Tech in Manhattan, Trace would show up at her lab. Security knew him so they'd give him access to the building. Trace walked back to the lab. When Avi saw him her face turned from pensive to joyous. Trace kissed her and tucked a magnolia blossom in her lab coat next to her pens. "I'll see you when you're done," he said. He pecked her on the lips and retreated outside. Trace loved to visit, but he always respected her space. Later, Avi left via the iron-and-glass front entrance. She had changed into jeans, boots, and a sweater, her lab attire left inside. Trace grabbed her arm. "C'mon. Let's try that new tapas spot on Spring."

We need to get back to that life. Trace walked into his office, flopped down in his chair, and fixated on the dusty awards jumbled on top of the shelves adjacent to his desk. The quake had shaken them into an entangled pile of gold plastic, plexiglass, and wood veneer; others lay broken on the floor. Trace and his operating team had earned the awards for safety and training, but now he wasn't sure if they'd lived up to them. Had the reactor exploded he would have swiped the awards clean into the trash. There were months ahead of intense restoration efforts for the New York metro area and the care of injured and displaced residents from the earthquake, years of reconstruction to put damaged communities back together. Once again New York would be okay—bruised and scraped, Trace and the tristate area would carry on. The earthquake and the nuclear scare would become another wound that would heal into a caterpillar scar the city and state would run their fingers over for eternity.

Trace rifled a desk drawer and surfaced with a power cable, using his house key to cut the wire casing open. He pulled out the colored strands and stripped the coatings off, leaving him with bare copper, which he twisted together down the six-foot length. Trace wondered if Bear Mountain and the industry would survive. He thought about Fukushima. All reactors in Japan had been taken offline, but four years after the disaster they slowly started coming back. He believed the U.S. might do the same considering nuclear constituted twenty percent of energy production for the country. Many states couldn't handle the impact of its absence. There were millions without power dealing with rolling blackouts in the dead of summer. People were having heat strokes across the country. Utilities already couldn't keep up with the demand, and once they saw the costs of pulling in extra coal and natural-gas energy streams they would beg the Department of Energy for fission. He believed the industry could rebuild and restructure. After the BP oil spill in the Gulf of Mexico they didn't stop procuring oil. This was similar, but he didn't agree with it. Antiquated reactors made nuclear too risky. The training and safety protocol didn't matter. *If someone drops a bomb it doesn't matter how prepared you are. It's going to detonate and devastate everything in its path.* New technology has shown significantly safer reactor systems. However, they aren't used. Natural methods like solar, wind, and water power are nothing in the world's production portfolio compared to fossil fuels and nuclear. It's a money game. *And for what? So some people can have five homes, an island, a jet, cars, jewels—material satisfaction to inflate vacuous egos?* Trace believed ego, industry, and consumerism had created monsters in modern society, poisoning the earth we walk on and the air we breathe. *How's that help the next generation to live on the planet? This is hell full of brainwashed idiots, me included. People don't deserve to live in fear.* Trace wouldn't put his family through it again. It wasn't worth it. Even though Gener8 employed thousands, hundreds alone in New York communities, it didn't matter. Even though their motto was to provide safe, clean, affordable energy to illuminate the path to the American dream, it didn't matter. Trace had been sure their safety systems were secure. Then when the quake hit the light spilled out of the holes. It wasn't perfect as he had seen it. It was human—riddled with bravado, error, and carelessness. No one could precisely predict what Earth was going to do and when it was going to do it. *She's fightin' back. That's what she's doin'. And she'll win.* He saw Earth like a graceful mare atop a prairie hill. She's there to ride, she's there to provide, but if you wrong her she'll trample you to protect herself. *Changes need to be made—global changes.*

Trace curved the twisted wire strands into a heart. Avi's and Brooklyn's love was all that mattered. What once was his passion had become his poison—goo inside his guts festering slowly, killing him. *I may've sacrificed my life for nuclear energy.* Tension in Trace's neck and shoulders eased slightly. *If Imma die, at least I know we saved the reactor and the land and the people. I'll be okay. Brooklyn... She's the one that suffers. Quit it!* He chuckled to himself. *Avi might be glad to get rid of me.* It wasn't true, but she deserved better. *She deserves the old me.* Tears pushed to his lids. He wished he could sleep more. It wouldn't happen until power was restored to the New York metro area and other nuclear-reliant areas of the country, using a safer production method. That's when he would be content; that's when he would sleep. At the Gener8 company conferences in New Orleans Chris Barnes had said, "I am energy. We are Gener8. We are now, we are the future." Trace shook his head. *We're a dinosaur.* He folded the remaining length of wire attached to the first heart into a second, conjoined heart and set the creation down on his desk.

CHAPTER 40

Trace sat in the emergency operations center with Ken Bramini looking at the large flat-screen TVs at the head of the room. Trace and Ken were on one-half of the screens. Gener8 CEO Chris Barnes, Governor Pagano, members of New York Emergency Management, health commissioners, surrounding county executives, emergency medical personnel, law enforcement, fire, parks, social services, communications, and the NRC stood on the other half at the Joint Information Center in Westchester in front of a crowd of reporters. Trace tried to instill some semblance of confidence within himself. He had won the jackpot, yet exhaustion and embitterment made his face sag, kept his lip curled. He was relieved they had dissipated the bubble. However, he knew it was a half-court shot in overtime at the buzzer—skill and luck, potentially a higher power guiding them. He kept thinking if Barnes and Ken didn't agree to stop venting to appease the governor, a hydrogen bubble may not have formed and they would've stabilized the day before. Containment held a massive amount of radioactive isotopes from the partial core melt, thus an evacuation would've been necessary if they had vented. The land around Bear Mountain would've been contaminated. However, early on containment held a fraction of the radiation it currently housed and it may not have caused an issue. Trace wasn't sure what was worse: the venting or leaving the containment building as they had sitting like a bomb, praying it could be dismantled without evacuating anyone. His initiative had worked, and of course everyone applauded themselves for making "the right decisions", but he wasn't sure it had been worth the risk. *Who cares!* He wanted to see his girls.

"After this you're going to decontamination and the hospital," Ken said to Trace.

"Imma find my girls after this," Trace answered.

Ken stabbed his finger at Trace. "You're gonna do what I—"

"Okay, we're live in five seconds," an operations-center staff member shouted.

"You'll follow fucking protocol, dammit," Ken said. If Trace's eyes were lasers they would've melted Ken's face.

"In three... two..."

Trace and Ken turned away from each other.

Trace watched Chris Barnes step to a gaggle of microphones with every news acronym in the country jammed together on the podium. He wore a double-breasted, window-pane suit over a white-and-purple plaid shirt sans tie. His wire-frame glasses dangled from his jacket pocket. "I'm here to tell you... the crisis is over. We're out of danger. I want to assure residents working and living around the Bear Mountain Nuclear Energy Center that the hydrogen bubble has been dissipated and the reactor is heading toward stabilization and cold shutdown. My company, Gener8 Corporation, has been working hand in hand with the DOE, NRC, EPA, and other local, state, and federal agencies to ensure the safety of the public." Barnes spoke in an even tone, a notch upbeat, his poise anchored with a tinge of Southern twang. "I myself have been in and out of the site over the last three days, and I can tell you firsthand that we are stabilizing the reactor and the release of radioactive isotopes into the environment has been minimal and has not exceeded federal limitations outside of the Bear Mountain property line. This positive news is a testament to the safety and emergency protocols that the dedicated teams from New York State, local agencies, and Gener8 have trained so extensively in."

"What about the high radiation levels that've been recorded over ten miles from the plant?" a journalist shouted.

Harvey Asner came to the podium, swept his falling combover out of his face, and leaned into the microphones. "Harvey Asner here from the Nuclear Regulatory Commission. What was told to the press was a hoax. What was printed was sensationalized. The hydrogen bubble has been relieved. Radiation levels outside the perimeter of the facility have not risen with any significance. There's less radiation out there than you'd get from a dental X-ray." Harvey stepped back from the podium.

"Thank you, Mr. Asner." Barnes turned back to the journalists.

"And the victims with radiation exposure?" a journalist asked.

"That's not a confirmed report." Barnes looked back to Asner, his director of media relations, and his other staff behind him. "Has anyone?…" Barnes turned back to the press. "We've heard it, but it's not true. It's not possible. People are trying to sell newspapers out there and it's a lie. My home is barely twenty miles from the plant. My family is all in this area—my friends, and my business associates. People close to me that I'd never put in harm's way. None of them has left and none of them have been exposed to threatening radiation levels. So, I can assure you our information is forthright and accurate and what some press outlets are printing is not."

"THAT MAN TELLS LIES!" a woman yelled.

"LIAR!" a man stood and jabbed his finger in Barnes' direction. Six more men and woman stood from the sea of reporters. Some held signs with X's drawn through nuclear steam-stacks. Others held signs with NRC, Gener8, dollar signs, and the words ENVIRONMENTAL ASSASSIN! MURDERER! SWINE! GREED! NUCLEAR HOLOCAUST! BLOOD MONEY! POISON POWER! One of the younger women removed her top to reveal 'NO NUKES' painted across her breasts.

"NO NUKES! TELL THE TRUTH! NO NUKES! TELL THE TRUTH!" they chanted.

Local police and security quickly moved in to grab the protestors. They continued to hurl allegations. "You've poisoned our community!"

"The truth shall set you free!"

"It's a coverup!"

"LIES! He LIES! Can't you see it?"

"We're being blanketed with fallout!"

"There'll be black rain!"

"We need to evacuate everyone!" Authorities dragged the protestors out of the room, their allegations continuing to echo from the hall.

Trace wasn't surprised by protestors. He'd seen them that morning outside the plant, in Manhattan, and dozens of times before. His first encounter when he started the job years ago was the most jarring, then he calloused to it. Now he understood where the people were coming from. He wanted nothing to do with nuclear either. However, he hoped people could see that he and his team worked hard to mitigate the disaster and keep the East Coast safe. The pro-nuclear attitude that had made up part of his soul until over forty-eight hours ago still wondered how the protestors could display anger on a subject they knew nothing about. He was still hurt that people attacked Bear Mountain, Gener8, and the nuclear-energy industry with such hostility. Even though it wasn't serving his life it still hurt to be subjected to the protestors' venom. The bitter poison from the public made Trace think he and his team were worthless. *No... That's what they want us to think.* The public should be grateful that he and the industry had provided them with electricity and a low carbon footprint. He thought he and his team might be seen as heroes. Not that he wanted to be labeled as one, but recognition for his team would be nice. He hoped residents would consider that he and his crew took their jobs with the hope to help support positive societal infrastructure. They didn't shake the earth or ask the reactor to malfunction. They did their best to respond to unexpected circumstances. No one was mad at firefighters after a building burned down and they had tried their best to save it.

"I'd like to see if control-room supervisor Trace Crane would like to say a few words. Trace personally turned the valve to dissipate the hydrogen bubble. He and his team are heroes and everyone here should applaud them for their incredible efforts." Barnes clapped his hands and turned to the government personnel behind him to get their hands moving. "Trace? Go 'head."

Did I just hear my name? Instinct drew Trace's attention to the screens at the front of the room. Barnes, Governor Pagano, and all other personnel stared at him on the screen behind them. *Are they waiting on me?* Ken Bramini's fierce eyes spun like pinwheels at him. Seconds passed. Silence over the airwaves. He saw his bloated, bruised, bloody face on the TV, eyes black, puffed, and sunken—no makeup this time around. Embarrassment dampened his energy. The world was waiting. *Say something, you idiot!* Trace cleared his throat. "Thank you. Umm… Public… public safety has always been… has always been our number-one priority. We *care* about this community. I care about it. My team here cares about it. It's our home. We live here. We live… close. Most of us, just a couple miles from the plant. We understand what everyone has been going through and we appreciate the support. We are grateful we were able to rein in the reactor and dissipate the hydrogen bubble. I haven't seen or heard from my wife since yesterday… my daughter in over two days… Avi, Brooklyn, if you're out there call the plant, get in touch with me." The video feed of Trace and Ken wavered. Trace's chair vibrated. He looked at Ken. His scowl asked if he had felt the tremors. Ken didn't seem to know what Trace was referring to. *Maybe it's the radiation inside me.* "If… If a… If any law enforcement or emergency-management staff can help me find my wife and daughter it would be greatly appreciated. We look forward to continuing to serve the community and… monitoring the reactor to continue its cooling and stability. Umm… Thank you."

The main bout had ended. He thought Chris Barnes should send champagne and cigars to the control room. *What was that shaking?* He didn't see Barnes' side of the screen move. He touched his chest and felt his heart still beating rhythmically. *Still alive. Fingers and toes work. Speech works.* Jerry's voice squawked over Trace's radio. "Crane, you finished in there yet? We got some sort of seismic event that we recorded—" Trace cut the volume. Ken scowled at Trace for having his radio on. *They felt it, too.* Trace stood calmly and smiled so he wouldn't startle anyone. The camera cut from him. "I better go see what's happening," he told Ken.

CHAPTER 41

"There's been an explosion at reactor three." The crewman's voice cut through Trace's radio as he tromped down a corridor pulling gloves on. "Something's exploded. I don't know if it's a transformer or what. Over."

The word 'explosion' howled through Trace's entire body like a poltergeist scream. "Copy that." He burst into the control room, tightening his respirator mask around his face. "What's happening? I got radio of an explosion? They think it could be a transformer?"

"The pressure in containment changed," Sinclair said.

"Elaborate. I felt the floor rattle in the EOF."

Sinclair pointed to the meter. "Pressure gauge spiked and then lowered."

Trace tossed his hands. "Was there combustion inside containment?"

"Seismic meter did record." Sinclair motioned to the seismometer. Trace saw the spike the weighted pen had drawn on the paper.

"Containment's intact as we can see on the surveillance

cams," Jerry said, pointing to the flat-screen TVs suspended from the ceiling.

Trace scowled at the seismogram and then turned to Jerry and Sinclair. They looked at him and shrugged. The pressure spike in containment worried Trace. *Can a transformer explosion spike the pressure?* Trace was confident the hydrogen had been piped out of the core directly into a sealed tank in auxiliary. The containment building was intact. Trace's pulse knocked in his ears, a presaging intuition howling in his head. "Jerry. Do we have a three-sixty view of containment and all reactor-three infrastructure?"

Jerry shook his head. "Nope. We have several cameras out from the quake."

"I'm going out with a team to take a look."

Trace walked swiftly around the concrete containment dome with Gary Harrell and two other crew. The two-hundred-and-fifteen-foot structure looked like a dirty, gray pill jutting out of the earth—one Trace didn't want to swallow. The sky was overcast and the spotlights on the dome coupled with the white protective suits Trace and his team wore made them look like astronauts on a lunar landing. Steam and smoke wafting became increasingly dense, blowing over his head. *Everything looks good. Everything's gonna be fine.* He saw the transformers. They were intact and the smoke wasn't coming from them. Trace stormed ahead, rounding the containment building and approaching smaller adjacent buildings. Small bits of concrete rubble appeared, then larger chunks. His boots froze to the ground. Gary and the other crew stopped and pointed.

"NO!" The roof and one wall of the auxiliary building attached to containment was blown apart, opening a hole in containment where the buildings joined. Adrenaline released with sharp stabs in Trace's abdomen. His arms weakened—a bizarre, cold, empty sensation down to his bones. *What's happened? This can't be...* It was as if he was staring at a double murder of his wife and child. The gun was in his hand, blood spattered on his clothes, but he had no memory of what had happened. His life stopped. It was over. Lifetime imprisonment or death was next. There was nothing else. *But why?* "Val, it's Crane, we've... Val, we..." His chest surged with breath and tightened. He couldn't speak.

"Spit it out!" Valdern shouted over the radio.

In his state of shock Trace couldn't comprehend how hydrogen had leaked into the oxygen-rich auxiliary building and exploded when it was supposed to have drained into a sealed tank. Trace closed his eyes and calmed himself just enough to speak. "Auxiliary's exploded and we've breached containment," he said into his protective-suit walkie. "Repeat. Containment is breached, auxiliary's exploded." Static swirled. Trace swallowed a large breath. "Large cracks in containment, part of the wall between auxiliary and containment blown out, most of the roof and part of a wall of auxiliary is missing. Goddammit. Fuck." Trace gawked catatonic at the destroyed concrete and protruding rebar. *We've poisoned everyone... everything... Did I do this? Did I turn the wrong valve? Did Valdern misdirect me?* Now Trace really needed to make sure Avi and Brooklyn were leaving town if they hadn't already. *Where are they?* An explosion in the auxiliary building was one of the worse possible scenarios because the building housed most of the control and safety equipment for the reactor. If Trace and his team lost control of the reactor they would face full meltdown, which would ratchet up fallout exponentially and make the containment of the disaster nearly impossible. The reactor would be a 767 with no wings until coolant was circulated around the core, but if the core melted completely it'd most likely become a mass of periodic-table elements in the substructure of the containment building with everyone praying it wouldn't leach out into the earth.

Trace burst back into the control room. "We need a team to patch the cracks in containment and cover auxiliary. How the fuck, Val? Seriously, what the fuck!"

"I read the fucking blueprints. I didn't come up with the idea."

Trace stepped up to Valdern's toes. "Well, you didn't read it correctly. Goddammit!" Trace jabbed Valdern's chest.

"Don'tchu put a damn finger on me!" Valdern grabbed Trace at his shoulders and shoved him. Trace stumbled back, his weight anchoring him. He stepped forward, eyes scorching, quivering—a man with nothing more to lose. Trace lunged for Valdern, grabbed him at the front of his suit, and shook him. "MOTHERFUCKER, HOW COULD YOU! I'LL FUCKIN' KILL YOU GODDAMMIT!" Spit leapt from Trace's mouth onto the inside of his respirator mask. Valdern wrestled against Trace's hulking frame. Jerry jumped between the two and pushed them back. "Stop it! Stop it, goddammit! We gotta active situation here!"

"Imma kill that motherfucker!" Valdern stared back at Trace, fists clenched.

"Calm down! Both of ya!" Jerry barked.

"How could you not read that schematic correctly?" Trace snapped.

"I did! I did! I just double-checked it," Valdern said. "We turned the right valve."

"Lemme see that goddamn thing!" Trace demanded. Valdern slapped the schematic down on the table and unrolled it. Trace looked at the paper, confirming Val's accuracy. "Damn pipes must've been compromised from the quake! Either that or the rush of coolant and hydrogen ruptured the holding tank." Trace shoved the schematic off the table. "Fucking Christ!" Trace slammed his arms to his side and paced. *You idiot, Crane. What the fuck were you thinking? You didn't know. You didn't know. You thought it'd be okay. I fucking blew up the auxiliary building. I'm fucked. FUCKED!* Trace was glad he had radiation poisoning that would most likely kill him because he knew his career was officially over. *Doesn't matter what I say. I did it. I turned the wheel. It was my idea.*

"Don't beat yourself up on it," Valdern said. "We had no other options. We would've never known that would be the outcome."

Trace continued to pace. *He's right. The whole thing's a booby trap.* They hadn't seen any indication in the control room that those specific pipes were compromised or an exorbitant amount of coolant would rupture the holding tank. Further, the auxiliary building wasn't equipped with hydrogen-detection alarms. *Think. Think. Think. You need a plan, motherfucker. Whaddayou gonna do? How you gonna fix this?* Trace stopped pacing and walked back toward Valdern. "We need to patch containment."

"What we gonna stuff in there?" Valdern said.

"Cotton?" Jerry remarked.

"Jerry, shut the fuck up," Valdern said.

"Our crew can get started on the cracks. Then we need some kind of lead-lined sheeting to lay over auxiliary and the compromised containment wall until we come up with a stronger solution. We'll need two cranes to bring it in place and guys on buckets to secure it. Call Radical Services; they'll have something or know where to get it. And in the meantime let's get boric acid spraying from the chopper and trucks on the ground," Trace said.

Valdern went to a phone on the opposite side of the room.

"Jerry. Do we still have control of the reactor?" Trace asked.

"I don't know. I don't know… Pressure and temperature are rising. Give me a minute."

"We don't have a fucking minute! You got seconds. Seconds!" *If we've lost all control so help us God.*

"Crane, come in, it's Greco," crunched in Trace's ear.

"Go 'head," Trace responded.

"I'm out in the surrounding area and exposure has increased greatly. I've found 3,425 millirem per hour in Cortlandt and Martin's got 1,963 millirem in Ossining."

Trace's face contorted. He ripped off his respirator mask, pulled his glove off with his mouth, and scratched the side of his face until it seeped blood. "Are you certain?"

"Certain. Double-checked everything and retested."

Trace wanted some kind of ointment to soothe his face. *More radiation exposure... sure, why not!* It was worth the scratch. He pulled his mask and glove back on. They'd had a major release. Trace knew licensed nuclear reactors shall not expose any individual of the public to more than 100 millirem per year. EPA guidelines also set individual absorption to 100 millirem, air exposure limits to 10 millirem per year, and water limits to 4 millirem. With the new field readings residents living between five and ten miles from Bear Mountain could achieve 1,000 millirem in less than an hour, one hundred times the EPA and NRC's yearly limits. At twenty-five miles out, 1,000 millirem could be reached in less than two hours from the time of release, also having the potential of exposing individuals to several hundred thousand millirem for the year, thousands of times beyond EPA and NRC standards. With more than 10,000 millirem of exposure per year known to significantly increase the chances of cancer, the situation was dire. Potassium iodide could be taken, but it would only protect individuals from the absorption of radioactive iodine in the thyroid. If the level of exposure Greco reported was accurate and rising, potassium iodide would have a minuscule effect.

"Crane, do you copy," Greco said.

"Copy. Keep testing," Trace replied into his radio. Greco's report of the gargantuan release of radioactivity lodged in his throat. He'd choke to death before ever being able to swallow it down. "Clyde, get the maps out on the table in my office." He headed for the room. The Korean-Caucasian hustled behind him with a collection of rolled paper under his arm and a fistful of pencils.

"Take a look." Clyde pointed to the map. "With 37,000 rem leaving the auxiliary and containment buildings and being disseminated via a north and northwesterly wind, I'm ending up with a forty-eight-hour dose projection of 226 rem within five miles, 164 rem at ten miles, 94 rem at twenty miles, 56 rem at fifty miles."

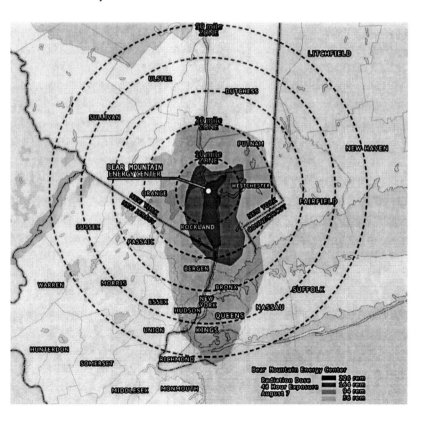

The dosages were desperately, sickeningly high. Trace's sternum burned, his stomach so tense it felt frozen. "They need to evacuate Manhattan?" It was a question and a statement. He hoped Clyde would say no, but he already knew the answer.

"Definitely. This plume is gonna blow right through and into Long Island before it hits the Atlantic."

"My god." Almost twenty million people resided within a fifty-mile radius of Bear Mountain and the projections Clyde showed Trace threatened many of them. That type of fallout could force a mind-boggling, economically paralyzing abandonment of New York City. *Water in the area would be contaminated. Drinking water would need to be cut from the supply chain. The Hudson River would carry contamination from Bear Mountain down between New Jersey and New York and out into the Atlantic Ocean, spreading the fallout to a much larger area, impacting marine life and the human food supply of fish. In the wild, marine-life reproduction could not be stopped, and therefore newly created life would suffer from defects as radioactive isotopes affected living organisms down to their DNA.* Life could be changed forever. He took a deep inhale and leaned on the table in his office. "Ken, come in, it's Trace," he said breathlessly into his suit radio. *He's gonna kill me.*

"Yeah," Ken said.

"Where are you? We've got a containment breach."

"What? I'm still in the EOF. Whaddayou mean we got a containment breach?"

"Hydrogen blew inside auxiliary. Most of the roof's missing and a portion of a wall. Containment wall is also compromised. Val's calling Radical Services to find lead-lined material to patch it. But we've got a major release. You need to recommend an evacuation immediately. You need twenty miles around plus a keyhole punching through Manhattan into Long Island."

"What?"

"Yes, Ken."

"Jesus."

"No. He can't save us now. We're fucked," Trace said.

"How? I thought we dissipated the bubble?"

"We did and it went into the auxiliary building and blew out the top like a fucking torpedo!"

"How did this happen?" Ken barked.

"Trace!" Jerry called out.

"Yeah?"

"Pumps are up and I'm trying to circulate coolant."

"You have control?

"Yup, we got somethin'," Jerry said.

"Thank god." Trace spoke back into his suit radio to Ken. "Call the governor."

"How did this happen?" Ken asked again. Trace cut his volume down. He'd explain it to Ken later. He figured Ken was going to launch off when he saw him because Trace had stopped Ken from pursing his own initiative. It didn't matter if the piping was compromised or the sealed tank ruptured. It was Trace's idea *and* he turned the valve with his own hands. Trace couldn't believe they had just been on TV reporting the crisis was over. It was similar to what had happened with the morning show only exponentially worse. It was the bottom, a burial under the substructure. Now again Gener8, Bear Mountain, and Trace had their pants around their ankles. *I just lied to the nation. But you didn't know. You didn't know! It doesn't matter. Everyone's going to think we lied.* Trace rubbed his hooded head. He should've told the governor to evacuate everyone yesterday. It wasn't Trace's authority to make the decision, but just saying it would've been better than sitting there and being sanguine. *Oh yeah, everything's great. No problem. We got this. How could you let this happen?* Trace realized he was dealing with one of the worst atomic accidents ever to occur in the world. It was Fukushima in America and he prayed it wouldn't turn into Chernobyl.

CHAPTER 42

Trace braced himself on the central desk inside the control room, unable to stop himself from hyperventilating. The room spun under his feet as if he had vertigo. He inhaled deeply and paced, staggering, tugging at his suffocating radiation suit while he and his team waited for consulting crews to arrive with the containment patch. He wanted to unzip his body and pull his soul out of his skin. He wanted to evanesce into another realm, run far, and expunge his name from Bear Mountain. Regret of ever stepping foot into nuclear energy deluged Trace. The guilt was little blades cutting at his viscera. *Why call it a control room? I haven't been in control this entire time! I've been tethered to this beast and dragged along.* Sweat dripped in his vision. He pulled off one of his gloves, reached under his mask, and swabbed his lashes and lids. *Some more isotopes for me, why not?* He hacked, his cough resonating like compressed air howling through a metal pipe. When he had been dressing after his shower he had noticed red blotches covering his arms and abdomen. *I definitely picked up more crawling around in auxiliary. And what was the point of that? You poisoned yourself more AND you caused the entire New York metro area to have to be evacuated.*

"Trace!" Skip Sinclair grabbed Trace at his shoulders. He twisted away from Skip, grabbed his hooded head, and paced. He wrestled with wanting to run out and get help since his symptoms had progressed, but instinct told him he'd be dead in a few weeks and medical attention wouldn't really matter. *Am I exaggerating again? You don't deserve it anyway! How could you! I'm an irradiated vegetable.* He chortled. *A microwaved potato. Ha! Nuked!* He wondered if he'd be tasty if someone bit into him. *I certainly've plenty of marbling.*

Trace sat at his desk and navigated to a website that hosted live news feeds. He was curious to know what was going on in the outside world. He landed on a channel that was running clips and commentating on the press conference he had been involved in. He saw himself—sallow, cut, bruised, eyes bagged, sunken, and black. "Uhh…" He flipped the channel.

A mid-forties woman with sunken cheeks spoke into a field journalist's microphone. "This whole thing's given me a wake-up call on immortality. You know, you go through everyday life and you're not worrying about the dangers that are looming in the background. You worry about car accidents, criminals, maybe fires, but not radiation. This has been eye-opening for me. Makes you value life more. Makes you wanna go and do things you enjoy and spend time with the ones you love. People don't do enough of that."

Trace agreed with the woman's sentiments. It showed how his home life had deteriorated over the past few years. *This is the time everyone starts kicking themselves.* It was exactly the moment when people start praying to god for another chance even though they never stepped a toe into a sanctum of any denomination. Everyone always waits until it is too late and wants a retraction and a do-over. *Fuck it. I'm not prayin'. I shoulda just been present. It's my fault.* Trace turned the channel.

Footage ran from the Diablo Canyon Nuclear Power Plant in San Luis Obispo, California. Throngs of protestors, some with gas masks on their heads and signs with red X's, surrounded the facility's mountainous entrance, while others marched back and forth chanting, "No more omission, decommission! No more omission, decommission!" A phalanx of police in riot gear stood in front of the vehicular swing-arm gates with black shields, batons, and pepper spray at the ready.

Live aerial footage of Bear Mountain flashed onto the screen. "We're receiving reports that there was an explosion in the auxiliary building and the containment building has been compromised. Just after the press conference declaring the crisis was over things have taken a turn for the worse. Smoke and steam are billowing everywhere. And it looks like an evacuation will be issued by Governor Pagano." He changed the channel. "People are going to want to know, what is the responsibility of Gener8 Corporation in this situation? Should they be responsible for paying for the clean-up efforts and evacuation costs that go along with a disaster of this magnitude? Trace buried his face in his hands. "A disaster of this magnitude… Who is responsible? Is Gener8 responsible? What does their CEO have to say? People are asking questions… The public wants to know. Who is responsible? Confirmed reports are saying indeed the auxiliary building of reactor three at the Bear Mountain Nuclear Energy Center has exploded. New York Emergency Management has told us Governor Anthony Pagano will be addressing the public immediately and we will cut to that feed as soon as they're ready. This may very well be the worst disaster the United States has ever seen. If a large amount of radiation has been released from the auxiliary and containment buildings, and experts are telling us it certainly would be given the explosion. If that happens and a wide-scale evacuation is issued this trumps 9/11, Hurricane Katrina, the BP oil spill, Three Mile Island, and all the California earthquakes combined. This is absolutely awful." He changed the channel again.

"If the reactors were found to not have been properly maintained should the company and its executives face federal charges? Is radioactivity blanketing the Northeast? Who is responsible?" *Who is responsible? Me, me, me, me...* "Is this a control-room operator error? Experts say Bear Mountain could cost billions to clean up... Billions of taxpayer dollars." *Control-room operator error? Control-room operator error...* The newscaster's voice was an unceasing tattoo needle on Trace's skull. "Will nuclear energy survive?" Trace grabbed his computer screen and hurled it across the room, cables ripping from its back. The monitor crashed to floor and slid into the wall. "What a tragedy this is—" Trace ripped the computer speakers from their cables and threw them across the room. They impacted the cinderblock wall, plastic shattering onto the carpet.

Trace's chest heaved. *I need to get out of here. Just leave. Just go. Your work is done.* Almost sixty hours without knowing if Brooklyn was okay in the wake of an earthquake and a nuclear catastrophe was a prison sentence. Every time he thought of his girls his stomach ratcheted further and his mouth grew more arid. *Walk out. No. See it through.* He still had to map out evacuation projections for New York Emergency Management. *You're crossing the finish line. Yeah. Finish line. You did everything you could. You made all the right moves. Stop blaming yourself.* Trace righted himself. His entire body throbbed and he felt unusually hot. *Fever?* He walked back into the control room and was met with looks regarding the commotion from his office. He blew it off. "Jerry, how we looking?"

"Coolant is circulating. We're up to three hundred inches. Pressure is at fourteen hundred psi. Temperature at seven hundred and falling."

Was the positive response of the reactor real? Trace didn't know. The crisis wasn't over by any stretch. He had to get the temperature of the core below six hundred. He wouldn't believe anything the reactor told them until it was entombed in concrete. No more celebrating before the check has cleared. The gaping holes in the auxiliary and containment buildings were the transpiration of one of his most deplorable worries. The immense amount of radioactive isotopes being released into the Hudson Valley was the reaper behind the twinkling clear night sky; it was an imperceptible, precipitable, emblematic EF-5 tornado. Ionizing radiation was walloping the DNA of innocent humans in the New York metro area like a gamma-ray burst pummeling the atmosphere. Trace hoped Avi and Brooklyn were gone. He hoped an evacuation had been ordered as he walked back into his office and dialed Avi's cell phone. "Hi, you've reached Avi—" Trace slammed the phone down. Blood from his nose dripped onto his lips. He tasted iron. He grabbed a tissue from a box on the floor and stuffed it under his respirator. He pulled the tissue out. *Blood*.

His desk phone rang. He picked it up. "Did they order the evac yet?"

"Umm... Hello? This is Flynn at New York Emergency Management."

"What? Ken?"

"This is Flynn at New York Emergency Management. Is this Bear Mountain control room?"

"Yeah, control room. How can I help ya?" Trace said abrasively.

"I'm looking for Trace Crane."

"Who's this?"

"Flynn from Emergency Management."

Trace's feet glued to the floor. *Flynn?* "Umm…" He centered himself. "This is Trace."

"Trace I've located your wife and daughter."

Flynn's words sent ripples of adrenaline through Trace's viscera. "Uh… What?"

"Avi and Brooklyn."

Located? Alive? Dead? Injured? He wondered if his girls' names being spoken into his ear was an auditory hallucination. When he looked at the phone the green, line-three LED told him he was connected to the outside.

"I can patch them through to you," Flynn said.

Patch? Patch? Containment patch? Patching. Control and patching. We're out of control. There's no patch on my wounds. Patch them through? That means they can talk! "Yes… Please!" His voice trembled. Trace had received a call from the lottery, a call from the heavens.

"Trace." Avi's voice quivered. Trace's hand trembled, the vibration of his wife's voice making his grasp on the receiver limp. "Avi?" Her voice seemed as if it was being beamed in from a distant galaxy. *Are you real? Are you here?* "Are you okay? Did you get my messages?"

"Hey, honey," Avi choked out. Her sobbing and breath distorted the receiver. Trace wanted to hold her against his chest. "Where are you? Where's Brooklyn?"

"I have her. We're at the hospital."

"Hospital? Are you hurt? Is she hurt? What's going on?" Alarm flooded Trace. *She's gravely injured, she's paralyzed, she has brain damage, she's…*

"I'm fine. Brook was caught inside the school when it collapsed and she has a broken leg, broken ribs, head trauma…

but she's okay. She's right here next to me and she's gonna be just fine. Hold on."

Trace heard rustling. "Hello, daddy." Brooklyn's sweet voice filled his ear. *My little girl. Thank god...* Emotion enveloped him in hot waves. His pulse throbbed in his neck.

"Hi, baby. How are you?" His voice was tight and cracking. Tension fell off his back, neck, and shoulders. The despair he had been harboring since the disaster started turned to euphoria. The aches of his injuries and the presence of radiation sickness subsided.

"I'm hurted a little."

Trace clenched his eyes closed, his body shuddering from the emotion he held back. "It's gonna be okay, honey. You hold onto mommy tight, okay?"

"Okay. When you coming back, daddy?"

Trace pulled the receiver away from his face, covered it, and choked up. Brooklyn's question was hard. He didn't know if he was going to make it out of Bear Mountain alive, and even if he did the dose of radiation would most likely take him out shortly after. Trace couldn't fathom not being around for Brooklyn, but until that time came, if it came, he would be a rock for her. He returned the receiver to his mouth. "Soon, honey. Soon. I love you," he said crisply.

"I love you, too, daddy."

Avi came back on. "What's going on with you? Are you okay?"

"I'm..." Flashes inundated him: the stress to be sagacious under tremendous duress, radiation exposure, Vic Hanson's death, the hydrogen explosion and containment breach, the risk to the environment and population. "I'm... I'm fine."

"Oh thank god. I miss you, terribly, Trace."

"I miss you, too, babe," he said.

Trace flopped into his desk chair and buried his masked face in one of his hands, thrilled his wife and daughter were safe.

"What's going on over there?" Avi said.

Trace wanted to tell her everything, but it wasn't appropriate long distance. Plus, it would upset her more than she already was. He would tell her the details later. "We're stabilizing the reactor." *Maybe.* He glanced into the control room and lowered his voice. "Listen to me. Take Brook and get out of town. Two hundred miles away at least. Go anywhere but toward the coast."

"Why? What's going on?"

Trace realized she hadn't heard about the explosion. It would take time for the evacuation directive to be piped through the governor's office, emergency management, and out to the media. "Just listen to me. Go. Get a hotel out of town if you have to."

"We can't, Trace. Brooklyn needs to be in the hospital here. She can't walk and she needs medicine."

"Pick her up and go. Take what you need. Get someone to help. Get her transferred. Whatever you gotta do."

"No, Trace. I wanna be here when you get out of there. It's going to be soon, right?"

"Soon, maybe… but don't worry about that." The truth was Trace didn't know. The reactor seemed to be stabilizing, but it was unpredictable; some of the controls and systems had been compromised from the explosion. There were days, weeks, months, years of work ahead. *I'm supposed to be in charge!* He feared he might die at the facility and never get to see Avi and Brooklyn again. He had to push them out of town. If he never saw his girls again he'd be fine knowing they were safe and out of the contamination zone. "You have to listen to me." Trace lowered his voice further. "There's radiation everywhere. There was an explosion. We breached containment. They're going to issue an evacuation."

Avi gasped. "Oh my god. But I thought the bubble was dissipated?"

"It was, but there was a problem. I'll explain later. Get Brooklyn and go. Doesn't matter where you go, just go the distance. Somewhere safe and then I'll be in touch and we'll meet, okay?"

"Trace, you're scaring me."

"Avi, please. Trust me and go. And remember those white pills I showed you in the foil. The potassium iodide? Take one, give a half to Brooklyn, too."

"Okay. Okay! I love you."

"I love you, too."

Trace hung up. He hadn't wanted to tell Avi, but she wasn't going to listen otherwise. She'd see it on the news anyway. Trace hoped she could figure out how to get Brooklyn out of the hospital and leave town. He saw himself at home with his girls, smiles stretching all their faces as the three of them embraced. The sweetness of Avi's olive skin, the musky smell of her hair comforted him. Her lustrous eyes appeared before his face, Brooklyn's luminous smile pushed beams of light around them, her giggle echoing. *What am I going to do?*

CHAPTER 43

Panic imbued Avi as she watched live aerial footage of the reactor steam-stack, columns of smoke, the decimated auxiliary building, and the compromised containment building flash on the TV. The newscaster appeared. "Minutes ago an explosion was heard coming from Bear Mountain. Live aerial footage is showing smoke and steam billowing from the auxiliary and containment buildings of the troubled reactor. We have calls out to Gener8, the NRC, and New York Emergency Management waiting on confirmations of what has taken place. Ladies and gentleman, this has us very nervous right now. An explosion at Bear Mountain. Just when we were delivering confirmed reports that the hydrogen bubble was dissipating something has clearly gone wrong. My god." There was commotion in the newsroom behind the anchor. "If you're in the area, please, stay inside your homes with the windows and doors shut until we know more."

Avi twisted in circles and grabbed at her hair. News of the auxiliary building explosion and containment breach was a hammer her intuition told her would eventually drop. *I knew it. I knew it! And I wish I hadn't. What did New York do to deserve this? No one welcomed an exploding meth lab as a neighbor. Why a nuclear plant? This is what happens when nobody says anything.* Her conversation with Trace had provided comfort and fear. His live voice overjoyed her. She wanted him with her at the hospital; she wanted to flee town with him. Avi was scared for her extended family and friends—for everyone in the area. *I can't believe he couldn't fix it.* She hoped Trace had left to come find her and Brooklyn. *What else is he gonna do there? It's all over now. What's done is done. Be with your family.* She looked at Lea. "How are we gonna move Brooklyn?"

"I'll see if I can get her an ambulance transfer." Lea turned for the door.

"Hold on." Avi held up her hand. She rifled in her purse and came out with a foil package of potassium iodide. From her own research and Trace's instruction Avi knew the potassium iodide would fill her thyroid, keeping out radioactive iodine that escaped from the plant. Since Avi's thyroid had already been compromised from Hashimoto's disease it was imperative for her to take the iodide to prevent the decimation of her thyroid and cancer. Avi pushed a pill out and placed it in Lea's hand. Lea washed the pill back with water. Avi stared at her pill. *You better keep me safe.* She washed it back.

"Okay. I'm going to see about a transfer." Lea exited. Avi went to Brooklyn's side. "Hi, sweetie. Take this."

Brooklyn opened her mouth. Avi dropped half a pill of potassium iodide in and gave her water to wash it back.

"What's going on, mama? Are you sad?"

"Mama's a little upset, but she's okay." Avi's stomach felt like a speed bag—jab, jab, left, right, fear, panic. She wanted to get on the hospital PA and tell everyone to grab their loved ones and get out of town, but she'd cause hysteria. Avi was torn. She hoped the governor would issue the evacuation soon and get everyone out safely while she focused on her own family.

Lea shot back into the room. "There're no ambulances available for transfer service. However, I was able to secure a private service. It's gonna cost you, Av. Like five, six thousand," Lea said.

"I don't care. I'm doing it. When can we go?"

"They need an hour or two to get everything together and get up here."

"Faster the better. I'm not sure we have that long," Avi said.

"I'll order it. Then I should leave, go get my dad and the boys. Then we'll drive back down this way and catch up with you at whatever hospital you land at."

Avi embraced Lea. "Thank you. I'll see you soon."

CHAPTER 44

Trace was eviscerated right there in his chair at the conference table inside the emergency-operations center—the same chair he had sat in broadcasting to the world, receiving applause and praise for his efforts in dissipating the hydrogen bubble. *You don't even deserve to sit. You should be waterboarded.* Governor Pagano, Chris Barnes, and other state-agency heads had applauded the destruction of the plant, the environment, and their own health on live television without even knowing. *They applauded my professional demise. It's your fault, not theirs! No! It's the system's fault.* It was the design, the tremendous risk in operation and lack of human control during malfunction that were to blame. Deep in Trace's heart he knew it didn't matter who was behind the controls. No one could predict how the system would react to an endless combination of possibilities and roadblocks in malfunction mitigation. Textbook solutions didn't work half the time, and experts could only use their knowledge and experience to craft what they believed to be the best resolutions. Reactors were unpredictable at times, and no one ever knew for certain what the result of their decisions would be until they deployed them. What was expected wasn't always the outcome.

Trace doubted he had the fortitude to persevere while invisible, silent, tasteless, odorless radioactive particles wafted into the respiratory systems of innocent men, women, children, and animals. It was happening to New York, the financial hub of the United States, the unofficial capital of the U.S., the cultural and financial center of the world. Clyde entered. "Put the maps on the table," Trace told him.

Trace and Ken Bramini had to pass along specific evacuation information to New York Emergency Management, the governor's office, and the NRC. The problem was the state was ready for an evacuation for a ten-mile radius around Bear Mountain, not an evacuation spanning fifty miles that included the four boroughs of New York City and part of Long Island. New York City itself was prepared to move between one and two million people on short notice—four boroughs was entirely different. *It's going to be a disaster. It's already a disaster. First we declare everything is okay and the crisis is over, then the situation does a one-eighty.* Trace was mortified. The governor had to safely move close to fifteen million people out of the New York metro area.

Ken Bramini's arrival sent Trace's head back. *Here it comes.* "When I ask you over the radio what's happened you respond over the radio about what's happened."

"Either the piping was compromised or the holding tank ruptured," Trace said curtly.

Ken shook his head, his fury seething behind his rising and falling voice. "You just cost… you just cost us this reactor. You… you…" He stepped to the conference table. "The evacuation is because of YOU!" Ken placed his hands on the table and leaned toward Trace. "What's wrong with you, man? Seriously. We're all gonna lose our jobs because of you. I should've never listened to you. It was too good to be true. We should've done the blowdown."

"Oh blow me." Trace sneered.

Ken scurried around the conference table, latched onto Trace's radiation whites, and glowered into his eyes. He felt heat radiating from Ken's reddened face. Clyde came between them. Ken positioned himself close to Trace's ear. "If the radiation don't kill ya when this is all over, I will. Believe me. I will."

"You've got a lot of gall to place blame on me. I did what was right. I didn't build the reactor. I didn't cause the malfunctions or break the pipes. I came up with a feasible initiative when no one else did! It was all we had left, dammit!" Trace smashed his fist into the table. "You put faith in me for a reason. You think I did this on purpose? You think this is a good fucking time! Think about it, Ken!"

Ken stepped back. "The whole thing is fucked up."

"Well, no kidding! I've barely had a real meal in three days. You've dragged me around to meetings and press conferences. I've had no rest. I've been injured all over my body, rescued men, taken in at least a thousand rem. What else do you want! I've got nothin' left! Nothin'. So if you wanna come over here and strangle me, go 'head. Do it. Let 'em do it, Clyde. I'm not gonna fight back anymore. Get your jollies off. Make yourself feel better. Because I'm at the bottom. We gotta move people now and that's the situation we're in and the situation we gotta focus on."

Ken acquiesced and sat across from Trace. "Everyone's been notified and we're gonna call into Marc Alberti at New York Emergency Management to shore up details. Get Alberti up on the screen," Ken barked to the staff at the cubicles in the front.

Trace, Ken, and Clyde huddled over the maps on the table. New York Emergency Management Director Marc Alberti appeared on the screen at the front of the room—stocky and mustachioed with brittle, receding, ebony hair. "Alright, gentle-man. Let's do this."

Trace looked up at the screen. He felt raw and embarrassed. *Marc knows. They know I turned the valve. They're gonna get the information from me and then they're gonna take me down. I'm guilty. I'm the guy that ruined the East Coast of the United States on planet Earth... Wow...*

"Trace," Clyde whispered.

Trace realized everyone was waiting. He cleared his throat. "From the field team's data and projections we're recommend-ing a two hundred–mile radius."

"A what!" Marc said.

"Twenty mile." Ken glared.

"Sorry. Twenty-mile radius around the plant, plus a hole and a key. A key... a keyhole." Trace pointed to a circle on the map indicating the twenty-mile zone. "We need to move all of Westchester County—New Rochelle, Mt. Vernon, Yonkers, Scarsdale, White Plains, Tarrytown, Tuckahoe, Ossining, Pleasantville, Hawthorne, Chappaqua, everything. Parts of Orange and Dutchess County, all of Rockland County, all of Putnam County west of Interstate eighty-four. All boroughs of New York City except Staten Island, and parts of Nassau County." Trace felt like he was delivering a death sentence to every single person he knew and loved.

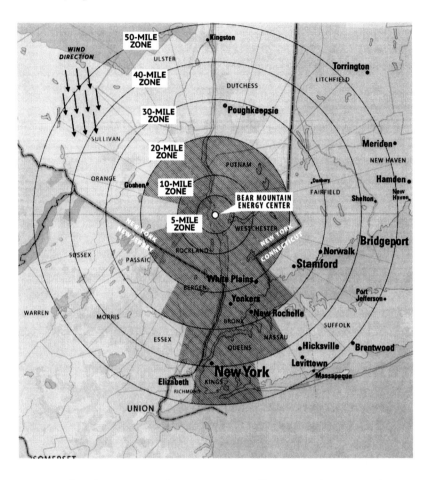

"You'll need to order a civilian no-fly-zone radius around Bear Mountain plus a halt on all civilian air traffic inside the radiation-plume keyhole." Trace dragged his finger over the map; when he stopped, it trembled. "Ess… Essentially down the Hudson and through four boroughs."

"Very well," Marc said. "Inbound air traffic to JFK and LaGuardia'll be diverted. Water traffic down the Hudson below Constitution Island to the Lower New York Bay'll be stopped by the Coast Guard. It's the summer and the weekend so luckily regular school programs aren't in session. We have approximately sixty hospitals and around three hundred nursing facilities to clear out. All of those facilities have their own evacuation plans. However, with everything needing to be emptied out it's going to take hours, and it's going to exhaust all transportation methods. How long do you think it'll take to get everyone out?"

"Everyone?" Trace said. "Every single person out of the city? I…" *Impossible.* "I… I honestly don't wanna guess. With most people south of Bear Mountain being able to only evacuate south and west, and with clipped roads, rail lines, and other quake damage, our evacuation time is greatly increased. It's probably going to take at least… at least twenty-four hours for the bulk of everyone to be moved and that's with everyone working 'round the clock." *It's going to take longer… much longer…*

"Jesus."

"You gotta move 'em safe," Trace said.

Marc sighed. "I know… Alright. All ambulance fleets are being dispatched along with all school busses. Critical patients will leave via ambulance. Non-critical patients will leave via bus. All patients will be dispersed to various hospitals outside the evacuation area—upstate, in Pennsylvania, New Jersey, and Connecticut. Some FDNY and EMS will be available for any potential evacuation injuries. NYPD will be dealing with traffic and mass transit."

Patients. Brooklyn. Mass. Critical. Critical mass. Yes… that's it… that's what started this… the minimum amount of fissile material needed to maintain a nuclear reaction. Ha! My girls have to get out. "You're converting all inbound lanes of tunnels and bridges to outbound?" Trace said.

"Exactly. We'll have some shelters around Bear Mountain that need to be evacuated and relocated. Red Cross and FEMA will be working on those. New York correctional facilities are a problem. My problem. Not yours. There's no large-scale evacuation plan whatsoever. We have almost sixteen thousand prisoners to move—Sing Sing, Bayview, MDC, Rikers, and the smaller homes. Prisons will be last priority behind hospitals and nursing facilities, and my team is going to arrange for an allotment of busses to be sent to each facility to transport prisoners. We will be dispersing inmates to random facilities throughout upstate, New Jersey, Pennsylvania, and Connecticut. It's going to be a joyous fucking experience. We're going to encounter employees of state agencies, hospitals, etcetera, that are going to leave their posts and evacuate. National guard has been deployed and will be filling in when this happens. They'll be available to assist in all facets of the evacuation from driving busses to moving people to first aid, and directing traffic."

Trace envisioned an apocalyptic free-for-all ensuing—prisoners running wild in the streets, looting for valuables and food, police and state employees joining them to save themselves and their families.

"What about the general public?" Ken said.

"MTA and New Jersey Transit are making all trains available. All inbound Manhattan tracks will be converted to outbound. Many northern rail routes have been damaged by the quake; therefore, trains will be traveling west and south only, greatly increasing evacuation time. Greyhound and all other bus carriers are opening up their entire fleets for us."

"That sounds good," Ken said.

"USDA should issue a moratorium on all crop and livestock distribution," Trace said.

"Already on it." Mark scribbled on his notepad. "Speaking of stock. The stock exchange luckily is not open today because it's Saturday. And they'll stay closed until they figure out a temporary solution. That's the least of our priorities, but thought you guys might be curious."

Trace envisioned the lights shutting off in the Theater District and Times Square, the hum of Wall Street falling to an eerie silence, Central Park, Riverside Park, Union Square, Washington Square Park, Carnegie Hall, Rockefeller Center, Radio City, Empire State Building, NYU, Columbia University—desolate. The most populous city in the United States was about to be evacuated under his watch. Home of the United Nations, the immigration gateway to America, a fifty-five-million-tourist-per-year metropolis that's residence to top artists, actors, musicians, politicians, banking and industrial juggernauts, renown scientists, socialites, new money, old money, hundred-million-dollar townhouses, and rutted-out projects. The gridded island filled with eight million voices speaking over eight hundred languages was going to be silenced. The heart of America was going to be left to stop beating, the blood draining into the sewer. *What's America without New York City? A lion without courage, an atom without a nucleus? Soulless.* An evacuation and radioactive isotopes blanketing New York City was a catastrophe that was going to alter the world. *I'm a terrorist. The biggest terrorist the world has ever seen. With the turn of a valve I've taken out an entire section of the eastern seaboard. I've single-handedly destroyed a city that took centuries to build. You didn't know. You did all you could! What are you gonna do now? You better stay here and suffer, that's what you better do. You better do your goddamn job and do it right!*

CHAPTER 45

Trace staggered around his office picking up papers, books, pens, pencils, paper clips, and other accoutrements that had been shaken to the floor during the quake. He stacked the items on shelves and his conference table in no particular order. He hated the mess but couldn't handle figuring out proper locations for the items. His office looked better save for the dust and ceiling-tile shards spread over the carpet. *Somebody'll bring a vacuum. Or not. Does it matter?*

Trace sat on his desk chair and looked at the damaged ceiling—debris hanging, wires exposed, light fixtures dangling. The ceiling resembled the current state of his chest—heart ripped out, ribs broken, nerves exposed, raw emotional pain jangling his bones. With the announcement of the evacuation Bear Mountain was going to be entombed in concrete never to operate again. Further, Gener8 as a whole would probably be obliterated. Stocks would continue to plummet. Gener8 was going to accrue tens of billions in losses within months due to the nationwide reactor shutdowns, disaster cleanup costs, and restitution. The worst of it would be financial affliction to the fourteen thousand employees of the company, many of whom had their retirement assets invested in company stock. Trace needed to pull his money out immediately to minimize damage. *Isn't that insider trading? Fuck!* He slammed his fist onto his desk. He believed his role at Bear Mountain was over. He had done everything he was expected to do and more.

Trace's duty was to make good on the disaster, he owed a lot for gambling with science and putting all living organisms in the metro area in jeopardy. If you're a firefighter you can't get scared after a building burns and you pull out dead families. You can't quit then. You can't quit the war after you see your partner's head get split by high-caliber rounds and an IED blast. *You CAN quit! And people do. No one can fathom the emotional and physical impact of such traumatic events until they've lived them. Post-traumatic stress follows. People realize the job isn't what they thought it was and they don't want it any longer. They see the truth behind it. Very few stay strong and keep believing. ...Or keep being fooled!* Trace believed he was no better than a terrorist who hit the detonator on a nuclear warhead. The only difference was his intention, but the result was the same—widespread mutation and annihilation of healthy biological cells—CANCER, SICKNESS, DEATH, POISON! *I'M A FUCKING TERRORIST!* Trace choked back tears. *I still deserve to see my family. If not for me then at least for them. Especially for Brooklyn.*

Trace stepped into the control room with a bag over his shoulder. "Val, what's the deal with the lead cover?"

"It's here. Radical Services gave us a whole crew, too. They're preparing to put it up now. Our guys've been spraying boric acid and patching containment cracks."

"Fantastic. Jerry?"

"Coolant at three hundred fifty inches, temperature at six hundred fifty, pressure at eighteen hundred psi."

All the data told Trace the reactor was continuing to stabilize, which was surprising given the damage to the auxiliary building, controls, and safety systems. "I'm steppin' out."

"Where?" Valdern asked.

"Goin' to see my girls. I hope you both understand. There's nothin' left for me in here and the exposure is eatin' me away. If I wait until discharge, if I would even make it 'til discharge, and go through decontamination they'll hold me and I'll have a hell of a time trying to see my girls. I wanna see them while I'm still lucid. You know this exposure's gonna take me down in another day or so," Trace said.

Valdern stared at Trace, his eyes cold. Trace waited for his negative response.

"Getcher ass outta here," Valdern said.

"God speed, go," Jerry added.

"Val, you're in charge," Trace said. They shared reverence for a moment. They had taken it to the bone, the loincloths were off. Man saw man at his nucleus. Valdern saluted Trace.

"I gotchu covered. But you know I can still whoop your ass."

Trace smirked. Valdern would never disrespect him again after he had gone into auxiliary and turned the valve. "I look forward to it," Trace said. He stepped to the door then turned back and took in the control room, feeling he might never see it again. He hacked behind his respirator. His nose bled, streams running, making him look like a prizefighter after fifteen rounds. Lord knows he'd had back-to-back bouts. Trace hustled back to his office, Valdern and Jerry watching him. He snapped up Brooklyn's broken mug from his desk and put it in his bag, then took a last look at his office—the cream block walls, gray berber, Formica-topped desk, laminate-wood shelving, and metal-tube, vinyl guest chairs. The leaning shelf with the dangling plant collapsed onto the couch, dirt spilling onto the sunken orange fabric. *Exactly how I feel. Fuck it.* Goodbye. He headed out the wheel-locked door.

Trace strode along the faded pavement between towering concrete casks and buildings, stepping over puddles of water. Stars dotted the newly darkened sky. Hoses snaked the plant grounds. A crewmember dumped sand on oil slicks. Suited men moved past him, guiding vehicles to the unit three auxiliary and containment buildings to hoist the lead shield over the holes. Trace's guilt deepened when he saw the crew working, the steam and smoke billowing from the damaged buildings. He stopped and watched. Forklifts, backhoes, and supply trucks sputtered past crew yammering, "Let's go, let's go, let's go." *You're a coward for leaving your crew behind.* He had no choice if he wanted to see Avi and Brooklyn. He had done the right thing, but if they needed a scapegoat they'd have no problem jailing, interrogating, and putting him before congress. *It's about my family now.*

He neared the parking entrance gates and stepped between buildings, out of sight, stripping his respirator off and unzipping his suit. He stood on one foot to step out of the protective ensemble. When he did he felt dizzy and clutched the wall, steadying himself. He dropped the items onto the ground and removed his rubber overshoes.

Blood tickled his face. He reached for it and looked at his hand. *Damn.* He grabbed a tissue from his pocket, tore it in half, rolled it into torpedo shapes, and stuffed them into his nose. He dipped another tissue in ground water and wiped the rest of his face. Trace took his smartphone from his pocket and tilted the blank screen, using it as a mirror to make sure all the blood was off his face and stared at his visage. His eyes were sunken, puffed, and gray—adrenaline clearly keeping them wide. Stubble had grown on his face, the psoriasis on his nose scaly and crimson. His lips were cracked and peeling, his cheeks ashen, scribbled with cuts and scratches. His chin was bruised purple and swollen, his temple and forehead bandaged from the ceiling-tile gash. *I look like a corpse.* Trace pocketed his phone and fished in his other pocket, extracting a car key. He'd taken Vic Hanson's keys, the crewman that Trace had rescued from the pipe-dislodging accident. He felt lucky that he didn't die like Hanson had but wasn't sure what was worse: the slow death or the instant. He slung his duffle back over his shoulder, smoothed his hair to the side, and juggled the key to Hanson's truck in his hand. *I'm ready.*

Trace arrived at the facility gates. The security guard from earlier in the day when Trace tried to flee stepped from the booth. "Crane."

Trace smiled.

"I don't see you on the discharge list nor do I see you on decontamination clearance."

Trace stayed silent. He realized he hadn't thought his approach through. *You're slippin'. You're not sharp.*

"You did go through decontamination, right?"

"Of course," Trace said. He felt unprincipled and injudicious, but security would never let him go free to the outside with the dosage he had taken in. He was certain his contamination would only affect him as long as he didn't spend periods of time in close contact with anyone else. Still he felt unprepared for the guard's challenge.

"Gate one to interior decontamination. I have Trace Crane here. Need an all clear for discharge."

Trace, you idiot. You're not thinking. You're not calculating. He believed the radiation dosage hindered his mental acuity. Then he considered the lack of sleep and the spate of emotions overwhelming him. If security tried to stop him this time he'd battle to the death. *They'll have to shoot me, drag me off like a trophy kill.*

"Where you goin' anyway? Bramini hasn't cleared you for

discharge. Are we all clear in there or something?"

Breathe. "They're patching up auxiliary and containment. Reactor is stabilizing. I've been summoned to the governor's office."

A voice blared from the guard's radio. "Guard one this is interior decon. That's a negative on Crane. He did not come through our station. Over."

"Roger that." The guard squawked off, his eyes analyzing Trace. "Which decontamination you go through?" the guard asked skeptically.

"Uh... Ummm... Operations center."

"Guard one to operations decon, over."

"How you gettin' on anyway? Your wheels are a pile over by the front somewhere."

"Umm... One of the guys is letting me take his car. He's getting a ride."

"Guard one this is operations decontamination, go 'head," blurted from the guard's radio.

"Need a clearance for reactor supervisor Trace Crane, over," the guard said.

The guard eyed Trace dubiously. *He knows I'm lying.*

"Guard one that's a negative on Crane for decon. Please send him back to our station."

"Roger that." The guard glared at Trace. "What is this? You lyin' again?"

"No... Not at all. They must be mistaken... I've been summoned to the governor's office."

"They're not mistaken. You need to hustle back to decon, and I need to call Ken Bramini for authorization. What, you're afraid they're gonna hold you or somethin'?"

"No... I've been summoned to the governor's office. I talked to Ken. He's the one that told me to get out to Westchester. I told him he's nuts pullin' me out of the control room again." *I will not be detained!*

The guard studied Trace, incredulity in his eyes. "Why didn't you mention that before?" the guard said.

"Because it's supposed to be confidential."

"I'm not buyin' this shit. You'd have gone through decon then."

"I did! I'm a goddamn supervisor here. Don't you think I know what I did?"

"I don't give a fuck that you're a supervisor. You go back and follow protocol. You go on your own or we're gonna drag you back there."

"No... I... No..." *Steady.* "They're mistaken. I went through decon..."

The guard waved over the two other guards. The men marched over, automatic rifles held pointed at the ground, fingers parallel to the triggers.

"What's it gonna be? You walkin' or're we draggin' you?" the guard said.

NO! Trace backed toward the pedestrian gates. He would rather the guards shoot him dead than drag him back inside. Either way he saw it as the same. He wouldn't be able to see his girls while he was lucid. Avi and Brooklyn would just be standing over his lifeless body. "No..."

The guards pursued him.

"NO!"

"Cuff him up," the lead guard said.

The two guards slung their rifles over their shoulders and reached for Trace.

"NO! STOP! IT'S A MISTAKE!" Trace's chest heaved. "NO!"

The guards lunged for his wrists. Trace flailed, his duffle bag dropping to the ground. "NO!" He turned sideways to the gate and pushed on it. It rattled in its latch. "NO! Call them back. It's a mistake." The guards grabbed Trace, hands snapping at his wrists like cobras. They spun him around and pushed him up against the gate. The handcuffs ratcheted. The warm steel bit down on his skin. "NO! Please. This is ridiculous. Call them back. Let me talk to them. You don't realize what you're doin'!"

The guards spun Trace around. He fought against them but was no match for four hundred pounds of muscle and military training.

"You're bleedin'?" The lead guard eyed Trace. "How long your nose been bleedin'?"

Trace scowled. "I wasn't. Your goons just threw me up against the fence."

"I see tissue in your nose. You been havin' nose bleeds? You might need to be checked out."

"No," Trace said.

"Let's go." The guard pointed. "Forward. Pick up your feet."

The guards lifted Trace under his arms. "Please. I'm telling you." If a Geiger was put anywhere near Trace it would blare; he'd be raced to quarantine. "Let me go!" Trace couldn't understand why the past three days had been so brutal. Why was *he* poisoned? Why couldn't *he* see his wife and daughter? Why was *he* being punished? He had given everything he had, borrowed more from the universe, and gave that. He was indebted in energy to the spirit world for giving to terrestrial society. Being dragged away like a prisoner was unimaginable. He'd put his life at risk and now was treated like a pariah. *I'm nothin' but yardbird to them. No one's your friend, not in security.* Trace didn't know how he could say hello to these men for fifteen years and get treated like an intruder. He realized they didn't know he was poisoned, they didn't know he wanted to get to his wife and daughter, they were just doing their job. Even still he abhorred them.

"Guard one, this's operations. Come in," squawked through the guard's radio. Trace snapped his head up. Everyone stopped moving. The lead guard faced Trace and glared. "Guard one. Go 'head."

"Decon was mistaken. Crane was through earlier. He's clear for discharge."

Trace thought he recognized the voice. *Gary?* Relief teetered on the precipice for him. He felt like his head was being held over an escarpment, a third party pleading to save him from having a smile cut into his throat and his body dropped into the ravine.

"Identify yourself, please," the guard said.

"Gary Harrell."

"You're *sure* Crane's been through decon?" The guard said skeptically.

"Positive. There was a mishap and I ended up washing and scanning him myself."

The guard sneered at Trace.

"Trust me he's good to go. Not sure how his wife puts up with him anyway. Man's got a wimpy lookin' dick, but he's clean now."

The assisting guards looked at Trace and busted up laughing.

"Shit, Crane…" The lead guard shook his head. He put his walkie to his mouth. "Roger that, Gary." He nodded to his men. They took the cuffs off Trace. Astonishment set in as if he'd been released from a life sentence. He rubbed his wrists in relief. *How did Gary know?* He figured Valdern and Jerry must've mentioned something or Gary had seen him leave. Trace took tissue from his pocket and wiped the blood from his face.

The lead guard handed Trace his duffle bag. "You still shouldn't be on the grounds without protective gear." The guard returned a particle mask and handed it to Trace. "At least wear this until you've gotten further away."

"Thanks," Trace said. He stuffed the mask into his pocket and approached the pedestrian gate. The lead guard saluted him. The gate buzzed and unlatched. Trace felt like he had been liberated from an internment camp after decades of oppression. He found Hanson's quad-cab pickup and hit the remote. He slung his duffle onto the passenger seat, hopped inside, and pushed the key into the ignition. A picture of Vic's two boys sat on the dash. Sadness welled inside him. *Someone could've been staring at Avi and Brooklyn's picture on my dash. I'm sorry, Vic. I'm sorry.* Trace would make sure Vic's family was taken care of by Gener8 after the disaster cleared. *I gotchu man, don't worry.* He started the truck and pulled out.

Trace arrived at the final guard gate and dropped his window.

"Oh, Mario Andretti here," the guard said.

Trace's lips stayed in a flat line.

"You passed decon?" the guard said.

"Yeah. Didn't they radio you?"

"No. Nobody radioed me. All I heard on the radio was you *didn't* pass decon. So how you get up here?"

"I did pass. It was a mistake."

"Perimeter to interior one. Is Crane clear?"

"Clear," squawked from the walkie. The gate arm lifted. Trace punched the gas and turned onto the main roadway. *I'm free!*

CHAPTER 46

"This is Governor Anthony Pagano. Based on the recommendation from Bear Mountain owner/operator Gener8 and the Nuclear Regulatory Commission, I am advising everyone within a twenty-mile radius around the Bear Mountain Nuclear Energy Center to leave the area until further notice." Pagano stood behind a podium at New York Emergency Management in Manhattan wearing his emergency attire—jacket, polo shirt, hat, cargo pants.

Avi watched the TV's reflection in the window of Brooklyn's hospital room. She turned directly to the flat-screen. Then she paced. *We gotta go. We gotta go. We gotta go.* She pushed her hands together in prayer. *Fuck.* On edge was an understatement. She was shackled at the escarpment of hell, fire scorching her heels, watching New York get raped and tortured. She felt like an accomplice just for knowing Trace.

Officers from the national guard stood behind Governor Pagano along with his press secretary, the head of New York Emergency Management, New York Health Commissioner, county executives, and other New York state-government agency heads. Pagano's sign-language interpreter flanked his left side. His devastation showed in a grim sickle on his face. He composed himself. "That radius includes the following areas, which are also listed at the bottom of your screen—all of Westchester County, all of Putnam County west of Interstate eighty-four, all of Rockland County. In Orange County—east of and including Sterling Forest, Bellvale, Chester, Rock Tavern, Stewart Airport, and Balmville. In Dutchess County—south of and including Castle Point, Fishkill, and Shenandoah. Beyond the twenty-mile radius we are evacuating all of Bronx, Manhattan, Brooklyn, and Queens. Lastly, in Nassau County, Long Island west of and including Garden City.

"Additionally, my office has been in communication with the governors of New Jersey and Connecticut. The following areas should move. In Connecticut, Fairfield County west of highway fifteen north to highway one-o-four behind the hearts of Greenwich and Stamford. In New Jersey—Bergen County north of and including Harrington Park, Westwood, Waldwick, Allendale, Ramsey, and Ramapo Mountains. In Passaic County north of and including Ringwood. Please listen carefully to the following evacuation protocol. Please do not ignore this protocol as it is imperative that we all work together to ensure the safety of one another in leaving the area."

The governor's voice echoed in the hall. It was the saddest speech Avi had ever heard. Every Borough, town, city, and county he mentioned stabbed at her stomach—the enormity of the evacuation too much to digest.

"I'm advising residents in the twenty-mile radius to move outward from the radius. Residents of Westchester County between Yonkers and Tarrytown please move west or north. Please do not come south toward Manhattan. The rest of Westchester County should move north or east. Residents of the four boroughs of New York City and parts of Long Island,

I'm asking that you all evacuate to the west and then south. Areas west of the Hudson you will move west and north. East of the Hudson you shall go east and north With that direction everyone will be moving away from the area without crossing through the evacuation zone. If you must travel to a friend or relatives in another direction please circumvent the evacuation zone when doing so. Emergency teams will direct those in need of shelters from main roads and highways to those locations."

Avi dialed Lea's cell from the hospital phone. Lea's voicemail picked up. She figured Lea had entered back into the disaster zone where cell service was still down. She dialed Lea's house.

"Hello," Lea's father answered after three rings.

"Tim, it's Avi."

"Hey. I saw the evacuation's being issued."

"Yeah. I'm here at the hospital with Brooklyn. I can't get Lea on her cell. Did she get home yet?"

"I thought Lea was with you?"

"She was, but she left a while ago to pick up you and the boys."

"She hasn't..." Tim paused. "Who is it?" Tim yelled into the house. His voice came back deep into the receiver. "Hold on. She just walked in."

Lea came to the phone. "Hello."

"Governor just issued the evacuation; we're not going to have time to wait for a transfer for Brooklyn." Commotion echoed in the hallway. She went to the door, phone still to her ear. Nurses, doctors, and orderlies moved swiftly, sneakers squealing on polished flooring—orders were barked, wheelchairs splayed, gurneys wheeled. Voices blurted over the intercom, pages going off back and forth, codes, alarms. Avi dashed back into Brooklyn's room. "People are moving fast around here. Seems like they're going to evacuate this place."

"Yep. They sure are. They're gonna prioritize the patients by ailment. Intensive care gets the ambulances and helicopters and then it's busses. The patients will all be disseminated to hospitals outside the evacuation area."

"I'm gonna need to take Brooklyn myself," Avi said.

President Tim Ramey appeared on the TV behind a podium in the White House press room. "Good evening, everyone." His Midwestern voice turned Avi's eyes to the screen. "For the last three days the American people have been concerned about the developments in Peekskill and Buchanan, New York. Governor Pagano and his emergency management teams are doing a fine job. Gener8 and its workers at Bear Mountain have worked tirelessly to stabilize the reactor. Unfortunately, their efforts have been overpowered by the reactor and a hydrogen explosion occurred, forcing an evacuation in the surrounding area. We've declared a federal emergency in New York, and I want to ensure people on the East Coast that we are supporting New York and the governor's efforts and are available to help in any capacity that we can. We have sent federal emergency coordinators to our great city, and I have been in touch with Governor Pagano and the Nuclear Regulatory Commission the entire way and will continue to do so until we know everyone is safe. Further, I want to assure the American people living near other nuclear reactors throughout the country that they are not in danger. All reactors have been shut down and are stable as we focus on helping New York. If you're in the area surrounding Bear Mountain and aren't already aware, please check with local news and authorities for evacuation details."

"Av, you with me?" Lea asked.

Avi pried her stare from the TV. "The president's on TV."

"Mama, what's happening?" Brooklyn squealed.

Avi turned. "Don't worry, sweetie. We might have to leave." Avi put the receiver back to her lips.

"Are we going home?" Brooklyn said. Avi looked back and nodded.

"Can I move her myself?" Avi asked Lea.

"Not ideal. You'll need supplies to keep her treated and a wheelchair. She can't walk on that leg," Lea said.

"Got it. I'll get her together then can you come pick us up?"

"We'll get our things packed and get back on the road to you ASAP."

"Thanks. I'll see you soon." Avi hurried into the hallway. In throngs of moving staff she searched for a wheelchair. Nothing. Nothing. She saw one folded next to the wall and went to it. She gripped the handles and began to wheel it back to Brooklyn's room. A female nurse built like a gorilla skidded into Avi. "Miss, I need that chair."

Avi held the chair tightly. "I need it!"

"No, miss, you don't. Let go of the chair. I need it for a patient."

"Well, I need it for my daughter. She can't walk."

"I'm sorry, miss, but we'll get to her. We're prioritizing this movement."

"No."

"Miss." The nurse stopped the chair from rolling. "You let go of this damn chair. Franklin!" she yelled.

A male nurse the size of a linebacker scurried over.

"Don't you touch me!" Avi snapped. Franklin grabbed her in a bear hug. She wriggled against his powerful arms.

"Miss, you need to calm down. We're not tryin' to hurtcha. We're tryin' to do our jobs here. Please," Franklin said. The female nurse ripped the chair from Avi's hands. "Please, miss. Imma let go a ya now," Franklin said. His pythons uncoiled.

"I needed it for my daughter, dammit!" Avi took off back to Brooklyn's room.

"Mama, what's going on?" Brooklyn asked.

"Everything's okay, honey. We have to leave the hospital. Mama's gonna carry you, okay?"

Brooklyn nodded.

Avi peeled monitoring cable tape from Brooklyn's skin. "Owww..." Brooklyn cried from the stinging.

"It's okay, honey. It's okay." Avi caressed Brooklyn's head and placed the IV bag in her hands. "Hold this, honey. I'm gonna pick you up now." Avi lifted her, her cast leg dangling.

"Ahh..." Brooklyn yowled. Avi brought Brooklyn into her shoulder.

"What happened?"

Tears welled in Brooklyn's eyes. "My tummy and my leg." She put her cast wrist around Avi's neck.

"Okay. Be tough for mama, okay?"

Brooklyn nodded, her hair falling in her face. Avi headed for the door.

"Mommy!" a girl cried out. Avi turned to Brooklyn's roommate, Sarah. Tears cascaded down her freckled face under her curly auburn hair. Avi went to Sarah's bedside. "Hey there. Hey. You're okay." Seeing Sarah scared harpooned Avi's heart. Avi wanted to take her, but she didn't know the extent of her injuries and didn't want to keep her from proper care or make it difficult for her family to find her later. Avi brushed Sarah's forehead and hoped if Brooklyn were in Sarah's position another mother would give her love. "Your mom'll be here. Don't worry." She caressed Sarah's face. The best choice was to leave her.

Avi trotted through the hospital sliding doors with Brooklyn in her arms, spilling into the night onto 165th Street and Broadway. Lights were out along the road and many buildings not connected to the hospital were dark. It was because of Bear Mountain, which made up twenty-five percent of the city's power sources. Ambulances and police vehicles strobed in epileptic pulses like carnival lights exploding in her face. Stretchers rattling across asphalt and emergency workers' shoes pattering with pavement grit were acutely present in her ears, as if her face was to the ground. Hospital staff shouted commands and discussed evacuation plans. The irony fascinated Avi. There was an emergency at the hospital. Everything that made sense to her had been inverted. Normality was in the teacup ride whipping, whirling. She felt she might vomit. She sat at a bench near the sidewalk, keeping Brooklyn against her chest, kissing her on the forehead attempting to shield her from the commotion.

"Aunt Lea's gonna pick us up." An ambulance siren blared and roared away. Helicopter chop was in the distance, then close. She saw the MedEvac landing on the roof. She shut her eyes. Trace pulled bloody bandages from Avi's chest while she lay in their bed. She looked down at the stitches criss-crossing her breasts. "Uh… god…" Tears welled in her eyes. "It's awful. Look at me." Trace placing fresh gauze on her wounds felt like gelid wind on her bones. She writhed.

"You're gonna be okay. I'm with you. This is the good stuff here. Sickness and in health. I got you." He caressed her arm and kissed her on the forehead. "You're so beautiful right now," Trace said. Avi smiled, his sentiments dulling the pain.

A police car ripped past, wailer so loud it flung Avi's eyes open. Her phone buzzed in her pocket. She answered. "Hello."

"Can't get back in the city. They're not letting anyone in. All lanes've been converted to outbound," Lea said.

Avi lurched forward. *Can't get in? Can't be!* "You tried the GW and…"

"Tappan Zee first and the cops told me GW was the same. Radio says traffic is being diverted. Can't get near it."

"Fffffuck…"A string of ambulances and other emergency vehicles pulled in and out of the hospital, lights twirling. A handful of NYPD and NYFD vehicles arrived. Broadway filled with more civilian cars, evacuees came out of their pre- and post-war buildings and scattered. *Pandemonium rising. Must go.*

Panic came in undulations through Avi's chest.

"You're gonna have to meet me out here. Maybe try a cab over the bridge. Let me know. I'm sorry, Av."

"It's okay. I'll…" She took stock of chaos in front of her. "I'll figure it out. I'll be in touch." She hoisted Brooklyn onto her shoulder, walked to the corner, and waved at darkened passing taxis. Not a single car had its service lights on. The cars she could see inside of were full, silhouettes of evacuees lucky enough to catch a lift, others empty with cabbies' faces hardened in determination to get to their families and evacuate the city. Avi waved frantically, frustration increasing with every dash of yellow. *Should I swim across the Hudson? Walk the GW bridge? Hitchhike?* She decided the subway to Penn Station and a New Jersey Transit line across the river was more reasonable. She dialed Trace on his mobile and never detested the sound of ringing so much. He was still at the plant and thus didn't have a signal. She called the control room. The dreaded busy signal hummed. She hung up and squeezed her phone like she wanted to crush it.

A compact SUV taxi pulled over. "Where you going?" the driver said.

Oh my god. Avi looked to the sky. *Thank you.* "Need to get across the Hudson," she said.

"I'm going straight down Broadway if you want a ride. My family in Queens. I take you as far south as you wanna go, no charge." It was better than the subway. Avi opened the door with her free hand and slid onto the vinyl seat cover with Brooklyn. The cabbie hit the gas and they shot down Broadway.

"Your daughter sick?" He glanced in the rearview.

"Injured from the earthquake."

"Ah… Is terrible," he said solemnly, weaving through traffic. "I have three daughter. Nine. Twelve. Sixteen."

"Oh my." She composed a text message to Trace. *Evacuation*

issued. Stuck in city. Trying to get out. Lea can't get in to get me. She's waiting outside. Bridges all diverted to outbound. Call me.

"My wife call. She have no car so she and the kids trying to get on a train and I meet them somewhere south and pick them up and we go out of the city."

"I hope you find them."

"I drive nineteen years in this city. I never expect this. It's… It's insane. Crazy. All for a power plant." He leaned on the horn. "Go! Go! Go! You idiot! My god they can't even drive in an emergency."

When they reached 98th Street traffic came to a crawl. Avi rubbernecked, but couldn't see over the gridlock.

"Oh… this's bad… This really bad," the cabbie said.

"You don't wanna take the Westside Highway?"

The cabbie glanced in the rearview. "All the highways are converted to outbound." He pointed west toward the Hudson. "I got guys in Brooklyn and Queens telling me there's no way to get east on the highways… everything going out. They can't get to their families. I don't want to risk not being able to get to Queens. So I'm staying city streets."

At their current pace it would take them hours to get to Penn Station. Avi couldn't fathom how long it would take the cabbie to reach Queens or if he'd ever make it. "I'm gonna get out here and head to 96th Street station."

The cabbie nodded. "Okay. I wish you the best."

"You, too," Avi said. "I appreciate the ride, and I hope you get to your wife and daughters quickly."

"Thank you. God bless you."

"You as well." Avi slid out of the cab with Brooklyn and loped down Broadway between throngs of evacuees toward the 96th Street subway station, her pulse throbbing in her temples, her knee burning against her pants. *Which train do I take to Penn Station? The one? No, no, no… the two or three express.*

Millions had come out of their stacked abodes, spreading out on one plane making the entire city look like New Year's Eve in Times Square. Cheers of excitement were yowls of terror. Primped women with teacup pooches, bankers, lawyers, and wealthy creatives scurried into chauffeured rides. Lower class and middle class of all ages moved on foot, pulling and pushing pets, luggage, strollers, and wheelchairs.

"I told y'all it was comin'! This is it! The rapture is here! I'm goin' to heaven. Take me up fatha!" a vagabond preached. A woman held her hands high, rosary beads around them, praying in Spanish. Every strata and ethnicity of the Upper West Side had scattered—confusion, fear, and desperation in their faces. A helicopter buzzed overhead. Police sirens, garbled voices over bullhorns, and flashing lights abounded.

"PLEASE LEAVE THE AREA CALMLY. DO NOT PANIC," echoed over a megaphone. A car had crashed into a taxi, the owners of each yelling at one another. *Why aren't they helping each other?* Light lanced through Avi's eyes, cacophony in her ears, the smell of body odor and fear singeing her nose. People hung out of their apartment windows who had decided to wait out the crowd or hunker down and stay. Avi knew a mandatory evacuation meant they had to leave immediately. She figured they'd find out when emergency workers banged on their doors.

She hustled with the stampeding crowd funneling into the 96th Street station, holding Brooklyn tight against her chest. Brooklyn buried her face into Avi's neck. "It's okay, baby." There were so many bodies in the station that not even an inch existed between each person, making the crowd move as one leviathan entity toward the tracks. Avi feared she would be trampled, swallowed up by the crowd and macerated. She reached the platform and attempted to move near the edge, but the crowd was a fortified wall of flesh and bone. Yammering voices, crackheads yelling, and a dreadlocked man playing the steel drums set a paradoxical underscore to the pandemonium. The warm, acrid gust of a downtown two train whipping into the station enveloped Avi's face. The doors spread. She pushed forward. In front of her a stocky man squeezed himself onto the stuffed train, forcefully shoving riders back. Others tried to do the same and found riders shoving them out of the cars. Avi tried to wedge herself and Brooklyn onto a car.

"There's no more room!" someone barked.

"Get the fuck out!" another yelled. The crowd shoved her and everyone else back. The doors closed. Through the car windows wet eyes stared back, grim visages like those on prison-camp trains. The train launched.

A downtown three train whisked into the station on the opposite tracks. Avi hustled toward it with the crowd. The doors spread. People tried to push on, but bodies were condensed so densely no one could move. That train passed on and another two train swept in. Full. It was impossible to get to Penn Station. Cabs or any car were out of the equation. Sliding onto a subway train seemed an inconceivable feat. Avi considered walking but feared it would take hours. She needed to get to Lea on the other side of the Hudson as soon as possible. She didn't want Lea and her boys to be at risk of absorbing high levels of radiation because they had to wait for her. Several more brimming trains ripped into the station, doors opening and closing like factory machinery, robots on a conveyer. In. Out. In. Out. Open. Close. Open. Avi closed her eyes.

CHAPTER 47

Trace crawled in bumper-to-bumper traffic in Hanson's tan pickup truck. The endless red glow floating above the traffic-clogged highway looked like low-lying aurorae he wished he could tether himself to and evanesce. Ten-mile-radius evacuation sirens reminiscent of air-raid horns cried omnipresently. Northbound lanes were redirected south, vehicles lining the road shoulder to shoulder facing the same direction. *Maybe the sky has fallen? Maybe I've already died and gone to hell?* Trace hoped to get to the Tappan Zee Bridge and cut west to the Garden State Parkway where he hoped traffic would be less egregious. The last thing he wanted to do was get closer to Manhattan. He didn't understand why more people weren't driving north. He didn't have a choice because he wanted to meet Avi and Brooklyn. Avi was already positioned south at the hospital and, therefore, it was best for her to continue south and not drive back past Bear Mountain. Trace would've headed north and gone over the Bear Mountain Bridge, except a section had fallen out of it.

Emergency vehicles were parked at various intervals along

the roadside, others weaving through traffic, lights and sirens blaring. Two green national guard humvees passed on the shoulder. *I've started a war. I created this. And no one around me knows. I'm the terrorist fugitive everyone's looking for, hiding in plain sight among the crowd. Maybe someone'll figure it out and execute me. Stop it! Stop blaming yourself.* Trace dialed Avi from his mobile. The line rang... two rings... three... four... six... "Dammit!" Trace coughed, a dry resonation in the recesses of his chest. He felt the radiation sickness vibrating inside his body. His head throbbed, the pain mostly dulled by the four pain relievers he had swallowed after leaving the plant. His stomach was slightly nauseated, his bowels bubbled. He hoped he wouldn't have to pull over to relieve himself.

Digital beeping inside the truck drew Trace's attention. He thought Hanson must've had a watch buried somewhere in the vehicle. Trace opened the center console and fished around—pen, mints, sunglasses, change. He closed the console and went for the glovebox. The steady beeping became louder. Trace reached inside—manuals, receipts, registration, insurance. He grazed across something small, rectangular, and plastic. A dosimeter. Trace looked at the screen—498.1 millirem. The device had been absorbing radiation sitting in the plant parking lot. Since it was increasing, the dosimeter told Trace a significant amount of fallout existed around him and everyone else in the area. He wasn't concerned with himself since he had already been severely contaminated, but he was gravely worried for those surrounding him. It was jack-in-the-box radiation that could rear its head as cancer at any time. *Surprise!*

Trace cracked his passenger window. He reset the dosimeter, leaned over and clipped it on the window. The readout started to rise—12.6 millirem, 34.9, 56.3. The dosimeter beeped. Trace surveyed the vehicles around him—sedans, vans, SUVs—families inside, children bouncing on the seats, driver's heads pressed firmly into headrests, their faces taut with perturbation, vexation, and trepidation. He looked at the dosimeter—148.2 millirem. Trace hoped everyone had taken potassium iodide. He and everyone on the roads inside Westchester heading south were in the plume pathway. He had traveled six miles in two hours. According to Trace's calculations everyone in traffic was getting hit with 56 to 60 millirem per minute. He figured evacuees could potentially absorb 10 to 30 rem or more by the time they cut over the Hudson via the Tappan Zee or at worst the George Washington Bridge. It all depended on how well sealed their vehicles were or if they had the vents and windows open. Thousands around Trace would absorb enough fallout to contract acute radiation poisoning. Some would get lucky and stay asymptomatic, others would fall ill and need hospitalized detoxification, others would receive a merciless hit to their thyroid, pregnant women would have birth complications, some would form latent cancers. Thoughts of radiation invading the bodies of the children crushed him. Children having their thyroids removed would be headed for a life full of biological imbalance—weight gain, plummeting energy levels, anxiousness, and pills. *Fuck*. Guilt for telling Vijay that everything was okay and his family was safe imbued Trace in repetitious recollection. "Trace, you must tell me. Is my family safe here?"

"Yes, anything changes you'll see it on the news." Trace was shocked that he ever believed in the evacuation preparedness. Here he was, in it. Damaged freeways and several million additional vehicles on the roads weren't factored in. Even if they were, it didn't matter. The move was impossible. The only practical solution would be to remove the threat and any possible need for an evacuation. *Decommissioning of reactors.*

Trace inched forward in Hanson's pickup. A purple minivan with its windows cracked, a man and woman in the front, children in the back idled next to him. Trace dropped his window and tapped his horn. "Hey!… Hey!" he yelled to them. The couple looked. "Close up your windows and shut your vents," Trace said. "There's radiation out here." The couple quickly raised their windows and slid their air vents shut. The wife mouthed 'thank you.' Trace looked at his reflection in the rearview mirror. He was surprised the family didn't think he was crazy considering the bandage across his head, blood seeping through, cuts and bruises on his ashen face. He slid a small comb from his shirt pocket and slicked his hair down to the side, then hacked blood into his hand. He wiped himself with a tissue. *Gettin' worse.* Trace was a toxic experiment that had escaped the lab. He was glowing uranium that should be kept inside a glass and steel-reinforced cask.

Trace peered down the sinuous line of vehicles and noticed more parted windows, cigarette smoke curling out, arms dangling. He realized that much of the population didn't understand how radioactive isotopes traveled in the environment. The wind was blowing iodine, cesium, strontium, and plutonium over them, sending it all silently into their bodies. Even with windows and vents shut isotopes would penetrate the vehicles to some degree. Trace turned the air conditioning fan up. He looked at his arms; more light-red blotches had surfaced, the older spots crimson. *I'm turning into one of those weird diagnosis pictures.*

His smartphone buzzed. He looked at the screen hoping Avi would tell him she and Brooklyn were on the road. *Evacuation issued. Stuck in city. Trying to get out. Lea can't get in to get me. She's waiting outside. Bridges all diverted to outbound. Call me.* He had a draining feeling in his abdomen. He immediately dialed her. The phone beeped back at him. "Damn!" He composed a reply. *I've left the plant. In car on way. Let me know where you are. Traffic gridlocked, but I'll get there. Text or call when you get this. Love you.* He wanted to get out of the pickup, sprint across the tops of the vehicles, run over the George Washington Bridge into the city, and save his girls.

An SUV with large, studded tires ripped by, straddling the shoulder and the roadside gravel. Trace thought it was a fine idea; he couldn't stand to dawdle in traffic when his girls needed him. He cut onto the shoulder and zoomed off, the pickup bouncing over the uneven blacktop. After a mile, Trace saw the truck with the large tires cutting back into traffic, revealing a late-model Nissan sedan with its hazard lights flashing. The hood was up, steam wafting. He saw the back of a head inside. Trace stopped behind the sedan and hurried out. A petite pregnant Latino woman sat inside, jabbing at her cell phone. Trace tapped on the window. The woman turned, terror and pain twisting her face. Trace waved for her to crack her window. She did. "What's going on?"

"I'm having contractions," she said, breathless.

"You traveling alone?" Trace said.

She nodded.

"Okay. Alright. I'm gonna get you to some help. You gotta get in my truck, though."

The woman shook her head. "No… No…"

Trace realized his bruised, bloody appearance was probably scary. It was no hunky fireman rescue, that was for sure. It was a sallow, black-and-blue white dude who looked like he'd been on a bender of bourbon, smack, and Tastykakes for years. "Look. I'm headed to my wife and daughter. I can help you. You stay here your chances of getting medical help are slim. Plus, there's radiation everywhere. You've gotta think about your child."

The woman stared at him for several seconds and then nodded. "Okay… Please…" Trace opened her car door and helped her out. She staggered, screaming in pain.

"C'mon. Just a little further. You're gonna be alright. I gotchu."

Trace helped the woman inside his truck. He navigated around her sedan and sped down the shoulder, her cries howling in his ears.

CHAPTER 48

I'm giving it one more shot. One more. This's never gonna work. Avi's muscles burned, Brooklyn feeling like seventy pounds in her arms. She was soaked with sweat, the night humidity and the density of evacuees making the station feel like a clothes dryer. She touched others at her shoulders and back, felt their body heat radiating, and sensed where the different flavors of acridity came from. Avi thought she might contract a bacterial infection from the inhalation of the stench. *I want a shower.* She feared she'd be stuck inside the exclusion zone and then she and everyone else would be left behind, sealed on the island, quarantined like a pack of zombies. Half a dozen different languages sounded like lyrics over the steel drums. It was an apocalyptic Mardi Gras and Avi wished everyone would just be quiet. *This all could've been avoided!*

The three train tore into the station and pinned to a stop in front of Avi and Brooklyn. The doors split revealing available space. Avi's heart lurched. She dashed forward, the titanic crowd pushing her from behind. She was thrust into the steamy car, worried eyes of every nationality ballooning in her face. She held Brooklyn tight against her chest, her IV bag sloshing. "Ah! My tummy!" Brooklyn winced. Avi rubbed her back.

"Sorry, honey." The train doors slid shut. Standing in the center without a hand bar concerned Avi, but it was impossible to move toward one.

"OPEN THE DOORS!" A young Latino man pounded on the exterior door. Avi saw his white t-shirt stuck in the sliders. "OPEN THE DOORS!" He hammered on the glass.

"Pull the emergency cord!" Avi yelled. "Someone's stuck in the door!" A muscular man pushed his way to the doors and tried to pry them open with his hands.

"Pull the emergency cord!" a man yelled.

"PULL IT!" Avi screamed. Those standing in front of the cord didn't react.

"Don't pull it!" a man bellowed. "It'll get us stuck here!"

"PULL IT!" Avi shouted. Nobody acted. The train launched. Avi fell back into the drove behind her. Then shot forward into the drove in front of her before being uprighted by four sets of hands. She trusted in the help of strangers and was grateful they provided. She believed others thought she was looney holding a child dressed in a hospital gown with an IV. *Did she steal that girl?* Avi watched the man sprint alongside the train, his shirt in the door. "Stop the car!" she yelled. "STOP IT!"

"PULL THE CORD!" Men and women shrieked. "STOP IT!" A tall black man in a business suit tackled the Latino, successfully tearing his shirt and freeing him from the train just before he reached the tunnel wall. The train occupants responded with shrieks as the train plunged into darkness.

Avi was stunned, her eyes still affixed to the door window, tunnel lights whipping by. She almost had watched that man get crushed by the train. *Why didn't anyone pull the emergency cord? Do we no longer care about each other?* Any other day the cord would've been pulled without hesitation. Evacuation fear had rendered most of the population catatonic, veiled with selfish injudiciousness. "Three express making all stops. Eighty-six street next," the conductor fired in a thick Staten Island accent. Avi couldn't conceive how a single other human would fit into their car. She felt tapping on her lower back.

"Miss. Miss."

She turned to see an octogenarian, khaki pants, Hawaiian shirt, hair so wispy it looked like bits of goose down feathers from his pillow had stuck to his head. "Take the seat, kid," he growled. Avi was impassioned by his kindness. "Take it." He waved her emphatically to the molded orange plastic and shuffled forward. Avi sat, relieved to be off her feet. Her leg muscles pulsated.

"Thank you." *One nice person.*

The warmth of Brooklyn's body on Avi's chest kept her from panicking. The occupants surrounding her were silent, earbuds dangling to smartphones. People were loud on the platform, quiet on the train. It never made sense to her. Avi's nose crinkled at a whiff of feces. She realized it was halitosis from a yellow-toothed Greek man next to her who had a jowly face that looked like hairy caramel melting. An acoustic guitar struck up from the far end of the car, a young black male with dreadlocks fingerpicking Bob Marley's *Redemption Song.*

A baby near the guitarist began to wail. The musician belted, "Won't you help to sing these songs of freedom? 'Cause all I ever have: Redemption songs; Redemption songs." The subway tunnel lights blipped through the windows like a series of camera flashbulbs, the train leaning into a curve. People clutched backpacks, rollaway luggage, duffles, and plastic shopping bags. A punk-rock kid with a mohawk in studded leather stared despondently out the window, a transgender man with no pants, a garter belt stretched to black stockings tucked into heels with a tribal tattoo covering one thigh, and a midriff

Grace Jones t-shirt grinned coquettishly, a black woman with cornrows argued with her brother that had voluminous hair with a pick stuck in the side. An elderly couple clasped their liver-spotted hands together, two chiseled men in their forties wearing workout shorts and tees locked arms, one rubbing the other's shoulder, the other rubbing his thigh. A Dominican man wore a black cowboy hat, another man wore a white rabbit-head mask. Women in hijabs spoke softly in Arabic. A young woman in a leopard fedora pressed her glossed lips. A Samoan man with a face like a St. Bernard had a wooden cane resting between his burly legs, his dismal stare at the floor showing his reflection of an arduous life that he'd be happy to end in a train crash.

Look at these wonderful people! Avi was surrounded by New York, by the world, all on that train. Everyone was going through the surprise and consternation of the evacuation. She wished all the different walks of life could step together. She kissed Brooklyn on the side of her head and stroked her back. On summer weekends many usually left the city for upstate canyons, edges of the island, the Connecticut coast, or airline destinations. However, because of the Friday quake not many left town. Avi wished she and Trace had planned something international. *Don't nuclear accidents know they should happen on holidays? Then no one would be in the city.*

"Eighty-sixth street," the conductor blurted over the PA. The train screamed into the station, brakes grinding. No one left. No one could board.

At Penn Station Avi rode the hordes of people pushing through the underground labyrinth past subpar fast food, newsstands, and imported tchotchkes. ICE COLD BEER, HOT DOG, SMOOTHIE, PIZZA. Some vendors still rung items as if the station influx from the evacuation was a sales opportunity. Avi considered a bottle of water and a snack for

Brooklyn. But she couldn't stop, not a second could be wasted. Phalanxes of armed national guard troops held submachine guns. Avi imagined it would be just the same if a terror attack had occurred. A man's screams penetrated Avi's ears. She saw him flailing, police slapping cuffs over his dirty wrists. It might be a good idea to get arrested. He might get off the island before her. Avi realized Brooklyn had never been exposed to the underground of New York City. During any slow weekday afternoon the sensory inundation would be shocking to her. During an evacuation it must've felt like a Benghazi uprising with mortar rounds and AK-47s. Brooklyn kept her face buried in Avi's neck.

They arrived at the New Jersey Transit concourse. People of every ethnicity snaked out of the escalators to the underground tracks. A woman's voice crunched over the PA. "PLEASE STAND IN LINE CALMLY. TRAINS WILL BE LOADED ON A FIRST-COME, FIRST-SERVED BASIS. NO TICKETS ARE NECESSARY. PLEASE STAND IN LINE CALMLY." Avi stood in line for a moment until she felt they would be waiting for hours with the risk of being contaminated by fallout. She headed toward the 8th Avenue and 33rd Street exit, fighting against the incoming crowds like she was running through sand against a stampede. A man knocked into her and Brooklyn spinning them around. Brooklyn squealed. Avi's eyes flared—a mother and her cub. She put her open shoulder into people.

"WATCH IT! C'MIN THROUGH! WATCH OUT! C'MIN THROUGH!" She made it to the exit and spilled out onto the sidewalk. Her vision was hazy. Droves of evacuees filed past her in purple blobs, emergency sirens squawked, lights glinting off buildings. Police wearing gas masks on horses and motorcycles directed intersections full of cabs, busses, and cars that weren't moving. Avi stood still waiting for her pupils to dilate.

Pedestrians overflowed the sidewalks and street shoulders,

bags slung over their backs, children in their arms, scarves wrapped around their noses and mouths in a futile attempt to stop fallout inhalation. Media vans had pulled up on sidewalks. Crews were omnipresent—filming, interviewing, the field reporters wearing particle masks. People shot video with their smartphones. Avi's eyes adjusted; none of it was an illusion. *Are you sure you're not still strapped to the hospital bed hallucinating?* She hoped she'd wake up to Trace standing next to her, and him saying, 'It's all over. The reactor is saved.' Avi saw a man wearing a robe and slippers hobbling on a cane. The evacuation had to be the hardest on the elderly, sick, and disabled—a kick to the gut when they were already doubled over. More than fifty percent of the city's residents didn't own a vehicle. That meant at least four million were leaving on foot or public transportation. *Insane.* EPA and New York Emergency Management busses were at opposite ends of 33rd Street. Field technicians in radiation-protective suits tested the air, their presence adding to the panic of the evacuees. *We're being contaminated and they're not! Wow... Lea can't get into the city, Trace is unavailable.* Instinct sent Avi down 33rd Street.

Twenty minutes later the illuminated, square-glass, midtown ferry terminal at 34th Street and 12th Avenue beckoned like a divine star. *Yes!* One boat departed full, another in embarkment, the line snaking down the dock. Avi contemplated waiting and calculated the time it would take for ferries to drop people and return for more. She must've been behind six or eight boats' worth of passengers. *No.* She acquiesced to her last option.

Eight minutes later she overlooked the north tube of the Lincoln Tunnel at 39th and 11th avenue. She dialed Lea from her smartphone. "Hey. I'm heading into the Lincoln Tunnel."

"You got a car?"

"No. Going on foot."

"What!"

"No choice. Trains and ferries all full, traffic gridlocked."

"Be careful."

"I should be on the other side in about thirty or forty minutes."

"I'll get as close as I can. Call me when you're there."

Avi hung up. With traffic crawling she found the walk less daunting. She wasn't the only pedestrian. Droves of New Yorkers descended into the underground in an attempt to flee the island. Avi danced between steaming vehicles, stood at the mouth of the dimly lit tube and took it in—a black leviathan, mouth agape, it seemed necromantic. The beast hissed steam across her face. She held her breath, disappeared into the abyss behind lines of evacuees. *Swallow me.*

CHAPTER 49

Avi jogged away from the Lincoln Tunnel exit, thrilled to see Lea wearing a particle mask, sliding back the door of her van on the roadside. Avi stepped inside with Brooklyn and placed her on the bench seat next to Lea's masked boys. "Mama's gonna get in the front, okay?" Avi kissed Brooklyn on her forehead and placed a mask over her face before strapping one over her own. "That tunnel's about eighty times more disgusting on foot than from inside a car." Avi wanted to bathe her skin and respiratory system in chlorine to rid herself of the filth. Her phone buzzed. A text from Trace. She replied telling him that she was with Lea and he didn't have to worry about picking them up and they could meet far south.

They drove down Palisade Ave in Lea's slate-blue minivan. Avi grazed her hands across the vehicle's air vents, making sure they were shut even though she knew radiation would still seep in. She drove so Lea could tend to Brooklyn's injuries and change her saline bag. Lea had brought supplies from her home, including crutches from when one of her boys had hurt his ankle. The roads were filled, Avi navigating aggressively through traffic. "Where's your dad?" Avi asked.

"He stayed behind, gun strapped to his hip. He said he wasn't leavin' until the evacuation was done and he knew looters wouldn't be coming through the neighborhood."

"Seriously?"

"Yeah. I gave him a mask after I yelled at him. Said he's already old and it didn't matter if he absorbed fallout because he couldn't possibly live that much longer anyway. He was hellbent on staying with the house."

"Sorry, Lea." The low-fidelity radio broadcast boomed through the car speakers. *"The following message is being trans-mitted at the request of Westchester County, Orange County, Rock-land County, Putnam County, Dutchess County, New York City, and Nassau County Emergency Management. County and state officials are directing citizens and residents to leave their homes calmly and evacuate the following areas due to a general emergency at the Bear Mountain Nuclear Energy Center: all of Westchester County, all of Putnam County west of interstate eighty-four, all of Rockland County. Oran—"* Avi cut the volume. "I can't stand to hear it again."

"We should listen just in case something changes," Lea said, returning to the passenger seat. Avi turned the radio back up.

"Reception centers have been established at locations listed in your county's emergency-planning guide and signs will be posted along major thoroughfares for those outside the planning area. Stay tuned to local television and radio for further instructions and updates."

Avi wiggled west hoping to get to Interstate 95, but the grid of Jersey City was jammed and she realized there wasn't an ex-peditious route out. She considered traveling into Staten Island and then cutting over since that area wasn't being evacuated, but she wasn't sure it would matter. Police cruisers, ambulances, fire trucks, and special emergency units whizzed by, eight- and twelve-cylinder engines roaring, lights flashing. The chop of the helicopter cruising overheard sounded like a sneaker in a dryer. "PLEASE EVACUATE THE AREA. Remain calm. PLEASE EVACUATE THE AREA. Please remain calm." Avi rounded a curve. An emergency SUV barreled toward them, headlights glaring through the windshield.

"SHIT!"

"OH MY GOD!" Lea screamed.

Avi stamped on the brakes and swerved onto the shoulder, the velocity of the SUV shaking the van as it zoomed past. They skidded to a stop. Avi and Lea checked on the kids in the back, they were fine. Avi's pulse beat in her ears. She dropped her head against the headrest and puffed out a breath. Blue and red flashed—emergency lights lancing into Avi's eyes. She closed her lids. If they had collided with the SUV they all would've been dead or severely injured. She wiped her sweaty palms on her t-shirt and grabbed Lea's hand. They both started chuckling out of delirium. Avi was glad to be with one of her best friends for the experience, grateful to not have to go at it completely alone. Avi's arms trembled when she gripped the steering wheel. *Gotta keep going.* She pulled back onto the road.

An endless millipede of vehicles with luggage, cribs, strollers, gas cans, and other gear strapped to the roofs crawled in front of them on the house-lined street. It seemed most of the people leaving the area believed they might never return, immense sorrow radiating from the sinuous line. Families rushed out of their homes, piling into their cars, vans, and SUVs, worry twisting their faces. Avi wanted to call her friends and extended family to make sure they were evacuating. Considering the collapsed overpasses near Peekskill, Avi worried how long it would take others to evacuate the area. She hoped they would be able to get on the freeway.

Groups of residents walked both sides of the road heading away from the city, bags on their backs, children in their arms.

Some wore particle masks, while others had garments wrapped around their noses and mouths. Avi saw a little boy dragging a stuffed Spiderman, confusion across his face. The wounds the disaster would leave on the little ones would take years to scar and would shape the rest of their lives. She wished they had more room in Lea's van and could invite others for a ride. However, Avi noticed most of them moved faster than the SUV.

Avi noticed a bus parked on the roadside, people fighting each other to get on, police trying to break up the melee. The whir of sirens and flashing lights never abated. A helicopter ripping by sent vibrations up her seat, through her body, and into her hands. "PLEASE EVACUATE THE AREA. Remain calm. PLEASE EVACUATE THE AREA. Please remain calm," echoed from the bullhorn. Avi found the directive to stay calm paradoxical as radiation wafted over them and their children were injured and in danger. *Easy to say when you're wearing a respirator.* An ambulance drove up the shoulder. A police car split between two lanes trying to get through, sirens whooping. Horns surrounded her—deep, high, angry, friendly toots.

Avi knew she would never live in Peekskill again. She had said goodbye to her home the morning of the quake; she had known then she wouldn't return. Her life with Trace and Brooklyn had been there. However, she could never live in proximity to a nuclear power plant again.

"The air is circulating internally, right?" Lea said.

"Yes." Avi checked the dash to be sure. "Yep." She nodded to Lea. "We need gas." The fuel needle laid on 'E', the LED next to it flashing.

"There's a station coming up here," Lea said. They crawled ahead. A large piece of cardboard taped on the station sign read *'Out of Gas.'*

"Damn... another station's out... The gas light's been on since this morning," Avi said.

"There's another across the street." Lea pointed.

A line of approximately fifty cars coiled around the station. The pumps might run out of gas by the time they made it to them. Avi didn't want to risk waiting while fallout blew their way. Two men fought at one of the pumps, one trying to pull the nozzle from the other's car and fill his gas can. The violence deterred her and they rolled past. *I can't believe people are fighting instead of helping each other.*

"Mama, I'm hungry," Brooklyn said.

"Okay, honey. We'll stop for something soon."

Five miles further down the road the van lurched. The engine sputtered and seized. The dash gauges and headlights faded down like sad closing eyes. "Shit!" Avi smacked the steering wheel.

"Oh my god. Are we outta gas?" Lea said.

"Yup!" Avi coasted to the shoulder. Cars honked behind them. "Oh, shut the hell up!" she snapped.

"What're we gonna do now?" Lea said.

"Mama, why we stopping?" Brooklyn asked.

Avi looked in the rearview and caught Brooklyn's eyes. She tried to smile, but what came out on her face was a flatline. *Radiation is blanketing us. We're all gonna get cancer. God, no... Please...* "Dammit! Dammit! Dammit!" She slammed the steering wheel.

CHAPTER 50

The pregnant woman's cries tore through Trace's stomach like a machete. He barreled down the highway shoulder with his four-way flashers on. Trace, who always had a solid core of uranium in the left of his chest, was melting down after the past three days. The coup de grâce was the woman next to him writhing, forced to give birth in his pickup during an evacuation that was his fault. She held the child she had just pushed out, blood soaking her dress, seat, and legs. Trace feared the woman had lost too much blood. She trembled, slipping in and out of consciousness, her chest surging with breath. "Hang in there. Stay with me." He rubbed her arm.

If he lived long enough he would be summoned to Washington where he'd be interrogated by the NRC, DOE, White House, and congress. His face would be published in every media format worldwide. He saw himself on the cover of *Time Magazine*, his visage superimposed over the face of Satan rising out of the exposed rebar holes in the auxiliary and containment buildings. He feared business, technical, and environmental articles that would analyze every millimeter of the catastrophe, his and his team's psychology, and the aftermath. *The End of Gener8—How They Went from Multibillion-Dollar Energy Conglomerate to Bust. Fission Has Fizzled. Bear Mountain—the Mistakes. Nuked. The End of the Atomic Age. The Decision on Fission. Bound by Meltdown. Nuclear Fear. New York, No More. The Lights Have Gone Out on Broadway.* All the headlines glared in Trace's mind. He couldn't shake them.

He figured media and protestors would camp twenty-four seven outside whatever temporary housing he and Avi found. He saw the media timelines of the entire incident starting with the earthquake, speculation of how it all unfolded, facts intertwined with sensation, personal stories about struggling evacuating families. Pregnant women and injured evacuees wouldn't be able to receive medical treatment and might die trying to flee. People were going to lose their businesses and their homes. Families living check to check were going to run out of money within a few weeks and have to live in shelters while searching desperately for any job. Even though Trace felt like he had failed his company and its employees, the government, and the people of the East Coast, he feared what was ahead for himself. Electricity costs in the New York metro area alone'll rise by almost three billion a year without Bear Mountain, the burden of the cost resting on the public.

His phone chirped. Avi: *Lea's got me. We can meet south.*

Relief vibrated through him. He had gone through so much up and down he felt like an amphetamine and barbiturate junkie. Amid his distress now Trace felt like he had actually done something worthwhile. Avi could've been the pregnant woman on the roadside. He was glad he crossed the woman's path and could take her to find medical attention. If he delivered her to a hospital or EMT in time it'd be one redemption for his soul to the vast debt he believed he owed. Blue and red lights flashed in the darkness ahead of him. He approached an intersection. A fire truck blocked the crossing road. Trace came to a hard stop at the foot of it. Firefighters and law enforcement frantically waved at him to return to the road, flashlights beaming at his truck. Trace popped out of the pickup. "I've got a woman here that's just given birth!" The firefighters hustled into action. Trace leaned his head against the doorjamb. *Thank god.*

CHAPTER 51

Avi felt like a strumpet in the wee hours on a shadowy stretch in Newark. Cars moved past her, faces obscured by darkness and headlight glare, anonymous ignorers secretly watching, judging, considering. *She might be evil... might hurt us... take our supplies... steal our car.* She couldn't connect with them. She was the crazy lady waving from the periphery of the roadside wearing a particle mask, labeled as unprepared for running out of gas. Unbeknownst to Avi her mobile buzzed in the center console of Lea's minivan—two missed calls from Trace. Dozens of cars had gone by, leaving her perplexed that not a single person had asked her if they needed help. *We can't get stranded now. In the fucking dark to boot.* Avi's head ached with every throb of her pulse. *C'mon, people.* The heartlessness of fellow evacuees passing by caused her indignation she had never experienced. She would stop for someone on the side of the road; even if she couldn't help them. She understood the fright that pervaded fellow evacuees; it plagued her, too. It was time for strangers to band together and support each other, not time to be selfish. Airborne radiation surrounding them petrified her. She didn't want Brooklyn to be contaminated like she had been when she was young. She didn't want her little girl to have to deal with cancer or autoimmune and thyroid issues from Hashimoto's. Avi hoped she'd see Trace soon. She needed his arms lashed around her.

A three-decade-old, faded-red pickup truck with one headlight pulled in front of Avi behind the van. An older gentleman exited—well-sunned, skin rugged like a rhino, jeans, t-shirt, and a leather biker's vest.

"You break down?" he asked.

"Ran outta gas," Avi replied.

"Ah…" He went to the bed of his truck and returned with a red container. "I got five gallons. That should get ya where you need to go. At least outta harm's way."

"Oh my god. Thank you." Avi smiled.

"I'll fill it for ya." The man opened the gas cap and put the yellow nozzle in.

"Thank you." Another kind older gentleman like the one she had encountered on the subway. *What's wrong with people under sixty? No one values strangers anymore.*

Avi pulled back onto the crowded road. "Alright, we got at least seventy-five miles in the tank."

"Thank God," Lea said.

An EPA van surrounded by workers in radiation suits taking air samples blipped. *It's really happening. Radiation's everywhere.*

"Mama, I'm hungry," Brooklyn said.

"Yeah, me too," Lea's boys said.

Avi looked at Lea. "We should get some food."

"There's a convenience store there." Lea pointed.

Avi saw a sign in the window with *Closed* written on it. People in the parking lot looked in the windows and banged on the doors. A man in a business suit threw a log through the front glass. "They're breaking into the store." Good people who would never steal partook because there was separation of the inanimate store facade from a human. Therefore, they could justify the action to themselves. Everyone had regressed to survival; mammalian instincts superseded intellect. *There may be no other choice.* "There's a large grocery store up on the other side. I see the sign." Avi pointed. They approached. The parking lot was jammed with vehicles and people running in and out with carts and bags. "Take the wheel," Avi said to Lea. "I'll get us some things while you stay with the kids." She pulled up to the front of the store, hopped out of the van and scurried to the entrance. Lea slid into the driver's seat and locked the doors.

Avi searched for a basket or empty cart. The store was trashed, lines of angry shoppers winding down aisles. Avi passed plants, candy, patterned napkins, and other superfluous items. The morning of the quake when she had ran out of the store in Peekskill confused, nauseated, and bloody flashed in her mind. An empty cart sat ahead of her. *Yes.* She gripped the handle. The cart screeched along the floor, the front right wheel broken. "Damn." She ditched the cart and headed for the produce section. The refrigerated shelves were bare, nothing but broken stems, rubber bands, and leaves from bundles of vegetables that had been taken. *Fruit.* She looked at the center bins—bruised, split open, and half rotten. A smattering of apples, pears, bananas, and berries lay along the floor. Avi tore off the last few plastic bags from a roll nearby and put the fruit inside one. What else could she go for? *Canned goods...* Avi dashed down the perpendicular aisle. The shelves were barren save for a can of coconut milk and a can of peas. *Frozen?* Avi whipped around into the frozen section. Bare. *Bread? Peanut butter and jelly?* Avi saw the sign for bread and jams and raced into the aisle.

Every shelf had been plundered. Avi came upon a loaf of sourdough and took it. She saw chunky, unsalted peanut butter in the back of the shelf along with a jar of apricot jam. She took both and put them in the other plastic bag. Avi hustled to the front of the store and swiped a box of plastic knives and a pack of napkins from the display table.

A woman latched onto Avi's bag of bread, peanut butter, and jam as she passed.

"Hey. Those are mine!" Avi pulled back on the bag.

"Hey, bitch, getcher own!" the woman lashed.

"What are you talking about? Those are mine," Avi snapped back. "Let go!"

The woman ripped the bag from Avi's hands. "Why're you tryin' to take my food? Getcher own."

"Whaddayou crazy?" Avi lunged for the bread and peanut butter. The woman pivoted away. "Give that back," Avi yelped.

"It's mine!" the woman said.

Avi swung the bag of fruit, clocking the woman across her face and knocking her down. She grabbed the peanut butter and jam bag. "Give it back, dammit!" She slapped the lady across the face. "Give it back! Give. It. Back."

"Hey, STOP!" Someone shouted. Avi recoiled. Blood seeped from the woman's lips. Avi stood over her, stunned. She had never hit anyone in her life. She felt savage, an unbridled beast. The woman's hand uncurled, releasing the bag. Avi snatched it and ran for the doors. With every step her anger turned to remorse. She had done what every other looter had—telling herself she had children to feed and there were no employees to collect money. Survival had engulfed her. *I'm one of them.* Avi rapped on the passenger window of the van. Lea unlocked the doors and Avi hurried inside.

"What happened?" Lea asked.

"Drive. Drive!" Avi said.

Lea hit the gas. Avi bawled.

"Av… what?…" Lea said.

"I just stole from the grocery store and some lady tried to take my food and I hit 'er."

"God. Well, don't worry about not paying. There's nothing we can do. We need to eat. And don't worry about her either. We have kids to feed."

"It was awful."

"Mama, why you crying?" Brooklyn said from the back seat. Avi wiped her eyes and turned back to her.

"It's okay, honey. I got food for you guys." Avi's phone buzzed and danced in the central cup holder. She saw *'Trace'* on the screen and snapped it up. "Honey."

"Hey. There you are. I've been trying to call. I left the plant."

"Oh my god. You did? We ran outta gas and then went to the grocery store to get food for the kids and…"

"Avi, get out of town. Drive. GO!"

"We're goin'. When will we see you?"

"Drive south and I'll call you back with a place to meet."

When Avi hung up she saw lipgloss and blood on her hand. *I'm awful. Awful! How could I do that? I had no choice!*

CHAPTER 52

The pickup truck bounced over the decomposed granite drive when Trace pulled into Lake Ridge Park in Virginia. Blood from his nose had dried like petrified, crimson, swamp narrows in the stubble around his mouth. His eyes were sallow, his lids and sockets ashen. It was 10:00 a.m. and he had been driving all night in evacuation traffic. What would have typically been a five-hour drive to Virginia had taken him fourteen. Avi waited outside Lea's minivan next to Brooklyn, who bounced up and down with excitement from the open door of the passenger seat. Seeing his girls in front of him helped suppress his nausea. The smile stretching Trace's face would expand to the periphery of the galaxy if his skin could cope. Sadness and joy engulfed him.

Trace threw the pickup in park. His legs wobbled when his feet touched the ground. He touched his face; it was hot. *Fever. Get it together.* Trace steadied himself and focused on his girls. Seeing them in the flesh had been unimaginable until then. For the past three days he hadn't been sure he would make it out of Bear Mountain. He had thought the reactor might explode into an inferno. He had thought he might get sent to decontamination and then directly to the hospital where he'd be quarantined. He didn't want Avi and Brooklyn to see him in that condition. He wanted his girls to see him as they knew him, standing on his own feet, their reunion free of pity. Trace rested his eyes on Avi, her hair tousled over a bandage, her emerald eyes radiating underneath. She staggered when she moved, something wrong with her knee, a bandage on her chest. Still, she luminesced.

Brooklyn wore a hospital gown, her leg in a cast, bandages on her arms, stomach, and head. He wanted to take the pain and injuries away from both of them and put it on himself. Innocent and ethereal, Brooklyn didn't deserve the trauma delivered to her from the disaster. Trace couldn't comprehend how her rapturous, elegant soul could deserve such affliction. He believed there had to be something existentially awry with the divine for it to happen. He pondered what he, Avi, Brooklyn, and any others stricken in the disaster had done wrong to deserve malign karma. He wondered if it was the five dollars he had stolen from a friend's wallet when he was nine years old or the time he and another group of friends had left derogatory messages on a fat girl's locker door. Was it the time he cheated on his history test by referencing a cheat sheet on the floor under his desk? Was it the time in middle school he sat in the cafeteria and harangued attractive girls because he didn't know what else to say? Or the time he took his friend's car to go visit a girl and didn't return until 3:50 a.m., getting him grounded? Trace hadn't a clue. He, Avi, Brooklyn, and countless others had never done anything wrong to deserve the deleterious repercussions of an earthquake and nuclear reactor meltdown. Tears pushed against Trace's lids; he held them back. *Be strong for them.* Trace adored Brooklyn's butterscotch hair, her hazel eyes, her tiny face gleaming, her arms outstretched toward him. He scanned the park, surprised to be standing in nature. He breathed deeply.

"Daaadddyyyy!" Brooklyn screamed, hobbling on crutches toward him.

Trace waved. "Hi, pumpkin!" He looked at Avi. "Grab her. She can't touch me yet."

Avi's face twisted in confusion.

"Daadddddyyy!" Brooklyn crutched toward him.

"Grab her. I've been exposed!"

"What?"

"Do it!" Contact with Trace wasn't life threatening but could definitely expose them to high levels of radiation compounding with what they had already received near Bear Mountain.

Avi scurried and stopped Brooklyn.

"You both can get about ten feet away."

"What's going on?" Avi said.

"I want Dadddyyyy," Brooklyn squealed.

"I've been exposed. I can't touch either of you. But I brought a clean suit and once I put that on I can. I wanted you to see me in normal clothes." It was the closest Trace had been to his girls in three days. He was desperate to wrap his arms around them. His heart was bleak without their love. He had no career and acute radiation poisoning. He was a spindle of DNA, a pile of flesh on a mineral-rich sphere. Modern society, material possessions, and superfluous subjects no longer mattered to him. Cars, his house, clothing, golf clubs, electronics, music, beer, sports, nuclear energy—none of it mattered.

"Daddy'll be right back, okay, honey?" Avi said to Brooklyn.

"Daddddyyy…" Brooklyn reached out for him.

Trace shuffled to the passenger side of the pickup, opened the door, and reached into his duffle bag. He took a clean radiation suit out, unfolded it, stepped inside, zipped it up over his distended gut, and taped the seams. Trace pulled the hood up and secured it around his neck. He pulled a particle mask over his nose and mouth and snapped vinyl gloves onto his hands. Then he walked around to the driver's side of the truck where Avi and Brooklyn were.

He moved within five feet. Brooklyn buried her face into Avi's neck. "Why's daddy wearing that?"

"Daddy's hurt and he has to protect himself, okay? Don't be scared."

Trace crouched down with his arms outstretched. He didn't anticipate their meeting to be like that, but he thought it better than her seeing him in a hospital bed. He knew it was hard for her to understand that he was radioactive.

Avi took Brooklyn's crutches and supported her with her hands. Brooklyn moved toward Trace. "Daddy…" She fell into his arms. Trace embraced her tightly. *Finally.* She felt like a warm ball of love splashing into his universe. Misery he'd had in his soul dissipated. He kissed her on her forehead through his mask.

"I missed you, you little monkey." He rocked her back and forth squeezing her. "I love you so much."

"Love you, too, Daaaddddyyyy."

Trace stood. He turned to Avi and gazed into her eyes. His bride, his love, his partner, his soulmate. They fell into each other. Her heart beat strongly against his chest, his beating against hers creating a single rhythm. Brooklyn clung to his leg. Trace looked down and saw her wrapped around Avi's as well. They were all finally united. He never wanted to be away from his family again. They were first from that point forward. Every day, every hour, he'd consider them before anything else.

Avi hadn't been sure if she would see Trace again after running into him outside the plant. In her husband's hulking embrace, resting on his voluminous, warm chest, she felt secure. She hadn't felt protected and connected in Trace's arms for years. The feeling proved to her how much love existed between them. Avi's anger toward Trace was distant. As soon as she had seen him she had forgiven him. She could see he'd been awake for the past three days trying to stabilize the reactor. She had never seen him so riddled with agony. For the entire road trip she had feared he could still be injured or killed. He could've gotten into a car accident, gotten called back to the plant and decided he had to stay.

Avi had dropped Lea and Lea's two boys off at a local hotel before speeding over to the park to meet Trace. She had found it odd he wanted to meet there, but now she understood. He didn't want to risk contaminating anyone or any establishment. Avi had her husband in her arms. She didn't want to fight with him any longer, she wanted to just be with him, sit with him, drink in the essence of their union. "I thought I was never going to see you again," Avi choked out.

"Same here. I tried to call you several times. I tried the house, your cell. I thought about you and Brooklyn the entire time I was at the plant. I love you so much. I wanted to leave the plant and come and find you, but... I'm so sorry," Trace said.

"Sorry for what? Don't be sorry."

"I'm sorry I didn't listen to you."

"It's okay. We're all safe now and we can move forward."

Trace nodded into her neck. "Yeah. We're not going back, and I'm quitting my job."

"Are you okay?" Avi asked. "How much exposure have you had?"

"Quite a bit," Trace said solemnly.

"Shouldn't you get medical attention?"

"I'm fine."

Avi looked into Trace's eyes. She took his hands and put them on her stomach. "I'm pregnant," she whispered.

"What? How?"

"They tested me at the hospital. That night with a few bottles of wine…"

"Wow…" Trace threw his arms back around Avi. "I…" His body began to tremble. "I'm…" Anxiety enveloped him, a strange draining feeling in his bones. His entire body felt weak as if his blood was let out. He shuddered. "I was exposed to a lot of radioactivity." Waves of heat undulated from his chest to his head.

Avi pulled back from Trace, keeping her arms around him. "What does that mean?" She searched his eyes. "Trace? Weren't you decontaminated?"

"I've…" Trace stepped back from Avi's embrace. "Step back…" He put his hand out to her. "Step back," he said, breathless.

"Trace… What?…"

Trace slid his particle mask off his nose and mouth onto his forehead. "I…" His lungs seized. "I can't breathe."

"Trace!" Avi reached toward him.

"Mommy." Brooklyn looked at Avi for comfort.

"Stay back," Trace said his right hand on his chest, his lungs constricting. He dropped to his knees.

"Daddy!" Brooklyn shouted.

"Trace!" Avi said, her face red with panic.

Trace held his hand out, trying to keep them at bay. He turned and vomited. He fell to his fists, his mind starkly clear. A high-pitched tone blared in his ears. Trace's arms shuddered and folded. He collapsed to the gravel, his particle mask squished into his face, tiny stones piercing his skin. The two wire hearts he had twisted together at the plant the day before fell from his hand.

"Mama!" Brooklyn tugged at Avi's arm.

"Trace!" Avi sprang to his side.

On a park bench in Brooklyn under an oak tree lit by dozens of candles Trace handed Avi a pumpkin muffin. "I made it for you," he whispered. She split the muffin in half with her hands. Inside she saw something shimmering back at her. She reached into the muffin and surfaced with a diamond ring. Avi covered her mouth with her empty hand.

"Trace..." her voice cracked. Trace plucked the ring from her fingers, a spec set into white gold, and took Avi's hand.

"I wanna wake up every morning with you. I want us to sit by the beach on the weekend and always when we're old. I wanna *be* with you."

Avi smiled.

"I wanna get street-truck coffee with you. Drink wine by the fire. Whatddaya think?" It was only the two of them under the foliage, the drone of a waterfall nearby. Dampness from an earlier rain released the scents of cypress, hickory, and pine into the night air. Trace felt like they'd been teleported back to a medieval garden on a Scottish countryside.

Avi nodded and Trace slipped the ring onto her finger. She dove into Trace's arms, kissing his neck, holding his face with her fingertips. The warmth of her cardigan against his cheek was like snuggling up to a warm living-room fire. She smelled like home, like family. Avi disappeared, Trace still hugging the space where she had resided. A gust of wind blew over him. "Aviiiii!" A baby was thrust into his arms. Inside Avi's hospital room Trace cradled Brooklyn. "I love you." He stroked Brooklyn's cheek. Trace sat at the edge of Avi's bed, leaned over, and kissed her on the forehead. "This is perfect. You, me, Brooklyn."

The doctor entered. "Your daughter has spina bifida."

"What?" Distress mounted on Trace's face.

"Spina bifida." The doctor's words echoed.

"No! Why?"

With a blast of light Trace wriggled on the passenger seat of his mother's car. "Mama, look!" He pointed at the Bear

Mountain reactor steam-stack across the Hudson.

"So you wanna work for Bear Mountain?" A balding man with unruly eyebrows sat in front of Trace inside a stark, cinderblock office. Trace, twenties, stared back at him from across the man's desk.

"Have since I was a kid," Trace said.

"Welcome to the team." The man extended his hand. Trace reached for it. The man disappeared before Trace could touch him. Avi took the man's place sitting across from Trace.

"Trace, I have cancer," she said.

"Cancer?" he echoed.

"Cancer..." Avi lay on a hospital bed, Trace gawking at her bandages and a slew of tubes and wires running from her.

"Cut the pumps!" Trace barked at Avi.

"Pressure's falling!" Avi said, Jerry's voice coming out of her mouth. Alarms blared.

"Did you hear that boom?" he said inside the control room.

"No," Valdern replied.

"No?"

"Temperature in the vessel's rising," Valdern said.

"We've got a hydrogen bubble," Jerry said. Trace stared catatonic, envisioning Brooklyn blowing a soap bubble in his face that expanded twice the size of his head. The bubble popped, liquid spraying across his face. He was on the floor of the valve room, knocked over by the pipe dislodging. Radioactive coolant spewed on top of him, melting his face into a puddle on the floor.

"I can't find my wife and daughter. You have to help me," Trace spat into his office phone. He ran to the front interior gates of Bear Mountain. *I must find them.* "You have to help me!" he shouted to the guard. He violently shook the gates. "LET ME OUT!"

Trace wrenched the squeaking handwheel inside the auxiliary building in an attempt to dissipate the hydrogen bubble. He grunted with every turn. The wheel morphed into a cell phone. Trace frantically punched in numbers. He pushed Avi's name. BOOM! Standing outside he watched a hole blow out the top of the auxiliary building like a volcano, chunks of concrete raining onto him. Static hummed in his ears. *I hit the detonator! I nuked my country!*

"We've breached containment! You need to issue an evacuation. NOW!" Trace shouted at Ken through the receiver. "Get out! Go at least two hundred miles," he told Avi. "The auxiliary building's exploded! Explo-a-lo-a-lo-a-lo-aloded!" his voice echoed. Evacuation traffic surrounded him, the pregnant woman dead, blue and cold on the seat next to him, her child still in her arms, blood covering all of her as if she'd been shot and beaten two dozen times. "AVI!" Trace raced down the highway shoulder, pedal to the floor, engine roaring. "C'MON!"

Trace stood on arid, cracked earth, a spiral of light encircling him in the darkness. Omnipresent murmuring rose in his ears, spliced by smatterings of discernible speech, his father's voice. *Do what's right, not what's easy. Do what you love. Be passionate about it. Don't worry about the money. Just do something that matters! Don't worry. Don't worry... worry... worry...* "I did... I DID!" His voice reverberated. "What happened? I tried! I tried to save Bear Mountain!" he yelled, falling to his knees. "I tried..." The spiral turned into an orb. "Please," he begged. The orb exploded. The earth below him lifted and fractured. He stumbled back. Apparitions of his dead friends and family appeared from the darkness. He saw his father in the navy chinos and polo he had worn on the day he died. He saw Hanson's face, his grandparents, his mother.

"C'mon," they all whispered. "Come with us." Trace stepped forward. He turned back, Avi and Brooklyn behind him.

"Trace!"

"Daddy!" they cried out. The earth under him lifted violently, sending him to the ground. He stood on a mountain, a large crevasse in front of him, majestic clouds above. Blue, purple, green, red, and white auroral hues showered him. Trace's body began to liquify into the beams of light, the different colors absorbing him until he dissipated.

Black.

CHAPTER 53

Trace... Daddy. Mr. Crane? Voices echoed between pulsating tones. *Mr. Crane. Trace? Daddy...* The horizon glowed, the blackness fading ever so slightly. Apparitions appeared. *What?* "Hello?"

Stark images revealed rapidly. Crisp, full images. Faces and objects. Black. The light brightened with every flash. The apparitions morphed into ridged ovals, feathery oculi blinking, darting. *Trace.* Walls of white moved between red crescents. *Trace, honey?* He felt a rubbery clasp on his arm. Then a small, excited creature pounced on him. *Daddy...* Two males in white lab coats and an elderly man and woman in the background gawked at him. Gray tufts of stiff hair. Sad faces. The objects flashed to black again. *Mr. Crane...* The mouth of a man in a white coat moved in slow motion, the words out of sync with his movement. Trace feared the man's jaw would chomp down upon him, his teeth like massive sheets of drywall moving up and down. Unbounded darkness was inside his mouth. *Did I come from there?*

Trace's left arm burned. It left a warm trail moving along his shoulder running across his chest. A rush of oxygen shot through his nose. "Trace," a woman said.

"Mr. Crane," a man said. Trace's eyes flung open. *I know her.*
"Avi?"

"Trace," she said.

Avi moved closer to him like she was coming out of a fish-eye lens. "What?" His stomach twitched. He vomited. "Ahh…"

Avi pulled the cotton-lined plastic sheet over him, rolled it up, and removed it with her gloved hands. Two long, slender, bloody, blackened alabaster objects with tubes running from them lay beside him. *What are those?* He couldn't recognize his arms.

A male in blue scrubs tipped water into Trace's mouth. Trace unconsciously rinsed and spit into a basin. He must've done that before. It seemed so natural. A multitude of cables ran from his chest, although he couldn't identify the area as his. His body was dead. He hovered above looking down at himself. *What exactly is me?* He scanned the room. Six faces looked back at him. Big faces, inflated like comedic cartoon balloons wearing particle masks. Trace tried to move. He groaned. His body had a numbing ache to it as if every bone had been beaten with a bludgeon.

Through her mask Avi kissed Trace on his forehead. "Trace, can you hear me?"

Trace's heart pulsated in his head, tension so tight in his skull it radiated to his jaw and throat. He only felt the pressure; the pain was numbed out by something else. His body swayed. He saw the ocean next to him. *I'm on a cruise. I'd love a mojito and a beer.* He nodded to Avi, his mouth agape.

"You're in the hospital," she said.

"Hosp…?" he said lethargically.

"The hospital."

Trace nodded. "Hospital…" He didn't understand, but it seemed as though his subconscious did. "How long?"

"Three weeks."

"Three… weeks…?" he said slowly. Memories of his stay and declining health came in flashes—his hair falling out of his scalp, no longer being able to walk, pain in his bones until the morphine kicked in, the inability to move, feeling held down to his bed and trapped in his body.

"You've been in a coma for the last seventy-two hours," Avi said.

"Coma?" Trace responded, confused. He looked at Brooklyn. She clung to her grandmother, her face red and teary. Trace caught a glimpse of another man in a mirror on the bathroom door. Trace noticed when he moved his fingers the man's moved. He was cadaverous, his face ashen, his eyes sunken and jaundiced. He was completely bald—no eyebrows, no facial hair, no body hair, no eyelashes. His limbs were spattered with crimson blotches, his skin black and flaying off in areas, revealing bloody tissue. Trace reached his hand up toward his face. The man in the mirror did the same. His emaciated arm felt like it weighed fifty pounds. Weakness radiated in his bones. He touched his face and felt nothing. He didn't recognize the man who weighed less than one hundred pounds, but subconsciously knew it was him. Avi reached for his arm.

"It's okay, honey. Look at me." She tried to position herself in front of the mirror.

"No." He pushed her arm away. "What's happened to me?"

"You're sick, honey."

Trace ran his fingers across his face. "Why?"

"He doesn't remember, again." Avi's father said in the background.

"Geez…" her mother sighed.

"You were in a nuclear accident. You saved the nuclear plant, but you got sick."

Trace nodded. His eyes searched the room. Flowers stacked

the windowsill and table surfaces. He saw bubbles floating, strings dangling. *What are those things? Loons? Saloons... Ball oonsss...* His body undulated, tingling with warmth. *I'd like to go for a swim.*

Trace envisioned himself, Avi, and Brooklyn moving into another Victorian home in a lush neighborhood. Flowers bloomed, grasses swaying in the breeze, elm trees twisting over the roads. The scent of nature was sweet, the air clean and crisp, hints of gardenia in his nose. Trace glimpsed himself carrying boxes into the house, a slight must of the old home lingering. The floors creaked when he stepped. He delivered a box to the living room. If Brooklyn wasn't around he'd tackle Avi onto the living-room planks and undress her as he had when they signed on their first home in Peekskill. Trace saw Avi hoist Brooklyn up onto the white-marble counter and feed her snacks. Trace had his arm around Avi, leaning against the French doors to the backyard, a glass of wine in each of their hands. They watched Brooklyn chasing butterflies and hummingbirds in the grass yard. He pictured himself at a new job for the state power grid. No more nuclear. No more living near a nuclear reactor. Avi was in her office researching, then in the lab, business prospering. Later, Brooklyn was off to school, Trace and Avi taking turns dropping her off in the morning. Trace was slender with streaks of gray at his temples, Avi ageless save for light crow's-feet. They had both climbed into their early fifties, appreciating each other every day, just as content as they had been when they first married. Brooklyn was a teenager dressed for the prom in an indigo chiffon dress, a boy in a tuxedo picking her up in a black limo.

Trace looked forward to helping Brooklyn move in with her boyfriend, probably in Brooklyn or the Upper West Side. He and Avi helped Brooklyn set up her apartment, a one bedroom in a pre-war walk-up; air conditioners hanging from the windows stacked up the storeys like stairs to heaven. They sent her off in a new pantsuit and designer bag for her first day at work. Trace walked her to the altar, gave her away to a gallant gentleman. Later there were grandchildren. Trace and Avi were in their sixties, both retired, still living happily upstate. Brooklyn and her husband visited with the grandkids.

Trace was ready to get out of the hospital, ready to start their new chapter. A hot wave rippled through his chest. His eyes spread. He gasped.

"Trace." Avi's voice quivered.

He was back floating in the dark expanse. The light he fell toward dimmed. Gelid air chilled him. *Hello? Avi? Brooklyn?* Avi and Brooklyn were on Earth. Trace watched over them. Weightlessness ensued.

CHAPTER 54

Six Months Later

Avi could smell the lush hills of wavy juniper set behind the water of Lake George. In the foreground a home with wood docks crept into the banks. A flagpole strapped to the end of the dock stood strong, an American flag hanging from the top. On the right side small islands dotted the lake, a white sailboat swayed.

Avi wished she was there, except she wanted to be away from nuclear power plants. All U.S. reactors were still shut down, but she had heard talk of the possibility for many of them to come back online. The decision to keep nuclear up and running after what had happened at Bear Mountain wasn't surprising to her. Avi and Lea with her two boys had decided to stick together in Denver until they could make a decision about where each of them wanted to live in the future. They didn't know what areas were truly safe; reports said winds were blowing fallout from Bear Mountain hundreds to thousands of miles away. Reports of radiation on the west coast of Ireland, England,

France, Spain, and Africa had surfaced. No one wanted to be near nuclear power, and since most of the reactors in the country were along the East Coast Avi and Lea went west.

Avi rested in a recliner, her feet on the floor, her newborn son, Bear, wriggling in her arms, Brooklyn next to her on a white nurse's stool. Avi watched the IV dripping, the crimson and clear liquid filled tubes coiling to her forearm. Her hair had gone dry, left unkempt, a few strands of gray showing. Her eyes were puffy and gray from lack of sleep, her sparkle gone. According to her the only positive about her current appearance was she hadn't put on weight. Stress and anguish had squelched her appetite. Avi was surprised Bear had received enough nutrition during her pregnancy. She had assuaged her fear of miscarriage by choking down protein shakes.

Avi hadn't had too many nights of solid rest since Trace had died and Bear was born. It didn't matter the type of sleep aids she had tried—herbs, medicinal—her mind was a constant spate of past events replaying on a loop, impossible to quell for longer than a few moments. She raced into the hospital to find Brooklyn, raced through the streets of Manhattan trying to escape, ran out of gas, beat a woman bloody in the grocery store. The destruction inside her home played over and over— the smashed dishes and picture frames, the structure leaning. Sometimes the house would start shaking and collapse on her. Almost nightly she had dreams where she tried to call Trace and when he answered the phone exploded. In other instances she had blissful moments where she and Trace were together, living happy, deeply in love. She woke up, rolled over to hug him only to find pillows, and she realized she wasn't in her bed in Peekskill, but in a strange bed in a strange place. They weren't her sheets, her pillows—her *anything*. She rushed into the next room to check on Brooklyn and Bear. Brooklyn was awake, eyes pinned open. "Mommy, I'm having bad dreams again." Sometimes she woke up mesmerized. "Mommy, daddy was here." Other times she woke up wailing. "Someone's chasing me!" Occasionally her leg ached.

"Trace!" Avi lurched for him, eyes wide and quivering as he dropped to his knees in the park clutching his chest. She had had him for just a moment in that park hugging her. After, he was never the same. She sat next to his hospital bed for weeks watching him waste away. *What did he do to deserve that kind of departure? He gave himself to providing power to New York and got a kick in the ass for it.*

Avi's aura had become dim. She looked sidelong down the rows of chairs full of people ranging from their thirties to eighties, most receiving chemotherapy. She was receiving a blood transfusion and DTPA (diethylenetriamine pentaacetate) in continued efforts to detox her body from radiation exposure she had received while evacuating from Peekskill.

Avi turned to the newscast on the wall-mounted LCD TV. "Six months later the tragedy of the Bear Mountain nuclear disaster is still fresh. Over fifteen million have been evacuated from the New York metro area. NRC officials confirm millions of curies of radioactive isotopes have been released from Bear Mountain, contaminating soil, crops, livestock, streets, structures, and ground water. The NRC says the release of radioactive fallout from the reactor is now dwindling. However, in the process of the reactor meltdown and the aftermath of the hydrogen explosion, over six hundred thousand gallons of radioactive wastewater had been dumped into the Hudson River, contaminating the Upper and Lower New York bays and neighboring Atlantic coastal regions. An exclusion zone of twenty miles has been cordoned off around Buchanan, New York, and the crippled Bear Mountain Nuclear Energy Center. That zone extends through all of Westchester County, Bronx, Manhattan, Brooklyn, Queens, and part of Nassau County,

Long Island, northern New Jersey, and western Connecticut.

"There've been five hundred and twelve confirmed dead, over six thousand injured, and another fourteen thousand one hundred and three confirmed stricken with radiation sickness. Experts from the NRDC and the Union of Concerned Scientists predict more than half a million latent, terminal cancer deaths, over a million cancer-related diseases, and more than one hundred thousand radiation-related birth defects to transpire over the next few decades for residents who've lived within fifty miles of Bear Mountain. The cleanup costs are estimated to total around fifty billion. Gener8 Corporation is to be hit by at least seventy billion in losses and the entire economy within a hundred-mile radius surrounding Bear Mountain is to suffer north of three trillion dollars in economic damage over the next two years."

The greatest city in the world—gone because of nuclear power. Avi turned away from the TV. Anxiety gripped her chest. She looked sidelong down the row of recliners again and hoped no one would recognize her from all the news shows and articles that had talked about Trace and showed her picture. *The villain.*

Major corporations had shuttered their Manhattan headquarters, most had satellite offices and the capital to set up in other cities. Hit worst were the locally owned businesses—restaurants, furniture, textiles, grooming, personal accessories, car washes, gas stations, liquor stores, farms—businesses that ran solely off their neighborhoods. People were forced to start over. A class-action suit backed by fifteen million–plus evacuees had been filed against Gener8 for fifteen trillion dollars with the hope to at least supply all with enough money to rebuild years of their lives. Insurance companies in the area were bled dry. Claims had far exceeded the 12.985 billion accrued under the Price-Anderson Act, a law enacted to gather insurance funds from reactor owners to be held in case a nuclear disaster affected the public. The federal government had stepped in with bailout money to assuage the situation. The uninhabitable real estate in Manhattan alone was estimated to be worth eight hundred billion dollars prior to evacuation. The four boroughs of New York blanketed with fallout were undergoing cleaning, but the Nuclear Regulatory Commission and the government had declared the area temporarily uninhabitable. Some experts said two years for rehabilitation, some said five, others said fifteen, twenty, thirty. Nobody really knew. *How do you rebuild? Who'll move back and live there?* Avi was certain her family wouldn't. If the state didn't let people reinhabit the city in a few years, there'd be a resurgence a decade or more later. It would be the hip artist thing to do—move into an old exclusion zone.

Above the George Washington Bridge into Westchester County, and twenty miles around Bear Mountain, had been declared uninhabitable for a minimum of thirty years to give time for radiation levels to dissipate. There would still be hot spots that would be uninhabitable for decades longer; the ten miles around Bear Mountain were declared indefinitely uninhabitable. Experts estimated it could be hundreds, if not thousands of years until the ten-mile radius was safe. The presence of Plutonium-239 with a half-life of twenty-four thousand years meant the area wouldn't see life until an entirely new era. The U.S. had experienced its Chernobyl, its petrified forest, its black scar.

Avi had heard the food supply hundreds of miles around Bear Mountain and deep into the Atlantic coast was turning up contaminated. Even though the land was technically habitable for humans, the threshold of allowable radioactivity in the food supply was significantly lower. More farms were shuttered, animals disposed, drinking water rerouted, and fishing waters cordoned off as radiological contamination continued to be discovered in new areas, seeping through the soil, and dispersing through moving waters. Despite regulatory agency, farmer, and fisherman testing efforts contaminated seafood, animals products, and produce were still being shipped around the world until authorities or civilians stitched the loophole and that line of goods was halted. The government and EPA had elevated the maximum permissible levels of radioactivity in food products in an attempt to not completely cripple the market. However, those elevated permissible levels, even though considered low, were still detrimental to human health. Avi knew no level of radiation above natural levels present from space and Earth were safe. The elevation of government-allowable limits baffled her.

Avi had believed that at her age she and Trace would be nearing the cruising era. The machine they had slathered oil on for years would finally stop sputtering and purr harmoniously. They'd have everything material they needed. Their children would be growing and they'd be socking money away for everyone's future—no drastic changes, just a graceful ascent to the apex. Avi was sure almost every middle-aged and elderly person from the New York metro area felt the same. No one had thought they'd be starting over—no house, no job, family members deceased, chronic illness, in a new town, no possessions—nothing. *THIS is a midlife crisis.* She wanted to get back to her advanced renewable energy initiatives. She hadn't progressed professionally since the disaster. Every time she looked at her research there was no inner fire burning to rekindle the magic needed to move the projects forward. Avi had paramount work to accomplish. Work that wasn't just for her—work that was for humanity. Her device that harvested zero-point energy was a crucial concept that could change energy for the planet. She just wasn't sure she would ever regain the fortitude to move forward.

Avi was grateful her newborn son had somehow been unaffected by radiation she had absorbed. Avi believed he had been spared because she had started detoxification treatments immediately after the evacuation. It was that or a miracle cast by

Trace from the heavens. Brooklyn and Lea's boys had finished several rounds of Prussian Blue to help detox their systems. Everyone felt and tested healthy, though latent cancers would be a concern for the rest of their lives. Avi drew Brooklyn in under her arm, pulled her close, and kissed her on the head. "I miss daddy," Brooklyn whispered.

"Your daddy was a hero," Avi told her.

"What's a hero?" Brooklyn asked.

"You were there when I was rising. You were there when I had fallen. You were there when I departed this world. You were everything until I became nothing."

-Trace Crane

GP James is a writer and musician living in Los Angeles. He has written four screenplays and two novels. As a music producer and sound mixer/engineer he has worked with artists such as Snoop Dogg, Amy Winehouse, Patti LaBelle, and many other Grammy Award winners.

CPSIA information can be obtained
at www.ICGtesting.com
Printed in the USA
FFOW02n0429200318
45902294-46781FF

9 781948 018074